last of the tuath dé

A Novel

Scott R. Larson

www.ScottLarsonBooks.com

**Books by
Scott R. Larson**

The Fantasy Novels

The Three Towers of Afranor

The Curse of Septimus Bridge

Last of the Tuath Dé

The Dallas Green Novels

Maximilian and Carlotta Are Dead

Lautaro's Spear

Searching for Cunégonde

Copyright © 2022 by Scott R. Larson

ISBN 13: 978-1-7331947-6-1 (paperback edition)

www.ScottLarsonBooks.com

Cover illustration
by
Tamlyn Zawalich

To

Teresa
for giving me space and support to write my books and blogs,
for not minding (too much) when I appropriate
your culture and language,
and for being my sole reference point
when it comes to love and romance

Maggie
for keeping me young(ish),
and for being my cultural, intellectual,
and interpretive guide in this strange world
I've traveled to — the future

the various artists whose works were among
the sources of inspiration for this saga,
including J.R.R. Tolkien, H.P. Lovecraft,
Robert E. Howard, Baran bo Odar & Jantje Friese,
and Chris Marker

Many thanks to

Dayle Moss
not just for giving extraordinary amounts of time,
care, attention, thoughtfulness, and help to my manuscripts
but for doing it over and over again — all the way
through six books that not only would have been
less professional without your support but
also not nearly as satisfying for me to have written
or for readers to peruse

Michael Morrow
for being there for the entire journey to date and always
offering encouragement, validation, and that one little detail
(multiple times) I should have thought of myself or, perhaps
more importantly, that lets me know that maybe
I'm not the only crazy one

Marcella Peralta Simon
and Sandee Tyler
for your interest in my work, for taking the time
to read through an imperfect iteration of the manuscript,
and for giving me your considered thoughts and reactions

Contents

1
Hathus

WHEN THE TAVERN'S double doors flew open, raucous noise spilled out onto the street. The doors swung back again, but not before a woman staggered out onto the sidewalk. Her long hair was straight and black, and it was tossed in one direction while her feet stumbled in another.

The hour was late, and the few people on the street avoided her nervously. She weaved uncertainly on the sidewalk, cursing angrily and tugging at the rope circling her torso. Her furious struggle with the rope, which held her wrist tight against her back, did nothing to help her balance.

Casual observers might have thought she wore spandex, but her black bodysuit was made from no ordinary synthetic fiber. A shirt of light chain mail covered the top of it. Her brown boots, each sporting a large brass buckle, were almost the height of her knees. A cobalt blue crystal—symmetrically shaped with sharp edges—dangled at the end of the slender leather strap around her neck. On her left hip was an ornate metal medallion the width of a large hand. On the other hip hung a leather pouch, partly covering a sheathed seven-inch knife.

As she lurched down the street, she reflected on her extra-ordinarily long life. She thought of the various mentors she had had over the years, in particular the one she would most like to see again.

When she came to the alleyway's entrance, she did not notice the curb and nearly fell. She saved herself, but only momen-tarily, by weaving into the darkness of the alley's shadows. After several seconds of awkward dancing, she flopped onto a pile of plastic trash bags. Cursing all the time, she rolled over onto some empty cardboard boxes.

As the stench of rotten food filled her nose, her complaints grew louder. Then she heard something and immediately went quiet. The sound had come from behind the bags. Several seconds later, she heard it again. It was like a bleat or a whine.

"Who's there?" she demanded.

Silence.

"Show yourself."

No reply. She struggled to sit upright and batted at the boxes with her free hand.

"I know you're there. It'll be better for you if you don't try to hide."

Still no answer.

"I warn you. Don't think you can take me by surprise."

She tried to stand, but her foot slipped on something slimy. She grunted as she strained at the rope.

A small figure burst from the pile of bags. He headed for the alley's exit, but she grabbed his coat and jerked him back. She pinned his arm to the ground. He cried out.

Getting a better look at him, she relaxed her grip slightly. Her anger softened.

"You're just a kid."

"Let go. You're hurting me."

"What were you doing in there? Are you alone?"

"Let me go. I wasn't bothering you. I was here first."

"It's dangerous to startle people. Especially in a dark place late at night. It's particularly dangerous to startle someone like me."

"You were the one who startled me. I wasn't bothering anyone. I was sleeping."

"Why are you sleeping in an alley? Did you run away from home?"

He did not respond.

"Answer me. Do you have a home? Or are you living on the streets? You know, Pioneer Square isn't the safest place for someone like you this time of night."

He stared at her defiantly. The more he studied her, the more curious he became.

"Why do you have a rope around you?"

"That doesn't matter. Answer my questions."

"Let go of me. I'm fine. I can look after myself. I've been doing it for a long time now."

"If I release my hand, do you promise not to run away?"

"Why? What do you care?"

"I need someone to untie this damned rope for me. If I release your arm, will you do that for me? Then you can go."

"I suppose—if you tell me why you're tied up."

"That's none of your business. What's it to you anyway?"

"I want to know. It only seems fair if you want my help."

"Okay, I'll tell you, but help me with the rope first."

She released her grip slowly. Eying her warily, the boy got to his feet. He looked as though he might bolt, but his curiosity overcame his fear. He sniffed loudly, and a look of disgust came over him.

"Are you drunk?"

"What does that have to do with anything?"

"You reek of alcohol."

"It's my own business if I had a few drinks. And what if I did? No one's ever accused me of not being able to hold my liquor."

"You smell like a drunkard. You sound like one too."

"Stop delaying and help me with this rope."

"The abuse from drink is from Satan."

"What?"

"I remember hearing that once, though I can't remember precisely when or where just now. 'The wine is from God, but the Drunkard is from the Devil.'"

She reflected on the sound of his vowels.

"You're not from around here, are you?"

"Why do you say that?"

"Because of the way you talk. Look, we're wasting time. Go behind me. I can't quite reach the knot, and it's very tight. See if you can undo it."

He dropped to his knees and did as he was told. He pulled at the knot, but his slender fingers could not loosen it.

"It's quite snug."

"Keep working at it. You only have to get it started. If you can do that, I'll be able to do the rest."

"You said you would tell me why you're tied up."

"Why do you care?"

"Because I want to know, and you promised to tell me. Why are you tied up?"

"Because I'm stupid."

Try as he might, the boy could not wedge his fingers into the knot.

"That's not a very good explanation."

"Look, there were some men in a tavern. We had a few drinks. We made a few wagers. In the end, they became angry because I won every single one. They wanted to fight. I preferred to avoid that."

"Because you were afraid?"

She trembled with anger, and her free hand slapped the boy to the ground.

"No, you little brat. I didn't want to fight them because it wouldn't have been a fair contest. There were only three of them."

Annoyed, he got back on his knees. He grudgingly pulled on the rope some more.

"You don't make any sense. If there were three of them, then you're the one for whom it wouldn't be fair."

"You only say that because you don't know who I am. You don't know what I'm capable of. Trust me, they were the ones with the disadvantage, but they were as ignorant as you are. Like you, they thought I was afraid. I assured them I could beat all of them with one hand tied behind my back. That's when they proposed one more wager."

"And you agreed?"

"Of course, I agreed. It was easy money. Are you having any luck at all with that knot yet?"

"So you actually allowed them to tie your hand behind you?"

"Are you slow or something? I don't often come across suckers like that."

"Did you win your wager?"

"I certainly did. I left two unconscious. Last I saw of the other one, he was heading for the back exit. You know, I'm starting to think you aren't really trying with that knot."

"How much did you win?"

"How much? Well, nothing in the end. That fool of a bartender called the police. It's a policy of mine to stay out of the way of law enforcement, so I chose to make a hasty exit. We had done quite a bit of damage to the place."

"I think it's beginning to loosen now."

"Finally. Just a bit more. Then I can do the rest."

The boy grunted in frustration.

"Those men in the tavern," he said. "What did they look like?"

"They looked like men. Why do you ask?"

"Did any of them look like that?"

She turned her head to follow his gaze. In the alley entrance stood a hulking figure. His hair was long and black, as was his beard. He wore a heavy coat and carried a wooden club.

"No," she said apprehensively. "He wasn't one of them."

The man stepped closer and stared at her. His voice was like a gravel mixer.

"Izanami?"

She stared back. He took another step forward.

"Hathus? Is that you?"

The boy shrank behind Izanami, though he continued working on the knot.

"What are you doing here?" asked Hathus.

"You know. Just having a night out. What about yourself?"

"I'm on an errand. An important one."

He continued to stare.

"I'm surprised to see you," he said.

"Really? Why?"

"I heard you were dead."

"Dead? Why? Where did you hear that?"

"The was a story going around about you and that other Hant Oppressor. They said things went badly for you in the Atacama Desert, that the pair of you took on one hant too many."

"You have that part right. Things did go bad at the Licancabur Rim. Really bad. That's definitely one place I won't be going back to. Tell me something, what do you mean by Hant Oppressor?"

"It's what you are."

"Well, it's not a term that I or any other Demon Hunter has ever used. Tell me, what kind of errand are you on? Are you still with the Condottieri?"

"There is no more Condottieri. Most of us have a new purpose. So you're still oppressing hants then?"

"It's called demon hunting, and it's a funny thing you should ask, Hathus. There has been no sign of any demons for ages now. It's as if the fiends lost all interest in this world. There was a time Sapphire and I could barely keep up with them. We had our work cut out for us. There were just the two of us, you know. The last two Demon Hunters. Something has definitely changed. It almost makes me nervous."

"Oppressing hants was always a sucker's game, Izanami. You should have known that. That's why the oppressors are all gone now. They're all either dead or in hiding."

"I'm still here."

"For now. What about the other one?"

"She's still around. At least as far as I know. I haven't actually seen her for a while, but that's a long story. Why do you keep calling me an oppressor?"

Something about Hathus made Izanami apprehensive. She turned nervously to the boy.

"What's taking so long with that knot?"

"You should join us, Izanami. Everyone else has. We're the future."

"Join who? What are you talking about, Hathus?"

"The Zen'ei."

"Zen'ei? That's a Japanese word, but I bet you didn't know that. Who are they? I haven't heard of them before. What's their angle?"

He took a step closer.

"No angle. Just preparing the way for what's to come."

"And what's to come?"

"Join us and find out."

"I prefer to find out those things *before* I join. Anyway, I've never been much of a joiner."

"There's a war coming, Izanami. Can you not feel it? When the end comes, everyone will be on one side or the other. No one will be able to sit it out."

"A war? What are you talking about?"

"Between those on the right side of history and those who aren't."

He now stood directly over her.

"What's your errand, Hathus?"

He stared hard and said nothing.

"Is it me? Did you come looking for me?"

"No." His eyes focused on the boy. "It's him."

"Him? What do you want with him? He's just a kid."

"That's not your concern."

"Unless you can convince me you're taking him to his parents, I don't think I can let you have him."

He laughed.

"That's a good one. Who are you trying to kid, Izanami? I remember you from the old days. You always hated children."

"I still do. Look, I honestly don't want to get involved here. Just make me believe you're taking him to his family, and you can have him."

As the boy tugged desperately on the rope, he whispered, "He's not..."

"Fine. I'm taking him to his family. Come along, boy."

"That wasn't convincing, Hathus. What are his parents' names?"

"I don't know. It doesn't matter. I'm taking him."

The boy's efforts with the knot became frantic, and at last the rope moved. In a quick, fluid motion Izanami arched her back, and with her left hand she reached behind her. As the rope fell away, she sprang to her feet.

"I don't think so, Hathus. I have a definite feeling you don't have his best interest at heart."

"You're making a mistake, Izanami."

"The mistake isn't mine, Hathus. I'm giving you a chance to avoid injury—or worse. Just tell me what this is about. Who wants him and why?"

Hathus raised his club.

"It didn't have to be this way."

"Actually," she said, "I have a nagging feeling it probably did."

He grasped his weapon with both hands and swung it at her. She avoided it but barely. Not only did her midsection and right arm still ache from the rope's tightness, but she knew her reflexes were slower than they should have been thanks to her night of drinking.

Fortunately, she had ways to compensate. She extended her arms straight outward and clenched her fists. A blinding light formed around them, and an energy pulse burst forth.

Hathus laughed as he raised his forearms. The energy was deflected in several directions all at once. Nearby trash cans clattered as they bounced against the brick wall.

"Is that the best you can do, Hant Oppressor?"

"What are those on your wrists?"

"Everyone has these now. They're energy dampers, and they're standard issue in the Zen'ei."

This is not good, she thought. Her ability to channel energy was her chief advantage over a mortal foe. Her knife would be little use against his protective clothing. Of course, there was the diabolusbane, but to use it against a human being was unthinkable.

He struck again. Once more she avoided the blow, but the way he had swung the club unnerved her. He had done it with such an angry force that the wind it made had strength of its own. His brutish determination alarmed her. He was not the same man she had known before.

She leapt into the air and bounced her boots against the side of his ribcage. Taken by surprise, he staggered but did not fall. As she landed awkwardly, she took note of the boy retreating behind the pile of black bags.

Wasting no time, she made another leap, but this time Hathus was ready. He latched onto her ankle, and she tumbled gracelessly to the ground. Before she could get up, he pressed his boot hard against her hip and raised his club. The boot was too heavy to move, so she twisted her legs and kicked his other one. It was enough to make him shift his weight and allow her to avoid the oncoming club. He had swung with such heedless force, his loss of balance forced him down on one knee—but only for a moment.

She rolled away from him, but before she could get to her feet, he struck again. A glancing blow caused her shoulder to explode with pain, as Hathus's reckless effort again left him on one knee.

Her anger mounting, she scrambled to her feet. Hathus stood as well, warily noting the resolute look in her eyes. For his own good, he was determined to finish her quickly. He spun his body completely around, building momentum as he raised his club. Before she could move her feet, he swung it forcefully at her head. She threw her upper body in the opposite direction, but she could not avoid the blow entirely. The pain in her temple almost caused her to black out, but she had at least avoided disaster. As she felt warm blood drip slowly down the side of her face, she was blind with fury.

She threw the full weight of her body against him, forcing him to take three awkward steps backward. As he struggled to regain his balance, she wrested the club from his hand. He stared in alarm as she raised it above her head with both hands and brought it down with all her might. He twisted his head in an attempt to avoid the impact, but she was aiming elsewhere. He screamed in pain when the weapon landed solidly on his knee.

Teeth gritted, he strained for the club, but she had already raised it again. This time it landed against his jaw, and two teeth flew through the air. He dropped to his knees, compounding the pain in the injured one. Izanami swung around and struck him on the back, forcing him forward onto his stomach. She stood on his back.

"We could have done this the easy way," she panted. "I had no quarrel with you. I only wanted answers."

"You're making… a mistake," he grunted. "You've taken a side now, and it's the wrong side."

She almost pitied him as she heard his labored breathing.

"You should have stayed out of it," he gasped. "You don't know what you've done."

"Just tell me why you want the boy. Come on, Hathus. It's me you're talking to. What's this about?"

Before Hathus could say anything, the boy sprang out of the pile of rubbish bags and sprinted away. Izanami stepped off Hathus's back and gave him a quick kick in the side before pursuing the child. He was fast, but even after a rough night, she was faster. She grabbed the neck of his jacket. His feet flew in front of him as she jerked him back.

"That's not very smart. If Hathus's friends want you, you're better off with me—at least until we sort this out."

"Let me go!" he implored, struggling against her grip. "I can look after myself. I don't need you."

"Believe me," she sighed, "I'd like nothing more than to be rid of you, but I can't in good conscience let you go knowing that those people are after you. Just tell me where your family is, and I'll take you to them. Then you and I will never have to see each other ever again. Just tell me who's responsible for you."

"Nobody's responsible for me. I'm entirely on my own."

"What did Hathus want with you?"

"I don't know. I swear it. I've never seen him before. I don't know anything about him."

"You don't have any idea at all?"

"I swear I don't."

"Damn. As much as I don't want to, I'm going to have to take you home with me. We'll try to figure it out there."

She turned to look at Hathus, lying motionless on the ground with his eyes closed. He would not give her any more trouble—for now anyway. She turned back to the boy.

"I'm Izanami, by the way, but you probably figured that out already. What's your name?"

He stared at the ground and spoke in a half-whisper.

"I'm Peter."

2
Peter

THE HOUSE WAS not merely modest. It was withdrawn. Set well back from the sidewalk behind an overgrown lawn, it was lost in the dark shade of the surrounding trees. With its cladding of cedar shingles, it melted into the foliage.

Resignedly, Peter followed Izanami up the walkway to the porch. When she opened the door and stepped inside, he held back. For the moment she had forgotten him as she stood silently. This had become her habit: standing for a few minutes just inside the door and listening. She tried to sense whether someone had been in the house during her absence, whether someone might be in the house now.

"Who's Sapphire?"

"How do you know about her?" she asked suspiciously.

"You mentioned her," he said, stepping into house. "You told that man you hadn't seen her for a while, that it was a long story."

"This is her place. I've been living with her."

"Where did she go?"

"I don't know. I thought I would have heard from her by now."

"Maybe she wanted to get away from you. You can be rather frightening, you know."

Izanami glared at him. "You have no idea."

Her face darkened. The tone of her voice unsettled him.

"Look, I've got no choice but to let you stay here for now, but you're going to have to look after yourself. I don't know anything about children. You can sleep in that room over there. If you need something, you can try asking me, but you'll be better off if you can just deal with it yourself."

11

The boy looked lost. She did not like the way his face made her feel.

"Are you hungry?"

"I don't get hungry," he shrugged.

"Everybody gets hungry."

"I don't."

"If you say so. Well, when you decide that you're hungry, you can help yourself to whatever you can find in the kitchen."

"Thank you, but I won't."

"You won't help yourself?"

"I won't decide that I'm hungry. I told you, I don't get hungry."

"Fine, but just so you know, I don't actually care if you starve."

Peter sat on the couch and watched her quietly. His gaze made her uncomfortable.

"Look," she sighed, "I'm no good in this situation. I need help with this, but I don't have anyone. I wish Sapphire were here. She likes children."

She glanced at the wall clock. It was almost two in the morning.

"What time would it be in Ireland?" she wondered aloud.

Peter shrugged.

"It must be daytime there already. It might be worth a try."

She sat down at a computer on a desk in a corner of the living room and switched it on.

"This machine is Sapphire's," she said, waiting for it to boot. "I hardly ever use it."

She glanced at the boy. He looked bored.

"You can help me if you want."

Peter got up and stared over her shoulder at the flickering monitor.

"I've seen these," he said, "but I don't understand what they're for."

"You don't know what a computer's for? I thought every child your age was an expert at these things."

"I'm not."

"Damn. Sorry, I mean, darn."

"What's wrong?"

She stared at the screen. The name ParyDymeOS had appeared along with a prompt for a password.

"She's changed the software."

"Are you Chinese?" the boy asked.

"What kind of question is that? Why would you ask me that?"

He shrugged. "You look the way I imagine Chinese people look."

"My mother would have taken great offense at that remark. She was Japanese."

"Oh, so you're Japanese."

"I'm Canadian. I don't take offense at anything, but I do lose my temper sometimes."

"You're awfully pretty, you know. I mean, when you're not being scary."

Each new word he uttered annoyed her more than the previous one.

"I should have just let Hathus take you. Look, you need to keep your mouth shut because I'm this close to killing you. Stop talking while I figure out what her password is."

He fell silent, and Izanami reflected. After a few moments she typed "Chiharu." The screen filled with a scenic photo of Puget Sound.

"She can be so predictable sometimes," she said under her breath, as she watched various icons appear one by one.

In the middle of the screen, a dialogue box appeared with the message "Want to Save the Planet? Click Here!"

"Why does it do that?" she grumbled, as she closed the box. "What does that mean anyway?"

She found the icon for video chat and launched the app. She scanned the list of contacts and clicked on one of the names. After a few beeps, a blurry image appeared on the screen, accompanied by some fumbling noises from the machine's speaker.

"Lola? Is that you?" asked a sleepy voice.

"No, it's the other one."

"Is something wrong?"

"You weren't asleep, were you?"

"I was, of course." The reply came in a hoarse whisper. "It's flippin' two in the morning."

"You mean, in Seattle. What time is it where you are?"

"The same. We're in Seattle now. How do you not know that? Did Lola not tell you?"

Izanami's eyes widened at the mention of the name Lola. So did Peter's.

"No, she didn't… wait, have you heard from her? Maria, have you talked to Lola?"

The image on the computer screen swayed in one direction and then another. Maria was carrying her phone to a different room.

"Sorry there, Chiharu, I didn't want to wake Kyle. He gives out bangs to me for not turning my phone off at night."

"Tell me. Have you heard from her?"

"No, it must be a couple of months now. Do the two of ye not talk to one another? I got my Green Card."

"She had to go away for a while. I haven't heard from her for a few weeks."

"Really? Is that like her?"

"Yes, it's exactly like her—except she has never gone this long before."

"Jeepers. You don't think she could be in any trouble, do you?"

"I don't know what to think, but I called you about something else. I have a little problem."

"You have a problem? And it was me you rang? What sort of problem?"

"You know all about children, right? I mean, you Irish people all have large families and are comfortable around kids."

"What's this about, Chiharu?"

"I've picked up a boy, and I'm not sure what to do with him."

"To be clear, when you say boy…"

"I don't know how old he is," she said, turning around to look at him. "How old are you?"

He shrugged.

"Oh, come on. You have to know how old you are."

He shook his head.

"He's strange. If I had to guess, I'd say, I don't know, eleven? Twelve?"

"That's certainly old enough for him to know how old he is. What's the story on him?"

"He was sleeping in an alley in Pioneer Square. I wouldn't have bothered with him, but someone is after him. Someone dangerous."

"Why are they after him?"

"I don't know. It makes no sense. Like I say, I would have left him there or maybe dropped him off at a police station, but if Mercenaries are after him, this is something serious."

"Mercenaries? What do you mean?"

"They're… well, all you need to know is that they inhabit the same world as Lola and I. The less you know about that, the better. Look, could you come over and talk to him? You might get something out of him that I can't. I don't know how to talk to him."

"I suppose I could go to you in the morning. I just need to know… I mean, you need to tell me if this is going to be something dangerous. I don't want to get mixed up in… you know."

"To be honest, I don't know exactly what we're dealing with, but there's no need for you to worry. I'll guarantee your safety. The first step is for us to get whatever information we can out of him. Then we'll see what happens after that."

"Grand. I'll see you in the morning so."

As Izanami shut down the computer, Peter said, "Lola's a funny name, isn't it?"

"It's not funny to me."

"I met a woman named Lola once."

"Of course, you did. You need to go to bed now. We have to be up in the morning because we're going to have a visitor."

"I'll go to bed, but I don't sleep."

"Of course, you don't."

A few hours later, Izanami stared across the table at the boy as she sipped her coffee and munched on some toast.

"Are you sure you don't want anything? I can't understand how you're not starving."

"I told you..."

"Yeah, yeah. We'll see how long you can keep this up."

There was a knock on the front door.

"That will be Maria. Go let her in. I'll boil some water. She'll probably want tea."

Obediently, Peter ran out of the kitchen. Izanami heard him open the door. As she put the kettle on the stove, she was surprised not to hear their voices. As the strange silence persisted, she stepped into the living room. Maria and Peter stood staring at each other through the doorway. A look of shock was on Maria's face.

"I know you," said Peter. "You had white hair before."

"What's he talking about, Maria?"

The Irish woman struggled for words.

"I'm sorry. It's just so unbelievable."

"Did you honestly meet him before?"

"Yes," she said quietly. "I did."

As if to convince herself the boy was real, Maria ran her fingers gently through his hair and along his cheek.

"I'm sorry," she repeated. "It's just that it's a double shock. You see, he's like an identical twin to my cousin Fionn. Poor little Fionn who died. He's not Fionn, but it's still upsetting to see him... again."

"How do you know him?"

"He was on the island. Riesgado Island. He was there along with two other children."

"Really? What were they doing there?"

Maria seemed not to hear.

"How have you been, Peter? I never expected to see you again."

Peter said nothing.

"What are you doing here? Are Celia and Audrey with you? Are they here too?"

He shook his head gravely. "I don't know where they are. I don't know where they've gone."

"Chiharu," said Maria, "I need to talk to you. Just the two of us. Peter, pet, do you think you could look after yourself here while Chiharu and I go out to the garden for a bit of a chat?"

"All right, but she told me her name was Izanami."

"That's because you're special," said Izanami sarcastically. "You get to call me by my working name."

The two women stood next to the fir tree. The grass was wet from a recent shower. Maria was visibly upset.

"Chiharu," she said urgently, "that poor lad is dead."

"Your cousin? Yes, I'm sorry about that, but…"

"No, I mean that child in the house. Peter is dead."

"He seems alive enough to me."

"No, you don't understand. Septimus told Lola that the children on the island had died and that he had brought them back to life—so he wouldn't be alone on the island."

"Are you sure?" mused Izanami. "I never figured Orpheus for being fond of brats."

"That's what Lola told me. She also said he sent them and the housekeeper all back to the afterlife."

"He had the power to do that? Even after he's gone, Orpheus continues to be full of surprises—and secrets."

"What does it mean that Peter's come back? How is that possible?"

"Are you sure Lola said they were dead?"

"I swear on my life. I mean, it seemed impossible, but with so many other impossible things happening, I just accepted it so."

"Well, that would certainly explain a few things about him, like why he doesn't eat or sleep and why he has no family, but how do the Zen'ei know about him and why do they want him?"

"Who?"

"I heard about them for the first time last night, and I have a bad feeling about them."

"Chiharu, should we be worried about Lola? Do you truly not know where she is?"

"That's how our relationship works. I ask no questions when she goes away for a while, and she does the same for me. It's just that…"

"What?"

"She's never been away this long before—not without getting in touch. I don't know what it means."

"Perhaps it's time the two of ye recognized you're in a relationship now. At some point ye have to make some compromises with your ideas of personal independence."

"This is the only way it works for me. I've been alone most of my life. Not being alone is hard for me. In my old life I never had to worry about anybody else. About where they were. How I would manage if they didn't come back. Things were simpler then."

"And you have no idea where to go looking for her?"

"No, not really. She sometimes goes in search of the Masters. The ones that still survive. Only a few are left now, and they are ancient at this point. She looks for their help in perfecting her skills and recovering memories of her past lives."

"Do you think that's what she's doing now?"

"Maybe, but something she said made me think that this time it might have had something to do with her parents. She always thought their deaths had been an accident, but more lately she's had suspicions there may have been more to it. Look, I shouldn't be talking to you like this. This is Lola's and my business. It's just that I know she trusts you, so I feel I can too. Besides, sometimes I have a need to..."

"Not be alone?"

Unconsciously, Izanami fingered the blue crystal hanging from her neck. Maria had been admiring it.

"That's lovely," she said.

"It's a gift from her. Well, it was going to be. I found it hidden away among her things. The anniversary of the day we met is coming up, and she likes to make a fuss about things like that. I think it's silly."

"That's so sweet."

"She's ruined me, Maria."

"I'm glad we had a chance to talk, Chiharu. If I'm being honest, I've sometimes had the feeling I'm not your favorite person."

"Why would you think that?"

"Until now you've always avoided talking to me. I mean, you were invited to my wedding, and you didn't come."

"You shouldn't have taken that personally. I can't stand gatherings. Besides, I knew there would be dancing."

"And…?"

"I don't dance."

"You're a fierce peculiar woman, Chiharu."

"Look, I knew you only invited me because you had to. Believe me, Lola had a much better time without me there. I heard later that the reception went on for days. I would never have survived it. Is that normal in Ireland?"

"So are you and I friends then?"

"I wouldn't go that far. I don't have friends. Look, I don't dislike you at all, but as long as we're being honest, then you should know that being around you reminds me of what happened. You know, what happened in the Netherworld."

"I can never stop thanking you for what you did, for rescuing me. It's strange, but I'll never truly believe it ever happened. It must be some sort of defense mechanism in my brain, but I'm eternally grateful and will always feel terrible about your friend."

"He was a comrade. I do miss him. It's more than that. That experience in the demon world changed me—and not for the better."

"So tell me, Chiharu, if you don't have friends, then what is Lola?"

Izanami's countenance changed. Maria detected—or thought she did—the faintest trace of a smile.

"I would not use the word friend to describe what Lola is to me. I do not have a word for that." Izanami was anxious to shift topics. "Look, can you take the boy home with you? He would be much better off there, and I need to be free to go on a search. I have to find out what the Zen'ei are all about."

"I don't want to say no, Chiharu, but…"

"Then don't."

"It's just that…"

"You're scared."

"Yes, I am. You have to understand, Chiharu. I'm not like you and Lola. Your world is so different from mine—from most people's really. I'm simply not fit for it."

"Yet you're still friends with Sapphire—after all that happened."

"Yes, and I'm still friends with you. I know you 'don't have friends,' but I don't believe that. Lola and I have bonded forever—not in spite of what she and I went through but because of it. I could never turn my back on her, but I'd be lying if I said that spending time with her isn't sometimes difficult—because of the memories she evokes. Still, I owe her so much. Not least is the fact that, if not for her, I would never have met Kyle. That has made all the rest of it worth it. I suppose the lesson is that you don't get the biggest rewards without sometimes going through the biggest tests."

"So you'll take the boy then?"

Maria had no chance to respond. The two of them were blinded by an intense light, then deafened by a thunderous roar. A powerful shaking forced them to the ground. Izanami fought to not lose consciousness, and it was an effort to raise her head. She could not see, and a fierce heat roasted her face. Gradually she made out the rough outline of the house. It was consumed in flames.

3
Inferno

IZANAMI STRUGGLED TO stand but only got as far as her knees. A few feet away Maria lay motionless. The Demon Hunter gasped for breath. She tried to work out what had happened. Then she remembered.

"The boy!"

She forced herself to her feet and staggered toward the blazing house, but the heat's intensity was too great. She leaned over and rested her hands on her knees.

"Someone will pay for this!" she panted. "And dearly!"

She stood straight and pulled her black hood tight so that it covered her head entirely. She retrieved her gloves from her pouch. Her suit would provide protection from the flames—just as it always had against demons' fiery blasts. The hood's wondrous fibers repelled the heat yet were sufficiently diaphanous to allow a gauzy view. She tapped the medallion which hung from her belt. In her hand materialized a long iron lance with an intricately woven pattern of sculpted metal on both ends. A glow emanated from its entire length. When in motion, the diabolusbane's supernatural power could also ward off some heat.

She now found herself regretting her missed opportunity. Since recovering her memories in the Netherworld, Sapphire had mastered uncanny skills. She had offered more than once to share her knowledge and to train her, but Izanami had let pride and stubbornness stand in the way. Some of those skills would surely be useful now.

She rushed headlong into the flames, whipping the blade in one direction and then another, creating a draft to dispel the heat. Despite her garment's supernatural quality, she could feel

21

the flames' ferocity through its membrane. She held her breath, as the fire consumed all oxygen.

She shielded her eyes as best she could and scanned the inferno for any sign of the boy. Normally, live cremation would be an extremely unpleasant way to die, but at least in this case it would have been instantaneous. She would not forgive herself for taking on responsibility for his safety only to fail miserably.

She saw no sign of his charred corpse. Could he have possibly escaped before the blast? Unlikely. She lasted only a few minutes before the heat and lack of oxygen threatened to overcome her. She retreated toward the street and gasped for air. Her throat burned as she coughed. She found a surviving patch of grass and sat. Rage consumed her—not only because of the loss of life but also because of what the house had meant to Sapphire. It had been her childhood home.

Much of the anger was directed at herself. Why had she not seen the threat coming?

Cautiously, she tried taking air into her lungs only to have the resultant coughing burn the length of her throat. A distant whine tortured her ears. She feared she would pass out, but then she was suddenly alert. A figure stood over her. As she struggled to stand, a hand touched her shoulder.

"It's okay. You're safe..."

The elderly man jerked his hand away in shock.

"Good Lord!" he cried.

Her suit had burned his fingers. He rubbed his hand frantically on his leg.

"How are you still alive?" he exclaimed.

"Who are you?" Izanami demanded. "What do you want?"

"Take it easy, young lady. It's just me. Oley."

"Who?"

"Oley. Your neighbor."

"Neighbor? Why should I believe you? I've never seen you before."

"No, I can't say you've been particularly friendly," he said, staring wide-eyed at his blistered fingers. "I've seen you plenty of times, though. Even tried to say hello once, but you didn't notice. I've known Lola ever since she was a little girl. I was already living here when the Blumquists bought the house. An awful shame to see it gone like that."

His blue eyes were kindly beneath the bushy eyebrows. Izanami remembered now she had indeed seen him before, but it was a habit of hers to ignore and forget strangers who posed no threat.

"You're darn lucky, young lady, that you weren't inside when the lightning bolt hit. Where's Lola? I sure hope she wasn't in the house."

Izanami rubbed soot and tears out of her eyes. She remembered Maria and tried to stand again.

"I've got to see if she's all right."

"I called 911 right away. You should wait for the ambulance. By the sound of the sirens, I'd say they'll be here any minute."

The distant whine that had bothered her ears had now become a combination of high-pitched wails.

"At first I thought that was Lola lying over there, but then I saw that it's that friend of hers. I've seen her before, but not lately."

The old man's constant chatter annoyed Izanami. She made another attempt to stand.

"Is Maria okay? Is she moving?"

"Hard to tell from here, but I'd say she's not too bad, all things considered. The little fella's holding her hand. He's trying to take care of her."

"Little fella?"

Izanami rolled over for a better look. Maria had begun to stir. Her moans were low and pained. A boy was indeed kneeling next to her. He held her hand and spoke to her. Despite all the soot that covered him, she could tell it was Peter.

"Thank God, he got out. I bet the little brat sneaked out of the house to eavesdrop on us."

"Here's the ambulance now. Don't you worry. They'll take good care of you."

"No ambulance. I have to go. I'm taking the boy and getting out of here."

"Lie back, miss. You're in shock. Just wait for the medics. They'll take care of you. That's what they're here for."

The sight of the ambulance and the fire trucks spurred Izanami to her feet, and she rushed toward Maria and Peter.

To her alarm, three hulking figures approached from the opposite direction. The nearest was Hathus. He grabbed Peter by the wrist.

"Ow!" cried the boy. "You're hurting me!"

"Let him go!" Izanami shouted.

"I'm done with you, Izanami," sneered Hathus. "I warned you to stay out of this."

Enraged, she drew the diabolusbane. Hathus stepped backward apprehensively, still gripping the boy's wrist.

"Easy there, fiend-chaser. I thought you never used that thing on your own kind. I'm not one of your hants."

"Aren't you?" she hissed threateningly. "Whatever it was that you did to the house... it has every sign of being supernatural. You've crossed a line, Hathus. Release the boy or lose your sorry head."

The Mercenary hesitated but only for a moment. With one hand and little apparent effort, he tossed Peter into the waiting arms of his comrade. He raised his club in anticipation of Izanami's next move.

"Stupid fool!" she shouted, dropping her weapon.

Her fury had replenished her strength. She broke into a sprint and threw herself at him headlong. Caught by surprise, Hathus tried to shield himself, but it was too late. Her body's momentum forced him to the ground with her on top of him. The club fell from his hand and landed near her foot. He immediately reached for it, but she kicked it away. He pushed her away roughly and crawled in the club's direction.

By this time his companion was disappearing down the street with Peter under his arm. The third man had slipped behind her, and she knew what he intended. For once, in the heat of a fight, she had maintained her concentration on the diabolusbane she had released. It had not yet dematerialized. It lay on the ground like a tempting prize.

She smiled at his agonized cry. The searing pain in his hand had shocked the breath out of him.

"Not very bright, are you?" she shouted at him as she stood and gave Hathus a kick in the side. She turned toward the would-be thief. "The diabolusbane knows its master."

Angered by her taunt as much as by his throbbing palm, he swung the spiky mace in his other hand at her. A swift kick knocked it from his grasp while giving him a new injury which prompted a thunderous bellow.

Despite his pain, he was game to pursue the fight, but there was no longer any point. Their mission was accomplished. He retrieved his weapon and fled after his compatriot.

Hathus had retrieved his club and was back on his feet. They both glanced around. A crowd had gathered in the street. A team of firemen doused the smoldering remains of the house while keeping a wary eye on Izanami and Hathus. Two paramedics approached Maria cautiously.

Though tempted to continue his fight with Izanami, the Mercenary instead bolted down the street. The Demon Hunter let her diabolusbane dematerialize as she gave chase. She reached the end of the block, then turned the corner where she saw Hathus joining the other two Mercenaries. They stood next to a large, rust-colored Humvee. Two of its huge tires rested squarely on the sidewalk in front of a brick apartment building. It not only blocked the sidewalk, but it took up half the street's width. Annoyed drivers waited impatiently for their chance to drive past.

As she raced toward the Humvee, one of the Mercenaries bundled Peter into the rear passenger compartment while Hathus clambered into the front passenger seat. The driver started the engine. Before he could put it in gear, Izanami had climbed the vehicle's grille and onto its hood. Through two thick windows, the pair in the front seat stared at her in disbelief. The driver angrily floored the accelerator.

The sudden vibration from the powerful engine beneath her almost caused Izanami to lose her precarious grip. The driver shifted into forward gear, but before the machine could build up speed, she pulled herself higher and pressed her body against the driver's window. Though his view was blocked, he continued forward at an alarming speed. He then slammed the brake, causing Izanami to slip backward down the hood and onto the ground.

The driver accelerated again, driving over her. Given the Humvee's ample width and clearance, there was little danger of her being crushed. Rather, her fear was that she was about to lose them. Once the vehicle had cleared her prostrate form, she leapt to her feet and ran after them. She froze when the Humvee jerked to a stop and then reversed. She leapt out of its path, but the spiky mace came flying out of the rear passenger window and struck her squarely on her head.

She blacked out.

When she came to, she had no idea how long she had been unconscious. Her head throbbed with pain. The vehicle's rolling motion and occasional bump only added to her discomfort. She was wedged between a door and a burly figure smelling of sweat and dirt. When her eyes focused, she saw it was Hathus. She tried to move, but strain as she might, she could not. She was bound by a rope so tight that the cords dug into her flesh.

"Not again," she complained under her breath.

She could not move, and she could not draw the diabolusbane.

"So you're awake. I bet you've got one hell of a headache. I actually thought Belenus had killed you."

She glowered at him.

"I had no quarrel with you, Izanami, you just wouldn't back away. Looks like you're going to meet Alaric sooner rather than later."

"How long was I out? Where are we?"

She heard something like a whimper and craned her neck to see around Hathus's bulk. Between him and the other door sat the boy. He looked sullen and dazed.

"Not long," said Hathus. "He only got you with a glancing blow. There was hardly any blood."

"Where are you taking us?"

"You'll see soon enough. Just take it easy. You don't need to worry."

"Don't I?"

"There's no need for us to fight, Izanami. Once you understand, everything will be different. You'll see."

"Understand what? You've got my attention now, and we have some time to kill. Tell me what this is about. What do you want me to understand?"

He laughed.

"I don't think you're ready to hear it yet. I think you just want to get me talking so you can learn something you can use against me. Believe me, you'll think differently once you know."

"Once I know what?"

"The path the world has been on. The disaster we've all been heading for. There's only one hope. It means we all have to change our ways, and it's already getting late. We're almost out of time."

"Definitely sounds urgent. What do we need to do?"

"Mock us all you like, Hant Oppressor," said a voice in the front seat. It was the mace-wielder Belenus. His voice was higher-pitched than Izanami would have expected. He sounded eastern European. "But I'll answer your question. Great sacrifices will be required. We shall all have to change our ways. It won't be easy."

"He's right," said Hathus. "Not everybody will want to accept the sacrifices that must be made. Too many people think they can just keep following the old ways, but they're wrong. We can't afford to think like that anymore. None of us."

"I'm still not any the wiser," said Izanami. "And what does this have to do with the boy?"

"He's special. Can't you sense it?"

"Him? Give me a break. He's just a kid—and kind of an obnoxious one at that."

"He's the key, Izanami. He's the link to the Old Ones."

"Old Ones? Really? Do you have any idea at all what you're talking about, Hathus? Are you mixed up with some sort of religious cult?"

"Religion is just another word for the supernatural. Isn't that your realm, Izanami? But I'm not talking about magic. I'm talking about facts, hard evidence."

"What do you plan to do with the boy? I have to know you're not going to hurt him."

"You're missing the point, but that's okay. I didn't understand at first either. Once you've met Alaric, everything will be clear. The world needs saving, and we have to do it in spite of all the ignorant people who don't understand."

"Look, if I could just get a straight answer out of you, I might actually agree with you. Maybe I'd even help you. Right now, all I can see is a group of thugs abducting a kid—and now me. You're not going to convince me of anything as long as you have me tied up and held against my will."

Hathus sighed with impatience and said nothing. Izanami tried again.

"Last night you said something about a war. Who's going to war?"

"It's already started. It's always been going on. The war is older than time. We've just been sheltered from it. Our ancestors knew about it, but the knowledge got lost. Now the old struggle is heating up again. Time is catching up with us."

"Just tell me the boy will be safe."

"His destiny is foretold and inevitable."

"That doesn't reassure me."

"I'm not here to reassure you or any other truth-denier."

"I'm not denying anything. You haven't told me anything. Just promise me that, whatever happens, the boy won't be hurt."

"My word is good."

"You give your word he will be safe?"

"Whatever you say."

"Why are you making this so hard?"

The mace-wielder had lost his patience.

"Don't waste your time with her, Hathus. She's a denier. I know her type. They pretend to listen, but in the end they always place their stubborn independence above the common good."

Belenus rubbed his hand—the one burned by the diabolus-bane—continually. The pain would not leave it. He noticed Izanami watching him and, despite the pain, he grasped his mace with the burned hand. He extended his arm into the rear compartment and pressed one of the mace's spikes against her throat.

"She's against us. I can see it in her. There's no point taking her to Alaric—and we definitely can't let her go."

He pressed his weapon harder against her neck.

"You didn't know her in the old days, Belenus. She's a formidable warrior and a worthy ally when she's on your side."

"That's just it," Belenus hissed. "She's only on her own side. Alaric wouldn't like it if he knew how much time we've wasted on her. He'd like it even less if we didn't stop her from getting in the way."

Hathus glanced at the boy. His face was turned away from the Mercenary.

"I don't understand, Izanami. What is this child to you? You never would have interfered in the old days. You wouldn't have cared."

"I'm not the one who's changed, Hathus. You were always a brute, but you were never the type to hurt a child."

"Say the word, Hathus," said Belenus darkly. "It would take only a minute to eliminate the problem. She wouldn't be the first casualty in the struggle, and she certainly won't be the last. Don't lose sight of what matters."

Hathus looked at Izanami mournfully.

"How much the world has changed, Belenus. Not long ago I would never have contemplated such a thing. It would have brought the wrath of all Hant Oppressors down on us. She would have soon been avenged. Now who's left to avenge her? I guess that's what happens when time passes you by."

"Can I do it?" said Belenus, a smile coming to his face. "I know *you* don't want to. You have history with her. Let's agree. I'll do it."

Hathus closed his eyes, lowered his head, and said nothing.

"You don't have a problem if I do it with my bare hands, do you? I really want to."

Hathus took a deep breath.

"Do as you like, but I'd advise against using your hands. If you insist on it, just make sure she doesn't get her arms free. If she gets to that hant blade of hers, we're all as good as dead."

"Her arms are secure all right. I think I might actually have cut off her blood when I tied the knots."

The driver stopped the vehicle. Belenus got out and yanked open the door, causing Izanami to tumble painfully to the ground. She squirmed and writhed as his hands reached for her throat. She resisted in every way she could, but she could not escape his assault. She strained against the rope with all her might in a vain effort to touch the medallion that would release the diabolusbane.

The absurdity of the situation fueled her anger. She had survived battles beyond count. She had fought demons. She had journeyed to the Netherworld and faced Astaroth himself. And now this was how she was to die? At the hands of a common Mercenary? Not in battle but as a helpless prisoner?

She gasped for air as his blistered and blackened fingers pressed against her windpipe. She struggled more frantically, but it was useless. She could not bear that the stink of his hot breath would be the last thing she smelled, that his hideous grin would be the last thing she saw.

She thought of Sapphire. The thought of never seeing her again broke her heart.

"Not so high and mighty now, Hant Oppressor!"

She began to slip into darkness. Her eyes rolled back. Above her in the vehicle she saw Peter pushing himself over Hathus's shoulder, staring in wide-eyed horror. She preferred him to be blind than to have him seeing her like this.

The boy buried his eyes into the Mercenary's shoulder. His body trembled. His black hair shook violently. His head flew upward, and suddenly he was unbound. His arms stretched outward. His mouth opened wide. Then came the sound.

The last thing Izanami remembered was the flash of light.

4
Grandfather's Trick

IZANAMI WONDERED WHETHER she was alive or dead.
Since she expected to be dead, it was a surprise to be aware and
thinking. She accepted she must be alive and wondered where
she was. She smelled oil and dirt. She saw a large vehicle's
dusty tire. This was definitely not the afterlife.

She ached all over. She felt a tug. It was uncomfortable and
annoying. It made the pain worse. She wanted to complain but
could not remember how to form words.

"You always seem to get tied up."

It was the boy. He was the one tugging. Why didn't he stop?
Irritating as ever.

"And you always need me to untie you."

She attempted to turn her head, but the aching stopped her.
She could only see the tire. She tried moving her head again
despite the pain. A man's inert body came into view. He was
close enough to smell. She recognized the clothes. It was
Belenus.

"These knots are tighter than the ones last night. I'm sorry. I
don't think I can undo them."

She groaned.

"Steady, there's something I might try."

Something burned her forearm. A flash of light hurt her
eyes. Her arm ached from the burning, but to her relief the rope
slackened.

"It worked!"

The boy sounded as surprised as she was. He tugged at the
rope enthusiastically until he had pulled it off her altogether.
That was a relief, but the pains persisted. He put his hand on
her shoulder. When she did not protest or resist, he gained

31

courage and rolled her onto her back. She stared upward into his large black eyes. His face was upside down, and he stared back intently.

"Are you all right, Chiharu?"

"I'd rather… you called me… Izanami…" She was relieved to be forming words.

"That other woman, Maria, she called you Chiharu. Why can't I? It's prettier than Izanami. Why do you have two names?"

"I told you. I have a working name—as well as the name I was born with."

"Which one does Lola call you by?"

"Neither. She has her own name for me."

"What is it?"

"I'm not going to tell you."

His face was way too close. His breath annoyed her. She turned her head to one side. She saw the rope a few feet away. It was in two pieces, the ends black and smoldering.

"What did you do to the rope?"

"I found a way to get it off you. Did I do well?"

"Yes, I have to admit you did."

She rolled over slowly, then tried putting her weight on one knee. Peter had gotten to his feet and offered his hand.

"I have to do this by myself," she said crossly.

"I'm only trying to help."

She stood on her feet unsteadily.

"Don't whine. I can't stand whining."

Hathus lay next to Belenus. Both were flat on their backs, and they were so still she thought they might be dead. She knelt to put her ear close to each of their mouths. They were both breathing lightly.

"What happened to them? And where's the driver?"

Peter pointed. The third Mercenary lay a few yards away. The hummer was parked on the shoulder of a two-lane road in a rural, wooded area.

"We're a long way from Ballard. How long was I unconscious?"

The boy shrugged.

"I need to understand what's going on," said Izanami. "You need to tell me everything that happened. All of it."

"He was hurting you. That one." Peter pointed at Belenus. "I was afraid he would kill you."

"Yeah, yeah, I know that part. What stopped him?"

"I… just… I was frightened." The boy cast his eyes downward. "I thought you were going to die. I didn't want you to die."

"What? Are you saying you did this?"

"It wasn't wrong, was it? You would have died. I couldn't let that happen. I just couldn't."

"But what exactly did you do?"

"It's difficult to explain. Can we go now? I don't want to stay here. Please?"

She stared hard at Belenus. "He was going to kill me." Her voice hardened. "In cold blood. I should do the same to him. It's what he deserves."

Izanami's anger alarmed Peter.

"Would you really kill him?"

"It's what he would have done to me." She spat on the fallen Mercenary. "As much as I want to, I have a code. I would only take a mortal human's life if it were to save my own or someone else's. He's no danger to me now."

"Isn't he?"

"It was my carelessness that put me at his mercy. I won't make the same mistakes again. I never had to fight Mercenaries before. Not until I met you."

"What if he wakes up?"

"If he were stupid enough to attack me again, then he would be a dead man. As long as he's no threat, I won't kill him… for now. Still…"

She placed her boot firmly on his hand and stood on it with all her weight. Peter winced at the cracking sound.

"My code doesn't prevent me from severely punishing some-one who deserves it. He'll have to learn to wield his mace with the other hand. Come, let's go."

The Humvee's driver door was wide open. Izanami leaned in for a look.

"It doesn't use an ignition key. Just an on switch next to the steering wheel."

"Are you going to drive it?"

"What? Me? No, I don't drive. They're not going to drive it either."

She walked around to the other side and opened the passenger door. She released the two latches underneath the seat and leaned it backward to reveal a large battery. She stepped back and drew the diabolusbane.

"Where does that thing come from?" asked Peter, perplexed. "Why didn't you use it against those men?"

"This weapon is connected to the demon world. It has supernatural properties. It only exists in this world when I summon it. Unfortunately, if my hands aren't free, it can't get to me."

With the blade she sliced the battery cables into numerous pieces.

"How did you know to do that if you don't drive?"

"You ask a lot of questions," she said impatiently. "I've been in one of these before. Not exactly like this one but close enough. My comrade Ragnar once stole one from a band of desert guerillas in the southern Kalahari. They were not one bit happy about it, I can tell you, but it certainly got us out of a tight jam."

Peter was surprised to see her turn wistful.

"God," she said quietly, "I miss Ragnar. I'd give anything to have him back for one more night of drinking."

After removing the battery's restraining bolts, Izanami removed it from the vehicle, walked on the road's shoulder, and heaved it down the wooded hillside.

"They definitely won't be driving this for a while. Now we need to get out of here."

"Where are we?" asked Peter.

"I have no idea. We'll just have to walk back down the road and hope to get a lift. I'm starting to regret never learning that teleporting trick from Sapphire."

As they walked down the highway, Peter asked, "Who's Orpheus?"

"He was someone like Sapphire and me, but he's gone now. Never mind him. I want you to tell me exactly what you did to those men. The whole story. Don't leave anything out. That blast you caused was more powerful than anything I can do with my hands."

"I told you. It's difficult to explain. It's something Grandfather taught me."

"Grandfather? I thought you couldn't remember any of your family."

"He wasn't our real grandfather. We just called him that. On the island, the one that Maria was talking about."

"Riesgado Island?"

He shrugged.

"We didn't call it that. We didn't call it anything. It was just the island."

"What was your grandfather's name?"

"He was just Grandfather. Grandfather Bridge."

"Bridge? Septimus Bridge?"

He stopped in his tracks. His face went blank.

"Septimus," he said quietly.

"Was that your grandfather's name? Septimus Bridge?"

He shrugged and resumed walking.

"And what was it exactly that your grandfather taught you?"

"He called it his trick. Sometimes we would go down to the strand and take turns making the stones fly."

"Fly? You mean you threw them?"

"No. We made them fly. One time, after I had been practicing for a long time, I was able to make a rather large rock bounce high in the sand. It was great fun. I thought I had forgotten how to do it until today."

"But what does making stones fly have to do with what you did to those three Mercenaries?"

"I told you, it's difficult to explain. It wasn't only about making stones fly. It was about making things happen, you know, with your mind. Hurting people without actually touching them. Making things burst into flame."

"And he taught that to you?"

"Yes."

"And to anybody else?"

"No. Celia and Audrey weren't meant to know about it. Neither was Judith."

Izanami grimaced. "That's Orpheus for you. Always had a double standard."

"Orpheus? We were talking about Grandfather."

"Right. What else did he teach you?"

"I don't know. Different things, but the best thing was the trick. He said it was something I should never do without his permission—at least until I was much older. That was the rule." Peter thought for a moment. "Is your code like a rule?"

"Yeah, that's exactly what it is. A lot of rules. Your grandfather was a great one for making rules."

"You knew Grandfather?"

"Yes. He taught me a few tricks too, but not the special one he taught you. That one was apparently just for boys."

"Are you angry? Did I say something wrong?"

"No. Not this time. I wish one of these cars would stop. I'm not in the mood for a long hike."

Soon a car did stop. If the driver wondered why the woman and the boy were walking on a remote section of Woods Creek Road, he kept his curiosity to himself. He dropped them off in the town of Monroe. From there two more bus rides were required to get back to Seattle.

Peter pressed his face against the bus window. "Other people have their own automobiles. Why don't you?"

"Buses suit me," said Izanami. "There's something about being on a bus that almost makes me feel normal. On the Metro Night Owl buses, I don't even get any stares."

"Where are we going?"

"Back to Ballard."

"Why? The house isn't there anymore."

"There's something I have to do."

It was dark by the time they arrived. The smell of smoke was strong in the air as they stared at the pile of ashes. Yellow tape circled the site's perimeter.

Izanami went to the front door of the neighboring house and knocked.

"Hang on a minute!" shouted a voice from inside.

Oley opened the door. "You!"

He stared at Izanami and then at Peter. He looked more frail than before.

"The police were looking for you, you know. You and those other ones. They actually sent out a SWAT team, but you were long gone by then." He calmed a bit. "Are you all right?"

"We're fine. Look, I want to... thank you. You were kind. Sorry, I'm not good at this sort of thing, but I just wanted to... you know..."

"Yeah, sure. I understand. No thanks necessary."

"I'm sorry I wasn't a better neighbor. I'm not sociable."

"Don't worry about it. Is there anything you need?"

"Yes, there's something you can do for me. Lola's away. She's been away for a while now, but she'll be back. I don't know when, but when she comes back, she's going to find her house burned to the ground. Can you tell her what happened? And that I'm okay?"

"Of course, I will."

"That's important. She needs to know I'm all right and that she shouldn't worry. Tell her Chiharu is all right."

"Chee hah roo. I'll tell her. My, that's a pretty name."

Izanami gritted her teeth. "Listen, there's more. This is the important part. Tell her that something is up. Something is going on, and it's serious. Tell her that I had to go away. Tell her I went to find Tsuru."

"T'soo roo?"

"Tsuru. She'll understand. I mean, she won't understand completely, but she'll understand enough. Will you do that for me?"

"You bet I will, young lady. Is there an address or a phone number where you can be reached?"

"No. She'll just have to follow me the best way she can. She'll figure out what to do."

"You don't have a cell phone?"

"Not any more. Too much tracking software. I was getting paranoid. I keep telling Lola to get rid of hers, but she's addicted to the stupid thing. So, have you got everything?"

"I'll have to write it down. Otherwise, I won't remember."

"Yes, you do that. A couple more things. If anyone else—anyone besides Lola—comes looking for me or the boy here, just act dumb. Act like you don't know anything. Act like you never talked to me in your life. Understand?"

"I can do that. You bet I can all right."

"Thank you. I owe you a debt, and that's something I take seriously. Now, one more thing."

"Yeah, sure, Chee hah roo."

"The woman who was injured, the one who was lying on the grass. Do you know where she is? Is she okay?"

"I heard the medics talking all right. They said they were taking her to Harborview. I don't know anything else."

"Thank you again."

"Don't you worry, young lady. That's what neighbors are for."

"If Lola decides she wants to rebuild her house and we come back to live here again, I promise I'll try to be a better neighbor."

As Izanami and Peter walked back down the street, the boy stared at her. When he didn't stop, she became annoyed.

"What?"

"You seem different. I mean, since the man almost killed you."

"Different how?"

"I don't know. You seem nicer."

"I do, do I? Don't be fooled. I'm not a nice person."

An hour later a young man engaged in a wrestling match with a vending machine. Accepting that the small bag of chips would not drop for him, he sighed and dug into his pockets. He found only pennies and nickels. He opened his wallet and found only twenties.

"Damn!"

He struck the machine again with his fist.

"Having a bad day, Kyle?"

He had not noticed the woman and the boy as they approached.

"Sorry, do I know you?"

"No, I guess not. I saw you once, but you were asleep."

"And you are...?"

"I'm Chiharu, Lola's friend."

"Oh, right. I've heard a lot about you. How did you get in? It's way past visitors' hours."

"How's Maria? Is she okay?"

"Yeah, the doctors think so anyway. They're keeping her for observation. They said she's mostly suffering from shock."

"Would it be okay if I talked to her? I just need a couple of minutes."

Kyle stared at Peter. "Hey, I know you. You were on..."

"Caleb?"

"Yeah, that's right. Man, I had almost forgotten. You guys called me Caleb. It's all like a dream now."

"You got old, Caleb."

"Hey, I'm not that old. What about you? You haven't changed in, what has it been now, two years? You haven't grown a bit."

Kyle looked at Izanami curiously, as if she might explain it to him.

"I'll see Maria now if it's all right."

"Right. Let me go see if she's awake, but I don't know if she'll feel up to having company."

"It's important."

Kyle returned after a few minutes.

"Yeah, it's okay. She says she wants to see you."

They walked into Maria's room. Izanami was relieved to see her sitting up.

"I'm sorry, Maria. I should never have gotten you involved."

Maria gazed at Peter. "Look, Chiharu. I can't mind him for you. I know you wanted me to, but I just can't."

"I know. I shouldn't have asked you. I didn't realize how serious this was."

"Are we in danger?"

"No, not you. They haven't any interest in you, but the boy and I have to go away."

"Where will you go?"

"It's better if you don't know, but I need to tell you one thing—in case Lola returns and you see her. Tell her that Peter and I have gone to find Tsuru."

"All right. I'll tell her, and she'll know who or what that is?"

"That's all you need to say. She'll remember me mentioning the name. It's better if you don't have any other information."

"Will the two of you be all right?"

"We'll be fine."

"Chiharu?"

"Yes?"

"Why do I have such a bad feeling? I feel scared without knowing why."

"I know what you're feeling. I feel it too. I've felt it for a while now, but I ignored it. Something's happening out there. Something's coming. I don't know exactly what, but it's on its way. I have to learn more."

"Thank you."

"For what?"

"For being honest. For not trying to protect me. Promise me you'll be safe out there."

"Here's some more honesty. I'll do no such thing."

"Lola would want you to."

"No, she wouldn't. I'm doing exactly what she would do, what she would expect me to do. I just needed to leave that message with you—and to see with my own eyes that you're all right. The kid and I need to go now. Goodbye—and good luck."

As she and Peter left the room, Kyle said, "Uh, nice meeting you finally."

"You don't need to be polite on my account," said Izanami without stopping. "I'm sure you've had better meetings."

"Yeah, you're right."

Peter followed Izanami out of the hospital and onto 9th Avenue. The wind off Elliott Bay chilled them as they walked down the steep Yesler Way overpass above the freeway.

"Where are we going now?" asked Peter.

"We're going to hang around the train station until morning, and then we're going to get a train north."

As they turned onto 6th Avenue South, they passed a tall man with a long, gray beard. He wore a dirty, threadbare overcoat.

"Repent! Repent!" he cried. "These are the last days! Repent before it's too late!"

"What's in the north?" asked Peter.

"Home."

5
North

PETER STARED AT the passing scenery. He watched the morning light play on Elliott Bay's dark blue surface as the train skirted its shore.

"How far is it to your home in the north?"

"You should get some sleep."

"I don't sleep."

"Oh yeah, I forgot. Well, *I* need to sleep. I'm exhausted."

The boy was silent for five minutes.

"Why do you and Lola both have two names?"

"We have one name for when we are working and another for when we aren't working."

"Why?"

"It's an old custom. It also happens to be a rule your grandfather insisted on. He believed it was dangerous for our birth names to be known when we were, um, working."

"Why?"

"Names have power. That's what he told us. Sapphire didn't agree with him. Since your grandfather's been gone, she's stopped following that rule. As for me, I'm still trying to get used to the idea."

"What exactly is your work?"

"Look, I know you keep saying you don't need sleep, but I do. These questions can wait."

"I'm bored."

"And you're my worst nightmare. You're not just a child. You're a child who never takes a nap or goes to bed."

"Just tell me what your job is."

Losing her patience, Izanami pushed her face up against the boy's. Her voice was low and grave.

"Do you honestly never sleep?"

He shook his head nervously.

"Never? You've never slept?"

"I... I don't remember."

"So you've never had a dream? Never had a nightmare?"

The boy said nothing.

"Because if you've never had a nightmare, then you can never understand my job. My job is the stuff of nightmares. The things that terrify you when you are alone in the dark in the middle of the night and your mind is free to wander into the darkest corners of your fears and of your imagination. Those are the things I hunt and hopefully destroy—if they don't destroy me first."

The boy stayed quiet. So did Izanami, but she regretted her outburst. She worried she may have frightened him, perhaps traumatized him. She had trouble reading his face.

"They call us Demon Hunters."

"Hathus called you something else."

"For some reason he's taken to calling demons 'hants' and Demon Hunters 'Hant Oppressors.' I have no idea what that's about, but I'm a Demon Hunter. At least that's as good a name as any. Look, I don't want you worrying about demons. The truth is, I haven't seen one for a long time now. It's as though they've lost interest in this world, and that's a good thing. At least I hope it is."

"Why wouldn't it be a good thing?"

"I don't know. I'd just feel better if I knew exactly why they've stopped crossing over. I get nervous when I don't understand things—especially when it comes to demons."

"What will you do for a job if there are no more demons to hunt?"

"I don't know. Maybe I'll just take it easy. Take time to enjoy myself. You know, have a retirement."

"You're not old enough for a retirement."

"I'm a lot older than I look. A *lot* older."

"Thank you, Izanami."

"Huh? What are you thanking me for?"

"For answering my questions. I like it when you don't talk to me as though I'm a child."

"You're welcome, but I don't know any other way to talk to you. All I know to do is answer your questions when I can, although I'm not sure honesty about certain things is good for you. Now, listen. I need to get at least a few minutes of sleep. If I manage to doze off by the time the train stops in Bellingham, make sure you wake me up. That's where we have to get off."

"Is that where your home is?"

"No. It's just where we have to get off."

Izanami closed her eyes. It seemed only a few seconds passed before Peter tugged vigorously on her arm. She struggled to gather her thoughts, surprised at how soundly she had slept.

"You said Bellingham, right? This is Bellingham."

"Right. Good job. Let's go."

For a few minutes Izanami found the world operating in slow motion. She did not mind because it meant her nap, despite its brevity, had been deep and restful. Getting a restoring rest in a short amount of time was a skill she had spent years developing. She envied the boy for needing no sleep at all.

They left the train station and walked toward Harris Avenue.

"Now where are we going?"

"To the freeway on-ramp. We're thumbing from here."

"Why couldn't we stay on the train?"

"We have to cross a border, and that's a bit of a problem since I have no passport. I'm guessing you don't have one either."

"What's a passport?"

"Something border guards insist on when you want to cross a border."

"Why don't you have one?"

"Because you need a birth certificate and people no longer accept my birth certificate as being mine."

"Why?"

"Because I don't look my age."

"Why? What age are you?"

"None of your business."

"You're like me, aren't you?"

"What are you talking about?"

"You're not getting older either, are you?"

"Oh, I'm getting older all right. I'm just doing it slowly. *Very* slowly."

"How is that different than me?"

"As far as I can tell, you aren't aging at all. You act and sound the same age all the time. I can feel the entire weight of my years—even if I don't show it. I'm a normal living person."

"Am I not a normal living person?"

Izanami held her tongue.

"You said you'd answer my questions."

"The truth is I don't know what you are."

When they got to the on-ramp, Izanami was pleased that vehicles were inclined to stop for the two of them. Traveling with a child was actually an advantage, she realized. The third one to pull over, a pickup driven by an older man, was going in their direction.

The pickup driver took them east toward Highway 9. There they got another lift all the way to Sumas.

"You're handy to have along," said Izanami as they watched the car drive away.

"Now what?"

"This is where things get more strenuous. We'll be traveling on foot from here on. I hope you're up to it."

In the town they went into a market to pick up bread, cheese, and fruit.

"Are you sure I can't get something for you? Do you still insist you don't need anything to eat?"

The boy shook his head.

"Well, that makes things easier. You're definitely a cheap date."

As she paid for the food, he said, "You must have a lot of money in that pouch."

"Only as much as is needed," she said. "No more."

They left the market and walked out of the town on a two-lane road. The afternoon was sunny but crisp. Traffic on the road was light. They passed a large house that was shielded from view by a thick growth of trees. After that the view opened up. A large field of grass was to their right, and a cornfield was to their left.

Izanami heard a distant rumble and froze. "I don't like that sound. Quick!"

She grabbed the boy roughly by his collar and pulled him into the corn stalks. She dropped flat onto the ground, and Peter imitated her. The rumbling grew louder. From their hiding place they saw a large rust-colored vehicle pass by.

"Is that the same...?"

"Yes," said Izanami grimly. "I wish I could have disabled it permanently, but they make those things indestructible."

"Are they looking for us?"

"What do you think? It can't be a coincidence."

"But how did they know to look for us here?"

"That's a good question. Come to think of it, how did Hathus know where to find you the other night in Pioneer Square? Do you have any idea?"

Peter shook his head.

"Are you sure? Don't hold anything back from me. If you know anything at all about those Mercenaries or why they're after you, you need to tell me."

"I swear. I never saw that man before the other night. I don't have any idea why he was after me."

"This isn't good. We have to make it as difficult as possible for them to follow us. That means we have to avoid roads."

For a while they waited quietly in case the Humvee came back. Then they walked to the cornfield's nearest corner and headed up a dirt road dividing that field from another. They continued north and then east. They followed lanes and paths across one farm after another. By the time the flat land gave way to wooded hills, Izanami was impressed that the boy had not complained about the long hike. He actually enjoyed being in constant motion.

Trees concealed them as they climbed into the hills and then the mountains.

"We won't meet anyone up here, will we?" said Peter.

"We might. This area is popular with hikers and also with people doing what we're doing."

"You mean they're going to see tuh-soo-roo?"

"You don't miss anything, do you? No, they're not going to see Tsuru. They're people, like us, who are slipping across the border, but we're only doing it out of necessity. Most of them are doing it because they're smugglers. The problem for them is that a lot of the trails have motion sensors and other ways for the border agents to monitor them. Fortunately, I know about trails that most others don't."

"How do you know so much?"

"Long years of experience. We're going to be walking for a few days. Are you okay with that? You certainly have had no trouble keeping up so far."

"I don't mind."

"I hope you won't be cold. It gets cold up here at night."

"I'll be all right."

"Let me guess. Are you going to tell me you don't get cold either?"

"Not usually. Do you?"

"No, but that's because of what I'm wearing. My suit might not look that warm, but it's quite effective at protecting me from the elements—and other things."

Darkness descended as they climbed a series of switchbacks. The wide valley before them melted into shadow. On the distant horizon, they could see the top of the rising moon. Izanami selected a spot at a sharp bend in the trail. It had a clear view in several directions. Moreover, a slight recess in the mountainside provided shelter from the wind. Peter sat on a large, flat rock, while Izanami produced a blanket and laid it on the ground.

"You fit a lot of things in that pouch of yours," said Peter. "Is it magic or something?"

She smiled. "I'm just good at packing."

She took a good look up and down the trail as well as down the slope. "Normally, I would make a fire, but I don't think that's a good idea under the circumstances. It would only draw attention to our location."

She sat on a rock across from the boy. She cut off a piece of bread with her sheath knife and offered it to Peter.

"I don't eat," he said.

"Oh, yeah. I forgot." She sliced some cheese for herself. She studied him as she chewed.

"You're definitely a mystery. Are you sure you don't know where you came from? Why you're different from other people? Why those Mercenaries are after you?"

Peter shook his head. "All I remember is the island."

"And your grandfather never said anything to you about where you came from?"

"He got cross if I asked too many questions."

"That sounds like him all right."

She looked toward the east. The moon had cleared the horizon. "It's going to get cold. Really cold. That won't bother me too much, but I don't know what to do about you. You may find it too cold to sleep."

"I don't sleep."

She sighed heavily. "You said you usually don't get cold. Usually isn't the same as never."

"I do get cold. Sometimes."

She picked up the blanket and handed it to him. "Here. Wrap this around you. At least it's better than nothing. I don't need it. My suit will keep me warm enough."

"Thank you."

"You won't be thanking me in the middle of the night when your bones are freezing. I'm sorry about the fire, but those Mercenaries seem determined to find us again. I can't take the chance."

"I'll be all right."

"You know, maybe you will be. You've certainly been surviving on your own for a long time now."

She drew near him and knelt on one knee so that her face was close to his.

"Since it actually seems to be true that you don't need sleep, I'm going to make use of you. You're going to be the night watch. I'm counting on you to stay alert. Wake me right away if you see or hear any sign of somebody—or something..."

"Something?"

"Yeah, or something. I'm going to catch a few hours of sleep. Usually, I'm a light sleeper, but tonight feels different. I'm tired in a way I haven't been for a long time."

She curled up in the most sheltered part of the nook and used her pouch as a pillow. Her knife was underneath it with her fingers around the handle.

"Good night," she said.

"Good night," said the boy.

She was surprised by how quickly sleep began enveloping her. As her eyes closed, she saw the boy motionless on his rock. He stared straight ahead and, by some trick of the moonlight and her imagination, he glowed. He was quiet and still, almost as if in a trance. Was he watching something far off in the distance or merely lost in his own thoughts? What did he think about, she wondered.

That image was the last thing of which she was conscious before the dream overtook her mind.

She walked in darkness so complete she might as well have been blind. Because she could not see the ground in front of her, she stumbled repeatedly. She reached out in case she might run into something. Her hands found the rugged surface of a cave wall. She proceeded cautiously. Her progress was excruciatingly slow.

Something wrapped itself around her leg. It was a large snake. She reached for her knife, but the sheath normally on her belt was missing. She felt for the medallion that would summon the diabolusbane, but it too was gone. The snake wrapped itself around her waist. She tried to grab it with her hands, but it was too large and smooth to grip. She felt it slither up her back and over her shoulder. She recoiled as its forked tongue scraped her cheek.

She turned and twisted frantically, pressing against its body as best she could. She felt additional pressure on her feet. It was another snake coiling around her ankles. Desperate to keep it from entrapping her legs, she kicked wildly. She kicked with all the power she could muster. She flailed urgently.

Gradually, her reality shifted, and then her foot connected with the serpent on her legs. She gasped for air. From a distance she heard a loud, distressed cry that alarmed her.

She spent several more moments fighting the snakes before she grasped that they were not there. She saw the familiar rocks around her and realized it had been a dream. Still, the panic did not subside. The ground beneath her and around her was disturbed by her thrashing. She looked toward the rock where Peter had been sitting. He was gone.

She stood and looked in every direction. There was no sign of him. Then she heard his voice.

"Help!"

6
Canada

IZANAMI RAN IN the direction of Peter's voice. His cry had come from beyond the trail's edge, from somewhere below.

"Peter!"

"I'm down here!" he called back.

She sprang over the edge and slid down the mountainside. She dodged trees and rocks while skidding down the slope.

"Talk to me!" she shouted. "I'll follow your voice!"

"I'm here! Please hurry!"

She found him propped against the trunk of a large fir growing next to a small ledge.

"Are you hurt? Can you move?"

She studied him for any sign of injury. She peered into his eyes for any indication of shock.

"I think I'm all right. Rather sore. That was quite a fright."

"What happened? Did someone do this to you?"

"It was you."

"What are you talking about? Did you fall?"

"You kicked me."

"Kicked you? What do you mean? I was asleep."

"You shouted. You were thrashing about. I thought something was terribly wrong, and I went over to see if you were all right. I laid my hand on your arm, and then you kicked me. You kicked me so hard I flew through the air and over the edge of the mountain."

"Really? I did? Sorry about that. I didn't mean to. I had a terrible nightmare."

"You're awfully strong, you know. You sent me flying as if I weighed nothing."

"I said I was sorry."

"Next time I think I'll just leave you."

"That's probably best. Come on. I'll take you back up the mountain."

She let him climb onto her back, and he clung to her as she made the ascent. When they had reached the trail above, Peter scrambled away from her and sat well back from the edge. Izanami stood at the brink and had a good look in every direction. Her first thought on waking had been that the Mercenaries must have found them. She studied the dark landscape for any indication of other people traveling or camping. She also kept a wary eye for serpents.

She looked up at the moon. A few passing clouds created an illusion of it racing across the sky. It was well past the midpoint of its nightly trajectory. She had slept several hours, which was a lot more than she had thought.

"It won't be long till sunrise," she said. "We might as well start walking again. I don't think I'll get back to sleep now, and as for you, well, we both know you won't be sleeping either."

Izanami grabbed her bag and took out two apples. She offered one to Peter.

He shook his head.

"It just seemed polite to offer it."

"You don't strike me as someone who worries about being polite."

"You're right. I'm not. It must be Sapphire's influence."

The air was cold and still. The only sound was that of the Demon Hunter's teeth crunching the fruit. A few minutes later, there was a sudden, piercing screech in the distance. It was followed by softer calls of "hoo-hoo" from another direction. The sounds were ghostly in the pre-dawn moonlight.

"Are those owls?" asked Peter.

"Yeah. Great horned owls, I would guess. Ever see one?"

"No, I don't know that kind. I do remember seeing brown owls."

"Brown owls? Where was that?"

He thought for a moment, then said, "I can't remember."

After reaching the crest, they followed the trail down the mountain. They stepped carefully in the half-light of the setting moon. Before long, the sun peeked over the horizon, allowing them to see the trail more clearly.

"That dream you had must have been scary."

"I have to admit it unsettled me."

"What happened in the dream?"

"There were snakes. Lots of snakes."

"Is that why it unsettled you?"

"Because of the snakes? No, I've never been particularly afraid of snakes."

"Then why?"

"Because of something strange."

"What?"

"That's the first dream I can remember having in at least fifty years."

"Honestly?"

"Honestly."

"I guess that's something else we have in common."

"What?"

"I don't dream either."

"I guess that makes sense. If you don't sleep, then you can't dream."

"Is it much farther to Canada?"

"We're already in Canada. We crossed the border yesterday."

"We did? Where was it?"

"On the mountain."

"You might have told me."

"Sorry, I'm not a tour guide."

By late afternoon they had crossed another mountain pass and were again descending. Below them was a busy highway skirting the base of the mountain. As they walked down, Izanami did not take the shortest route to the highway but instead one that brought them to an interchange.

"Will you use your thumb again?"

"That's right. Our feet can have a rest for a while."

They stood near the entrance to the freeway and waited. As the sun sank toward the western horizon, Peter wondered if anyone would stop for Izanami's thumb once the daylight was gone. After a thirty-minute wait, a blinding pair of bright headlights heralded the arrival of a semi-trailer truck pulling onto the shoulder. The name T&X Transport was painted on the cab door.

Izanami asked the driver, "Where are you headed?"

"I can take you all the way to Calgary, if you're interested in going that far."

"We'll take a lift as far as Cache Creek if that's all right."

"Heading up Prince George way?"

"That direction, yes."

"Hop on, folks."

Izanami sent the boy climbing into the cab first so that he would be next to the driver. She knew the trucker would expect conversation in exchange for the ride, and she hoped he would give his attention to the boy. The cab was wide enough for the three of them to sit comfortably, and she hoped to manage a brief catnap.

"Where are you folks coming from?"

Unsure of what to say, Peter looked at Izanami, but she had already closed her eyes.

"Seattle."

The driver studied the pair of them with a few side glances. "You're not running away from home, are you?"

"Why do you ask that?"

"Well, you both look pretty young, and I'm guessing you're not related."

"She's my minder. She's a lot older than she looks, you know. She's taking me to visit a friend of hers."

"Where does her friend live?"

"In Canada."

"Yeah, well, I figured that much was certain. Are you coming from Vancouver?"

Peter shook his head.

"I thought maybe the two of you had decided get out of the city—with everything that's going on."

"What's going on?"

"Don't you listen to the news? I guess maybe not at your age. There are riots everywhere—and not just in Vancouver. It seems to be every big city. In the States too. It's like people are going crazy. Where did you say her friend lived?"

"I don't know where in Canada she lives. I've never been to Canada before. At least I don't think so."

"Are you English or something?"

"Maybe. I'm not certain."

"Not certain? You mean, you don't know what country you're from?"

"Could we talk about something else please? I'm not good at answering questions."

"Fair enough. I'm not always so good at it myself."

The driver had become distracted by something in his rear-view mirror. Peter saw bright lights reflecting off the truck's side mirrors.

"What kind of crazy driving is that?" said the trucker, glancing at his mirror with concern. "Is that a Hummer? I didn't know those things could go that fast. Must be one of the newer turbo diesel ones."

The boy shook the Demon Hunter's arm franticly. "Izanami! Wake up!"

She gasped, startled by how soundly she had been sleeping. "What?"

"It's them!" cried the boy nervously.

"Wait," said the driver. "Do you know those lunatics that're following us?"

Izanami maneuvered herself for a look in the side-view mirror outside her window.

"What the…!" She turned to the driver. "I don't suppose this rig can go any faster."

"I'm right at the speed limit as it is."

"Speed limit? Forget the speed limit. Can you go any faster or not?"

"No way I can afford another ticket! Hey, what are you doing?"

He had to shout over the wind that now roared into the cab. Izanami had rolled down her window. Mere feet away the Humvee had pulled alongside the truck in the adjacent lane. She slid smoothly into the window frame and crouched, bracing herself against the air current.

"If you're not going to go any faster," she shouted, "then you'd be better off slowing down!"

The driver turned his head back and forth, trying to watch the road in front of him and, at the same time, his unpredictable passenger. What kind of lunatic had he let into his truck? He lifted his foot from the accelerator, cutting the truck's speed, and was shocked to see her spring forward into mid-air. As his rig continued to slow, he saw his erstwhile passenger land on top of the other vehicle. Given the Humvee's speed, he wondered how she had the strength to cling to the rim above its windshield.

"Chiharu!" cried the boy plaintively.

The Humvee sped away as the truck rolled to a stop on the freeway's shoulder.

"I can't believe what I just saw!" exclaimed the driver.

"Why did you stop?" said the boy, anxiously. "We have to go after them."

"No way. I'm taking a few minutes to catch my breath, and then I'll take you as far as Hope. They have an RCMP detachment. I'll let them figure out what to do with you."

"Please. Can't we go after them? She's in danger. She may need us."

The driver put the truck in gear and pulled back out onto the highway.

"Who is she? What are you doing with her? Did she kidnap you?"

"No, she's trying to help me. If she gets hurt, it will be my fault. Can't you go any faster?"

"Settle down, son. I'll get you to people who can help you. Don't you worry."

"You don't understand."

A few miles down the highway, the darkness was split by a bright, burning ball of fire. As they approached, they could see that it was in a field next to the road. The trucker slowed to have a better look. In the flames they could see part of a vehicle's metal frame and the remains of a large radial tire.

"It's them!" shouted the boy.

The driver pulled the truck over a short distance past the blaze. Too impatient to struggle with the heavy door, Peter clambered through the open window and down to the ground.

"Hey, where are you going?" cried the driver, but Peter had already leaped over the guardrail and now ran toward the fire.

"Chiharu!"

The overwhelming heat stopped him in his tracks. Tears streamed down his face.

"Come back!" shouted the driver, standing on the shoulder. "There's nothing you can do."

Peter became aware of movement in the darkness on the far side of the fire. He circled around the wreckage for a better view. In the fluctuating light of the blaze, he could see two large figures standing at equal distances from a smaller third figure. The boy dropped to his hands and knees and crept closer. One of the men brandished a club, the other a large knife. Between them was Izanami, wielding her knife. As Peter stared at her, he noticed something was missing. The medallion was not hanging from her belt—the one she used to summon the diabolusbane.

"Have you not learned your lesson, Hant Oppressor?" said one of the men. It was Hathus.

"Have you not learned yours?" said Izanami. "If I am forced to choose between the boy's safety and your lives, then you Mercenaries are dead men."

"We are not Mercenaries," spat Hathus. "We are Legionnaires. Do not forget it."

"That's a reckless threat when it's two against one," said the other man.

Peter did not recognize him. Hathus gave him a cautioning look. Apparently, this new Legionnaire was somehow not aware of Izanami's reputation.

"Do you really prefer death," asked Izanami, "to disappointing this Alaric?"

"You don't understand what's at stake. If you grasped the truth, as we do, you would help us."

"I keep waiting for someone to explain this big truth to me, but you never quite manage it."

The man with the knife lunged at Izanami. She flung her fists in front of her and shot a blast of energy at him, but he deflected it easily with his forearms.

"Damn," she cried. "Does *everyone* have those things?"

He lunged again with the knife. She side-stepped his attack but not before Peter, in his fright, let out a gasp. Hathus's head swung in the boy's direction. He smiled as he turned and started toward the child. Peter froze in place as Hathus loped closer. Izanami pivoted for her own dash to the boy but was foiled by the other Mercenary's thrust of his knife. The blade bounced off her suit's impervious fabric, but the momentary distraction gave him a chance to grab her upper arm with one hand while attempting a knife thrust at her neck with the other.

With no choice but to defend herself, she deflected his knife hand with her forearm while thrusting a knee into his groin. While his trousers' padding shielded him from the full force of the blow, the impact was severe enough to make him wince and drop his weapon. He fell to his knees and gritted his teeth.

Now free to pursue Hathus, Izanami darted after him.

"I could use some help here," she muttered to herself. "Why did I have to outlive all my old comrades?"

Hathus now held Peter roughly by the wrist and made no move to flee. He raised his club as a warning to come no closer. She halted a few yards away, her knife at the ready. Hathus yanked the boy by his arm a foot off the ground.

"Ow! You're hurting me!"

Izanami wondered if Peter might again avail himself of Grandfather's trick, but given that the boy's concentration was consumed entirely by the pain in his shoulder, she figured not.

"Let him go, Hathus!"

"No! Leave now or face the consequences."

"What consequences? Whatever it is you want him for, you clearly want him alive. I won't let you leave with him. We're at a standoff. You may as well let him go."

Izanami was thrown forward by a sudden blunt blow to her back. The other Mercenary had recovered faster than she had expected. She hit the ground and rolled over to look up at him. She reached for her fallen knife, but her hand was immobilized by a heavy boot on her wrist. Her foe glared down, and it was clear from his face that he was still in pain. She squirmed and kicked at his leg. He raised his knife.

"Can I kill her, Hathus?"

His comrade looked warily as the boy dangled from his hand. "It didn't go well for Belenus when he tried it."

"I'm not Belenus. I'm going to do it."

"That suit she wears will protect her."

"It doesn't cover her entire neck."

Izanami writhed more furiously, but her movements were severely limited by the weight of his boot. He stared at her neck and raised his blade higher. He chose his moment, and she saw his hand jerk. She tried one last twist of her torso, but she knew it wasn't enough. Instinctively, she tightened the muscles in her neck.

A foot away from her face, the knife plunged into the ground. At the same time his body collapsed on top of her. His weight knocked the wind out of her, but it was preferable to a blade in the carotid artery. Her wrist ached, but it was now free. As she struggled to get a breath, his body flew up and away from her, landing a few feet away. She stared at his motionless form in disbelief.

She looked up to see another figure standing over her. His hands still held the rock he had used to attack the Mercenary from behind. He smirked and shook his head, causing his long, blond hair to sway.

"So it *is* you." The voice was deep, the accent of indeterminate European origin. "Once again you owe me your life, Izanami. Let us think of all the ways you might repay me."

She slid backward and blinked her eyes. "Koschei?"

"Who else? You always get into so much trouble without me. So, where is my thanks then?"

"But..."

"But what?"

"But you're dead."

7
Cariboo Highway

HATHUS TOOK ADVANTAGE of the confusion caused by the stranger's intervention. He dragged the boy as he fled. Fighting the pain in her wrist, Izanami retrieved her knife and leapt to her feet. She sprinted after the Mercenary and soon caught up to him. She dove for his legs and brought him rolling onto the ground. Free from Hathus's grip, Peter scrambled away from him. Hathus reached for the boy but was effectively immobilized by Izanami, who planted her knees firmly on his back. She pressed her blade against the back of his neck.

"Where did you think you were going with him?" she panted. "Your vehicle is wrecked. Were you going to run all the way back to your precious Alaric on foot?"

The Mercenary grunted and said nothing. She glanced at the boy who watched from a distance, crouching on the ground.

"Are you all right?"

He stood, rubbing his hand tenderly. He nodded solemnly.

Koschei strode over to join them.

"Who is that, Izanami? What's his quarrel with you?"

She stared at him with suspicion. "Who are you? Where did you come from? Why here? Why now?"

His high cheekbones sank into a frown. "Is that any way to greet an old comrade? We've known each other too long to play a game like this, Izanami."

"Koschei is one of the best comrades I ever had, but he's dead. Who are you?"

"Dead? Yes, you said that before. It's news to me. Do I look dead to you?"

"I saw you die. I was there. You were killed by a demon in the Netherworld. Like the fool you are, you sacrificed yourself for me. I'll never forgive you for that."

"The Netherworld? My dear Izanami, you've clearly lost your grip on reality. What on earth would you or I be doing in the Netherworld? Do I look like a suicidal idiot to you?"

"If you were really Koschei, then you would remember Orpheus convincing us to join him in a quest to rescue his precious Justine. He and Sapphire."

"Who?"

"You don't know who Sapphire is? Whoever you are, reveal your true identity at once. You're not Koschei, no matter how much you look and sound like him."

"Suit yourself, Izanami, but what do you want to do with these two? They would be Mercenaries if I'm not mistaken."

"Did you never meet Hathus? No, I suppose there's no reason you would have. He used to be with the Condottieri, but now he's with some group calling themselves the Zen'ei."

"Personally, I never had much time for the Condottieri and their strange ways. Why do they insist on using such antiquated weapons? Everything they do is out of pure greed. Look at the way they spend their time—charging wealthy eccentrics exorbitant fees to plunder ancient relics of dubious mystical power. They're a distasteful class of people. Who's the boy?"

Izanami was failing in her resistance to accepting this man as Koschei. Her every instinct told her, despite the impossibility of the situation, it was truly he.

"He was on Orpheus's island. He's like you—a conundrum that logically shouldn't be here."

"How is Orpheus? Have you seen him?"

"We don't have time for this. I need to make sure these two can't follow us."

"What can I do to help you, old friend?"

She hoped she wasn't making a mistake in deciding to treat him as the true Koschei—at least for the time being.

"Take the boy and walk back toward the highway. He shouldn't see what I'm about to do."

Koschei extended his hand to Peter. The boy nervously took it and walked away with him, looking back at Izanami once, then twice.

She waited until they were a good distance away. As she stared at the tall figure with the long, blond hair, she was more convinced, despite everything, he was her dead friend. It made no sense, but she had seen and experienced too many fantastic events in her long life not to understand that few things were truly impossible.

"Do you believe me now, Izanami?" said Hathus, fidgeting under her knees. "The world is changing. You've seen it for yourself. The dead are returning. We are in the final times."

"You know I can't let you go, Hathus."

"You have no choice. You have a code. You won't kill us."

"No, but I'll hurt you. You'll heal in time, but you won't be walking for a while."

"You'd disable us and just leave us here?"

"You were warned. What's the point of warnings if neither of us treats them seriously?"

"Do what you must, but it will change nothing. Your destiny is already written."

"Whatever you say, Hathus."

Koschei and Peter heard the screams. The Russian tried to distract the boy by asking him questions. Eventually, the howls stopped. Presently, Izanami joined them. She wiped the blood from her blade on the grass. Koschei eyed her curiously.

"So you cut the…?"

"The peroneal tendon. In both ankles. They'll heal in time, but with any luck, not before this is all over."

"You're harder than you used to be, Izanami."

"Not any harder than I need to be. Actually, I've become softer in a lot of ways. It's Sapphire's influence."

She touched the medallion, which she had restored to her belt.

"Lucky for those two that this was separated from me in the crash. I swear I would have used the diabolusbane on them."

"And you say you're softer?"

"So says the man who died and refused to stay dead. Come. We can catch up as we walk. We have a long way to go."

"So you want me to go with you—despite being under the delusion that I'm a dead man?"

"The boy and I are better off with you than without you. You've proved that."

Peter heard the two men's moans. "Will they be okay? Won't they need help?"

"Don't worry about them. They'll manage to crawl far enough to attract somebody's attention. I only wish I could see them explain who they are and what happened to them."

"Where are we going?" asked Koschei.

"I have to take the boy to Tsuru. If anyone can figure out what his story is—and for that matter, yours—it will be her."

"Your old Master? Is that woman still alive?"

As they neared the highway, Izanami spotted two large semi-trailer trucks parked on the shoulder a hundred yards down the road. She raced ahead of the others to read the name on the farther one. It was T&X Transport, and a familiar face was inside the driver's window.

"Did you actually wait for us?" she asked.

"When I saw the Hummer on fire, I pulled over. The other truck was already here. He called in the accident. The RCMP should be here anytime. They told him to wait so they could get a statement. I couldn't believe anyone survived that crash."

"I jumped off before the impact. The two inside scrambled out before the thing blew. They're lying over there. They may need some medical attention. Will you still take us to Cache Creek?"

"You should wait. The Mounties will want to talk to you."

"It will be better if they don't. Trust me, nothing will be gained by our staying here."

"Just what kind of trouble are you mixed up in?"

"No trouble. Everything's fine. Will you give us a lift or not?"

The faint sound of an approaching siren could be heard in the distance.

"Who's he?" asked the driver as he studied Koschei.

"He's with us. Are we going or what?"

The driver looked at Izanami and then Koschei again and then the boy. "I should have my head examined, but all right. Hop in quick. One of you can go behind in the sleeper."

The trio boarded the cab quickly as the driver started the engine. He checked the traffic in his mirrors and gave a quick toot on the air horn. As the other truck responded in kind, he pulled onto the road. Izanami leaned for a look in the side mirror. Two cars with flashing lights had arrived. To her relief they both pulled over behind the other truck. She settled into her seat.

"Thanks," she said to the driver. "I'll give you something for fuel."

"Don't worry about it. I have no idea what any of this is about, but I'm usually a pretty good judge of people. I'll drop the three of you off at Cache Creek, and then I'm going to do my best to forget any of this ever happened."

"You are a wise man," she said.

"So which one are you?" asked Koschei from behind them.

"I don't get you," said the confused driver. "What do you mean?"

"Are you T or are you X?"

"Neither. They're the ones paying for the fuel."

He continued glancing back at the imposing man with the long, blond hair, unsure what to make of him. They soon reached a place called Hope. Following the Trans-Canada Highway required an exit to a different road. Izanami gazed eastward somberly down the highway not taken.

"Are you all right, Chiharu?"

The boy's habit of watching her all the time annoyed her.

"I'm fine."

"You look... sad."

"I spent some time in a place down that other road. I was just remembering it. That's all."

"What was it called?"

She smiled ruefully. "Sunshine Valley."

"It sounds nice."

"It wasn't."

After a bit more than two hours, the truck arrived at Cache Creek. The driver offered to drive them a few miles up the Cariboo Highway despite it being out of his way. After a few miles, he turned into a side road to let them out. It was also a good place to reverse out and head back to the main highway.

"Thanks again," said Izanami when they had descended from the cab. "You've been a great help. Are you sure I can't give you something? For your time if not for the fuel?"

"No, thanks," said the driver with a smile. "I got a pretty good story out of it. That's payment enough."

"If you say so," she said, "but I'd advise you to tell your story only to people you know well. For your own safety."

He looked for some sign she was joking but he saw none. "Then again, maybe it's not that interesting a story after all. Good luck to you all."

As the truck disappeared down the highway, Koschei stared at Izanami. "Who are you and what have you done with my friend?"

"What are you talking about?"

"You never used to be so polite. It's not like you at all."

"I told you. Things are different now. Come on. We still have a lot of walking to do. With any luck we'll get to the trailhead by dark."

They hiked up the road, keeping to the wide shoulder on the right. It was a straight two-lane highway paralleled by one utility pole after another. The world around them was in motion. A brisk wind sent dark gray clouds gliding above them. It also made the acacia branches on the surrounding hills shake and the tall grass in the nearby fields sway.

Koschei looked at Peter. "What did those Mercenaries want with the boy?"

"I wish I knew, and the kid says he has no idea either. They belong to some kind of cult, and the boy seems to hold some kind of religious significance for them. What I'd like to know is how they always seem to know where to find him."

The Russian gave Peter a friendly shove on the back, which the boy did not appreciate.

"So, lad, are you a messiah? Come on, you must know something. What's made those soldiers of fortune so eager to get their hands on the likes of you?"

"I don't know," he replied crossly. "I just wish they would leave me alone. I wish everyone would leave me alone. I just wish I could go back to…"

"Back where?" asked Izanami.

"I don't know. Wherever I came from. The island maybe. I was happy there. With Grandfather."

"How exactly did you get off the island?"

"I don't remember anything about that. All I remember is Grandfather lying on the bed. He had got very old. He kissed me goodbye. Then it's all confusing. All I remember after that is being in that city. The place where I met you."

"Who's your grandfather, boy?" asked Koschei.

"The man he calls Grandfather," said Izanami, "it was Orpheus."

"Really? He never struck me as the grandfatherly type. Surely, he could shed some light on this. Why are we not looking for him instead of your old Master?"

"Because Orpheus is gone—for good. He's trapped in the Netherworld for all time."

"You're joking. How did that happen?"

"Do you honestly not remember us going to the Fiend's realm, Koschei? I'll never be able to forget it—as long as I live."

"It sounds like the sort of thing a person would remember, but I have no memory of anything like that happening."

"You don't remember Orpheus, Sapphire, and me finding you in Sussex? You had bought a castle and were calling yourself Alexei Mikhailov."

"Sussex? Really? What would I have been doing in Sussex? Are you sure? I'm beginning to worry about you, Izanami."

"Maybe you're right to. Have you gone mad or have I? What's the last thing you *do* remember?"

"Well, let me see. I have to admit things are a bit hazy for the last while. I do remember being in Budapest, but that was some time ago. Was that before I was in Montevideo or after?

Strange. I never had problems with remembering things like that before.”

“How did you come to be where you found us earlier? How did you come to Canada?”

“Yes, I thought this was Canada all right. Frankly, I’m at a loss. I have no idea why I’m in Canada.”

“The shock of what happened to you in the Netherworld may have wiped out your most recent memories. If you did somehow escape from there, I suppose it’s a miracle you have any sanity at all left.”

“Assuming what you are saying is true, Izanami...”

“Yes?”

“Let’s say for the sake of argument you’re right. What did happen to me in the Netherworld?”

“Frankly, I don’t know if I’m ready to talk about it—or if you’re ready to hear about it. It was bad.”

“And Orpheus didn’t come back?”

“He’s gone. About as gone as anyone can be, although seeing you here now makes me wonder if anyone is ever truly gone.”

“Izanami, do you think sometimes...?”

“Yes?”

“... that sometimes the entire universe has gone mad?”

“Yes, I’m definitely getting that feeling more and more.”

Izanami had almost forgotten about Peter, but he had been listening intently.

“Is the world going mad?” he asked. “Is that why there are riots in all the cities?”

“Riots?” she asked. “What riots?”

“That lorry driver said people were going crazy in all the cities.”

“Are you sure? I didn’t hear him say that.”

“You were asleep.”

“Maybe you heard him wrong. Weren’t we in Seattle just the other day? There weren’t any riots then.”

Peter shrugged. Izanami looked at Koschei, who also shrugged.

“How much farther are we going?” he asked.

"Not much farther. We'll be leaving the highway soon, and I for one will be glad about it. Then we'll follow a trail to Lost Gap. That's where we'll find Tsuru."

They walked a while in silence. The sky darkened, and a low roar announced the chilly wind that blew through the valley. Despite her suit's protection from the cold, Izanami shivered.

It was dark before they reached the trailhead. A waning gibbous moon played hide and seek with the soaring black clouds. In the gloom they stepped carefully along the uphill trail for almost a quarter mile. When they found a suitable spot, they stopped.

"I'm going to chance making a fire," said Izanami. "We can't be seen from any distance here."

Koschei stayed with the boy while Izanami collected sticks and branches. Once she got the flames going, they sat to enjoy their warmth. She pulled her bread and cheese from her pouch.

"I'm afraid there isn't much," she said. "The boy doesn't eat at all. I only brought enough for myself."

"It's not a problem," said the Russian.

"Don't be polite, Koschei. You must be famished after the day we had. I'll share what I have with you."

"It's not necessary."

"Don't be stubborn. Go ahead and have some."

"You misunderstand me, my friend. I'd gladly take some of your bread, but I'm not the least bit hungry. I have no appetite."

"Strange. Well, suit yourself."

She chewed on the bread and cheese by herself. The others watched her, and though neither looked the least bit covetous of her food, it made her uncomfortable.

"So the Demon Hunters aren't so close to extinction after all," she said between bites. "Sapphire and I thought we were the last two. Now you're back. That makes three."

"There was a time when we were many. The great ones are all gone."

"I take exception to that. Sapphire and I are as good as any of them."

Koschei chuckled at Izanami's lack of humility. "Remember Callan? Now he was truly great. He was the best of us. A true friend. I was certain he would go on forever. I still remember the day I heard he fell in the Sistan Basin. I couldn't believe it. I still can't."

"The worst was the afternoon when Ragnar fell. It haunts me to this day."

She looked at the boy and wondered if the conversation was upsetting to him. If it was, he gave no sign. He sat silently, watching the two of them with alert eyes that never tired.

"Yes, that was a bad day," said Koschei. "Do you remember Zeena?"

Izanami's face darkened.

"We're not going to talk about Zeena."

An awkward silence followed. Then Izanami spoke again.

"You know, I was wrong, Koschei."

"Wrong? About what?"

"About the day Ragnar died being the worst day. That's not right. That wasn't the worst day. Not anymore."

"What was the worst day then?"

"The day I saw you die."

The two comrades talked for a long while watching the flickering flames die down. Then Izanami found herself overcome by a profound weariness.

"Shall we take turns keeping watch?" she said.

"Agreed."

"Do you mind if I sleep first? I can barely keep my eyes open."

"That's fine. Sleep all you want. I can keep watch the entire night."

"You say that now, but you'll feel differently in an hour or two. Wake me then, and I will take my turn."

"I assure you, it won't be necessary. I have no need of sleep."

She wanted to ask him something, but it was no use. Sleep overtook her. The last thing she heard was the eerie, distant screech of the great horned owl.

8
Lost Gap

SHE WAS IN a house, but what house? Walking was difficult, as in the darkness she couldn't see where to put her feet. Voices from another room made her uneasy. Her disquiet turned to alarm. She had to get outside, but she saw no door or window. Something scurried over her foot. *Rats*, she thought. She had felt them on her skin. She wasn't wearing her bodysuit. She felt them against her ankles. She kicked madly to get rid of them. Now they had climbed her legs.

She wanted to cry out, but she could make no sound. Tiny sharp teeth nibbled at her neck. She tried swiping at the rodent on her shoulder, but something restrained her arm. She squirmed wildly, attempting to free herself. If only she could yell, but her vocal chords were frozen. In one last eruption of fury, she flailed in every direction at once. At long last sound burst from her mouth. Her body jerked in a spasm.

"I wouldn't do that if I were you." It was the boy.

"Ow!" Koschei cried in surprise and pain. "She's having some kind of a fit..."

"I told you. She kicked me halfway down a mountain the last time."

"Wake up, Izanami. You're having a nightmare."

Gradually, she calmed herself. "What?"

A dark expression on his face, Koschei rubbed his jaw. "You had no cause to strike me."

"Chiharu," said Peter. "Are you all right?"

"It was so real," she muttered, exhausted and struggling with lingering confusion. "After so many years with no dreams, why am I having them now?"

70

"Maybe it's that cheese you were eating. Eating strong cheese sometimes makes me have strange dreams. Or so it did when I used to sleep—and when I used to eat."

"Do you really not sleep anymore, Koschei, or eat?"

He shrugged and shook his head.

"It's like the boy. He doesn't either. What's going on? It makes no sense."

"Perhaps your old Master will have some explanation. How much longer until we reach her?"

"Not long at all, and now that we're all awake, we shouldn't delay."

Izanami walked to the nearby stream to wash her face in the icy water. Her heart still raced. She did not like dreaming. She hated the lack of control while asleep. She returned to the others and made a breakfast of the remaining bread and fruit.

When she had finished, the three continued their trek up the trail. The morning was bright, and the air was fresh thanks to a light breeze.

"Only a few more miles to the entrance to Lost Gap."

"How long has it been since you last saw her?" asked Koschei.

"Let me see. It must be about four years now."

"Are you certain she'll be there?"

"I have no reason to think she won't."

"She's quite old, isn't she?"

"I suppose, but you know the Masters. Age doesn't matter much to them."

"Yes, but most of them are gone now."

Izanami said nothing. She did not want to contemplate Tsuru not being there.

"The boy called you by a name."

She said nothing.

"Chiharu, I think he said."

Still no reply.

"Is that... your birth name?"

"I don't want to talk about it."

"Why would you tell him your birth name?"

"Everybody knows it now. That's the way things have gone. Sapphire thinks that owning our true names is a strength, not a weakness."

"What do *you* think?"

"Once I trusted Orpheus. Now I trust Sapphire. With my life."

"You and this Sapphire must be close."

"It's new for me, but yes, we're close. Closer than I have ever been to another person."

"Chiharu, eh? That's a pretty name."

"If I hear that one more time…" she fumed. "So what's your true name? You know mine. It's only fair that I know yours."

Unsure, he hesitated a moment, but then he said, "Alexei."

"So you were actually using your true name when we found you in Sussex? What's the rest of it? Alexei what?"

"Does it matter?"

"You won't remember this, but the time we were headed for the Netherworld, we were overcome by a strange enchantment. We all suffered hallucinations related to traumas in our earlier lives."

"No, I do not remember that."

"Sapphire told me later that you shouted something about Rasputin. Did you know him?"

Koschei took time to respond. "Yes."

"Are you going to tell me about it?"

"No."

As they continued their hike, Koschei and Peter gazed only forward, but Izanami found herself looking back at regular intervals. She could not shake the feeling that someone might be following them.

At midday they came to the foot of a steep hill. The trail continued upward, but Izanami led them off the trail. They traced the hill's base in a gradual circle toward the left. After a half mile they descended into a ravine and walked alongside a rippling stream emerging from a growth of old trees and bushes. Penetrating the woodland was like entering a cave. They were enveloped by shadow, the temperature dropped precipitously, and the birdsong they had heard all morning was absent.

"*Nifiga sebe!*" Koschei gasped. "I'm freezing. What kind of place is this?"

A quarter mile inside the woods, they came to a black pool. It was fed by water pouring over the rocks above. Izanami walked to the far edge where a stony pathway passed under the falling water. She stopped.

"What are we waiting for?" whispered Koschei.

"For permission. Be patient."

Her outward calm belied her inner anxiety. Normally by this point she would have detected Tsuru's presence, but so far she felt nothing. Koschei's question about whether her old Master would still be there gnawed at her. To her relief, after a few more minutes she felt the familiar and comforting mental connection, but she also sensed discomfiture caused by the presence of her two companions. It was not certain they would be allowed to pass.

"How long do we have to stand here?" complained Peter quietly.

She ignored him as more minutes passed. Then a wave of relief washed over her.

"We may continue."

She led them under the falling water and into the cave behind it. Now the darkness was absolute. The stone floor was uneven and slippery. As she stepped carefully, Izanami was surprised when Peter's clammy, desperate hand grabbed hold of hers. The walk through the damp cave felt endless.

All at once they were blinded by the sun. Dry heat enveloped them. Outside the cave the climate was entirely different.

"Was that a tunnel," wondered Koschei, "or a portal?"

The ground was rocky and bone dry. The pure blue sky contained not a single cloud. Not far away, atop a small hill, sat a stone cottage with a red-tile roof. The only vegetation around it was dry scrub and a few cacti.

Koschei and Peter could feel Izanami's relief.

"We are safe here," she said.

"Is this Canada or Italy?" asked an amused Koschei.

"You ask a lot of questions," said Peter.

They approached the house, but the two held back as Izanami ascended the stony steps to the front door. She waited at the threshold. After a few moments the door opened of its own accord, and she went inside and straight to the parlor. Open windows and a light breeze made the interior cooler than the outdoors.

In an old, overstuffed armchair next to the dormant stone fireplace sat the old woman. She was so settled that it was difficult to tell where she began and the chair ended. Her long, straight hair was more white than gray and long enough to reach her lap. She focused on her knitting and did not look up.

"So here you are," she said aggrievedly. "I thought you'd forgotten me."

"And I thought you had more than enough of me the last time."

"Well, if you've come back, it must mean you need something. You're lucky to have found me here, you know. I may not be here the next time. I have little enough time left."

"You say that every time I come."

"Go ahead and have your fun, but you'll see. So ungrateful."

"Look, I'm sorry. I know I'm not the most loyal disciple you ever had."

"Not the most loyal? You do make me laugh sometimes. You know, you could have been a Master yourself by now. You had the potential, but you did not have the patience—or the discipline. You let yourself be lured away by... him."

"No need to be jealous of Orpheus anymore. He's gone now. For good."

"Yes, I'm aware. To be honest, I felt a relief when I sensed his presence departing this world. Everything settled into a more tranquil state. That's changed now. I have a nagging feeling the earth is still disturbed by him somehow."

"I didn't come to discuss Orpheus or to debate the past. I need your help."

"First, put on the kettle for me. I tell you, some days I don't know if I'll be able to get out of the bed."

Izanami checked the wood stove. A low fire burned inside it. She filled the kettle and set it on the hob.

"Weird things are happening, Master. Do you know about it? Can you tell me what's going on?"

"What would I know? I'm here all on my own. I never get out. No one comes to see me. Are you going to invite your friends in?"

Izanami had forgotten about them. She went to the door and beckoned them to enter.

"Master, this is my comrade Koschei, and this boy is called Peter."

She squinted at the two of them and motioned for them to approach. When Koschei was near enough, she touched his hand, then recoiled.

"You're wrong," she said gravely.

"It's nice to meet you too, Master," said the Russian sarcastically.

She motioned for Peter to come to her. Upon touching his hand, her reaction was stronger. "You're wrong too. Very wrong."

"What do you mean, wrong?" asked Izanami.

Tsuru turned to her. What little color had been in her face drained away. "They do not belong here. They are wrong."

"Where do we belong?" asked Peter.

"I... I do not know, but it is not here. Not now."

Izanami drew close to her and whispered, "Tell me. Are they alive or dead? Are they ghosts? Are they resurrected? Tell me what they are."

For a full minute Tsuru studied the pair, saying nothing. Though impatient, Izanami held her tongue. The kettle was on full boil, and she went to take it off the hob. She located the teapot, gave it a rinse, put in the tea leaves, and then wet them.

Koschei knelt next to her chair. "Tell me, Master. The truth. Am I a ghost?"

She ran her fingers over his cheek and frowned. "You seem solid enough. Would a ghost not be incorporeal? I don't know. I've never met a ghost."

"So why am I here when Izanami says she saw me die? Why cannot I remember how I got here? Am I resurrected?"

"So many questions to pester an old woman with. I can't answer yet, but it's definitely not right. Not with you or the boy. Something is very wrong with the universe. With the whole fabric of existence. I've been feeling this for some time. These are not good days."

"Does it have to do with the riots?" asked Peter.

While pouring the tea, Izanami turned to Tsuru and said, "He insists a truck driver told him there were riots in the cities. Is that true?"

"How would I know? Do I look like a telegraph machine? On the other hand, I am not surprised to hear it. Things are unbalanced. I never expected to live so long I would actually see the end of times. Now I fear I may."

As she gave her old Master her cup, Izanami asked quietly, "Can you tell me where Sapphire is?"

"Who?"

"Don't play that game with me. You know very well who."

"I haven't seen you for years. How could I possibly know what you've been up to?"

"Just tell me what you know."

"Sapphire, you say? Is that her real name?"

"You know it's not. Her birth name in this life is Lola Blumquist. She's the reincarnation of Tyra Knagenhjelm, whose Demon Hunter name was Eurydice. In her first life she was called Justine de Bruin."

"Interesting. Are you certain that was her first life?"

"Yes. I mean, I suppose it was. I never thought about it before. What does that matter at this moment? You know who I'm talking about. Can you tell me anything about her?"

"Very well. Come close and focus your mind on her. I shall see what I can divine. Closer."

Izanami dropped to her knees next to the old woman, who now took a sudden interest in the blue crystal hanging from her neck. She put her spindly fingers around it gingerly.

"Interesting. Where did you get this?"

"It's a gift from Sapphire. I mean, she got it for me. She just didn't have a chance to give it to me yet."

"So she didn't tell you about it? She didn't tell you what it is?"

"No. Why? It's just a crystal. What else would it be?"

"Now that you have it, keep it safe. Do not let it out of your possession—under any circumstances."

"Tell me about Sapphire."

"Very well."

Tsuru laid her spotted hand on Izanami's head.

"Well, you don't need to worry about her. At least not for the moment. What is she to you again?"

"She's my… friend. My comrade in arms. We're the last two Demon Hunters." She looked sheepishly at Koschei. "Well, we were until Koschei came back."

"And that is all that she is to you?"

"What does this have to do with anything? Can't you just tell me where she is and when I'll see her again?"

"You'll see her soon, I'm certain. She'll have much to tell you. In fact, she'll be able to answer your questions better than I. Sit still for a moment."

With her hand still resting on Izanami's head, the old woman closed her eyes and murmured a few words in a strange tongue.

"I've left a marker that will help draw her to you. She'll find you more easily now, no matter where you might be."

"Can you tell us anything else?"

"Yes, I can put things together better now after having felt your spirit and your connection to the one you call Sapphire. That combined with everything you've told me only confirms my fears."

"And what are you fears, Master?" asked Koschei.

Tsuru sighed and took a sip of tea.

"I suppose there's no point keeping my worries to myself. The coming struggle will be yours, not mine. My time is all but over. It's your destiny that will be marked—or terminated—by what is coming. I shall tell you all I know."

The three visitors settled around her on the floor. Peter stared at her in fascination. Koschei looked at him with concern.

"Should he be here? Will this be fit for his ears?"

Peter looked at Tsuru anxiously, his eyes imploring her not to send him away.

"The child is not what he seems. He's a key part of all this. The luxury of shielding children from harsh realities is not for times such as these. Stay, boy, and listen with the others to what I have to say."

9
The Old Ones

"YOU DO UNDERSTAND, don't you? The human race did not always hold sway in this world. In the grand scheme of things, our time here has been a mere blink of an eye."

Tsuru paused to take a long sip of tea. She was in no hurry. Izanami took a sip as well. Koschei and Peter sat patiently. Izanami had absent-mindedly given them tea as well, and their cups went untouched.

"Beings existed long before the arrival of our kind. Time had no meaning for them. We cannot fathom the expanse of time they knew. They were not flesh and blood. They did not have lifespans as we do. Linear time did not apply to them. That's a concept the human mind invented out of necessity so reality could be made to fit into our limited capacity for perceiving and understanding."

"Then they must still exist," said Koschei. "Where are they?"

"You know well, Demon Hunter, that ours is not the only plane of existence. It is only one of many. For example, you are aware of the so-called Netherworld where the fiends dwell. The Old Ones—the ones here before us—have their own dimension in the fabric of existence, but they are not constrained by it. They once roamed freely in this world and indeed considered it part of their own domain. We have no way of knowing what name they have for their domain, but those of us who study the old lore call it Tír nAill, the Otherworld."

"You said they *once* roamed in our world," said Peter. "Are they no longer here then?"

"That's the question, isn't it? Unlike the Otherworld, our dimension is—and always has been—subject to constant change. You might say instability. This ball of dirt and water on which

79

we dwell hurtles endlessly through the cosmos. As it circles its yellow star, it mutates. Its surface and atmosphere undergo perpetual metamorphosis. Living creatures emerged from the crucible of its sea. They thrived and evolved. They developed intelligence. While this new form of life was primitive compared to the Old Ones, it had a particular quality that fascinated them. The new creatures had physical form and knew their world through sensory experience. The Old Ones came to envy these new beings for their physicality and, as strange as it may seem to us, also for their mortality. They begrudged them their capacity for birth, death, and rebirth. Furthermore, they came to resent them because they found themselves becoming dependent on them."

"Dependent?" said Izanami.

"As the New Ones evolved, they developed self-awareness and then meta-awareness. Through their five primitive senses, they were cognizant of themselves and their physical surroundings, but in time they developed consciousness of that which could not be perceived through the senses. They became aware of the Old Ones and aspired to become more like them. They gradually formed a metaphysical link, and this link became a mutual dependency. Without understanding them, humans worshipped the Old Ones, and through a mysterious, transcendental need, the Old Ones came to rely on that worship. Through the New Ones' physicality, they could vicariously experience satisfactions and pleasures of which they had never before conceived. Each was able to have a tantalizing taste of what was beyond them. Thus the Old Ones and New Ones achieved an exquisite harmony. It could not, however, be sustained indefinitely.

"Humans continued to evolve. Their numbers grew. Their intelligence surged. Civilizations flourished. The balance between Old Ones and New Ones began to shift in favor of the New Ones, and this threatened the Old Ones. They foresaw a time when the physical world might threaten the quality of their own existence—if not their own very existence itself. They now viewed the New Ones as we might regard an infestation or infection: something to be removed in the interest of health and survival.

"This view was not universal among the Old Ones. They are not a monolith with a single mind. Just as humans have divided themselves into clans, tribes, and nations, so the Old Ones had formed themselves into two distinct circles. One accepted the risks, along with the rewards, of the New Ones' rise. The other did not. The discord between the two circles could not be reconciled. It led to a cosmic war of cataclysmic proportions."

"Forgive me, Master," asked Izanami, "but how is it possible to know about these things? I mean, given that they involve beings and occurrences beyond our human ken?"

"Long ago in the mists of forgotten times, certain particularly gifted humans were able to communicate with certain sympathetic Old Ones and gain fragments of knowledge, which were then passed down as sacred lore. No doubt, some gaps have been filled with logic and guesswork. As I have taught you, it is wise to be mistrustful of all stories. Yet, what I recount to you is our best understanding."

"How did the war end?" asked Peter.

"That is an example of a major gap in our knowledge. All we know is that something happened to stop the war and allow the New Ones to survive. The Old Ones retreated to the Otherworld and abandoned this corner of reality, but one must wonder for how long. Logic would suggest that they must yet covet this former part of their realm."

"Is that what's happening now?" asked Izanami. "Are the Old Ones coming back?"

"Perhaps," said the old woman gravely.

"All of them?" asked Peter. "Or just the ones who wanted to get rid of us. You know, the bad ones. Are they coming back? Sorry, do the two circles have names?"

"Whatever names they have for themselves are beyond our ability to conceive and enunciate, so we have had to invent our own names for them. The most useful names to have survived down through the ages are in the Irish language. It is in that tongue that the old stories have come closest to surviving intact. That's not to say that the Irish legends weren't embellished or combined with other historical events, but it's their names that have been adopted by Masters who research the lore.

"So to answer your question, lad, the circle of Old Ones that wanted to purge the universe of humans is called the Fomóire. The entity which guides them—their leader if you will—is called Balor. Many are the legends that have survived of Balor of the Evil Eye. We call the other circle—the ones who argued for our survival—the Tuath Dé."

"The 'two a day'?" asked Peter.

"Not too bad an attempt at the pronunciation."

"So," said Izanami, "are the Fomóire coming? To destroy the human race?"

"I cannot say with any certainty," said Tsuru. "All I know is that something fundamental has shifted in the balance between our world and theirs, and it's having a destabilizing effect."

"What do you know about a man called Alaric or about the Zen'ei?"

"That man's name means nothing to me, but I do know something about the Zen'ei. They have existed for a long time, and their strength has waxed and waned through the centuries. They draw their members from those sensitive to the distant will of the Fomóire. Just as there are cultists who act as useful human idiots for the demons of the Netherworld, the Zen'ei are the heralds of the Fomóire."

"They insist on their own language. Mercenaries call themselves Legionnaires. They call demons 'hants,' and for them Demon Hunters are 'Hant Oppressors.'"

"That is no accident. To control words is to control the mind."

"Well, whatever the words they use," said Izanami, "they're definitely on the rise. What do we need to do, Master?"

The old woman settled into her chair and closed her eyes. "Why ask me?"

"Who else is there to ask?" said a frustrated Koschei. "You're the one with the knowledge of these things. You must guide us. Tell us how to protect our world from this threat."

"This will not be my war," said Tsuru. "I am not long for this world—or any world. I have little at stake. You're the ones who must lead the fight for our kind's survival."

"That's not good enough," said Izanami. "You can't abandon us just because you're old and tired. We're not asking you to pick up a sword, but we need you to guide us."

"Don't you understand?" said the old woman. "I'm not being stubborn. I don't know what to do. I've done all that I can do, which is to tell you all that I know. I have nothing more to teach you, no more advice to give you. You're on your own. I wish you good luck and remind you that billions of souls depend on what you do next. If you succeed, you will be owed their gratitude, but you'll never receive it. They will never know your names or what you have done. If you fail, it won't matter. History will have ended."

Izanami jumped angrily to her feet.

"Then it's hopeless. I'm just one warrior on my own. Who's to help me? I have no idea where Sapphire is. The boy's just a child. I'm not sure he and Koschei are real. They shouldn't be here."

Noting the hapless look on Koschei's face, she added, "No offense."

"None taken," he replied sarcastically.

Tsuru calmly sipped the last of her tea.

"You always had a temper, Izanami. It was your main weakness as a disciple. It must surely be a vulnerability for a Demon Hunter."

Izanami fumed and said nothing. Then a thought occurred to her.

"We have to find out more about the boy. He's the key. The Zen'ei are desperate to get hold of him. What do they want him for?"

Tsuru beckoned Peter with a long bony finger.

"Come, boy. Let me try once more to see what makes you tick."

He approached cautiously. As she laid her hand atop his mop of black hair, he squirmed. Her fingers were like the legs of a large insect. Her smell was old and musty.

"You're a cypher. As if you're not truly here. Close your eyes and think of something that makes you smile. Or cry. It doesn't matter."

He did as he was told, and his face settled into a resigned grimace.

"Tell me what you see."

"I see water. Nothing but water. Everywhere I look is the sea. I'm drowning. I'm going to die."

"That's all?"

"I see the strand, but it is too far away. The tide carries me away. I wandered too far from the shore, and now I can't get back. I'm going to die!"

She withdrew her hand and clucked her tongue.

"Very well. That will do."

She turned to the two Demon Hunters.

"Not too helpful, I'm afraid."

"That's it?" said Izanami.

Tsuru sat back in her chair and sighed.

"There is one who is more suited to this than I. He may be your best hope. You need to find Hadrian."

"Hadrian? Who in the name of...?"

Izanami searched her memory for where she had heard the name. It had been quite some time.

"Wait, tell me you're not talking about Hadrian the Necromant. Are you serious?"

"Do you know him?" asked the old woman.

"I've never met him, but I know his reputation. The last time I heard anything about him, they were saying he was mad. That was decades ago. Even then he was the butt of jokes. He has to be older than you. You're having a laugh at my expense, right?"

"Don't underestimate Hadrian. He never burnished his reputation as so many others did. He's always avoided the limelight, but there is more to him than meets the eye."

"There has to be someone else."

"That's my advice, but do as you like. Take some time to think about it. I suggest we all sleep on it."

"You and I are the only ones who will do any sleeping, Master."

"Oh dear. You must forgive me. Where are my manners? You all must be famished. You're welcome to whatever you can find in my larder. It won't be much. I survive on little these days."

"Am I the only one left in the world who eats?" said an exasperated Izanami. "Look, I'll just find myself some fruit or raw vegetables to eat. Do you have any cheese? What about bread?"

"You never did learn to cook, did you?" sighed Tsuru. "Very well."

She struggled to her feet and took the cane leaning against the wall. She shuffled toward the kitchen.

"I'll make us a hearty soup. I don't know how you've lasted this long without basic survival skills."

Izanami was about to follow her, but Koschei detained her.

"Do you believe these wild tales about the Old Ones?" he said in a low voice.

"She may be a cranky old bat, but she definitely knows her lore. If she says a war with the Fomóire is coming, it would be foolhardy to ignore her."

"Do you really think the Fomóire exist? Like you, I've heard those tales for years, but I've never completely accepted them."

"Do you have another explanation for all the weird things that have been happening?"

He shook his head. "What do you know of this Hadrian? Is he someone we can trust?"

"It can't hurt to talk to him, but I'm not optimistic. I'm afraid we may be on our own, my friend."

"Orpheus is who we need. Are you certain he's gone for good?"

"I'm afraid so. It's so strange you don't remember what happened in the Netherworld. I hope your memory returns at some point."

Izanami gave Tsuru a hand in the kitchen. The larder had more food than the old woman had implied. After an hour of chopping and simmering, they had produced a rich soup of bacon, peas, leeks, potatoes, and cabbage. They also had home-made bread, causing Izanami to suspect her old Master was not as infirm as she insisted.

Tsuru slowly ate her small bowl of soup. Izanami consumed hers hungrily. She was delighted to have a hot meal again. In Sapphire's absence she had fallen into bad eating habits.

Koschei and Peter sat politely at the table, showing no interest in the food.

After the meal was eaten and the dishes washed, Tsuru announced she was going to bed. With a yawn, Izanami said she would do the same.

"Come, boy," said Koschei with no hint of fatigue. "Let's make a fire. We can sit up all night and tell stories. I have a few good adventures to recount, or perhaps you would be more interested in my childhood days in St. Petersburg. In exchange you can tell me any interesting tales you might have."

From her room, Izanami heard the cadences of the Russian's voice until she fell asleep.

In the morning she woke fresh and energized. Sunlight streamed through the window. It had been a long time since she felt so rested. She was relieved not to have dreamed.

She found Tsuru chopping vegetables in the kitchen. A pot of porridge was on the stove.

"You used to rise with the sun," said the old woman without turning around.

"These days I'm more prone to lie down with the moon, but that's my own business. Where are the others?"

"They went for a walk. It's a beautiful morning, but then it always is here. Those two are forming a bond."

"Good. I never know how to talk to the child. I wish I hadn't been landed with the responsibility of protecting him. Say, would you keep him here? I mean, while Koschei and I go looking for Hadrian?"

"So, you've come around to my suggestion?"

"I don't know what else to do. I'd go looking for Sapphire, but you've assured me she will find us when the time is right."

"She will."

"So, where will we find the Necromant?"

"The last I heard, he was holed up in his cabin deep in the Bialowieza Forest, somewhere near the Poland-Belarus border."

"Really? Bialowieza? Are you sure? The word among Demon Hunters has always been that place is full of negative energy. Why would he choose to live there?"

The old woman shrugged. "That's my best information. You're not afraid, are you? A brave Demon Hunter like yourself?"

Her old Master had a gift for roiling her. "Look, I'm sorry I didn't follow the path you wanted for me, but it was my path, not yours. It's all in the past now. Can't you let it go?"

"If you were truly secure in your choices, you wouldn't care what I think. In any event, it hardly matters. I'll be gone soon enough."

"Please stop talking as if you have one foot in the grave. It gets tiring."

Izanami helped herself to a bowl of porridge and sat at the table.

"I suppose you had your breakfast already."

"Hours ago."

"And you definitely ate?"

"Of course, I ate. My appetite isn't what it once was, but I do eat. Why? Are you worried about me?"

"Being around people who neither eat nor sleep has begun to unnerve me. More to the point, being around people who are supposed to be dead unnerves me."

"Are you worried that I might be dead?"

"No, I saw you eat last night, and I saw you go to bed. I'm just getting jumpy."

"Finish your porridge and go for a walk. You'll feel better."

Izanami followed the path down the hill. The sky was bright and blue, the air dry. The morning sun was warm. As she rounded a bend, she heard voices rise from below. Koschei and Peter were engaged in a chat. When he saw her, the boy ran to her enthusiastically.

"Koschei has such grand stories. Much better than yours."

"I'm not surprised. You see, he has an unfair advantage. He doesn't allow himself to be constrained by things like facts."

"Did you know he was born a prince?"

"No, I never heard that story. He must save that one for special listeners."

"And did you know that three Russian tsars had the same name as me?"

Koschei had now caught up with the boy.

"Where are we? I don't think this is Canada—at least not any part of Canada I've ever been."

"It doesn't matter. We'll be leaving soon."

"To find the Necromant?"

"It appears to be our only option. We must go to the Bialowieza Forest."

"You know what they say about that place, don't you?"

"Yes, I've heard the stories, but do you have a better idea? You're not afraid, are you? You've already cheated death many times—including the time you actually did die."

The Russian chuckled grimly. "It's not for myself I'm worried. It's you, my friend."

"Don't bother. Say, I just remembered something." She took his left hand. "Let me see your arm."

Puzzled, Koschei rolled up his sleeve to reveal his muscular forearm.

"No, I need to see the upper arm."

Amused, he removed his shirt.

"You do not need to invent pretexts, Izanami, if you want the pleasure of admiring my chest."

"I'm still looking for proof that you either are or are not the real Koschei."

She ran her hand along his brawny bicep.

"Resurrection seems to have been healing for you. I see no sign of that old injury."

"What old injury?"

"You know, the time the demon Agramon burned your arm at the edge of the crater on Tristan da Cunha. It left an extremely nasty scar."

"What are you talking about? I don't remember that."

"How could you forget it? I know I never will. Turn around."

Koschei obeyed willingly. He liked the attention he was getting. She traced a ragged line next to his right shoulder blade.

"Yet this scar is still here on your back. The one you got from Nergal on the Road of Bones going to Oymyakon."

"Of course, it is. I'll never forget it. I thought I was dead that time."

"Why do you remember some of your battles and not others?"

He shrugged and reluctantly put his shirt back on. The three returned to the house. Izanami helped Tsuru make the midday dinner.

As they worked together, she asked her former Master, "Have you thought about my suggestion of keeping the boy here?"

"I think you should keep him with you. This place may seem safe enough, but if the Zen'ei are determined to find him, they could track him even here, and I'm in no position to protect him. You and Koschei are much abler guardians than I."

"I've seen you wield your powers, Master. I think you're more than a match for anyone."

"Those days are past, Izanami. I'm not the woman I once was."

"Can you at least use your powers to send us to the Bialowieza? That would be a huge help."

She sighed. "It will exhaust me for days, but yes, I'll do that—or at least attempt it. Given the urgency of the situation, I suppose it's the least I can do."

"Thank you. When should we go?"

"Do your best to rest for a few hours after dinner. I'll pack some food for you. I'll send you away at the stroke of midnight. Given the time difference, that will put you there in the morning."

Izanami slept fitfully during the evening. When she rose, she was unsure whether she had slept at all. Her two companions were awake, alert, and waiting for her.

"If you're ready to go, then come outside," said Tsuru. "Teleportation sometimes makes a mess in the house."

The stars were bright and plentiful in the sky. The air was comfortable with a light breeze to mitigate the residual warmth from the day.

"You'll land us accurately, won't you?" said Izanami, mindful of Sapphire's occasional imprecision with her teleportation power.

"No promises," said Tsuru. "At my age, I'll be lucky to get all your atoms in the same place at the same time. Now join hands so you have more chance of arriving together. Close your eyes tight. It's been a long time since I've done this, but I can tell you it will be extremely disorienting if you're gawking about."

"Goodbye, Master," said Izanami. "Thank you for every..."

The old woman had not waited for the Demon Hunter to finish thanking her. The three tightened their grips on one another's hands and, at the first sign of a dizzying bright light, shut their eyes. They felt an exhilaration not unlike a sudden drop on a roller-coaster, then an uneasiness in their stomachs. Each felt the others being tugged in a different direction. They clung all the more firmly to each other's hands. After two or three disorienting minutes, their bodies landed abruptly on the ground.

10

The Battle of Bialowieza

AS IZANAMI LAY on the damp ground, the world refused to stop gyrating. She closed her eyes, then opened them—several times. When the whirling finally stopped, she saw the others sprawled nearby. By the looks on their faces, their heads were reeling as much as hers. They were surrounded by ancient oaks with gnarled trunks as well as some spruce and hornbeams. Sunlight barely filtered through the thick overhead cover of leafy branches. The air was cool and damp.

"Is everyone okay?" she asked.

"I'm all right," said Peter.

"Orpheus definitely had a lighter touch with this sort of thing," groused Koschei. "I'd say your old Master is well past her prime."

Unsteadily, they rose to their feet.

"Tell me, Izanami," said Koschei, "do you ever regret not staying with Tsuru and learning her arts? You yourself could be performing these wonders if you had stuck with it."

"Sapphire has offered several times to be my teacher, but the mystical arts aren't for me. Not the dark ones where nature is bent abnormally to one's will. The idea of it... makes me uncomfortable."

"And fighting demons doesn't?"

"That's different. Fighting is something I understand. Come, we're wasting time. We need to look for the cabin Tsuru told us about."

The ground was littered with broken branches and rotting leaves, and there was no obvious trail to follow. Izanami followed her instinct and proceeded in a direction where the trees grew slightly farther apart. She took care to identify two fixed points ahead to chart their direction. The forest's atmosphere was disorienting, and she wanted to avoid any possibility of walking in circles.

After a while they crossed the faint trace of a long-unused trail. She stopped and looked in one direction and then the other. Neither way looked better to her, so she chose the one that inclined slightly downward. They walked in silence for more than a mile before Koschei spoke.

"Something's foreboding about this woodland."

Izanami felt it too but was keen to avoid dispiriting talk.

"No point dwelling on subjective impressions."

"It is quite creepy," said Peter.

"You're not scared, are you, boy?" said the Russian. "Do not fear. I'll protect you from the lions and tiger and bears."

"Why would there be lions and tigers in a wood like this?"

"Have you never seen…? Never mind."

Izanami could not shake her apprehension. It was not helped by the temperature dropping despite the sun rising higher above the sheltering trees.

"Do you know any Polish?" she asked.

"A little," said Koschei. "Why?"

"I was wondering what the name Bialowieza meant."

"That I can tell you. It means White Tower."

It was unusual for Izanami to feel such disquiet, and she did not like it. She distracted herself with thoughts of Sapphire, but that only gave her something else to fret about.

"Izanami?"

The Russian's insistence at disturbing the quiet had begun to get on her nerves.

"Yes, Koschei?"

"Do you ever wonder…?"

"Wonder what?"

"Does it seem strange to you that, in all the years we've known each other, we never became lovers?"

"No."

"We've been comrades and friends quite a long time, haven't we?"

"We have."

"It just seems strange that, with all the experiences we have shared, something wouldn't, you know, have happened between us at some point or other."

She fumed. She glanced at Peter, saw that he was as interested in her response as Koschei, and fumed more.

"It's not strange at all. Why on earth are you asking this now?"

"So you've never thought of me in that way then?"

"It's never occurred to me to be in a three-way relationship?"

"Three? What do you mean? Who's the third person?"

"There's you, and there's your ego."

"Very funny."

"Why are you talking this way? Don't you know that best thing about our friendship has always been that we never have conversations like this?"

"Sorry. I think it's this forest of the White Tower. It's having an effect on my mind. Don't you find something oppressive about it?"

"It will pass. We just have to keep going. We have to find the Necromant."

"I... I keep having thoughts about my mortality. About the fleeting nature of time. It's like an omen."

"Why worry about death now? You've beat it once already."

"I still don't remember anything about the Netherworld. You insist my memory's flawed, but maybe it's yours."

"You think I imagined going to the Netherworld? I wish none of it ever happened, but it did."

"See it from my point of view. How can I know you're not delusional? Why should I assume your memory is better than mine? You keep going on about someone called Sapphire, but where is she? Is she even real?"

"She's real all right. You'll see. Peter remembers her. Don't you, Peter?"

The boy seemed to wake from a dream. "What?"

"You remember Sapphire. You know, Lola."

"You mean the strumpet?" he said with a sigh. "Yes, I remember her."

"Strumpet, eh?" laughed the Russian. "This gets more interesting all the time."

"I don't like this forest," said the boy darkly. "Can't we leave? I'd rather be anywhere but here."

As if in answer to the boy's wish, they emerged from the trees to find themselves in a clearing. The open space was a relief, as was the large patch of blue sky overhead.

Izanami was about to speak, but she froze. They all heard noises coming from the trees behind them. They were like the sound of marching, but not the consistent parading of a disciplined army. It was the cacophonous din of many boots hitting the ground randomly. It was the noise of a mob. The Demon Hunters exchanged apprehensive looks.

"Did Tsuru send us into a trap?" said Koschei.

"Not intentionally, but it doesn't matter now."

"You must wish now you'd let that Sapphire of yours teach you how to teleport."

Izanami drew her knife.

"If it's the Zen'ei, they'll try to take the boy. We can't let that happen. At any cost."

Koschei nodded grimly and drew his blade as well.

The noise grew louder. Izanami spotted a dead tree several yards away at the edge of the clearing. It had a large hollow. With her weapon she drew Peter's attention to it. He understood her silent command, ran to it, and concealed himself inside. Izanami and Koschei positioned themselves in the center of the clearing.

The Demon Hunters stood motionless, eyes darting from one direction to another, searching every gap in the trees for a sign of movement. Their breathing was slow and steady. The air smelled of decaying vegetation. The noise grew loud and close, yet they saw nothing. Izanami wondered if their opponents were invisible.

A figure appeared. Then another. Then many all at once. They were everywhere. Because of the trees, the number of men and women was difficult to gauge. They were mostly armed with clubs and knives, and they all had an unsettling fierceness in their eyes. Izanami recognized a few of the faces belonging to

Mercenaries whose paths she had crossed at one time or another. Others were fanatical cultists.

What she had never seen before was the monstrous beast bringing up the rear. Misshapen and scaly, it was easily ten feet tall. It lumbered heavily, waving its claws in the air and snaking its tail on the ground. For a moment Izanami took it for a demon, but then she saw it was an unlikely product of her own world—a pitiable abomination of nature bred by depraved minds.

As the horde closed in, Izanami shot a blast of energy at the nearest Mercenary. Stunned, he fell to the ground.

"Finally," she said, "someone who doesn't have those damn dampers."

She felled several others by the same method, but there were too many. She could not defend herself from every side. Glancing at Koschei, she saw his attackers were slowly overwhelming him as well. She shouted in his direction.

"Do we agree, my friend, times have changed? The old code no longer serves us. No longer can we be bound by our vow not to use demonic arms against our own kind."

"If you say it," replied the Russian grimly, "then I so agree."

The Canadian drew her diabolusbane and sliced through the midsection of the first Mercenary to reach her. Another, wearing chain mail, stepped over his body. That one wielded a proper sword and deftly parried her attacks. Yet it took only one miscalculation for him to be felled by a well-placed thrust to the thigh. Several others immediately took his place.

The Demon Hunters were now surrounded. Their opponents couldn't match their weapons and suffered mounting losses. Still, they had overwhelming superiority in numbers.

Izanami was sickened by the carnage the diabolusbane wreaked in her hands. Bodies were strewn on the forest floor, yet the attackers persisted. The Demon Hunters' protective clothing shielded them from serious harm, but the constant blows took their toll.

While fighting furiously, Izanami did her best to give Koschei an assist where she could. The battle brought back unwelcome memories of the fatal conflict in the Netherworld, and she was determined not to be the cause of his fall in this fight. Koschei was well aware of what she was doing, and it wounded his pride.

"Fight your own battle!" shouted the Russian. "I can look after myself!"

She nodded but continued casting a wary eye in his direction.

As the pressure mounted, Izanami's efforts became increasingly desperate. She swung her weapon wildly one way and then another. Despite the injury and death she inflicted on her foes, their enthusiasm for violence did not wane. Nor did her determination, but as the long minutes passed, she tired. The diabolusbanes could compensate only so long for the disparity in numbers. She blocked all thoughts from her mind lest her sense of reason lead her to despair.

After the exertion of felling two brutish women with a single furious stroke of the diabolusbane, she struggled in her exhaustion to draw her next breath. To her relief—and dread—no other warriors took their place. All activity ceased, and the surviving Mercenaries and cultists stood expectantly. While grateful for the respite, she did not understand what was happening.

Then she saw him. A tall, robed figure striding calmly through the parted throng. The monster followed him protectively, like a massive gargoyle version of a dog. Izanami and Koschei raised their weapons defensively.

"No need for those."

The voice was oddly soft, yet it reverberated through the forest. It had a calming tone completely at odds with the situation, and it was impossible to ignore.

"I merely want to see the Hant Oppressor who has caused everyone so much trouble. The one incapable of seeing reason. The one insistent on following old superstitious traditions while the planet perishes around her."

He stared intently into the Canadian's eyes. She focused on regulating her breathing.

"So you are the vaunted Izanami."

She stared back at the hooded figure's face. His skin was smooth, pale, and hairless. His round eyes were a nearly transparent shade of blue. His nose was aquiline, his lips thin and colorless.

"Alaric, I presume."

He closed his eyes, smiled, and bowed his head slightly. He extended an arm in a circular motion as if to acknowledge the surviving fighters.

"Can this many people possibly be wrong about something? Look at their numbers. Look at how few you are. They are willing to die to save the world. No matter how many you slaughter, more will replace them. It is time, Hant Oppressor, to be on the right side of history."

Unsure what to make of him, Koschei stared wide-eyed. He looked to Izanami for her reaction.

"I've never cared for that expression," she scowled. "History doesn't have a side. You speak of history, but what you mean is the future. The future has yet to be written. You may want to write my future for me, but don't waste your time. I'll write my own future."

Her words had become louder until they ended in a shout. A few of the Mercenaries had gotten uncomfortably close to her. Alaric replied serenely.

"I've seen your like before. You think your brain is every bit as good as anybody else's, but is it? You'll always be right as long as you think of no one but yourself. Fine. See how far that gets you. The world will not be saved by those only looking out for themselves. True wisdom is heeding the word of those who know much more than you do."

Her hand tightened on the diabolusbane as the Mercenaries edged closer.

"What happens now?"

"You know what we need. Once we have him, our quarrel with you is over."

"Tell me why you want him."

"What do you care? You're looking after yourself—and only yourself. You're writing your own future. You care only about what *you* want and about your precious free will. Go write your future and leave him to us."

"The fact you won't answer my questions tells me everything I need to know about you."

"I'd explain, but you're not capable of understanding. You cannot comprehend how the boy is the key holding reality's fabric together. Through him we can unmake the false path the universe travels. Everything can go back to how it was always meant to be. At long last we will reunify with the Old Ones."

"I don't like the sound of that," said the Demon Hunter.

She raised her weapon, but it fell from her hand. With jarring speed two Mercenaries had grabbed her arms. Two others did the same to Koschei. As the diabolusbanes reached the ground, they dematerialized. Alaric gave a subtle nod to a fifth Mercenary next to the dead tree trunk. He dragged Peter from his hiding place.

"Chiharu!"

"Let him go!" shouted Izanami, straining against the hands restraining her.

"Our business here is done," said Alaric. "Have a nice life and enjoy your free will."

"Peter!" she shouted. "Grandfather's trick!"

The boy closed his eyes and grimaced so hard the veins in his temples bulged. He shook violently, startling his captor. The Mercenary and the boy were thrown to the ground by a sudden, powerful burst of energy. Peter leapt to his feet and sprinted away into the trees.

"Get him!" shouted Alaric, his voice echoing in every direction.

Three Mercenaries rushed in pursuit. As the Demon Hunters struggled furiously, Izanami managed to deliver a sharp kick with her heel to the shin of one of her captors. His distraction let her free one arm and strike his head forcefully with her forearm. Alaric stepped back warily.

As the Mercenary struggled to regain control of her arm, Izanami pulled her knife from its sheath and plunged it into his side. She pulled it out again as he doubled over in pain. As her other captor tried to subdue her, she lashed out at one of the Mercenaries holding Koschei. Her knife didn't find its mark, but it was a sufficient diversion for the Russian to break free.

"The boy," she panted. "Go help the boy."

Reluctantly, Koschei left her struggling with a swarm of Mercenaries and darted away. He slowed upon hearing the boy's plaintive cry. Three mercenaries emerged from the trees, two dragging Peter by the legs. Koschei drew his diabolusbane.

"Let him go! Now!" he cried.

He rushed forward, but two Mercenaries had caught up with him from behind. One clubbed him brutally on the back, and the Russian dropped his weapon as he was forced to the ground. More men piled on top of him.

Izanami continued her own struggle with several Mercenaries. She dropped her knife and used her hand to summon the diabolusbane. By the time it could fully materialize, several pairs of hands had restrained her arms. The weapon melted into the air. She strained futilely against their combined strength. Alaric approached her.

"As I said, we have no quarrel with you. We only want the boy. Unfortunately, it's all too clear you will never cease your interference. Our aims are completely peaceful, but you leave us no choice."

He nodded to a bald brute nearby, who in turn drew a broadsword.

"Be aware," continued Alaric, "you have forced us to do this. You are entirely responsible for your own death."

The swordsman stepped to within three feet of Izanami. He examined his blade carefully, as if worried it might be damaged in some way. He tightened his grip on the hilt, balanced his body, and took a deep breath. He drew his arm back and then plunged the blade directly at the center of Izanami's belly.

She went limp with pain. The force of the blow had been severe and powerful. She fought hard not to black out.

The Mercenary staggered backward, puzzled over the pain in his hand and the lack of blood on the blade.

"You'll not be able to pierce that suit," said Alaric impatiently. "You must go for the neck."

Several yards away, Koschei squirmed furiously against his captors as he watched the swordsman prepare for another blow.

"No!" he cried.

The assassin gripped the sword's hilt with both hands. He leaned back, then practiced swinging the blade in a circular motion toward her neck. The men holding Izanami ducked their heads as low as possible, perhaps nervous about the accuracy of their comrade's aim. The sword swung through the air.

Then it stopped.

Everything stopped. It was as if time had frozen. All eyes were drawn to a tall figure now standing among them. He wore a hooded robe and wielded a heavy, gnarled staff. His face was shadowed by the hood. He pounded the ground with his staff.

"There will be no more killing here today."

Behind the newcomer, a Mercenary quietly raised a bloody club and swung it toward his back. Without moving his head, the figure extended an arm straight outward. The would-be attacker screamed in pain as his weapon fell to the ground. In awe, the others remained motionless.

Alaric surveyed his cowed army, sizing up the situation. He shouted.

"We have what we came for. It is over. Bring the boy to me."

"I'd prefer you left the child here," said the figure.

"You would, would you?" said Alaric.

The Mercenaries holding Peter delivered him quickly to their leader. Alaric took the child's hand. He studied the boy with famished eyes as if striving to memorize every detail about him and preserve that critical moment for all time. The Zen'ei leader took the child's chin in his hand and stared deep into his eyes. Peter resisted, trying to look away.

Alaric took a deep breath and again surveyed what remained of his forces. Many had fallen, but it had been worth it.

"Kehua!" he shouted.

The hulking monster, whose only role in the battle had been to protect its master, knelt so that Alaric, with child in tow, could climb onto its back. Once they were mounted, the beast rose.

"Halt!" shouted the hooded figure. "I said to leave the boy!"

The monster bounded away at surprising speed.

"Kill them!" shouted Alaric as he disappeared into the trees. "It is Balor's wish! Kill them all!"

11
The Necromant

"NO!" SCREAMED IZANAMI as Alaric disappeared with Peter.

The remaining Mercenaries shook off their consternation at their commander's sudden departure. The brute with the broadsword lifted his weapon, intent on completing his interrupted task. Izanami and Koschei struggled furiously.

"Close your eyes!"

Izanami heard the words in her mind, not with her ears. Every instinct told her to keep her eyes wide open, but she saw Koschei shut his eyes. Apparently, he had heard the instruction as well and decided to comply. She chose to close hers as well.

The hands gripping her went slack. She opened her eyes to see every Mercenary and cultist lying on the ground. Koschei staggered toward her. The hooded figure approached as well. Izanami retrieved her knife.

"Are they all…?"

"Asleep. At least the ones not slain by the two of you. I must say, you're quite a violent pair."

"We have to go after the boy! We're losing time."

"You won't catch them on foot. The creature is much swifter than its appearance would have suggested."

"Can you teleport?"

"I can. Where shall I take you?"

"I… I don't know, but we have to get Peter back. I don't know what Alaric has in mind for him. I can only hope he'll keep him alive."

"As far as I understand things, he will keep him alive."

"That's good news—if you're correct."

"But only until the ritual. Then the boy will be put to death. Rather painfully, I'm afraid."

"What? How do you know this? Who are you anyway?"

The stranger lowered his hood, revealing a head of thick, black hair. His skin was weathered and ruddy. His long face's most notable feature was a pair of deep-set, dark brown eyes. They were topped by bushy, black eyebrows.

Izanami took an immediate dislike to him.

"I am the one you came seeking."

"You're not Hadrian the Necromant."

"I'm not?"

"You can't be."

"I'm sorry. Have we met?"

"No, but I've heard the stories about Hadrian for decades. You're nowhere near old enough to be him."

"You of all people should know one's appearance does not necessarily correspond to chronological age."

"Yes, but people were already describing Hadrian as haggard in the middle of the twentieth century."

"Haggard? Really? Seems rather unkind."

"I think," interrupted Koschei, "we have more urgent things to discuss than how people look. How do we find the boy? Do they truly intend to kill him?"

"It would have been helpful," said Izanami, "if you'd showed up sooner and stopped Alaric from escaping with him."

"I'm sorry. I'm doing my best to catch up. I've only recently become aware of the situation."

"Has Tsuru been in communication with you?"

"Sorry, I don't know who that is, but it doesn't matter. We need to make a plan."

"Perhaps we could go to your cabin," said Koschei, "to pool our information and decide how to proceed."

"Cabin? What cabin?"

"Tsuru said you lived in a cabin."

"I still don't know who that is. Let's make our plan here and now. As you say, there's no time to waste."

"Do you know why Alaric wants the boy?" asked Izanami.

"He needs him for a ritual, but that is only for superstitious purposes. Balor's worshippers are best manipulated through ritual and narratives that inspire devotion. The main reason they need the child is so they can kill him."

"But for what purpose?" said Izanami. "Why him? How did they know about him? How was he chosen?"

"I could to try to explain, but it would only consume precious time, and it wouldn't directly aid us in what we need to do."

"We should introduce ourselves..."

"There is no need. You are Demon Hunters. His name is Koschei, and you are..."

Hadrian was distracted by her crystal. With something like reverence, he reached out and cradled it in his fingers.

"How long have you been wearing it?"

"This? I don't know, maybe a couple of weeks. Why?"

Warmth radiated from his hand as he turned the crystal one way and then another. The sensation was unexpected and not altogether unpleasant.

"Mind it carefully," he said. "Do not let it out of your possession under any circumstances. Now that you've worn it, you must not stop wearing it. At least not until the end."

"The end? The end of what?"

"The end. You'll know."

"What is it? Does it have supernatural properties?"

"It most certainly does, and it's what led the Zen'ei to the boy."

"What? I thought I was protecting him. You mean, all that time I've been drawing the Zen'ei to him? How stupid can I be? That means they can still track me. I have to get rid of it."

"No," said Hadrian sternly. "For good or ill, you and it are now tied together. It will be much worse for all of us if you and it are separated."

"Wait," said Izanami defensively. "If I was the one they were tracking, how did they know the boy would be with me in Seattle?"

"Because in that instant you, the boy, and the Grisial all became linked and thus traceable by the Zen'ei."

"Linked? How? I don't understand."

"You must trust me that all will become clear. For now, there simply isn't time..."

"What is the crystal? Why did Sapphire have it?"

"Who or what is a Sapphire? Never mind. Thankfully, having the Grisial is ultimately to our advantage. We can turn the tables on Alaric and use it to find *him* now."

"So you don't know who Sapphire is?"

"I'm afraid not."

"She's another Demon Hunter. How do you know about Koschei and me but not her?"

"As I told you, I'm still catching up. I've had to learn a great many things in a brief amount of time."

"How are you learning these things? How do you know about the… what did you call it?"

"The Grisial. I'm sorry, but you're still wasting time. It can all be sorted later—if we survive."

"I agree with you," said Koschei impatiently. "Let's go rescue the boy."

"Exactly right. May I ask you, Izanami, to kneel with me?"

"Kneel? Why?"

"It's only for my own comfort—and perhaps also for yours. I'm afraid you and I will have to maintain physical contact while kneeling."

"Really?" she said suspiciously. "Why?"

"I apologize. To locate Alaric, I need to probe the Grisial, and you have become its host. Because it has taken a human host, I can probe it through your mind."

"I don't like being touched by people I don't know."

"Or people she does know," coughed Koschei under his breath.

"I shall be respectful," said Hadrian.

"What if I give the Grisial to you? You could be its host. Won't that work even better? Seems more efficient to me."

"I'm afraid it's more complicated than that. Certain things have happened while you've been connected to it. If it's separated from you, we may not be able to put things back the way they were meant to be. Do you understand?"

"Not really. Sounds to me like an elaborate excuse to feel me up."

Hadrian was dismayed.

"With the fate of the universe in the balance, do you think my main concern is to take advantage of a strange woman I've only just met?"

"Strange?"

"Frankly, yes."

Izanami dropped to her knees and drew her knife from its sheath.

"Tell you what, Necromant. Do whatever you must, but if your fingers wander where I don't want them, this blade goes straight into your gut. Got that?"

Offended, the Necromant got down on his knees and drew near to her.

"Know this," he said. "If the world's fate were not at stake, I'd have nothing to do with you."

"Just get this over with."

Koschei stifled a laugh.

"She's a bit nicer," he said, "once you get to know her."

With a watchful eye on the knife, Hadrian extended his fingers and placed the tips at various points on her head.

"This requires a fair degree of concentration, and that knife is a distraction."

"Deal with it, Necromant."

He closed his eyes and went into a trance. The warmth she had felt before from his hand now emanated from his entire body. It gave her a comfortable, mellow feeling. She felt herself drawn into a dream state. She imagined herself floating through a dark tunnel. She could hear voices coming from all directions—too many to hear clearly all at once—and they were familiar. She emerged from the tunnel into a clear nighttime sky blanketed by stars. She looked down. Far below she saw Tsuru's cottage standing alone in a barren landscape. The sun quickly rose, and then she looked down at the Trans-Canada Highway. She saw herself and Koschei battling Hathus and the other Mercenary.

In the space of a moment, she was then over Ballard witnessing her battle with Hathus and Belenus next to the ruins of Sapphire's house. Now it was nighttime again, and she was over Pioneer Square where she saw herself again fighting Hathus.

The sun was in the sky again, and she returned to Ballard where she descended. She floated through the entrance of Sapphire's house, which was now restored. She was in Sapphire's office. She opened a drawer stuffed with papers and went through them. She found the crystal. It was beautiful, the way it sparkled in the light. She put it on. Now the crystal was gone, and she lay on her bed. The bedroom door opened, and she sat up. Sapphire came into the room, and she was overcome with joy. She didn't want this moment to end, but she felt herself slipping away. She used all her will to stay in that moment. Everything went black.

When she came to, Koschei and Hadrian stood over her. Koschei was concerned.

"Are you all right, Izanami?" he asked.

She was confused. She looked around and remembered she was in the Bialowieza Forest. She clenched her hand and panicked to see it was empty. She spotted her knife on the ground and retrieved it quickly.

"I'm sorry," said Hadrian. "I honestly did not foresee that effect on you. Are you all right?"

She felt Sapphire's absence keenly, and it angered her.

"I'm… all right. I'm probably just a bit tired from the battle, and I haven't eaten anything all day. Did it work?"

"Yes, I'm happy to say. Alaric is obviously working with someone versed in the mystical arts, and that person succeeded in making a link with the Grisial and you. That's how he always knew where to find you, but the link can be made to work both ways. I've traced it back to Alaric. I didn't pinpoint his location exactly, but he seems to be at a high elevation. He is traveling through the air and at great speed. I'm not certain what would account for that."

"Could he be on an airplane?" asked Koschei.

"Airplane? A vessel that flies? Interesting. Are there many of those?"

"Of course, there are," said Izanami. "How long have you been hiding out in this forest anyway?"

"This is good. We have time. He will not perform the ritual until he arrives at his destination. Then it will take a day or more to prepare for it. I'm afraid I'll have to probe the Grisial again after he has arrived so I may fix his location."

Izanami sighed. "If you have to."

"Once I know precisely where he is, I can take us there. That is when the real work will begin. The Zen'ei are numerous, and many of them are quite willing to die for their cause. There are only three of us. Is there anyone else who could help us?"

"The Demon Hunters are all gone now," said Izanami. "Except for Koschei and me. And Sapphire. She's out there somewhere, but I don't know where. If only I could get in touch with her."

"You did your best," said Hadrian. "I sensed you calling out to her while we were in our trance. I understand who she is now. I'm sure she will come when she's able. What about Orpheus?"

"You know Orpheus?"

"Our paths have crossed a few times... in the past."

"He can't help us. He's trapped in the Netherworld for eternity."

"That sounds like an interesting story," said Hadrian. "Perhaps you will tell it to me at length—when there is time. That's it then. It's only the three of us. You should have something to eat and try to get some sleep. We'll all need to be as fit and ready as possible once we know where we're going."

Izanami opened her pouch and took out some of the food Tsuru had given her. She looked at Koschei, who just shrugged. She asked Hadrian, "Would you like to share some of my food?"

"Don't worry about me. There is something I must do before we depart. I will return soon."

"Why am I the only one who ever needs to eat or sleep?" groused Izanami as she chewed on bread and cured meat.

Koschei sat next to her.

"For what it's worth, my friend, I would gladly share your dinner if I could. It looks tasty."

"What do you make of the Necromant?"

"Things would be much worse if not for him. I'd say Tsuru put us on the right path after all. If only we had not lost the boy."

"How is that she knows Hadrian, but he doesn't know her?"

"He does behave strangely, but that would come from being a hermit. To be honest, you're a bit odd yourself. You're not exactly the same Izanami I knew before."

"And you're not precisely the same Koschei, but that's probably because you're dead."

"You have to stop saying that."

"I saw her, Koschei."

"Who?"

"Sapphire. I saw her in my trance. The Grisial took me back in time to her. She was standing there as real and alive as anything. I miss her so much. Why is she taking so long to come back?"

"You should take the Necromant's advice and get some sleep. As bad as the last battle was, the next one will likely be worse."

"You're right. I'm exhausted. You'll watch over me, won't you? I don't feel at all comfortable in this forest."

"Yes, my friend, I'll watch over you. Always."

She found a comfortable, dry spot and pulled the blanket from her pouch for a bit of comfort. She had doubted that she would fully sleep, but she quickly slipped into a state where time had no meaning and memory played one trick after another. She was unaware when the dream began or that it was a dream.

She stood in the forest, but now it was pitch black. She was alone and filled with dread. She held her breath and listened. Wind rustled the branches above her. She heard a cry like a crow's. She couldn't shake her sense of an impending danger. The fact she had no idea what the danger might be only made it worse. Her heart pounded in her chest.

She felt a light movement on her foot. It was nearly imperceptible, but it was definitely there. It tickled the top of her foot in spite of her boot. She felt the same sensation on the other foot. She felt it in many places. She felt it move up one of her legs and over her knee. Now on the thigh of her other leg. In a panic, she swatted at her leg and felt small, hairy legs climb on her fingers. She swatted more furiously. Both legs were now covered by the creatures. They were spiders and, judging by their size, probably tarantulas. She kicked and swung her arms, but they swarmed over her in greater numbers. The legs brushed her lips. Others were tangled in her hair. She opened her mouth to scream, but there was no sound. Only more hairy legs probing inside her mouth.

She flailed wildly, but nothing she did stopped them. She tried again to yell, and again she failed. She tried again with more urgency. At last, in her increasing frenzy the roar escaped her lips. It was so loud she frightened herself. She tried to run, but brawny arms restrained her.

"Izanami! Wake up! You're dreaming!"

She struggled more, trying to work out how the spiders had somehow been transformed into Koschei. She saw his face, and that calmed her. Now if only she could catch her breath.

Beyond Koschei's shoulder she saw Hadrian. He stared at her with concern.

"Is she normally prone to nightmares? Or did they begin after she put on the Grisial?"

"I've never known her to have terrors like this before."

"We should try again to locate Alaric," said the Necromant. He added apologetically, "I'm afraid you and I shall have to go into a trance again."

"Do what you need to do," said Izanami resignedly.

The Necromant and the Demon Hunter knelt on the ground and looked into each other's eyes. He put his hands on her shoulders and stared intently. His irises looked like shadowy tunnels into another world. She found them more welcoming this time in addition to the comfortable warmth radiating from his body. This time the experience was less disconcerting, probably because she knew what to expect. She had more control this time of where her mind went during the trance. She called out to Sapphire in every way she could.

When the trance ended, Hadrian stood.

"I know where he is. We must go to the Swiss Alps. If you are ready, I can take us there now."

12
Lausanne

WHEN THE SPINNING stopped, all four landed on their feet. Izanami and Koschei were pleased not to have been thrown to the ground, as they had when arriving in the Bialowieza Forest.

"I must say," said Koschei, "your skill at teleportation is much finer than Tsuru's."

"It does work better when the one performing the teleportation is along for the journey," said Hadrian.

They took in their surroundings. They were in the shadow of a Gothic cathedral on a high hill. They walked down the street, and a vista opened up on the city below. A few medieval towers dotted an urban landscape of Belle Epoque buildings. In the distance was a large, dark blue lake. Beyond that, a range of rugged, snow-capped mountains. The air was cold, crisp, and invigorating. The oppressive feeling Izanami and Koschei had experienced in the forest faded.

They followed the street downhill. It led to a deserted shopping district. Plywood panels covered most store windows, and the panels—as well as the sides of buildings—were covered with graffiti in English and French. Many of the slogans were variations of "Save the planet!" and "Balor Is Coming!" Some shops had been gutted by fire. Rocks of varying sizes littered the boulevard along with a few abandoned police barricades.

The silence was eerie. A few blocks farther, they happened on a small electronics shop nestled on a side street. There was no board protecting its display window, and it had somehow escaped damage. Inside the shop, a small flat-screen television played. On the screen a newsreader spoke anxiously. Captions at the bottom of the screen were in French.

"Very impressive," said Hadrian in apparent admiration of the appliance.

"What's she saying?" said Izanami to Koschei. "I'm still trying to focus my eyes after the trance and the teleportation."

"She's reporting on riots that occurred overnight. Most of the violence was in Geneva and Zurich, she says, but also in smaller cities like Lausanne. That's where we are, no? Lausanne?"

"Yes," said Hadrian. "It has been... a long time since I was here. Much has changed."

Koschei continued reading. "Many were injured and several killed. The police have largely abandoned their posts. Some have joined the rioters. In spite of the casualties, she says, it's a great day for democracy. *Pour le pouvoir du peuple.* The power of the people."

"If it's like this in Switzerland," said Izanami gravely, "what must it be like in France and Italy?"

"Now she's saying that, despite the unrest, the Cythère Conference will go ahead as scheduled."

"The what?" asked Hadrian.

"She's explaining. Just a moment."

"I've heard of that," said Izanami. "The rich and the famous go to it every year."

"Yes," said Koschei, continuing to read the captions. "An economic forum bringing together executives of the world's largest corporations as well as many of the wealthiest international investors. Four of the five richest billionaires will be in attendance. That includes Bob Ware, co-founder and chief executive of ParyDyme Corporation, who is hosting the conference this year. Security will be extremely tight at Château Cythère."

"The wealthiest never need to worry about their safety," said Izanami, "even when the whole world is burning down around them."

Hadrian stroked his beard. "Where exactly is this Château Cythère, I wonder."

"Based on the way she speaks of it," said Koschei, "I would think it's close to where we are now."

"We passed a kiosk back there with a tourist map," said Izanami. "That may show it."

They walked back down the street to look at the map. It showed the château about forty miles west of Lausanne. Hadrian touched the spot with his finger.

"Yes," he said with certainty, "that is where Alaric has taken the boy."

"Are you certain?" asked Koschei. "In the middle of an international conference attended by well-known people from all over the world?"

"Yes, it makes sense. In order to return, the Fomóire will need unwitting and widespread cooperation from this world's current inhabitants. Gatherings of people provide the necessary concentration of human life force for their purpose."

"If Peter is in that château," said Koschei, "all that security won't make it easy to rescue him."

"You can teleport us in there, though," said Izanami, "can't you, Hadrian?"

The Necromant was doubtful.

"I don't know precisely where we would arrive. I cannot see a place exactly before teleporting. It's safer to go for open area rather than attempt going directly inside the château. One or more of us could end up embedded in a stone wall."

"Could that really happen?" asked Izanami.

"Oh yes. Teleportation is not without grave risks."

"So what's our plan then? How do three of us get in there and get out again with the boy?"

"Getting out will be the easy part," said Hadrian. "Once we have the child, I can teleport us anywhere we want to go. Locating him and liberating him will be the challenge."

"I don't suppose you have a way of making us invisible," she said.

"Very few have mastered that art. I hope to be among them one day, but I fear that lies far in the future for me."

The remark surprised Izanami. "How much more studying of the mystical arts is left for you to do? By this point, don't you measure your age in centuries?"

"I'm counting on my passion for knowledge to keep me young for a very long time," he replied, somewhat offended.

"Why wouldn't we simply march into the castle?" said Koschei. "Right through the front door?"

The other two stared at him.

"In addition to the world's attention being focused on the place," said Hadrian, "we would likely be confronting the full force of the Zen'ei."

"So? Can't you just pound the ground with that stick of yours and make them all unconscious?"

"If their numbers are what I expect, then I would be unable to subdue all of them. Moreover, I expect that Alaric is backed and supported by someone with powers similar to my own. Alaric himself is not a sorcerer, but he's clearly aided by someone who is."

"Given the circumstances," said Koschei, "I see no way to plan this operation with any precision. All we can do is have the Necromant take us as close to the château as he safely can. We will then have to improvise. Perhaps there will be an opportunity to apprehend one or more of the arriving attendees and take their credentials so that we may enter as guests."

"Frankly, Koschei, that sounds like something you saw in a movie."

"What if it is? What do you know about them anyway, Izanami? You don't watch them."

"Movies?" wondered Hadrian.

"I watch movies now. Sapphire likes to watch them, and I've seen some with her. I've actually learned to enjoy them."

"You always insisted you didn't like them."

"It was the idea of them. You watch one from the beginning, but its ending is already fixed and set. Characters whose fates are predetermined don't interest me. I prefer real life where one chooses one's own destiny."

"Ah, yes, as you told Alaric. Free will is important to you— even in a movie."

"Time grows short," said Hadrian. "I can think of no better plan than Koschei's. We should proceed and hope for the best."

"Agreed," said Izanami, "but I'd feel better, Necromant, if you sounded more optimistic."

"Optimism is worth less than preparation. Come, Demon Hunter. I must probe the Grisial one more time to learn as much as possible about what may await us."

"I'm getting tired of being this stupid crystal's vessel."

"You donned the Grisial by choice. By your own free will, if you like. Choices have consequences."

With a sigh Izanami resigned herself to another melding of her mind with the Necromant's. They knelt on the sidewalk. Hadrian laid his hands on her shoulders. She closed her eyes and braced herself for the discomfort of physical and mental proximity. She focused on again reaching out to Sapphire in the trance.

Her mind floated, and Izanami knew something was different. As much as she tried to focus on Sapphire, she was drawn in a different direction. The images in her mind, one after another, were like a rushing river carrying her downstream. She was swept, as if from one cascade to another, through the Necromant's innermost memories.

The sensation of being engulfed gave way to an awareness of floating. It was as if she were high in the sky. Below her was a wild mountain range covering a vast land more primeval than the Bialowieza Forest. Hadrian's knowledge was now becoming her knowledge. She understood this was the homeland of the Dacians, a people whose remote history and culture was a mystery to the rest of the world. The landscape was rugged and spectacular. Dense with dark forest, it was populated by malevolent creatures that roamed and preyed in the night. A wilderness home to one of the world's largest carnivore populations. A territory that would long resist outsiders and would-be invaders. Among its enigmatic inhabitants were those who had been there the longest. Mysterious even to the Dacians, they were the Usari.

The Dacians would eventually be conquered by the Roman warrior Trajan. After him would come further waves of invaders. They would have names like Goths, Gepidae, Huns, Visigoths, Slavs, Angars, and Mongols. The Dacians not assimilated by the outsiders would become a diaspora flung to all corners of the world. Deep in the Carpathian Mountains, however, one tribe survived in isolation. Wedded to the natural world, their sages would absorb the darkest secrets of the metaphysical world. Their gifts would include unnaturally long lifespans. Their skills would be so advanced that outsiders would see their arts as magic.

These were the people of the Necromant Hadrian.

As the strange memories filled Izanami's head, she was embraced by the warmth she had felt before from Hadrian's mind. It was pleasurable and relaxed her completely. Yet she resented the peace and comfort it brought. She hated the intrusion. Most of all, she hated the fact she did not want it to end.

The memories became disjointed. She would not recall most of them with any clarity. Only fragments. One, however, would remain in her mind clearly. Cobblestone streets at night in the weak glow of gaslight. Black carriages drawn by horses. She would remember a room with floor-to-ceiling shelves stuffed with ancient books and manuscripts.

As Hadrian and Izanami remained in their trance, Koschei was alerted by the sound of a distant rumble. Far down the street, a crowd worked its way slowly toward them. As they came more into view, the Russian discerned an unruly mob. Some carried signs, others sticks and clubs.

"I don't mean to hurry you," he said quietly to the oblivious pair, "but we have company. Now would be a good time to finish. Quickly. Now."

Neither Izanami nor Hadrian reacted. Koschei held his breath and weighed his options.

Izanami saw Hadrian at a desk amid piles of books and papers. Before him was a manuscript next to an inkpot. He scribbled furiously with a quill pen. A woman appeared in the doorway. She had flowing, black hair and intense, violet eyes. She wore an olive green riding habit with billowing sleeves. She held a riding crop. Izanami was taken by her beauty.

Distracted, Hadrian looked up. "So, you have returned at last, Miss Knagenhjelm. I hadn't expected to see you again."

"What you may or may not have expected is of no interest," she said. "I trust you're aware of what's happening—and what it portends."

"Now that you've returned, may I not at last call you by your *nom de chasseuse de démon*? Will you allow it? May I call you Eurydice?"

Her eyes flashed, and a slight smile played on her lips.

"So, Hadrian, is this how a Necromant flirts? Alas, we have not the time. There's not a moment to lose."

"What?" murmured Izanami.

"There's no time. We can't wait."

It was not Miss Knagenhjelm's voice. It was Koschei's. Izanami needed several moments to get her bearings.

"You shouldn't have done that," said Hadrian angrily. He was already on his feet. "You broke the trance. I wasn't able to end it properly."

Groggy and angry, Izanami got to her feet.

"You mean, you didn't have time to clear my memory. You didn't get to erase what I learned while we were in each other's minds."

"Look," said the Russian, shouting to be heard above the crowd encircling them. "I didn't want to do it. I had no choice. In case you haven't noticed, we've got company."

The angry mob consisted of young people.

"We're here to save the planet!" shouted one. "Are you with us or against us?"

"Are you part of the problem," cried another, "or part of the solution?"

"Are you with Balor or against him?" yelled a third one.

Izanami shouted back at them.

"We have no quarrel with you. We're not interfering with your march. Go on your way."

"Why don't you answer?" came the reply. "If you cared about the world, you'd answer. How can you be so blind? How can you be so uncaring about others? You're holding us all back."

"There's no point engaging them," said Koschei calmly. "Let's walk away quietly and hope we don't have to hurt any of them."

No matter what direction they headed, the crowd blocked them. After several minutes, Koschei lost his patience and shoved a pair of them out of his way. The reaction was a collective roar. The crowd pressed itself more forcefully against the three of them.

Two marchers were particularly stirring up the others. Izanami took aim at them with her fists and, as gently as possible, forced them backward with a light burst of energy. Five people fell to the ground. The crowd went dead quiet. All eyes stared in her direction. It was as if time stood still.

A loud voice broke the silence. "She's one of them! The learned ones have told us about them!"

Another voice. "Violence comes out of her hands! She's one of the oppressors!"

"There's no reasoning with them," said Izanami. "Any chance of teleporting us out of here?"

"I need to be able to concentrate," said Hadrian. "I won't risk taking some of them with us."

"So," said Koschei, drawing his blade, "we'll have to do this the old-fashioned way."

"Wait, Demon Hunter," said Hadrian. "I command resources beyond teleportation."

The Necromant placed the tip of his staff firmly on the ground and closed his eyes. The veins in his temples throbbed as he focused his mind. The pavement cracked in pieces, and energy radiated several yards in every direction. Those standing closest were knocked off their feet. Those farther back found themselves thrown against one another.

A few of the braver ones looked as if they might charge him. He raised his staff high in the air again, and the crowd stayed motionless. The standoff lasted several minutes. Then the marchers began to drift away, some casting menacing backward glances.

"Well done, Necromant," said Koschei. "Let's head to the château before any of them come back."

"We have to settle something first," said Izanami heatedly. "It's true, isn't it? I've been learning things about you when we go into those trances, and then you've been erasing my mind before I come out of it. I only found out because Koschei interrupted the last trance before you could finish."

"You're correct," said the Necromant. "I don't understand why you'd be angry about that."

"You've been messing with my mind, with my memory. Of course, I'm angry. Who wouldn't be?"

"Sharing our thoughts is an inevitable side effect of my accessing the Grisial. You have no entitlement to my personal memories. I have a right to my privacy."

"And I have a right not to have my mind tampered with. How do I know what else you might have been erasing?"

"Under the circumstances, I suppose you must trust me."

"I'm not a trusting person. What about *my* thoughts and memories? You must be able to see all of them. What about *my* privacy? I don't suppose you're erasing your memories of what you've seen in my brain."

"I would if I could, but it's simply not possible to erase one's own memories. I do my best, however, not to collect any of your thoughts that aren't relevant."

"Well, you're not doing it again."

"Very well. With any luck, it won't be necessary."

"Were you ever going to tell me?"

"Tell you what?"

"That you knew Eurydice?"

"Why? What do you know about Eurydice?"

"I think you know."

"I assure you, I don't know what you're talking about."

"You really don't know?"

"Know what?"

Koschei stood silent, keeping a wary eye in case any of the mob returned.

"You don't know that Sapphire and Eurydice are the same person? My Sapphire. The one I keep talking about."

"What? Tyra still alive? That isn't possible…"

"No, Tyra's not alive. She was reincarnated as Lola Blumquist. She's Sapphire."

"That's impossible," said Hadrian angrily.

"I swear it's true."

"There has never been a credible report of reincarnation," said the Necromant skeptically. "Not among mortal humans. What's your evidence?"

"My evidence is Sapphire. She remembers her life as Eurydice—and also the life she lived before that."

"I would need much more information to take this seriously. We haven't the time."

"It's true. If Orpheus were here, he'd tell you. He knew her in her first life."

Hadrian was astonished. "He knew Tyra? I'm not aware they ever knew each other."

"No, he only knew her as Justine and Lola. Okay, hearing myself talk about this out loud, it does sound crazy."

The Necromant reflected. "This is nothing short of astounding. Yet the more I think about it, the more it would explain."

"What were you to her?"

"Sorry?"

"What were you and Tyra to each other?"

"This is precisely the sort of situation I meant to avoid by shielding my memories from you."

"Sorry to interrupt this intriguing conversation," said the Russian, "but shouldn't we be using this time to rescue the child?"

"You're right, Koschei," said Izanami, "but we'll definitely finish this discussion later. For now, though, Necromant, take us where we need to go."

13
Château Cythère

IZANAMI, KOSCHEI AND Hadrian looked around to see where they were. It was a wide clearing surrounded by thick alpine forest. The scent of stone pine was strong in the cool mountain air. Beyond the tops of the trees, they could see a peak, perhaps four or five miles away. Atop it was a tall castle with at least four turrets of varying heights. Each had a distinctively pointed roof topped by a spire. Against the clear sky, they saw thin banners rippling in the breeze like ribbons.

"You couldn't get us any closer than this, Necromant?" said Izanami.

"Not safely."

"So we have a walk ahead of us," she groused. "And not the easiest terrain."

"At least the forest will provide cover so we won't be easily spotted," said Koschei.

Izanami grabbed the compass from her pouch and took note of the castle's direction. It was close to due east. The compass would be their guide once their view was obscured within the forest.

They set out immediately. Once they entered the forest, they lost the sunlight, and the temperature dropped. They made their way through the trees over uneven ground. Izanami led, followed by Hadrian, then Koschei. For the first half hour, they trudged in silence.

Alone with her thoughts, Izanami's mind returned to the memories she experienced during the trance. Though she didn't want the distraction, she couldn't help herself. She was still angry about Hadrian probing her mind.

She wondered what things the Necromant had learned about her. To what thoughts and feelings was he now privy? She could not get Tyra Knagenhjelm's image out of her mind. Her face was stunning, her smile magnetic. Her accent was vaguely British but with a Scandinavian inflection. Izanami would have been drawn to her no matter what, but knowing she was Sapphire's previous incarnation intensified the fascination.

Because Izanami had seen her through Hadrian's eyes, her feelings were confused. Her own emotional reaction was entangled with the Necromant's. She envied him for having known her in the flesh. She was also disturbed by the look in Tyra's eyes as she gazed at Hadrian. There was clearly something between them.

Izanami could no longer keep her thoughts to herself. She stopped and turned to the Necromant.

"Just tell me. Were you and she lovers?"

His expression was pained.

"If you would only permit it, there might be a way to remove those vexing memories from your..."

"No. You're not messing with my mind ever again. Just tell me."

He sighed. "I was warned this would happen."

"Warned? By whom?"

"It doesn't matter. Not now anyway. It's unnatural for two minds to merge the way ours have. I'm afraid it will bind us forever. I'll never be rid of your thoughts and memories, and you'll never escape what you've experienced of mine. Though we've barely had time to become acquainted, we've shared an intimacy few people achieve in a natural lifetime. I don't know if you fully appreciate this yet."

"What are you saying? That because I let you into my head a couple of times, we're suddenly best friends and always will be? Don't flatter yourself, Necromant. I choose my own friends, and I choose them carefully. You and I will never be friends."

"I'm talking about more than mere friendship..."

"Would you just stop!" she shouted. "Don't pretend you know me. No matter what you think you've seen, you know nothing about me."

Koschei had held back at a distance while they talked, but now he joined Izanami and laid a hand gently on her shoulder.

"I don't understand what's going on here," he said, "but now is not the time. We must keep moving."

"You're right. Let's go."

They resumed their hike. Hadrian deliberately lagged behind the other two.

"I hate him," she said. "How dare he."

"The force of your words concerns me," said Koschei.

"There's no way I'll hold my tongue about this."

"That's not what I meant. It's just that..."

"What?"

"I have to wonder what there is about him that provokes such strong feelings in you."

"What are you saying?"

"Only that he brings out passion in you. Sometimes there is a thin line between the passion of hatred and the passion of..."

"Don't say it. I'll kill you if you say it."

"There was once a woman who spoke to me with the exact same tone you have been using. She swore she hated me. By the next morning it was a different story."

"Are you serious? Are you really using this situation to brag about some old conquest? You're itching for a fight, aren't you? Because if you are, I'll give you one. I'll put that missing scar back on your arm."

"I don't want to argue with you. It just concerns me how this Necromant affects you."

"Fine. We won't talk about him anymore. Let's talk about you. Are you really a prince?"

"Did the boy tell you that?"

"Who else? I certainly never heard it from you. Is it true? Or did you just make up a story for him?"

"You and I don't talk about our childhoods, remember? Neither of us likes revisiting our most painful memories."

"That was always our understanding, but things are different now. I saw you die. Since that day I've had regrets. I'm sorry about the things you and I never talked about. About the questions I never asked you. About..."

"Yes?"

"Things I never told you."

"What things? That you've always been in love with me?"

"Can't you stop? You're intolerable sometimes. Just tell me. Are you a prince or not?"

Koschei's mood turned serious.

"Yes, but that was another lifetime. There's no point talking about it."

That put an end to the conversation. They tramped the next half mile in silence.

Hadrian caught up to the other two, intent on speaking to Izanami. Koschei fell back a bit to give them space, but she refused to acknowledge the Necromant.

"I'm sorry," he said.

"Don't be. I myself rarely make or accept apologies, but then you should know that—since we're so intimate, you and I."

"I just want to say that I understand."

"Understand what?"

"In spite of what you may fear, I didn't access every thought and memory you had. Certain ones, however, were unavoidable. I understand what you went through, I mean, as a child. I know about the internment camp."

"You do, do you? Anyone who's interested knows about it. It's in the history books."

"I know what that man did to you. I understand why it must be so difficult for you to trust people."

Izanami stopped in her tracks and turned to grab Hadrian's collar with both her hands.

"You have no right to talk to me about this!" she shouted. "You have no right to my history. It's stolen property, and I'll never forgive you for that."

She was shaking, and the fact Hadrian saw her in this state made her angrier. She clutched his garment more tightly.

"Just tell me one thing. Just because we bonded in a trance, that doesn't mean you can read my mind *all* the time now, does it?"

"Don't worry. We experience each other's thoughts and memories only while in the trance. Not any other time. Still, there is a telepathic link established between us—if we should both choose to use it."

Koschei worried about the delay caused by the discussion.

"I think it's best if we speak no more of this until after the child is rescued. Can we agree on that?"

Izanami slowly released her grip on Hadrian's robe and resumed walking.

"We must be almost there," she muttered. "It can't be much farther, can it?"

After a short while, the way turned steep. They had reached the base of the mountain. From that point the climb was arduous, and Izanami was glad of the physical exertion and the escape it provided from the thoughts churning in her head.

Nearly halfway up the slope, she felt a weakness. It occurred to her she had not eaten all day.

"Is no one else starving?"

The other two looked at her blankly.

"No, of course not. No one eats anymore except me. I can't go on unless I have something—even just a small amount. We'll have to rest a few minutes."

She searched her pouch and found the last of the bread and cheese as well as an apple. She was about to offer to share but then remembered there was no point.

"I can't understand how you can keep going without food or sleep, Koschei. I can only assume it's because you're dead, but what's your excuse, Hadrian? Are you dead too? Is that why you look so young when I know for a fact that you're as old as dirt? Am I the only one alive here?"

"I can assure you I'm not dead," said the Necromant.

"Then what's going on with the two of you and the boy? Why do none of you sleep or eat?"

"I can't explain it," said Koschei. "No more than I can explain not remembering certain things you insist we did together."

"I have no such memory loss," said Hadrian, "and I can explain my lack of need for rest and food. I have employed an old enchantment during this critical period so I won't be distracted by mundane necessities."

"Are Koschei and the boy also under such an enchantment then?"

"Not by me," said the Necromant. "It would not be wise for me to do that to somebody else."

"Frankly," she said, biting off a chunk of bread rather viciously, "I don't find your explanations satisfactory."

She chewed sullenly on the bread. She hated not understanding what was going on. Moreover, she found the Necromant condescending and she resented him for it. She finished her food and wiped her mouth with the back of her hand.

"Sorry for the delay. Let's go. I swear, if I don't keep moving, I'll go mad."

They continued scaling the mountain until they emerged from the trees. The castle loomed above them. They heard something and paused to listen. Combined with the breeze's hum was the faint sound of chamber music. One-hundred yards or less of bare, rocky mountainside was all that was between them and the base of the castle. The structure stretched high into the sky. On the outside wall were a few small windows, each protected by iron grilling.

They clambered closer to the edifice's base. Their ascent revealed an ever-expanding view beyond the trees. Below was a narrow, winding road. It was clogged with traffic—mainly sports utility vehicles—making its way upward toward the castle.

Having reached the castle wall, their climb would now be strictly vertical. From a distance it had appeared smooth, but up close they could see it was uneven enough to be scaled by a skilled climber.

"I'm going up," said Izanami.

"By yourself?" asked Koschei.

"That makes the most sense. I have experience with this kind of climbing. I'm fast, and I'm quiet. With any luck I'll be in and out before anyone knows what's happened."

"So why did Hadrian and I come?"

"You're the backup. If I'm not back in two hours, then you make your own plan."

"There should be a bit more forethought," said the Necromant, "than you simply barreling alone into an unknown situation and hoping for the best."

"I'm done talking. I have to act, and I need to do it now."

"Wait," said Hadrian. "Do what you have to do, but for your safety I must tell you something. Though you don't want to hear it, you and I are now mentally linked through the Grisial. If we choose, we can vaguely sense each other's thoughts. Use that so I may know where you are. So that Koschei and I can find you if necessary."

"I told you. I'm not letting you into my head again, and I definitely don't want to be in yours."

Without another word she scrambled up the castle wall. Her speed impressed the two men. She climbed deftly from one slight ledge to another, pulling herself up by grabbing hold of any bulge or jut she could find. As she ascended higher, her quick, agile movements resembled those of a spider. Koschei and Hadrian looked at each other, shrugged, and made themselves comfortable.

Izanami was relieved to have left them behind. She had always found too much time with others—men in particular—to get irksome. She now felt liberated.

Reaching for the next handhold, she glanced over her shoulder. Far below, her companions were tiny. Beyond them, the carpet of pines spread over the base of the mountain and down into the valley. An icy gust sent a shiver through her and coaxed her to reaffirm her hold. She could see a distance of perhaps twenty miles. To the north was a range of jagged, snow-capped peaks. To the south was another, somewhat smaller range. The sudden realization of being so high made her momentarily dizzy. Her foot threatened to slide off its meager perch, and she quickly rebalanced herself. She shifted her gaze upwards. Better to concentrate on finding the next handhold than to take in the scenery.

Her progress was slower than she hoped, and she wondered if she should have told the others to give her three hours before following. She continued to move one hand and then one foot after another, and soon enough she laid a hand on the ledge of the lowest window. With her other hand she reached up and grabbed the iron grating that protected it. The latticed pattern was easy to grasp and climb, and it was a relief not to have to worry about a sudden, strong gust blowing her away.

She climbed upward until her hands and feet were all safely lodged on the metal strips. She pressed her face against them and peered through the glass window. Luck was with her. The room inside, a bedroom, was unoccupied. She studied the iron grille for a way to loosen it so she could enter.

Powdery stone drizzled down on her from above. Alarmed, she looked up to see the grille's upper right anchor bolt come loose from the wall. Her weight caused the grille to lean outward on one side. She looked to the other anchor bolt above and saw it straining. She shifted her body cautiously, intending to regain a foothold on the wall, but her movement only added more stress to the remaining upper anchor bolt.

As if in slow motion, the bolt came free. She clung to the grille as it leaned farther outward. Only the two bottom anchor bolts, straining from her weight, held the grille to the wall. The grille's angle was such that the wall was just out of reach. Despite knowing better, she glanced down. A vast, empty space separated her from what looked like miniature trees hundreds of yards below.

She retreated gingerly back down the grille, hoping to get a foothold on the wall below it, but its slant would make that difficult. Without warning the lower right anchor bolt sprang loose. She clutched the grille as it spun in a half-circle around the axis of the remaining bolt. To her relief, the last bolt did not give way immediately. She hung from the grille, her feet dangling. The wall was within reach, and she wasted no time. She moved her feet and hands onto whatever juts in the wall she could reach.

She had no sooner secured her grip when the grille broke free and tumbled downward through the air. It seemed like minutes before she heard a faint echo of its impact far below. She hoped Koschei and Hadrian had not been unlucky enough to be in its path. From such a height its velocity would have been more than sufficient to kill a man outright.

She climbed back up to the window ledge. Her fingers trembled. She told herself it was from the alpine wind's chill, but she couldn't fool herself. She had stupidly allowed herself to become unnerved. Such a lack of discipline might prove fatal.

Holding onto the stonework bordering the window, she stood on the stone ledge and tested its stability by shifting her weight carefully from one side to the other. The ledge was secure. She examined the window and its array of rectangular glass panes held by a metal framework. Careful not to crack the glass, she pushed one of the panes out and caught it before it fell to the floor. She reached inside and unlocked the window.

Cautiously, she stepped into the room and satisfied herself that it was indeed unoccupied. It appeared not to be in use at all. Given its cramped size, spare furnishings, and the roughness of the stone walls, she judged she was in the oldest part of the castle. The modern window fixture notwithstanding, it probably dated from medieval times. The main part would doubtless be more modern and spacious.

She was relieved to be out of the cold, outside air. While her suit had kept her body warm, her face felt frozen. She took a few deep breaths and collected her thoughts. The castle was huge, and she had no idea where she needed to go. Relying on pure instinct, she would have to move quickly to find where the boy was being held.

She opened the room's thick oak door and surveyed the outside hallway. It was narrow, dark, and deserted. The stone walls and low, arched ceiling—not to mention the cool dampness—made it feel like a cave. She stepped stealthily down the corridor, listening for any sound. She climbed a narrow stone stairway. Despite the thick stone walls, she could hear the muffled sound of the chamber music. She crept higher and heard the faint, dull rumble of a room filled with conversations.

Satisfied that she knew where most people were gathered, she reversed course back to the corridor below and followed it in the other direction. Her hunch was that Peter would be held in the lowest part of the castle, perhaps in a dungeon within the mountain. The corridor ended at a thick, wooden door with a rusty padlock. She picked at it with her knife but soon grew impatient. She then drew the diabolusbane and sundered it easily. She pulled the heavy door open and peered inside. The residual glow from her weapon was sufficient light to see that the chamber was empty.

She retraced her steps back up the narrow stairs. On reaching the level above, she spotted the back of a man in a black suit. He was several feet away and striding in the opposite direction. She froze until he had disappeared around a corner. The music and voices were now more distinct. She tread warily in search of other ways to access spaces below. Finding none, she worried she'd be left with no choice but to explore the higher parts of the castle. That would be difficult to do without encountering people.

She tried handles of the doors she passed. They were all unlocked. When she peeked inside, the rooms were all dark. As she closed one of the doors, she heard the echo of footsteps heading in her direction. She reopened the door and slipped inside. As the footsteps passed, she felt the wall by the door. Despite the castle's age, it had been wired for electricity. She flipped the switch, and an overhead light revealed a man's dressing room. Trousers, coats, and suits hung on racks.

She turned off the light and left the room to enter the next one. It contained a selection of dresses and gowns. As much as she disliked the idea, she knew her best chance of exploring the castle was to blend in—something she could not hope to do in her own clothes. She could put on one of the dresses, but that would mean not having the protection of her suit. There was also the fact that she hated wearing dresses. She weighed the pros and cons and saw no other option. She went through the selection and settled on the plainest of the black dresses close to her size. It was strapless and lower cut than she preferred, but at least it allowed her to move with little restriction. She glanced at the mirror. She wore no makeup, and her hair was untidy. She didn't care. She knew from experience that confidence and body language would compensate for a lot in a crowd, and she didn't intend to linger anywhere long enough to invite attention.

Shoes were a problem. There was no way she would wear high heels. She found a pair with heels low enough for her to walk—or run, if necessary—comfortably. She would have to carry her medallion—the one that summoned the diabolusbane—in her hand. That and the crystal hanging from her neck might attract unwanted attention, but she chose not to worry about it. The sort of people here, the rich and famous, would have more than their share of eccentrics.

She hid her suit, boots, knife, and pouch in the back of a large, wooden wardrobe. She then stole out of the room and into the corridor. She had no sooner rounded the first corner when she met a tall, heavyset man in a black suit. He was planted in the middle of the hallway. His face was scarred, and one eye was glassy. His voice was like an industrial rock crusher.

"You shouldn't be here."

14
Bob

AS MUCH AS she hated doing it, Izanami batted her eyes and smiled. She contorted her throat muscles in an attempt to raise her voice an octave. She exaggerated her vowels to emphasize her North American accent.

"Thank goodness, you're here. I got completely lost. I've absolutely no idea how I wound up here. Where on earth is the ladies' room?"

His face was as emotive as a stone carving. His accent was Germanic. "There are no toilets here. How did you come to be here?" He stared her up and down. His lip curled as if smelling something foul.

Izanami forced herself to titter. "I just knew I shouldn't have had that second glass of champagne." She touched his arm. "Now be a good boy and point me back to where everyone else is, won't you?"

She promised herself she'd never get into a situation like this again. Her only consolation was the possibility she might get to kill him later.

"Come with me."

He stepped to one side, indicating she should walk ahead of him. She proceeded as gaily as she could, all the time feeling his eyes bore into her back. She made an effort to swing her hips, but she couldn't quite master it. Every so often she looked back with a smile she hoped wasn't too forced. His scowl was constant.

They climbed a set of steps, then walked through another corridor. Soon they met another man in a black suit. He was taller and not as heavyset.

"Who is this?" he asked.

"She was down there."

"But how? Without anyone seeing her?"

A slow head shake was the reply.

"How did you get past everyone?" barked the tall man. "What were you doing down there?"

She smiled her widest grin.

"Oh, silly, old me. I don't know where I am half the time. Give me a glass of champagne, and you never know where I'll wind up."

She put her hand on his arm.

"Can you please get me back to where I'm supposed to be? I'm sure they're missing me."

"Something's not right here," said the tall man, taking a mobile phone from his inside coat pocket.

"Screw this," muttered Izanami. "I'm never going to be a spy."

She grabbed the phone from his hand, slammed it to the floor, and smashed it with her foot. She grabbed both men's ties and jerked the two of them so hard that their heads collided. As they reeled in shock, she clenched her two fists together, raised them high, and then pounded with all her might directly at the tall man's sternum. He collapsed to the ground.

Dazed, the heavyset man put his thick arms around her and locked hands. She doubled over and fell to her knees, flipping him over until he landed on his back. She then extended her arms outward and slammed them against his temples. He moaned and attempted to stand. Forcefully, she shoved him back to the floor and locked an arm around his neck. She squeezed until his body went slack.

Panting heavily, she stood and watched to see if anyone else would come.

"Stupid," she muttered. "I shouldn't have bothered changing clothes."

She made a half-hearted effort to straighten her hair and smooth the dress. There was a small tear in the hem—one more thing that people might notice. She looked down at the two men. They had gone down easy enough. *Definitely not Mercenaries,* she thought, *just ordinary security guys.*

She hurried down the corridor, following the ever-louder sounds of music and conversation. After more turns and climbs, she came to the entrance of a great hall. It was spacious, high, and crammed full of people in expensive clothes. Everyone's hand held a glass, and all were engaged in earnest conversation. At the far end were the chamber musicians. To one side was a staircase leading upward. She made in that direction and dashed up the steep steps. It was a longer climb than she expected. At the top was a mezzanine overlooking the hall from a height of around thirty feet. She walked along the balustrade, surveying the scene below. She wondered if she might spot Alaric or any other familiar face. She found it difficult to believe she was surveying the best and brightest of the world's economic community. From this vantage they were tiny.

"I thought I was the only one who liked to sneak up here."

She had not seen the man standing nearby. He was in his early forties. His suit was Armani, and his shirt collar was open. His long but thinning hair was barely combed. His pale, blue eyes were magnified by oversized, smudged glasses. He swirled the ice in his tall tumbler of amber liquid.

"I don't care much for crowds," she murmured, turning to look down again.

"To be honest, I don't either. Does that surprise you?"

"Not really. Lots of people don't like crowds."

He looked at her quizzically, as if she'd missed the point of his question.

"Are you here with Kobayashi?"

"Why? Because you think I'm Japanese?" she said, hoping to put him on the defensive.

"Sorry, you're right. I made an assumption. So, who *are* you with?"

"Why do I have to be with somebody?"

"Well, because if you weren't, then I'd know who you are. You and I haven't met. I'd remember if we had. That's a fascinating crystal you're wearing, by the way. I bet there's an interesting story behind it."

"Not particularly. It was a gift from my girlfriend."

"I'd say she has good taste."

"Do you know this castle well?"

"I'd say by now I do. We've been here the past couple of weeks preparing for the conference. I'm sorry if I offended you, but I actually do love Japanese culture. As it happens, I am quite a *shinnichi*. I've studied for years with a teacher named Miyamoto. Do you know him?"

She took a deep breath and turned away from him. "Not everyone from Japan or whose ancestors are from Japan automatically knows each other, but then you should know that since you are educated enough to know the word for Japanophile."

"Again, I apologize. For some reason, I just thought you might know him."

"Can I ask you a strange question about the castle?"

"Please."

"If someone wanted to keep a prisoner here in secret, where do you think they would keep him?"

"You weren't kidding. That was a strange question. Is there a reason you ask?"

"Just humor me."

"Of course, but surely you don't suspect the Cythère Conference of holding prisoners, do you?"

"I'm just someone who sometimes wonders about odd hypothetical things. Think of it as a game."

"I like games. Come to think of it, there is a secret door—just above us, as it happens—that has piqued my curiosity ever since I arrived here. I happened to see someone go through it on one of my first days here."

He sipped his drink and grinned.

"Do you think the man in the iron mask may be hidden away in there?"

"Can we go see?" she smiled back at him.

He studied her for a moment.

"I like you. You're fun. What the hell. Yes, let's go have a peek at the mysterious room. I'm game if you are."

He led her down the walkway until they were in a narrow corridor.

"I have to say, you're refreshing. I get tired of people being intimidated by me."

"Really? You don't seem intimidating to me."

"I can see that. It's almost as if you don't know who I am."

"I could say the same about you."

"But that's the thing. I actually *don't* know who you are. You haven't told me your name."

"You haven't told me yours."

"Good one," he laughed. "Okay, I'll play. I'm Bob."

They came to a large, wooden wardrobe located hard against the wall. He winked at her and said, "Watch this."

The wardrobe appeared to have double doors, but that was a deception. Reaching around to the side, Bob opened the front to reveal it was single large door. Behind it was a passageway.

"Cool, huh?" He was as giddy as a child.

She followed him inside. The way was narrower than any of the other corridors she had seen. It brought them to an enclosed set of stairs leading upward. Izanami had to stoop as she climbed. At the top was a small antechamber and a heavy wooden door with a large padlock.

"This is it. Kind of creepy, huh?"

"I don't suppose you have the key."

"No, but I could get one of the staff to come open it for us."

"That won't be necessary."

She held up her medallion with one hand and touched it with the other. The diabolusbane materialized in her hand.

"Stand back," she commanded.

"Man, that's so cool! What the hell is that thing?"

She ignored him as she raised the weapon and brought it down. The padlock disintegrated from the blow. She grabbed the door's handle with both hands and pulled. Because of its weight, it opened slowly.

A single candle, in a holder attached to a wall, burned. Its light was barely sufficient for making out the shadowy room. In the center was a crude wooden bed with no mattress or padding. Curled in a fetal position on top was a small, white, naked body. The face was hidden under a mat of black hair. One ankle was restrained by a shackle attached to a chain.

"Peter!"

"My God," cried Bob. "What on earth is going on here?"

The boy's head turned slightly. "Chiharu? Is that really you?"

"Wait," said Bob, "do you know him? Who are you anyway?"

"You need to take a step back, Bob," she said, raising the diabolusbane. She brought it down on the chain, shattering it.

The diabolusbane dematerialized as she loosed her grip. Spotting a dirty blanket wadded up on the floor, she took it and wrapped it around the boy. He looked dazed.

"You came for me. I hoped you would."

"I said I'd protect you. I keep my promises. Come on, we need to get out of here. Can you stand?"

She got him to his feet. He was able to stand, but only unsteadily.

"Can you walk?"

He nodded. Bob stood to one side, watching with wide eyes. Peter took two steps before a hooded shape appeared in the doorway. The man lowered his hood to reveal a familiar face. She let go of the boy and rushed toward Alaric, but she could not reach him. She was frozen in place. She did not understand why, as Alaric had done nothing. She managed to turn her head slightly and saw Bob with his hand extended. He laughed.

"Sorry," he said. "I can't let you do that."

He turned to Alaric.

"Leave her to me while you find another place for the boy."

"I don't know why you went ahead with this silly conference. What does it matter now? It only delays us from taking the boy to the site of the Inhabitation."

"Patience, Alaric. I want to have some fun with my guest."

Izanami stared at him with an open mouth.

"Why so surprised?" he laughed. "Why do you think they call me the Software Wizard?"

She could not fight or flee. She cursed herself for having walked into another trap. As she stood immobilized, two men entered the room and grabbed Peter roughly. They left the room followed by Alaric, then pushed the door closed. Bob beamed as he grinned at her.

As much as she hated to admit it, she had only one hope. She would have to focus all her thoughts on Hadrian and try to lead him to her. She closed her eyes and thought of the Necromant. In the darkness she searched for his presence and revisited as many of the memories she had acquired from him as she could.

She was surprised to feel the warm, pleasant glow she had experienced in the trance. She sensed his presence and knew he felt hers as well. The sensation was vivid and gave her a distinct sense of knowing his approximate distance and direction of travel toward her. There was something else. Another presence. It was strong and powerful. It too was approaching. It was strange and new but, at the same time, oddly familiar.

His hand still extended, keeping her in place, Bob drew near. He circled her, studying her from every angle.

"My God," he said, "you're so hot. If you worked at my company, I'd definitely be dating you."

She felt the muscles in her jaw relax. He had loosened his control so that she could speak, but it was also sufficient for her to spit. Unfortunately, her saliva fell short of its target.

"You weren't offended, were you? Don't you understand it's a compliment?"

Her body was forced backward and downward until she was lying on top of the wood slats of the bed. Bob knelt beside her and ran his fingers through her hair.

"Who are you? How do you fit into all this? I suppose it doesn't matter. The entire world will be completely changed soon, and this will all be a forgotten memory. I regret our time together must be so brief. Perhaps we'll meet again in the new era."

"Why are you doing this? How can you do this to a child? Why him?"

"Do I need to understand everything perfectly myself? I have experts for that. I'm a big-picture kind of guy. Not every man gets to be the father of a new world. Not every man is up to the challenge."

He ran his hand along her thigh. She focused on the number of inches between her fingers, his throat, and his agonized death.

"Where did you get your powers?" she asked.

"Impressive, aren't they? I told you. I studied under Miyamoto. I'm one of his Augurers."

She laughed. "What's an Augurer? Do you mean Mage?"

"You betray your true character with that word. Don't you understand how offensive it is?"

"You're no Mage. You're just a chancer who's learned a few tricks you don't fully understand."

"Believe that if you want. I got to where I am today because people kept underestimating me. They don't underestimate me now. Now the press calls me the Software Wizard. They don't know how right they are."

"If you're talking about the Miyamoto I knew, he would never have mentored the likes of you."

"Well, he didn't exactly have a choice. It cost a lot of money just to learn that he existed and what he could do. It cost a lot more to lead an expedition to find his sanctuary in the Himalayas. I always wondered why he would have left Japan for that part of the world. It was so cold, the air was so thin, but no matter. He was old and frail. To be honest, I don't think he was mentally all there. How old would he be? A thousand years or more? It wasn't that difficult to convince him to teach me what I wanted to know. I just had to filter out all the antiquated morality lessons."

"Where is he now?"

"Don't worry about him. He's quite comfortable as a permanent guest at one of my properties. All his needs are met."

Bob stroked her cheek lightly.

"Don't you just hate it when you spend years looking for exactly the right person and then she finally shows up just as the world's about to end? On the other hand..."

He kissed her on the forehead.

"It's kind of the ultimate romantic turn-on, isn't it? We're like Romeo and Juliet about to take the poison."

She spit at him again. This time she hit her target. With a smile, he slowly wiped his face with his fingers, then inserted them into his mouth. He savored the taste.

"Yum," he said, licking his lips. "You know, I never believed in love at first sight before this."

He traced the chain around her neck with his finger. It came to rest on the crystal.

"So you're the one who has this. If only I dared to take it from you. How I wish it had come to me instead of you. The things I would have done with it. All the possibilities…"

"What do you know about it?"

"Only as much as you do."

Her blank expression intrigued him.

"Or do I know more? Is it possible you don't understand? If that's true, then it's even more unfair. I would have put it to good use. Perhaps you'll do that for me. Would you? Would you use it to do what I ask? There are so many people I'd use it to meet."

She struggled against the invisible force holding her, but it was useless. He pressed his face close to hers and stared into her eyes.

"Can I convince you? I'm certainly going to have fun trying."

They were startled by a dull, heaving sound. The room's door was pulled open from the outside. A blond head appeared through the gap.

"Koschei! Thank God!"

"AT LAST!" SHOUTED the Russian. "I had to hurt a great many people finding you, Izanami."

"Good," she said, "Free me, and together we'll hurt a lot more!"

Her freedom of movement returned. Bob had released control of her to direct his attention to Koschei. The Russian had begun to swing his diabolusbane only to find himself frozen. Izanami's medallion lay on the floor several feet away. She thought about attempting to retrieve it but chose instead to dive directly at Bob. She knocked him to the ground. If she had had her knife to hand, she would have plunged it into his chest. Instead, she held his wrists to the floor. That kept him helpless. Despite his supernatural abilities, he had none of the strength of a Mercenary or even a fanatical cultist.

"Who is he?" asked Koschei.

"I think he's the software guy we saw on the news," she said. "Somehow he's gotten some training in mystical arts."

"So you mean it wasn't an act?" said Bob with disgust. "You honestly didn't know who I was? Talk about being out of touch!"

"Say, Izanami," said Koschei, "is that a dress you're wearing?"

She ignored him.

"So, Bob, you're the one who makes that stupid software that drives me crazy. I hate the way it keeps popping up with messages about saving the planet. What's that about?"

"Just being a good corporate citizen. Let me go, Chiharu. We should be working together."

"Is everyone calling you by your birth name now?" asked Koschei.

"He heard Peter say it. Peter was here, Koschei. I found him, but they've taken him somewhere else. We've got to get to him."

"Right. By the way, you look great. You should wear a dress more often."

"Shut up, Koschei."

"So what do we do with him?" asked Koschei pointing at Bob.

"Leave him to me."

Hadrian had entered the room.

"You should have waited for me, Koschei. We agreed we'd stay together."

"You were slowing me down."

"I was neutralizing cultists and Mercenaries—as well as a few unfortunate economists who got in the way. I'll hardly apologize for that."

"So it worked," said Izanami. "You were able to find me through my thoughts."

"Yes, as much as you may dislike it, Izanami, the two of us are joined telepathically."

"We had to come through the main entrance," said Koschei. "That's why it took so long. We had to get past a hell of a lot of people. So much for sneaking in stealthily and getting out quick."

"Go," said Hadrian. "Find the boy. I'll stay here with him. Then we must depart as quickly as possible."

Warily, Izanami stood. The Necromant held his staff high and directed the palm of his other hand at Bob. The Software Wizard remained prostrate on the floor. She retrieved her medallion and joined Koschei in a race down the narrow steps.

"Hurry," she said. "They haven't had time to go far."

"I saw Alaric with a band of men on the way up," said Koschei. "They showed no interest in me, which I thought was strange."

"Where were they headed?"

"Follow me."

He led her down to the main hall and then through the corridors below where she had been before. They soon caught up to Alaric and the others. With the force of a madwoman, Izanami grabbed a Mercenary from behind and yanked her backward to the floor. Izanami seized her club, then gave her a hard, swift blow to the head. She then used the weapon on another and then another. Koschei had joined in the attack as well.

"Stop!"

The booming voice was Alaric's. All paused to look at him. He stood in the middle of the corridor. With one hand he pulled tight on Peter's hair. With the other he brandished a large knife.

"Stop or I'll kill him now! It makes no difference to me whether he perishes here and now or whether he dies at the appointed time and place."

Izanami wondered if he was bluffing. The Zen'ei wanted Peter to die, but according to Hadrian, the ritualistic aspect of his death was important to them. Would they kill him now after having kept him alive this long? Her instinct told her Alaric was engaging in brinkmanship, but she wasn't willing to risk the boy's life on her instinct.

"What about an exchange?"

It was Hadrian. He had brought Bob with him.

"What do you say? This one playing at being a Mage in trade for the child."

"What good is he to us?" said Alaric. "He was useful in locating and securing the Expiator. That was all we needed him for."

Bob glared at him.

"I know your type, Necromant," said Alaric. "You wouldn't harm him, let alone kill him—even if that were a concern of mine."

In a quick motion, Izanami grabbed Koschei's knife from the sheath on his belt.

"Hey!" shouted the annoyed Russian.

She stepped behind Bob, still under Hadrian's control, and jerked his head backward by his hair. She pressed the blade against his throat.

"Maybe he wouldn't kill him," she said, "but I would. In fact, I promised myself I would. I might change my mind if you give us the child."

Alaric showed no concern in the least.

"Go ahead. Be my guest. Soon it won't matter which of us was dead and who was alive at this particular moment."

Izanami studied him and then, reluctantly, lowered the knife.

"Damn," she said, "I hate dealing with fanatics."

Koschei grabbed the knife from her and sullenly re-sheathed it.

"I've told you before, Izanami, not to touch my things."

"Can't you do something?" said Izanami to Hadrian. "What's the use of us having a Necromant if you can't solve a situation like this?"

"What would you suggest? He has the blade on the lad's throat. Anything I might do would require relinquishing control of their Mage—if you would like me to risk that."

"So, what happens now, Alaric?" shouted Izanami.

"I'll tell you what happens. Your Necromant shall free our Augurer. Then you shall allow us to leave and not attempt to follow us."

"I'm afraid that doesn't work for me."

"Then we'll have our glorious sacrifice here and now. It's not my preference, but it is acceptable to me."

There were murmurings among the cultists around Alaric. There was apparent disquiet among them at the idea of not following the ritual.

"There is no need for concern," Alaric declared. "The prophecy allows for this possibility."

"I have never heard that before," complained a tall woman near Alaric. "Cite your authority for this deviation."

Alaric was annoyed. "Do you presume to understand the prophecy better than I? To question me is to question Balor."

More people began to speak up.

"You're not Balor."

"It sounds like you're making this up as you go along, Alaric."

Izanami wondered how the growing dissension might work to her advantage. Alaric looked worried, and that concerned her. Would he act desperately if he felt his authority slipping away? Would he kill the boy and accept the consequences? The more minutes that ticked by, the more she was convinced that was the case.

While Alaric was distracted by the now spirited debate, Izanami caught Koschei's eye and subtly motioned to a nearby door. His response was a confused look. She knew the door was unlocked and the room was empty because it was one she had checked on first entering the castle.

She had the germ of a plan, but it relied on Peter. He was miserable, numb, and dazed. She had no idea how he would react. As she watched Alaric grow nervous and impatient, she had no choice but to put her faith in him.

"Peter!" she yelled.

She drew everyone's attention. Slowly, Peter raised his head and turned his bewildered gaze in her direction. In reaction, Alaric clutched the boy tighter and secured his grip on the knife. His hand trembled in anticipation.

"Grandfather's trick!"

Everyone stared at her in confusion. The boy made no move, as if he had not heard her. Then, ever so gradually, his eyes brightened. He nodded slightly, then shut his eyes so tight his sockets disappeared. His face went red. A vein in his forehead throbbed.

A sudden blast of light and energy propelled everyone to the floor. All but Izanami who had been prepared. She regained her footing and dashed to the boy. She jerked him away from Alaric. She saw a spot of blood on his bare shoulder. The knife had grazed him when it fell from Alaric's hand.

She dragged Peter to the door. She shoved it open and pushed the boy inside. Then she all but pulled Koschei in after her. He had recovered from the blast, though not as fast as Izanami. She pushed the door closed and bolted it.

"What the hell was that?" gasped the Russian.

"It's something Orpheus taught him."

She listened for sounds from the other side of the door.

"So now what do we do? Or did you not think any further than this point? You should have dragged the Necromant in here instead of me. He could have teleported you out of here."

"I knew I could count on you to cope with the situation. I didn't know what to expect from him."

"Well, we both better hope for the best from him. He's our only way out of this."

They could hear the sounds of confusion and chaos, as those in the corridor recovered from the shock. Alaric barked orders at them, doing his best to restore some sort of order.

"Let's get him," someone said. "He's with them. Make him pay for them taking the boy from us."

They heard a crackling sound, something like electrical feedback. A few voices cried in pain.

"I wouldn't try that," said the Necromant's voice. "Not if you value your lives."

"Clementine," shouted Alaric. "Remember where we saw the axes? Be a dear and take a couple of the others to fetch them."

"They're going to try breaking through the door," said Koschei. "I wonder if Hadrian will be able to stop them."

As if in answer, Izanami heard a voice in her head.

"He won't. It takes almost all his concentration to hold Bob in check."

"Is he communicating with you right now?"

She nodded.

"Amazing. Too bad it's not of any use to us."

"Maybe it is. I'm going to try something. Luckily, I can let him know exactly what to expect."

"And are you going to let *me* know exactly what to expect?"

There was a clamor on the other side of the door. Clementine and the others had returned with the axes. In short order, there was a loud blow struck against the wood, and the entire door shook. There was another blow. They heard the wood splinter. Another blow. A bulge appeared in the door.

"It's a strong enough door," said Koschei "but at this rate they won't be long breaking through."

Peter, who had remained on the floor since Izanami threw him there, meekly got up and, the blanket draped over him, walked over to her. He put his arms around her waist and hugged her tight.

"Chiharu, what's going to happen to me?"

There was another hard blow on the door.

"Nothing's going to happen to you. I promise."

She put her hand awkwardly on his head and patted it. She glanced at Koschei who looked at her skeptically. She motioned him closer.

Another axe struck the door, and a corner of the blade pierced the wood all the way through.

She took the boy's hand and put it in Koschei's.

"Peter, Koschei will stay here. He'll protect you. No matter what. Isn't that right, Koschei?"

"What are you intending, Izanami?"

"I've told you what you need to know. Leave the rest to me. And Peter, don't pay any attention to what I'm about to say to those people."

"Izanami…" began Koschei.

Another blow hit the door. It was the loudest yet, and more of the blade came through this time.

"Alaric!" yelled Izanami. "Let's make a deal."

"We don't need a deal," he shouted back. "We just need the boy."

"That's the deal. You can have the boy. I just want to negotiate what I get in return."

"You don't get anything in return. We're taking him."

"Some of your people will die if you do it that way."

"I don't care."

She heard disgruntled mumblings from some on the other side.

"*You* might die."

After a moment's silence, Alaric said, "Go on. What's this deal of yours."

"I want money."

Alaric laughed. "Money won't be any good to you. Don't you understand?"

"Listen," she insisted, "I want a million dollars from Bob what's-his-name over there. In cash. Once I get a taste of money for once in my life, I might even be willing to be friends with him."

"You're not serious. You're mocking us. I don't believe you for one..."

"Shut up, Alaric," said Bob. "I want to hear what she has to say."

"Look, Bob, we got off on the wrong foot. I think I understand you better now. I'm willing to give it a chance if you are."

"Ware, you fool!" yelled Alaric. "Can't you see she's not serious? It's some sort of trick."

"Stay out of this, Alaric! I've done a lot more deals than you have in my time. I'm an old hand at risk assessment. Where's the risk here?"

"There's no risk," said Izanami. "Allow me to open the door and come out. I'll show you my good faith personally. I'll have our Necromant release you."

"This is the best deal I've ever been offered. I agree, Chiharu. Come out. As long as you're peaceful, no one will harm you."

"Wait a minute," barked Alaric.

"Shut up!" yelled Bob. "You're not in charge here. You're nothing without me."

Izanami took a deep breath. She unbolted the door and pulled it open. A large axe was embedded on the other side. All eyes were on her as she stepped into the corridor.

Alaric stood on the far side of the mob. He made a move toward the door but then froze. On the other side of the group stood Bob. Having been released by Hadrian, his hand was raised, immobilizing Alaric.

Bob's eyes were on Izanami. She smiled and approached him. She made sure to hold his gaze. She did not break eye contact as she walked right up to him and put her hand on his cheek.

"Isn't this better than fighting?" she whispered.

He nodded as he stared into her eyes.

"Go, Hadrian!"

In the blink of an eye, the Necromant swept past them and through the door, which was then promptly shoved close.

"Hey! What?"

The mob grew agitated. Alaric, now released from Bob's power, pushed his way toward the door. Meanwhile, Izanami felled Bob with a sharp kick to the groin.

"I told you, you stupid fool!" shouted Alaric. "She manipulated you."

From the other side of the door, Koschei shouted, "Izanami, what are you doing? You should have told me. I should be there with you."

"No!" she yelled. "You need to protect the boy. That's the most important thing. Hadrian, get yourself and the others the hell out of here!"

"Izanami, no! You can't do this! You can't fight them and their Mage all alone."

"Don't worry about it, Koschei. I owe you for saving my life in the Netherworld. I can never repay that. Hadrian, stop wasting time!"

Through the door could be heard a strange sound like a windstorm. Light shone through the cracks that the axes had made in the wood. Then all was still and silent. They were gone. Peter was safe.

In evident pain, Bob struggled to his feet. His face was red and contorted in rage. He placed his hand gingerly where she had kicked him and a healing energy flowed from his fingers. Judging from his restored posture and the look on his face, he had healed himself, but it did not soften his anger. He thrust his arm forward, and Izanami's body jerked suddenly. Her medallion dropped to the ground. She was in the all-too-familiar grip of his power. This time it was different. Not only was she paralyzed, but pain was coursing through every nerve in her body.

"You will pay for that!"

"We have no time for this!" shouted Alaric.

"Yes, we do," replied Bob. "The boy is gone. We'll have to hunt him down all over again, but it doesn't matter. His fate is inevitable. In the meantime, I'm going to enjoy myself. Leave, Alaric, and take your rabble with you. We'll make our new plan afterwards."

The crowd did not move. All were fascinated by the sight of the Demon Hunter frozen in place. Their interest only increased when she levitated a few inches off the ground.

"Okay, stay and watch if you want, but it won't be pretty."

Izanami braced herself for what was to come. Whatever happened, she was determined not to show him fear or desperation.

There was an unexpected shuffling of the mob. Each took a turn stepping to one side until they left a space through the group wide enough for a person to pass. Someone new had arrived. A figure in a purple hooded robe swept toward Bob and Izanami. The cultists stared and said nothing. The Mercenaries raised their weapons nervously and waited. Alaric remained motionless with a bewildered look on his face.

"Who the hell are you?" asked Bob.

"There's been a change of plans."

16
The Prodigal

THE NEWCOMER RAISED a hand and pointed an index finger at Bob's face. A stream of bright light traveled a jagged path from the finger to his head. He staggered backward.

Izanami was free. She grabbed her medallion from the floor and cautiously stepped back. Unsure of what was happening, she stared at the new arrival, then at Bob, and then back again. She warily summoned her diabolusbane and held it at the ready.

Flushed with anger, Bob raised both his arms and brandished his fists at his opponent. He attempted to shoot a blast of energy, but instead he chipped off bits of stone from the ceiling as he was thrown off balance by another bolt. This time the voltage had doubled—with painful results. Angrily, he raised his hands in another attempt to strike, but another bolt came immediately.

Judging Bob to be outmatched, Alaric shouted, "There is no more to do here! Time to depart!"

The cultists, Mercenaries, and their leader vanished up the corridor, leaving only Bob, Izanami, and the stranger. The last bolt had left Bob on the floor. Strangely calm, he sat up but made no attempt to stand. Instead he took his mobile telephone from his pocket, tapped it a few times, and spoke.

"I've sent you my location. Come at once. Is Reynolds still with you? Yes, bring him as well."

He put the phone away and looked at his opponent.

"Are you going to tell me who you are? Who are you working for?"

"I'm with her."

Izanami stared. "Sapphire?"

"Didn't you recognize me?"

151

Lola Blumquist lowered her hood to reveal a short-cropped head of white hair and a wide smile.

"The robe is new."

"So's that little cocktail dress. Looks good. You should wear things like that more often. It's a shame no one but me ever gets to see your legs."

"Stop."

Sapphire turned her attention to Bob.

"So, what are we going to do with this guy?"

"I have some ideas," said Izanami darkly, "but you probably won't approve."

The sound of footsteps reached their ears. A group in business suits approached from the far end of the hallway.

"Who are they?" demanded Izanami.

"Just my assistant and a few journalists she's been shepherding."

She let the diabolusbane dematerialize. "Really? You're inviting the press here?"

"I've kept them waiting long enough. They should have a camera operator with them."

Bob slowly regained his feet, all the time maintaining eye contact with Sapphire and keeping his hands visible.

"They'll be wanting my statement about the terrorist attack."

"What terrorist attack?"

"The wanton assault by violent extremists at the Cythère Conference where the world's financial leaders had come together in support of the movement to save the planet. A TIGRIS unit from Worblaufen is on its way as we speak."

"You're joking, right? They'll think you're crazy."

"Who? The television audience?"

"The journalists. They've been here the whole time. They know there was no terrorist attack. We came to rescue the child you kidnapped. I'll tell them myself if I have to."

Izanami was bluffing, but it didn't matter. Bob only laughed.

"Do you think they'd listen to you? Who do you think pays their salaries?"

"You own a television network?" asked Sapphire.

"No, but a good friend of mine does. Another owns a major newspaper. Others own the main social media sites. We're all united in the effort to save the planet."

"Do you know what you're supporting?" asked Izanami. "Do you understand what this whole thing is really about?"

"I know there's no point in having one of the largest chunks of net worth in the world if I don't use it for something monumental, something to fundamentally change history. If you want to debate specific merits, Alaric's your man. He's the vision guy."

The group was nearly upon them. A video camera was aimed in their direction.

"Uh, sweetie," said Sapphire, extending her hand, "we should go."

"Wait," said Izanami. "Follow me. I have to do something first."

She led Sapphire down the hall and into a room. She bolted the door behind them.

"I'm not wearing this one second longer."

She slipped out of the dress and donned her suit. Once her knife and medallion were in place, she turned to Sapphire.

"Now I'm ready."

Sapphire drew close and gazed into her eyes. She was about to speak, but instead she swooned. Izanami grabbed hold of her.

"Are you okay?"

"Well, that's embarrassing. Sorry. Just a little tired. I've gone a few days without sleep, and teleporting really takes it out of me."

"Are you sure that's all it is?"

"Careful. You risk losing your most attractive feature."

"Which is?"

"That you never waste time worrying about me."

"I've been extremely worried about you. I haven't stopped worrying since what happened at the Licancabur Rim."

Sapphire was surprised by the emotion in her voice, the concern in her eyes. She'd never seen Izanami like this. Sapphire put her arms around her and held tight. Izanami kissed her on the mouth and was loath to stop. Then she steeled her resolve and pulled away.

"There's no time."

"Tell me about it."

Izanami drew close again and whispered in her ear.

"You found me."

"You summoned me."

"So it worked? You heard me? I connected with you telepathically?"

Sapphire nodded. She put her fingers around the Grisial hanging from Izanami's neck and studied it thoughtfully.

"I take it this had something to do with it. I have to say, it flatters you. As a fashion accessory, I mean. Where on earth did you ever get it?"

"My girlfriend gave it to me."

"Girlfriend? You have a girlfriend? That's new."

"You don't make this easy."

"You mean me? You know, I didn't actually give this to you. In fact, I thought I had it well hidden."

"It was poorly hidden. Deliberately, I assumed, but maybe you're just bad at hiding things. I thought it was meant to be a surprise. That should teach you not to leave me alone for too long in your house."

"Yes, about my house..."

"You know about that?"

"Say, was that really him?"

"Who?"

"The guy who had you trapped."

"I wasn't trapped."

"You looked pretty trapped to me. He's the software guy, isn't he? Who'd have thought he'd be mixed up in this?"

A clamor could be heard on the other side of the door.

"Don Samuelson!" someone shouted. "ICN News! Do you want to make a statement?"

"What's your organization called?" yelled someone else. "Do you have a manifesto?"

Someone turned the door handle. The two women looked at each other and nodded. They joined hands, closed their eyes, and were gone in a flash of light.

They stood on a ledge halfway up a mountain. Below was a valley covered by a stone pine forest. They saw Château Cythère overlooking the valley's far end. At that distance it was tiny.

"You didn't bring us very far."

"No sense expending a lot of energy until we know what we're doing."

Izanami could not take her eyes off Sapphire. She examined every inch of her face, her hair, her hands. She threw her arms around her and committed her skin's scent to memory. She studied the sound of her breathing.

"God, I missed you."

"Me too. I honestly didn't know it would be so long. There's a lot to catch up on. I don't know where to begin. Things have… changed. We need to have a long talk."

"I don't like the sound of that."

"Of course, you don't. You don't like change, and there's been a lot of change."

"Do you know about the Zen'ei and everything that's been going on?"

"Some. How did you wind up in Switzerland?"

"We had to rescue Peter. The Zen'ei captured him."

"Peter?"

"Yeah, he knows you. He says he met you on Orpheus's island."

"That young boy?"

"Yes."

"He came back?"

"Yes. They say he's the key to everything. The Zen'ei are determined to get hold of him and kill him."

"So strange. Why him?"

"I was hoping *you* would have the answers. Maria said he was dead."

"You've seen Maria?"

"Yeah, I'm afraid she wound up in the hospital because of me. She was there when your house was destroyed."

"My God. Is she all right?"

"Yeah. So you knew about your house?"

"I went to Ballard before coming here. I no sooner arrived at the house—I mean, where the house had been—when Oley showed up. He gave me your message."

"Well done, Oley."

Sapphire laughed. "You had never talked to him before that, had you?"

"No. Did you try to find Tsuru?"

"I didn't have to. I began getting messages from you. They got stronger and stronger—I at last heard your voice in my head as clear as a bell."

"So many weird things have been happening. Impossible things. Koschei is back."

"He is? I suppose I shouldn't be surprised."

"Wait. How can it not surprise you that a dead Demon Hunter has come back to life? How is that less surprising than the dead boy from the island?"

"Because you and Koschei were close. You never met Peter."

"What does it matter how close we were?"

"So, you don't actually understand what the Grisial does."

"No, I didn't find a set of instructions with it, and no one has been able or willing to explain it to me. What does it do, and why did you have it?"

"It's the reason my parents died. The police said it was a burglary gone wrong, but now I know that someone was after the Grisial. If I hadn't spent that night at a friend's, I might have been able to save them."

"Or you might have died with them."

Izanami put an arm around her.

"What were they doing with the Grisial?"

"Someone left it with them for safekeeping. Someone who knew who I was—long before I knew."

"I'm... sorry."

Sapphire took a new look at Izanami.

"Is it my imagination, or are you more compassionate than you used to be?"

"I'm trying to be, but you're not making it any easier."

"Sorry. So where's Peter now?"

"I don't know. Hadrian teleported him and Koschei somewhere."

"Hadrian?"

"Yes."

"The Necromant?"

"Anything you want to tell me?"

"I... I've never met him."

"Haven't you?"

"Not in this lifetime. Why? Did he say something?"

"No, but I saw you in his mind. He and I have shared memories."

"He must be very old now. I'm kind of surprised to hear he's still alive."

"I'd say he's aged quite well. I'm wondering if he might be immortal, you know, like Orpheus. What went on between the two of you?"

"I think Tyra's entitled to take her personal memories to the grave."

"But her memories aren't in the grave, are they? From the look on your face, I'd say you remember it quite vividly. You told me you had only the dimmest memories of your life as Tyra. Yet that smirk on your face... God, you're blushing. I'd say your recollections aren't at all dim."

"That's what I need to tell you. I've learned much more about myself. About my past lives. There were more than just Justine and Tyra. Justine wasn't my first incarnation. Oh, Chiharu, there's so much to explain, so much you need to understand. I don't know where to begin. I'm not who I thought I was."

"Sorry to do this right now," said Izanami, "but I have to ask you to be quiet."

"What? I'm pouring my heart out."

"I know. I'm sorry. Hadrian is communicating with me. I have to listen."

"You and he share each other's thoughts? And you're worried about what he and *I* were up to a century and a half ago?"

Sapphire waited. Izanami closed her eyes and disappeared into her mind. After a few minutes, she returned.

"They've gone back to the Bialowieza Forest. Can you take us there?"

"Can you be more specific?"

"Yes, I can give you all the information you need. Come here."

Izanami wrapped her arms around Sapphire, and they closed their eyes and pressed their foreheads together. Izanami was distracted by the scent of Sapphire's hair.

"I can pass the information to you mentally. The most effective technique would be to maximize bodily contact."

"You made that last part up."

"Let's pretend I didn't."

She brushed her lips lightly against Sapphire's lips and felt the warmth of her breath.

"Are you concentrating?"

"Oh, yes."

"So you know where to take us?"

"Oh, yes."

"Are you sure?"

"Oh, you're talking about teleporting."

"You can start anytime now."

"You're still talking about teleporting."

"Funny."

After a momentary sensation of floating, the space around them went from bright light to darkness and then to the cool, damp air of a primeval forest. From the shadows emerged three figures—two men and a child.

Peter rushed to Izanami and hugged her waist.

"Chiharu! I missed you. They said you'd come, but I didn't believe them. I thought they only wanted to keep me quiet."

Sapphire laughed out loud at Peter's display of affection.

"Why, Chi–chi, who knew you were so good with children?"

"Chi–chi!" screeched Peter. "Is that her nickname for you? Chi–chi!"

He couldn't stop laughing. Izanami gritted her teeth.

"And we won't ever hear you say that name again, will we, Mrs. Lynch?"

"Mrs. Lynch? Is that your nickname for her? Why do you call her Mrs. Lynch?"

Izanami smiled. "It was her name in another life. Why do I call her that? Because she hates it."

"Hello, Peter," said Sapphire. "Do you remember me?"

"Of course," he said. "You're the strumpet."

The Russian stepped forward.

"He drove us crazy, Izanami, making us promise over and over that you'd come."

"Hello, Koschei," said Sapphire.

"The famous Sapphire, I presume?"

"One and the same. I take it you don't know me?"

"So I fear," he replied elegantly, "and the loss is definitely mine."

"Don't worry," she said. "You'll know me well enough before this is over, and though it makes no sense to you now, it's good to see you again."

Hadrian joined the group, his eyes fixed on Sapphire.

"So," he said, "are you really…?"

"Yes, or rather I was in another lifetime. As you see, I'm someone entirely different now."

"Oh, I think I see something of the ravishing Tyra in those eyes, that smile. Sorry, I've let myself get carried away. It's all so strange."

"Yes, and even stranger is the fact you look no different than the last time I… Tyra saw you. Does this mean what I think it does?"

"I'm sorry. I know you've only just arrived, but I must leave all of you a while. I assure you it's necessary and in support of our mission. While you await my return, I've arranged a place for you to rest and take nourishment—for those of you who need those things."

He led them down a forest path to a hollow where the trees were particularly thick. Deep in the glen was a small clearing where stood a house built of logs.

"So you have a cabin after all," said Izanami. "Why did you tell us you didn't?"

"It's not rightfully mine. You're quite welcome to it. I'm assured you'll find beds and ample food."

"Assured? Assured by whom? Who lives here if not you?"

"All in good time. When I return, I'll have a better idea of what to do next."

The Necromant bowed his head, turned, and disappeared into the trees.

17
The White Tower

THE CABIN WAS as comfortable as the Necromant had promised. There was an agreeable warmth from the wood stove and a hearty pot of stew on the hob. On the large, wooden table was fresh bread and red wine in an earthenware crock.

Izanami and Sapphire dug into the stew greedily. Izanami was thrilled to share a meal with someone—especially since it was Sapphire.

After having their fill, the women went to one of the beds and lay down side by side. Across the room by the stove, Koschei told Peter more stories.

"Did you know Koschei was born a prince?" asked Izanami quietly.

"I don't really know much about Koschei."

"How did he come back, Sapphire?"

"I'll explain tomorrow. I promise. It's just that I can barely keep my eyes open."

"Should I be worried about you? Something's different. That wasn't like you to almost faint back there in the castle."

"This is a nice change."

"What is?"

"You've started to worry about me."

"I'm glad you're back. I don't know what I would have done if..."

The rhythm of Sapphire's breathing changed. She had already fallen asleep and deeply. Izanami turned so she could gaze at her. Her eyes could not get enough of her.

Izanami's mind was too busy for sleep. She went over the day's events multiple times. Despite a few setbacks along the way, it had been a good day. The most important thing was that

Peter was safe—for the time being. The Zen'ei were still out there and would not rest until they had recaptured him. How would it end? She closed her eyes and listened to Koschei's low voice.

"So that was when Prince Felix and the others decided the Mad Monk must be stopped. They invited him to the Moika Palace for tea and cakes at midnight. That's in St. Petersburg, you know. The cakes had been laced with cyanide. As was the Madeira wine. In case the cakes didn't do the job."

She was too restless to sleep. Koschei's grim tale didn't help. She got up and went to over to them.

"I'm going out for some air. I need to clear my head. I won't be gone long."

"Be alert out there, but then I don't need to tell you that."

As she left, he resumed his story. "To the nobles' amazement the poisoned cakes did not affect him in the slightest. Nor did three glasses of tainted wine."

"He shouldn't have been drinking wine anyway," said the boy.

The path was as dark as a cave. The moon and stars were concealed by the trees. The blackness didn't deter her. She had been comfortable in darkness since suffering temporary blindness after a battle with demons in the frigid remoteness of the Kerguelen Islands.

The forest was dead quiet. No wind disturbed the branches above. No call came from any bird of the night.

She stopped. She detected the faintest sound of voices ahead. She stepped cautiously, straining to hear words.

"I shall go no further with you. Before I leave you, assure me again the Grisial is safe."

The gruff voice was that of an old man. Extremely old, she judged by the timbre.

"I assure you it is."

The other voice was Hadrian's.

"But is it in your *personal* possession?"

"No, but it's secure enough for now."

"It's essential that you… we… are the ones who have it. The only ones. Now and far into the future."

"I understand."

"Are you prepared for what lies ahead?"

"I can only hope that I am."

"What do you make of the Demon Hunter?"

"Izanami? She's daunting."

"She is indeed."

"You didn't tell me she knew Tyra, that Tyra would be here."

"Do not be confused by the metempsychosis phenomenon. Eurydice and Sapphire are not the same person. It would be a mistake to believe you've found Tyra again."

"No, this Sapphire is indeed different. I don't yet know what to make of her."

"I'll leave you. Remember all that I've told you—especially about the Grisial."

"I only wish I had your knowledge and experience."

"But you have it. That's why I'm here."

"I mean in my own head, rather than relying on you."

The old man laughed ruefully.

"I'd gladly exchange all my so-called knowledge for one hour of being your age again. There are limits to my knowledge. Like you, I am impatient to have the greatest mystery revealed. For more than a century I have waited to understand the riddle of the boy. Good night."

"Good night."

Hadrian's footsteps approached her. She turned and walked briskly back toward the cabin. He soon caught up with her.

"Yes, I thought I felt someone's presence. Funny to meet you here. You weren't spying on me, were you?"

"I couldn't sleep. I went for a walk."

"Were you not afraid to wander alone in the forest at night?"

Izanami laughed out loud.

"That's a good one. Who were you talking to?"

"So you *were* spying on me."

"Why so many secrets?" she said, holding the crystal close to her breast. "We're on the same side, aren't we?"

"Trust me. Things will be clearer tomorrow, but it will fall to your friend Sapphire to enlighten us all."

They returned to the cabin. Hadrian sat by the stove and, distractedly, joined Peter in listening to Koschei's stories. Izanami lay down and wrapped her arms around Sapphire. She closed her eyes and took comfort from the rhythm of her breathing. As she drifted off, Sapphire twitched. She was dreaming. Her light moans suggested it wasn't happy.

Soon Izanami also dreamed. She was outside again, wandering through the forest's blackness. The air was thick with insects. She couldn't see them, but their buzzing plagued her ears. They brushed her face, and she swatted at them uselessly.

She became aware of a massive structure before her. Its whiteness was so stark that it pierced the dark. A marble tower, its height dwarfed the surrounding trees. She approached and looked for an entrance. Seeing none, she looked up. On the tower's top was a turret where stood a lone figure. Staring through the gloom, she strained to make out who it was. Despite the distance, she could tell the woman had an imposing stature. She stretched her arms high above her. Though for Izanami the air was thick and still, the woman's snow-colored robe billowed exuberantly. She swayed from one side to another, as if taken by a glorious melody audible only to her.

Izanami strained her eyes. She wanted to see her more clearly. She was consumed with curiosity about her. In her obsession the Demon Hunter attempted to scale the tower, but its surface was too smooth. Every attempt ended with her sliding back down. She called to the woman, but the insects' droning drowned her voice.

She climbed the trunk of the nearest tree. She stepped up from one branch to another until no higher boughs would support her. She parted the branches in front of her and peered at the tower's crown. She still had no satisfactory view. Again, she called out, and this time her voice carried. The woman ceased her movements and turned in her direction. She extended her arms as if reaching for Izanami. She began to sing, and it was the most melancholic sound the Demon Hunter had ever heard. The volume increased, and the unearthly melody broke her heart.

The woman grew in size. She was so large the tower could no longer support her. She then floated away from the tower. At this new magnitude, her face was recognizable. It was Sapphire. She contemplated Izanami with overwhelming sorrow. Mournfulness coursed through Izanami's body. She tried to call out again, but now no sound came from her mouth.

Sapphire floated higher. Arms outstretched, she rose until the sky enveloped her in its darkness.

From her tree limb Izanami watched the tower also recede into the dark. The temperature dropped. A distant rumble grew louder. Her tree shook. Subtly at first, then violently. The entire forest shuddered. The ground convulsed. Cracks appeared in the now-faint tower's surface. They spread from top and bottom. Then the structure broke into pieces, crashing into a heap of jagged, chalk-colored rubble.

Izanami clung desperately to a tree branch, whipping in one direction and then another. She fought to hold on, but it was hopeless. She needed all her strength, but her arms failed her. They were paralyzed.

"Wake up, will you!"

The darkness turned to light. She was on her back. Someone held her by the upper arms.

"Wake up. You're having a dream."

Sapphire's face came into focus.

"God," said Izanami. "That was the weirdest one yet."

"Are you okay? You were screaming. Really loud."

"Was I?"

"You kind of freaked me out."

"Sorry. I've never done that before, have I?"

"No, you're usually an annoyingly sound sleeper."

"Did I wake everyone up?"

"Just me. The others weren't sleeping."

Izanami looked around. Light streamed through the window. By the stove Koschei, Hadrian, and Peter stared.

Peter said, "Are you all right, Chi-Chi?"

She leapt from the bed.

"I'll kill you. If you ever call me that again, I swear I'll kill you."

The boy laughed uncontrollably and ran behind Koschei for safety.

"I don't suppose there's any chance of a cup of coffee," said Izanami.

"You're in luck," said Sapphire eagerly. "Watch this."

She took two cups from the cupboard and put them on the table. She closed her eyes and held her hands flat a few inches above each cup. Izanami needed a moment to understand what was happening. Each vessel filled slowly with black liquid.

"How are you...?"

"Cool, huh?"

"Where did you learn that?"

"I've learned a lot of things since I last saw you."

"You've become a full-blown sorcerer, haven't you?"

"Things are definitely... different."

"You keep saying that."

"Let's talk. Grab your cup, and let's go outside. Careful, that coffee's industrial-strength hot. I'm still working on that, but I think I've got the bean roast down pretty good."

The coffee was indeed searing. Izanami could only manage by holding the cup delicately by the handle.

"Is this a beverage or a chemical weapon?" she said as they stepped out the door into the cool morning air.

"I had a strange dream too," said Sapphire. "I've been having them most nights."

"Me too. You were in this one. It was terrible. I was losing you. Something powerful was pulling you away from me. I know they're just dreams, but they've been freaking me out."

"I know what you mean."

"Tell me something."

"Yes?"

"You knew Hadrian in your past life when you were Tyra."

"Yes, I did."

"How well did you know him?"

Sapphire laughed. "Are you jealous?"

"We can have that talk another time. I just need to know if we can trust him."

"Why?"

"I heard him talking last night. Someone else is involved in this, and I don't understand how or why."

"How strange."

Izanami put her hand around the crystal.

"Tsuru told me to keep this with me at all times. Not to let it out of my possession."

"She was right. Now that you have it, it can't be separated from you. It would mean disaster."

"I think Hadrian means to take it from me."

"Are you sure?"

"I don't know who to trust. Except you."

"We'll figure it out. Should I be worried about you? You're… stressed. It's not like you."

"To be honest, for the first time in a long time I feel overwhelmed. The world's gone crazy. It feels like this could really be the end of things. Do you feel it too?"

"Chiharu…"

Sapphire cut herself short.

"What is it you have to tell me? Just say it."

"I don't know where to begin."

"Try the beginning."

"I've learned so much. About myself and about everything else. It's funny. I always thought I knew who I was. Then I went to Riesgado Island and met Septimus Bridge. I found out I didn't know who I was at all. It took a long time to get my head around the fact I had lived before. That I had lived twice before. That I had spent centuries trapped in the Netherworld."

"You've always seemed able to cope with it. Very well, in fact. Much better than I would have."

"Yeah, but you see, I've since learned my previous lives as Justine and Tyra were only the tip of the iceberg."

"You had other lives?"

Sapphire nodded. "A *lot* of other lives. I've been going from body to body for millennia."

"How did you find out about these other lives? Can you be certain the memories are all real?"

"I went from Master to Master. I discovered names of Mages you and I had never heard of before. I found scrolls that hadn't seen the light of day for centuries. Each new discovery awakened a new memory. Every new remembrance unleashed a fresh cascade of flashbacks.”

“I should have gone with you. You shouldn’t have been on your own.”

“No, I had to do it myself. You want to know something funny?”

“Yeah, I think I do.”

“When Septimus trained me to be a Demon Hunter, he said he suspected I might have been a man in a previous life. That made me angry. I was certain I could never have been anything but a woman. Now I know the truth. I have been many women, and I have been many men.”

“Really?”

“Really.”

“Interesting. I’m trying to picture you as a man.”

“You seem to be enjoying the picturing.”

“Sorry, it’s a lot to take in. I can’t imagine what it’s like for you.”

“It was overwhelming at first, but I understand now. Each life has been a different person. They’ve all been me, but they’ve all been different.”

“Well, I like the body you’re in right now. I like you as you are here and now. That’s what matters, right? The present moment?”

Sapphire hesitated. “There’s more.”

“More? How much more can there be? More than the fact you’ve been around forever? That you’re probably immortal? The important thing is you’re here now. The two of us are here now. You’re Lola Blumquist, the woman I…”

“Yes?”

“You know how I feel.”

“It would be nice to hear it—at least once.”

“They’re just words.”

“If you say so. Look, Chiharu, I wanted to give you the whole story like this—just the two of us—but that’s not how it’s going to be. I have to tell the others what I’ve learned, and there just isn’t time for me to go through it twice. Too much is at stake, so you're going to have to learn the rest of it along with the others. Please forgive me. At least I've told you this much on your own. I'm so sorry we don't have more time."

"Don't apologize. We're in a war. Not like any war anyone's ever been in before. It's no time to get sentimental. We'll have time for that later. After this is all over."

"There's one more thing I need to tell you. Something I won't be telling the others."

"What?"

Sapphire put her arms around Izanami and hugged her tight. She brushed her lips against Izanami's and then along her cheek and close to her left ear. She whispered softly.

"I love you, Chiharu Ito. I always will."

Izanami found no words.

"See," said Sapphire, "it's not that hard. You should try it sometime."

18

The Tuath Dé

SAPPHIRE STOOD CLUTCHING her coffee cup as the others took seats at the table. They waited while she took a long sip. Koschei broke the silence.

"Do you really know me?" he asked. "I thought Izanami was having some kind of mental breakdown, that you were a hallucination. Yet here you are now in the flesh. Why don't I remember you then? Is what she says true? Have I been resurrected from the dead?"

"No, Koschei" said Sapphire. "You're not dead, but the truth is no less fantastic. You're here by the grace of the Grisial. The crystal Izanami wears is one of the oldest and most powerful talismans to have fallen into the hands of mortals. Because of a series of circumstances I still do not fully understand, it lay many years in my parents' house in Seattle. It was there before I was born."

"That couldn't have been a coincidence," said Koschei.

"Someone gave it to them and convinced them to keep it safe. They never understood why, but they safeguarded it faithfully. In the end, it cost them their lives."

"So it was always meant for you then," said Izanami. "You should be the one wearing it."

"That's unclear to me. Also unclear is its exact purpose. Was it meant to precipitate the doom now hanging over us? Or is it meant to save us from it?"

"What precisely is its power?" asked Izanami.

"Haven't you worked it out? It bestows on its bearer an awesome command of time and nature. It summons people to you. It can transport them across space. Not only that but it can warp the flow of time to bring them anachronistically."

170

"Wait," said Izanami. "Are you saying...?"

"It's not restricted by linear time."

"How can that be?"

"The Grisial is infused with the otherworldly nature of the Tuath Dé. It's not bound by our primitive perception of the universe. It didn't bring Koschei back from the dead. It located him at a moment when he was alive and brought him to you. From your perspective, it plucked him out of the past. From his perspective, it transported him to the future. That's why his memories seem incomplete to us. This is Koschei before he met me. For him his first encounter with me lies ahead."

"Time travel?" said Koschei. "Are you sure? Every Mage I've ever known has insisted time travel is a fabulist's fancy. A logical impossibility."

"Insofar as our natural laws hold sway, that's true, but this goes well beyond any rule of nature."

"This is doing my head in," said the Russian. "If I've left my own time to come here in the future, won't that change history? Won't it affect everything that was supposed to happen from now on? I mean, from then on?"

"It's possible but not necessarily inevitable. What you're describing is an irreconcilable paradox. The fabric of reality could be shredded. If you survive our struggle with the Fomóire, however, then you may return to the moment from which you were plucked and live out the rest of your life. In that case there's no paradox."

"But history will still have been changed," insisted Koschei. "I'll know my own future. I'll behave differently than I would have. I certainly won't be going to the Netherworld."

"If and when you go back, you'll have no memory of any of this. It would be illogical for you to have memories of being out of your own time—just as it would defy reason for you to age or to need food and sleep while suspended outside your own time."

"So I'm going to die in the Netherworld? No matter what?"

"Don't dwell on that. If and when you resume your natural timeline, you will have no foreknowledge. Your journey to the Netherworld has already happened. All our futures have already happened in the grand cosmic cycle of time and space. There's no way to change it. Even if you could, would you? What would it gain you if the inevitable result is a reality-ending paradox that erases everything and everybody?"

"Well, when you put it like that..." muttered the Russian.

"I remember now," said Izanami. "When I fought the Mercenaries in Canada, I had a stray thought. I wished Koschei were there to aid me. I had already forgotten about it by the time he appeared. Did I actually make that happen?"

"Yes. The Grisial's power is difficult to wield. All the more so if you're unaware of its capabilities. That you succeeded in summoning Koschei to your side suggests you must have some affinity with it."

"You mean to make people appear I only have to think about them? That can't be right. I think about people all the time, but they haven't all shown up."

"It's not a simple matter of thinking about people—or even missing them. It requires a certain mental control which has to be learned. That you summoned Koschei demonstrated an instinctive, if inexact, understanding of this."

"What about the boy?"

"I have a name, you know," protested Peter.

"Did I pluck him from out of a different time as well? How could I have done that? I didn't know him. I never knew he existed."

"Yes, that's a conundrum," said Sapphire, perplexed. "My own understanding of the Grisial is still incomplete. Can you remember who or what you were thinking about in the moments before you first saw him?"

"I... I don't know. I don't remember what was going through my head. All I know is that I was angry. I had an arm tied behind my back, and I was drunk."

"She was," said Peter. "It was disgusting."

Sapphire sighed. "Really, Izanami?"

"Skip the lecture. Explain how could I have summoned Peter?"

"I don't know, but something you were thinking must have caused the Grisial to bring him to you in that moment."

"Hathus showed up immediately. Did Alaric know in advance the precise time and place it would happen?"

"We know Alaric can track the Grisial. Perhaps he can detect when it transports someone through time."

"If this thing is that powerful, it's good that we have it, right? Now that I understand its power, I can use it to bring back others to help us. I could bring back Ragnar."

"And Callan," said Koschei.

"We must be careful," said Sapphire. "There's immense risk in extracting people from their own time. It distorts the fabric of reality, makes it more fragile. Every time the Grisial's used, it increases the risk of cataclysmic disaster. Say for example, if Koschei should die fighting the Zen'ei, he'd never return to his own time. It would create a paradox. Perhaps the timeline could absorb such a change—but on the other hand, it might not."

"Is it necessary," said Koschei, "to speak so frequently of my death?"

"That's precisely what the Zen'ei are attempting to do. They're trying to create a paradox so irreconcilable that this plane of existence shatters, paving the way for the Fomóire's return. That's why they want the boy. He must play some indispensable role in the future that would be consequential if canceled out."

"Of course, he does," muttered Izanami. "I can already see how this is going to go. As always the Demon Hunters will take all the risks, fight all the battles, make all the sacrifices. At the end of it, will any of us matter? No, it will be all about the boy."

"I told you," protested Peter, "I have a name."

Izanami turned to him angrily.

"So, who are you, Peter? What makes you so damned important? What great thing are you going to do after the rest of us have been killed saving your scrawny neck?"

"I... I don't know. I'm sorry. I didn't ask for any of it to happen. I don't feel special. Just... scared."

"Take it easy, Izanami," said Sapphire. "This isn't his fault. It's none of our faults."

"Should the child be here for this discussion?" said Koschei. "These are dark matters for one so young."

"What do you say, Necromant?" said Izanami. "You've been awfully quiet. What can you add to this?"

"I'm afraid I have little to offer beyond what Sapphire has told us. It's clear we must keep the child safe at all costs."

"What's less clear," said Koschei, "is how all this ends. If the boy is indeed from another time, we must send him back to deny the Zen'ei the chance to cause a time paradox. Can the Grisial be used to that purpose, Sapphire?"

"At this point Izanami knows more about how the crystal functions than I do. She's its bearer. She's used it."

"Used it?" said the Canadian. "I thought it was just a fashion accessory."

"If the two of you don't know," said Koschei, "then who would? Tsuru?"

"I can think of only one who might possess the necessary knowledge," said Izanami. "Miyamoto."

"Who?" said Koschei.

"My first Master."

"I thought Tsuru was your first Master."

"She didn't accept us the first time we sought her. We then sought Miyamoto. He was the first Master to actually take me on, but it didn't end happily. It wasn't long before he kicked me out. He called me immature and headstrong."

"Sounds about right," said the Russian under his breath.

"You said 'we,'" interjected Sapphire. "You didn't seek Miyamoto alone?"

"That doesn't matter. I was with Miyamoto long enough to know he has profound knowledge of the cosmos's prehistory. More than anyone else alive."

"That's consistent with what I've heard," said Sapphire. "Of all the Masters, he was the one I most wanted to consult. I couldn't find him anywhere."

"The Zen'ei have him," said Izanami. "Alaric's Mage told me that he's holding him. That's how the software guy gained his abilities with the mystic arts."

"Are you certain?" said Sapphire. "I find it difficult to accept Miyamoto would be so easily captured."

"I agree," said Hadrian. "Is it possible he's cooperating with the Zen'ei willingly?"

"I can't believe he'd do that," said Izanami, "but I agree it makes no sense that Bob could gain power over him. We'll know the answer when we talk to him."

"Yes," said Sapphire, "he may well be the key."

"What about you?" said Izanami. "Your knowledge of the Old Ones must be greater than his—with all the lifetimes you've lived."

"How many lifetimes have you had?" asked an intrigued Hadrian.

"More than I can count," said Sapphire.

"And can these multiple lives of yours give us any useful insight into the Old Ones? What can you tell us?"

Sapphire drew a long breath.

"I suppose it's time to get into this."

"We know a bit already," said Koschei. "Tsuru told us what she knew of the Fomóire."

"And the two-a-day," added Peter.

"Tuath Dé," smiled Sapphire.

"Frankly," said Koschei, "it sounded like children's stories. You know, myths and legends."

"Where do you think myths and legends come from?" said Sapphire. "Do you never wonder why strikingly similar fantastic tales have been handed down by vastly different ancient civilizations with no apparent connection between them? Do you not suspect some primordial truth must lie behind all of them? Ironically, humanity is most prey to otherworldly forces in moments when, in its self-styled sophistication, it dismisses the old lore as mere figments of primitive imagination."

"Where's the proof?" asked Koschei.

"These are not things that can be proved or disproved," replied Sapphire. "Either you believe or you don't."

"Why believe?"

"For the same reason we believe anything. We choose to trust the teller. In this I am the teller, and I tell you the stories are true."

"Tsuru told us," said Izanami, "there was a war between the Fomóire and the Tuath Dé and that it ceased before all of reality was destroyed. Why did they stop?"

"Did she tell you about the link between the Old Ones and the New Ones?"

"Yes, she said it was the reason the Fomóire decided the New Ones had to be destroyed."

"Balor was convinced the Fomóire's salvation lay in stopping their assimilation into the physical world. To prevent it he was determined to fight until the New Ones were obliterated."

"What stopped him?" asked Hadrian.

"The Tuath Dé stood in his way. They were determined to protect the New Ones. It was a long, vicious war, and it ended in the only way it could. The Tuath Dé were wiped out."

"The Tuath Dé then no longer exist?" said Hadrian.

"They are all gone. Save one."

"But if the Fomóire won the war," asked Koschei, "how did humans survive?"

"Because of Clíodhna."

"Who?"

"Clíodhna was a child of Danu and first of the Old Ones to achieve incarnation."

"She became human?" asked the Necromant.

"She abandoned the battlefield and fled to the dimension of the New Ones. She found a way to make herself part of the physical world. I don't know if you could call her strictly human, but she acquired physical form. She succeeded in interacting directly with the natural world—including humans.

"She was pleased by her physical form and didn't want to abandon it. She chose to remain humanoid—even at the cost of her immortality. The first human being she encountered was Ciabhán, the son of a chieftain. They had no way of communicating, but they had an immediate and mutual attraction. Her provenance was well beyond his capability to comprehend, but in time she learned his language and was assimilated into his culture.

"Balor was enraged. The war had been fought to prevent the Old Ones' absorption into the New Ones' world. Clíodhna altered the Old Ones' reality forever—especially when Clíodhna and Ciabhán produced offspring. The link between Old Ones and New Ones was established for all time."

"Even so," said Hadrian, "what was to stop Balor from destroying the New Ones, as he had done to the Tuath Dé?"

"Clíodhna came to understand she was more powerful in her new physical form than she had been in her incorporeal state. She was now a bridge between two worlds. Her mere existence was sufficient to protect the mortal world from the Fomóire."

"But," said Hadrian, "you say she became mortal. Presumably, her protection endured only as long as her lifespan. She couldn't protect the New Ones forever."

"Forever? That's a misleading word. Linear time is an illusion humans necessarily constructed in an attempt to cope with their place in the cosmos. Clíodhna's unique state continues to protect this plane of existence."

"You confuse me, Sapphire," said Koschei. "You said she became mortal. Forgive my humble linear mind, but did she not die long ago?"

"Her physical body was mortal," said Sapphire. "Her metaphysical form was—and is—not bound by time."

"She's still alive!" said Peter.

"Then where is she?" said Koschei. "Never mind Miyamoto. She's the one we need to find. If what you say is true, she's the one to stop this crisis."

"Her spirit is timeless. Her essence is as primordial as the stars in the sky. The body she inhabits is only a frail vessel. It wears out in a brief amount of time. Then she must be reborn. Not only that, she must start over each time and relearn everything. Only rarely does she come to understand fully who she is, but it doesn't matter. The blood of her original mortal form runs through the veins of all humanity—as does her original metaphysical spirit. It is merely sufficient for her to be present in the world to protect it.

"Sometimes she becomes too curious. She pursues knowledge of her true nature but never quite achieves it. That is, until now. In learning the full truth, the magnitude of her self-awareness becomes more than her mortal body can contain. Her physical form weakens. The consequence is that the mortal world passes through a moment of critical danger. Her protection of this plane flickers like a candle in a breeze. That moment of fragility is Balor's opportunity to cross the barrier between physical and inchoate and to exterminate the New Ones at last. It's his chance to eliminate the last of the Tuath Dé."

"Is there any hope?" said Koschei. "We must locate Clíodhna immediately. Where do we begin?"

Sapphire put down her empty cup, walked to the bed, and sat.

"Are you all right?" asked Izanami.

"I'll be fine. To answer your question, Koschei, the key to all this lies with the Grisial and its bearer. I haven't worked out how exactly, but that is where we must concentrate. That's why we need Miyamoto. Sorry, I need to lie down for just a moment. I guess I still haven't caught up completely on my sleep."

"You three, go outside," said Izanami to the others. "Make a plan for finding Miyamoto. I'll join you in a minute."

"Are you sure you don't want to come with us, Izanami?" said Koschei. "I'd think you'd want to be in on this from the beginning."

"I'm coming. I'm just having a quick chat with Sapphire first."

When Koschei, Hadrian, and Peter had left the cabin, Izanami lay on the bed next to Sapphire. She put her arms around her.

"So this is how I get to find out?"

"I told you I didn't want it to be like this."

"I'm so angry right now. How am I supposed to feel about this? How am I supposed to feel about finding out my girlfriend's a deity?"

"I'm not a deity. How am I supposed to feel about the fact you're now calling me your girlfriend?"

"Did I understand all of that right? Did I hear what I think I heard? Did you just tell us that you're dying?"

"Not if I have anything to say about it."

"Because you can't. I won't let you."

"Well, that settles it then."

"Don't joke about this. Not about this. I won't let anything happen to you."

"I love you too, Chiharu."

19
Miyamoto

WHEN IZANAMI JOINED the others outside, Peter ran to her and wrapped his arms around her waist. She did her best to ignore Koschei's grinning face.

"I'm glad you're here," said the boy. "I was getting scared."

"Scared of me, you mean? After the way I yelled at you."

"No, not you. I know you didn't mean it."

He hugged her tighter.

"Don't be scared," she said. "You're safe from those people who took you. We'll protect you."

"It's not that. It's..."

"It's what?"

"I have a... creepy feeling. Like someone's watching us."

She looked around. "Do you see anyone? I don't."

"There... may be something to what the boy says," said Koschei, a bit sheepishly. "I feel it too. The sense of someone's eyes on us."

"A bit jumpy, are we, Koschei?" she laughed.

No one else laughed. Despite her bravado, she felt something similar.

The Necromant chose to change the subject. He drew close to Izanami and nodded toward the cabin.

"How is she?"

She eyed him suspiciously. "Are you reading my mind again?"

"I've told you, when we're not in the trance, we both must cooperate to share our thoughts. I do, however, have eyes, ears, and a brain. I heard the same things that you heard. I see from the look on your face you suspect—or perhaps know—what I suspect. She's Clíodhna, isn't she?"

"Did she already tell you?"

"No, of course not. I've only just met her."

"I mean, when you knew her before."

"I doubt Tyra knew anything of Clíodhna. Sapphire herself told us this is the first time any of her incarnations has achieved this level of self-awareness. Why is it so difficult for you to trust me?"

"I trust precious few people—and I still get deceived all too often."

"You've never deceived anyone?"

"We're not having this discussion, Necromant. Don't confuse an alliance of necessity with friendship."

"What are you two talking about?" said Koschei. "Are you saying..."

"Sapphire is Clíodhna," said Peter. "Weren't you paying attention, Alexei?"

"Do not call me that, pup."

"She's supposed to be protecting us," said the boy. "Why isn't she?"

"It's not her fault, child," said Hadrian. "This moment has been inevitable for eons."

He looked at Izanami and at the crystal she wore.

"Despite her otherworldly provenance and eons of knowledge, it doesn't appear that Clíodhna in her present state is the one to save us. That burden would seem to fall to the bearer of the Grisial."

"I didn't ask for this," she said crossly. "I don't know what to do."

"Yes, you do," said the Necromant. "You've already said it. We have to find Miyamoto. What exactly did Alaric's Mage tell you about him?"

"Only that he was a 'guest' at one of his properties."

"That man's a billionaire," said Koschei. "He must have properties all over the world. How can we locate your old Master quickly?"

Izanami put her hand on the crystal.

"I could summon him with this."

"Sapphire said it was risky to use," said Hadrian. "It's contributing to what's causing reality to break down. Besides, you don't know what Miyamoto you'd get, I mean, at what age."

"We might be better off getting him when he was younger than the age he is now. Bob said he was frail. If he's helping the Software Wizard, it might be because he's failing mentally."

"That may be," said Hadrian. "but we still need his help, and isn't rescuing him from the Zen'ei the right thing to do in any event?"

"You're right," conceded Izanami. "What about *your* powers, Necromant? Don't you have some way of locating him?"

He shrugged.

"I've never met the gentleman. I have no connection to him. You, on the other hand..."

"That was years ago."

"It doesn't matter. If you've met him even once, that may be sufficient. If I can get a bearing on him through you, I could teleport us there."

"I hope you're not suggesting what I think you are. Absolutely not. It's out of the question."

"Alternatively," said Koschei, "we could consult public databases to obtain a complete list of Mr. Ware's properties and then visit them all—one at a time."

"That would take forever," protested Izanami.

She glared at the Necromant.

"You're enjoying this, aren't you? You can't wait to get back into my head."

"You flatter yourself if you think your head's an enjoyable place, Demon Hunter. I wouldn't propose it if the circumstances didn't warrant it."

"Is there no other way?"

"You tell me."

Izanami fumed for several moments.

"Very well, but if I get any sense of you probing where you shouldn't, you'll pay dearly."

Koschei and Peter watched as Hadrian and Izanami assumed the familiar kneeling position. They closed their eyes, and the Necromant put his fingers on her temples. As she went under, the Demon Hunter studied his skin's pores and wondered how there could be so little sign of aging.

Izanami was determined to guard her every thought, save those of Miyamoto, though she had little idea of how to accomplish that. She focused on memories she had put away for decades. She recalled the day she and Shigeru scaled the mountainside leading to Miyamoto's Tibetan retreat. It was a painful recollection, but she forced herself to relive it. She felt Hadrian's presence as she re-experienced it, and she resented the intrusion.

She strove to push him away. On doing so, she was surprised to find she had entered his thoughts. The towering Himalayas melted away to be replaced by a single windswept promontory. The wind howled, and waves crashed against the rocks below. A crescent moon appeared and disappeared behind black clouds sweeping across the night sky. Several yards from the cliff's edge, a pair of horses whinnied nervously, stepping back and forth in a nervous dance. On the precipice was a woman whose taffeta dress rippled in the wind. It was Tyra. To Izanami her eyes were those of a stranger, but the emotion they conveyed was heartbreakingly familiar.

The image vanished, and Izanami found herself falling backward to the ground. Hadrian knelt before her, his head in his hands. He rubbed his eyes.

"I have what I need," he said. "I know where to find him."

He staggered to his feet. Izanami did the same.

"You have a gift for telepathy," he said bitterly. "You've quickly become proficient. It's a pity you never had the discipline to become a Mage."

"I was told I was too headstrong," she replied sourly.

"Clearly. For someone so preoccupied with her privacy, you have precious little regard for mine."

"If you would be honest about your relationship with Sapphire…"

"Tyra. They're different people."

"What are you hiding?"

Koschei had lost patience with the pair of them.

"Can you not put aside your argument long enough to tell us where to find the old Master?"

"Sorry, you're right. I know where he is. In fact, I know what he's doing at this moment."

"And...?"

"He's thinning leaves on a vine."

"He's what?"

"He's in Bordeaux, specifically Médoc. In a vineyard."

"He's not imprisoned? He's outdoors and performing manual labor?"

Hadrian nodded in response to the Russian's question.

"Is he under guard?" asked Izanami.

"Not as far as I can tell."

"Then let's go at once and bring him here."

"Could it be a trap?" said Koschei. "It seems a bit too easy, no?"

"If it's a trap," said Hadrian, "Izanami and I shall deal with it."

"I'll go too," protested the Russian. "If there's danger, you may need me."

"If there's danger, the most important thing is to protect the boy. Someone must remain with him here."

"Are you sure about this?"

"Hadrian's right," said Izanami. "He has to go because he's the one teleporting. I have to go because I'm the only one Miyamoto will know on sight."

"Then it's settled," said Hadrian.

"What's settled?" said Sapphire, appearing in the cabin's doorway.

"We know where Miyamoto is," said Izanami. "Hadrian and I are going to bring him here."

Sapphire steadied herself against the door frame, as if not certain of her balance. She hesitated before speaking.

"Be careful. We can't afford to miscalculate."

"Nor can we afford to delay," said Hadrian.

Izanami looked at him and then at Sapphire. She could not let go of the image of Tyra on the cliff.

"Agreed," said Sapphire, "but first tell me exactly where he is—in case you don't come back."

The Necromant approached her and extended a hand.

"This will be faster."

She understood and nodded. He touched her cheek with his fingers, and they both closed their eyes.

"I've got it," she said.

"Just like that?" said Izanami as he turned to her. "You can share thoughts with her so easily? What kind of connection exists between you?"

"We are both Mages. It is a common skill among our kind."

"She's a Demon Hunter. Like me."

"She's both things. Now, are you ready?"

He reached toward her.

"I don't want to hold hands."

Peter, who had stayed close to her, put his arms around her waist again.

"Do you have to go?"

"Koschei and Sapphire will look after you. Don't worry. You're safe."

"It doesn't feel safe. I still feel like we're being watched."

Sapphire was amused—not only by the boy's attachment to Izanami but by the fact that she indulged it.

"We're wasting time," said Hadrian. "Now take my hand."

"I said I don't want to."

"It's safer if we have physical contact."

She eyed him stubbornly.

"Please. It's only our hands."

She reluctantly allowed him to entwine his fingers with hers. They closed their eyes and were engulfed in the familiar sensation of a dark whirlwind.

When they opened their eyes, heat radiated from the sun high above in a cloudless, blue sky. In contrast to the dank forest, the air here was pleasantly warm and dry. It carried a floral, fruity smell. They were surrounded by rows of grapevines held up by steel wires. Because of the hilly terrain, there was an illusion of the rows rising and falling like sea swells. At the far edge of this grapevine ocean rose a tall sea pinnacle. It was a château in the French Renaissance style, complete with ornate chimneys and turrets.

Izanami drew Hadrian's attention to the small figure toiling away two rows over. He wore a black robe much too warm for the weather. The stooped laborer worked meticulously at thinning the vines' leaves with hands covered by well-worn gloves.

They looked around and saw no one else. They squeezed between the wires, forcing their way through one row of vines and then another. They were now in the same furrow as the diligent worker. He continued his task, giving no indication that he knew they were there. They approached cautiously. Without moving his head, he spoke in English with a Japanese accent.

"You've damaged the vines."

"We're sorry," said Hadrian. "It couldn't be helped. We've come on urgent business."

The man did not deviate from his task or reveal his face. Izanami circled round, trying to enter his line of sight.

"Master? Is it you?"

"What a question. Who else would I be?"

"Do you remember me?"

He still did not stop or look up.

"Of course, I remember you, Chiharu. Did you think I was feeble?"

"Do you know why we've come?"

"Do *you?*"

"We need your help. We have questions only you can answer. Will you help us?"

"I am long past helping."

"Master, I'm curious. Why do you toil in a vineyard of all places? One thing I remember clearly about my brief time with you is that alcohol never passed your lips."

"Nor does it yet. One can like the grapes and not the wine."

"Are you well, Master? Tell me, are you here of your own volition or are they holding you against your will?"

"Ah, my poor Chiharu, you still wrestle with the question of will."

"May we take you away from here? To ask you our questions?"

"If this is urgent, why not ask your questions here and now?"

"To be honest," said Hadrian, "we fear for your safety while you are here."

"Fear for your own."

"Will you not look at me, Master?" said Izanami. "I would like to see your face again after all these years."

"Why waste your time with that? They come."

The Demon Hunter and the Necromant swung their heads around. Three large men strode toward them. They were about fifty yards away.

"Let's not waste any time," said Izanami to Hadrian. "Take us all back."

"I... I need his permission."

"Really? You'd rather get into a fight with Mercenaries than appear discourteous?"

"It's a requirement. Teleporting with an unwilling participant can lead to disaster."

"Master, Hadrian is going to take us all to a safe place. Do you understand? You're okay with that, right?"

"No place is safe, but I think you know that."

"Okay, a safer place."

"Was he always like this?" asked an exasperated Hadrian.

"Come to think of it, yes, he was. Master, I need a definite 'yes' or 'no' from you right now."

Izanami had had enough talking to a hood. She needed to see him. Gently, she took hold of the cowl's brim and lowered it to his shoulders. Upon seeing no head, she jumped backward.

"What the...?" said Hadrian. "Is he invisible?"

She laid a hand on his shoulder.

"He feels solid enough. Master, why can't we see you?"

"Have you mastered invisibility?" asked Hadrian. "That's a skill I have long tried to master. Perhaps you might teach me?"

"We're not here for tutoring, Necromant," said Izanami crossly.

"I have indeed mastered the skill you covet," said the old man's voice, "but that is not what this is."

"Then what is... this?" asked Hadrian.

"I am out of phase. I think you know something about that yourself, don't you, Necromant? My reality is constant, while the world around me slips away. But what explains your shift, young man?"

Izanami's eyes bore into the Necromant.

"What's he talking about?"

"I have no idea."

The approaching men had closed half the gap between them. Izanami was relieved to see they were not Mercenaries after all. They were run-of-the-mill security personnel. Still, they looked well capable of a fight.

"Can you teleport him and us when he's like this?" asked Izanami.

"I... don't think so. I wouldn't chance it without his cooperation."

"Master, please say you'll come with us. Now."

The movement of his shoulders suggested he was shaking his unseen head.

"My part in this is now all but done. I wish you good fortune, though that is a meaningless gesture of courtesy. Chiharu, I never would have dreamed you would be the one. I never saw it in you, and that reflects on my own lack of wisdom."

"Please, you have to tell me how to stop the Zen'ei. How do we prevent the Fómoire's return once and for all? Tell me what to do, Master."

The black robe's right sleeve rose toward her. Slowly, an ancient, bony hand came into view from the shadow of its floating cuff. It reached out to touch the Grisial.

"I thought I might survive the end times," said the voice wistfully, "but that was hubris on my part. It would have been at the cost of everything else. Instead, I have preserved myself just long enough to do this."

In the left sleeve appeared his other hand. It came to rest on Izanami's forehead.

"Master, why did you teach that man the power of the mystic arts when you knew his purpose was evil?"

"Evil? Do you still believe in evil, Chiharu?" He sighed. "You would have profited so much from my instruction. I regret now having sent you away. Even at my age there is still something to learn. As for that man you ask about, isn't it obvious?"

"What?"

"If I had not taught him a few tricks, how would you and I have found each other?"

"But he fills the world with lies. He should have been stopped."

"Do you remember none of my lessons? You can't stop lies. If you begin suppressing lies, it is not long before every uncomfortable thing you hear sounds like a lie."

"But there had to be another way. They almost killed Peter, and that would have destroyed everything. If we hadn't gotten there in time..."

"Yes, time. The ultimate illusion. Even I cannot escape it—especially now that I have come back into phase for you. My time is up."

In the shadowy hole between the robe's shoulders, a head materialized. Izanami saw the face of her old Master. Though recognizable, his hairless head was far older than she remembered—not unlike a skull. He smiled at her kindly. Then the head was gone, as well as the fingers that held the Grisial and touched her forehead. The crystal fell back to its normal resting position. The robe fell in a heap on the ground.

"Wait," she cried. "What happened? Is he gone? For good? He said he had preserved himself long enough to... do what? Did he do it? Or did I distract him with my stupid questions?"

She grew agitated.

"What do we do now? He was our only chance to end this, and I squandered it."

Hadrian took a step toward her. He wished for a way to calm her, but she pushed him away.

"Go ahead, say it," she hissed. "I let us all down. I let the entire universe down."

Her attention was diverted by the cocking sound of three handguns. The security men had their weapons aimed at Izanami's and Hadrian's heads.

20

In the Master's Wake

"WHAT DID YOU do to him?"

The shortest of the three security guards had spoken. His accent was North American, Boston to be precise. They were all squarely built and had similarly wide jaws. Their physical similarity suggested they might well have been brothers. To a man, their black suits appeared a half-size too tight. Hadrian admired their handguns.

"Their weapons are impressive. Compact yet clearly powerful."

"Quiet!" barked the shortest man. "Back away!"

Obligingly, the Necromant retreated a few steps. Izanami stood her ground, but the shortest man glared at her until she sighed and stepped back too. He kicked the robe on the ground a few times to assure himself it was empty.

"Answer me. What did you do to him?"

"Spontaneous combustion," lied Izanami. "It's rare, but it happens."

"Don't give me that bull," said her interrogator. "You think I'm stupid? It'd have scorch marks or something."

She tried to catch the Necromant's eye. Even with their firearms, the security men would be easy enough for her to take, but there'd be less risk if he would use his powers. She didn't understand why he didn't.

"We're as confused as you are about this," said the Necromant. "Perhaps if you take us to whoever is in charge, we can sort it out."

The shortest man reflected a few moments, then made a decision.

"Okay, but no tricks."

190

He motioned to his colleagues, and they frisked the detainees. The one examining Izanami confiscated her knife but showed no interest in her medallion or the crystal.

"Walk ahead of us. In that direction."

The shortest man picked up the robe, and the group walked toward the château.

"Nice property," said Izanami. "Does it belong to Bob? He and I are old friends, you know."

"I'm not answering any questions."

She glanced at Hadrian. Why was he wasting time with this charade? To her annoyance, he winked at her.

At the château's portico stood a slender man with sandy hair and black-rimmed glasses. He wore an expensive, gray suit and appeared no older than thirty. His posture suggested a healthy self-confidence.

"Where's the old man?" he demanded impatiently.

"Gone," said the shortest man.

"What do you mean, gone?"

The shortest man shrugged.

"People don't simply disappear."

"Apparently, they do. This is all that's left of him."

He handed the robe to the young man, who stared at it blankly.

"Bob's not going to like this. Who are these people?"

"They were there with him when he disappeared."

The young man took a mobile phone from his inside coat pocket and made a call.

"We have intruders on the property. Double-check security in the server rooms. Bob doesn't want anything to hinder the app downloads." A pause. "Are you certain? Very well." After another pause, he lowered his voice. "There's no point telling me. Bob does what he does. You know that."

He returned his phone to his coat pocket and addressed Hadrian. "Who are you? How did you get on the property?"

"Your property was quite easy to access. No one stopped us."

"Stop playing games. Why are you here?"

Izanami was baffled by Hadrian and his insistence on engaging the men in conversation.

"Perhaps we're concerned citizens," said the Necromant, "wondering why you would force an elderly man to perform strenuous, agricultural labor."

"That's none of your concern. It's his own choice. He's a guest here. Wait a minute. I know who you are now. You were both on the security footage. You're two of the terrorists who attacked the Cythère Conference."

"Do you honestly think that's what happened?" asked Izanami. "That it was a terrorist attack?"

"Of course. Reports from every news outlet have been uniformly consistent. The police have already been called. They'll be here shortly." A bit nervously, he asked the shortest man, "Are you positive they're unarmed?"

A confident nod was the reply. One of the other men held up Izanami's knife triumphantly.

Izanami said, "Now that you're feeling safe, whoever you are..."

"I'm Chad Burberry. I work for Bob Ware."

"Well, Chad," said Izanami, "were you aware a child was held prisoner at the château and was intended for a ritual sacrifice?"

"Don't be absurd. Is there no lie you people won't make up? How ludicrous to suggest something like that would happen at Cythère. The world's most prominent and successful people were present. Bob was in charge of the event personally."

"Why was the old man here?"

"Mr. Miyamoto is Bob's spiritual adviser."

"Has he ever mentioned the name Alaric to you?"

"Look, you're in no position to be asking me questions." He glanced at his watch. "I wonder what's keeping the gendarmes."

"I heard there are riots again in Bordeaux, Mr. Burberry," said the shortest man. "They may have been diverted."

The strains of Pink Floyd's "Money" emanated from Chad's coat.

"Damn," muttered Chad as he retrieved his phone. "Sorry, Bob. I didn't mean to bother you with this. That message was only an FYI. Things are under control here. The gendarmes should be here any minute. What? Yes. The Japanese one? Yes."

"I'm Canadian."

"You want to talk to her? You mean, on my phone? Is that safe? What if she uses it to detonate a bomb or something? Really? Okay."

Chad reluctantly handed his phone to the Demon Hunter. It was gold-plated and encrusted with tiny diamonds. She saw Bob's face on its screen.

"Chiharu!" he smiled. "If I'd known you were coming, I'd have made a point to greet you personally. Did you come to see my Acharya?"

"Your what? Wait, don't tell me that's your word for Master."

"That word's offensive, but what else could I expect from a Hant Oppressor. Tell me what you've done with the Acharya?"

"No, you tell me, Bob, what will it take to end this? To make you give up your cult and end this obsession with the Old Ones?"

Bob winced. "Don't you understand how disrespectful your language is? They're called the Primogenitors. Soon they'll return, and then you'll see. Humanity will realize its destiny. The planet will be saved."

"There isn't any reasoning with you, is there?"

"Please, return the Expiator to us so he can fulfill his destiny and humanity's."

"Do you think anything can justify murdering a child?"

"Society makes tradeoffs with lives all the time. People die every day on the roads so we may have the convenience of automobiles. Why wouldn't you sacrifice a single life if it means the salvation of the world?"

"So further talk is hopeless then?"

"Talk is never hopeless. Start by purging yourself of your hateful words. Then open your mind. Join us. It's not too late, Chiharu. You can be part of it. You can be on the right side."

She ended the call and Bob's face was replaced by undulating geometric patterns. Chad was dumbfounded by what he had heard.

"You mean, they were really going to murder a child? I didn't know that part. I swear." He thought better of it. "Wait, this is a trick. You've found a way to mess with my head. They wouldn't do that. Journalists would find out and tell us."

Izanami turned to Hadrian. "I'm getting bored waiting for the gendarmes. Can we go now, Necromant?"

He shook his head in dismay.

"I thought we might learn something useful, but it's hopeless, isn't it? The twentieth-century mind is even more pliant to the forces of indoctrination than I feared."

"Twenty-first-century."

"What?"

"This is the twenty-first century."

"Right, of course. Yes, let's go."

Hadrian waved his right arm, startling the security men. They raised their weapons but found themselves unable to stop them from falling from their hands to the ground. They made clattering sounds as they landed on the stone tiles. Izanami's knife also fell from the hand that had held it. Their eyes widened with panic. Chad and the security men struggled to move. Izanami retrieved her blade and returned it to its sheath.

"Take my hand," said Hadrian.

"Do I have to?"

He furrowed his brow, not unlike a disapproving parent. Reluctantly, she took his hand.

"Oh," she said, remembering the device in her other hand. "Your phone, Chad."

She tossed it in his direction. Unable to move, he watched as it slammed with a loud smack onto the tile in front of his feet. Its screen went black, and the glass filled with tiny, jagged cracks. A few of the diamonds popped out of their settings. He looked up to see a few leaves and bits of dust swirling around the intruders. Within seconds they faded from view.

"They're back!" yelled Peter as he saw them materialize in the exact spot from where they had departed.

Sapphire and Koschei looked at them expectantly. Izanami took a moment to catch her breath. She knew they were waiting for an explanation, but all she could do was shake her head in frustration before uttering two words.

"Miyamoto's gone."

"Gone?" said Sapphire. "What happened?"

"I don't know. Maybe Hadrian understands it better than I do."

"There was little time," said the Necromant. "It was as though he had been hanging on just long enough to impart... something to Izanami. He touched the Grisial and her head. Then he was gone."

The others looked at Izanami. Her face was blank.

"Did he plant some thought in your mind?" asked Sapphire. "Did he impart some knowledge to you?"

"I don't know what he did. I don't know if he did anything. I stupidly kept pestering him with questions that, in the end, didn't matter. I was just trying to satisfy my curiosity. I must have distracted him. I don't think he got to finish what he was trying to do."

"Don't be so certain," said Hadrian. "His manner of communicating was by no means straightforward. It shouldn't surprise us his purpose wasn't immediately clear. I'm not inclined to believe he waited centuries for that final encounter and then simply, as you say, got distracted."

"Then why don't I know what I'm supposed to know?" said Izanami. "Why don't I know anything?"

She put her hand around the crystal and squeezed it. She would have crushed it if she'd had the strength.

"It's a mistake. This wasn't meant for me. If I'm the one who wears it, then the world's doomed. Any one of you would have been better than me. Sapphire, take it."

She tugged at the strap.

"Don't!" shouted Sapphire. "The only way you can fail us is by taking it off."

With a glance from her, the others understood they should leave her and Izanami alone.

"I understand you didn't want this," she said softly, "but none of us wanted any of this to happen. Someone told me once that we don't get to choose our burdens. We only get to choose how we carry them."

Izanami smiled weakly. "Who told you that? It wasn't Orpheus, was it?"

"No, it was my ethics professor at U–Dub."

"You know, I keep meaning to tell you something. It's annoying sometimes when you keep talking about your time in college. Nobody cares."

"Sounds like someone may be a little jealous because she never got to finish her education."

"What would your know-it-all professors suggest I do with this stupid crystal?"

"Unfortunately, U–Dub didn't offer a major in Mystical Arts."

Hadrian approached them and cleared his throat cautiously. "I might have a suggestion."

"No," said Izanami emphatically.

"I haven't told you what it is."

"You don't have to. I already know."

"So, now you're the one reading *my* mind?"

"I don't have to. You always have the same solution to every problem."

"If Miyamoto did put something in your mind, wouldn't we have a better chance of discovering and understanding it if we put our minds together?"

"I don't like it when you're in my head or, for that matter, when I'm in your head."

"What does any of that matter when our entire world hangs in the balance?"

Sapphire put her hand on Izanami's shoulder. "He has a point, you know."

"You're taking his side?"

"It's not sides. We're all on the same side. It's down to a simple choice of existence or non-existence. Can anything else matter?"

"You don't know what it's like. The intrusion. The crippling feeling of loss of control."

"Don't I? For a while now, I've been haunted constantly by former lives. A few millennia's worth."

"That's not the same. It's different when someone else invades your mind. Especially when it's someone you don't trust."

"Do you have a better idea then?"

Izanami's shoulders slumped. "No."

"I promise," said the Necromant, "I will only look in your mind for information that your old Master may have put there. I swear I'll ignore everything else."

Koschei and Peter had returned and were listening to the conversation. Izanami felt everyone's eyes on her. She felt she had no choice, and she hated that feeling.

"Okay, let's get this over with."

She and Hadrian knelt on the ground. He touched her temples lightly, and they closed their eyes. Izanami trembled. More than any previous time, she dreaded this mental encounter—and she didn't know why.

She entered the now-familiar dreamlike state. Her mind filled with Hadrian's presence. Her natural instinct was to repel him, but it was impossible. She felt like a puppet. Her body was not her own. Her mind was not her own. Childhood memories came flooding back. Her life unfolded like a strip of film, doubling back on itself over and over. She raced through one frame after another until there were no more. At the end of it all was Miyamoto. He was younger than she had ever seen him. She sat with him, and he spoke to her.

For the first and only time, he patiently explained everything she ever wanted to know. He answered all her questions— even anticipating her queries before she thought of them. She was overcome with relief and satisfaction. She basked in the comfortable feeling.

A shadow then appeared. It was the Necromant. He stood between her and the Master. She felt the information she had acquired slipping away. The shadow that was Hadrian grew larger, dwarfing her. She struggled to flee but could not move. She was like a drowning woman being sucked underwater. Everything went black.

Her eyes opened wide, and she gasped for air. The trance had ended, and she lay on the ground. Sapphire, Koschei, and Peter looked at her with concern. Towering behind them, Hadrian stared darkly.

"I have it!" he cried. "At last I have it!"

They all looked at him in shock. He settled his gaze on Peter.

"Come, boy," he commanded.

"Peter, no!" cried Koschei, but the boy had walked obediently in the Necromant's direction.

Hadrian took the child's hand and then reached deep into a pocket inside his robe. He took out an object. Izanami stared in disbelief. It was the Grisial. He studied it carefully, then put it back. He closed his eyes and bowed his head. Within moments a breeze had rushed over all of them. Hadrian and Peter faded from view.

Sapphire and Koschei looked at each other in shock. Then they looked at Izanami. Their eyes were full of questions.

21
Betrayal

SEVERAL MOMENTS PASSED before Izanami could speak, as she struggled into wakefulness.

"I was right," she gasped. "I knew I shouldn't trust him. If only I'd listened to my instinct."

"He had the Grisial!" said Sapphire in dismay. "How is that possible?"

"He must have taken it from me," said Izanami, sitting up, "while I was in the trance. What does this mean?"

"But he didn't," said Sapphire, pointing at Izanami's chest. "Look."

Izanami looked down. The Grisial still hung from her neck. "How...? You mean, there are two of them?"

"What happened during the trance?" asked Sapphire.

"He double-crossed us. He found what he was looking for in my head, and then he fled—taking the boy with him."

"To do what?" asked Sapphire. "What possible reason could he have for doing this?"

"He's betrayed us."

"Betrayed us? But why? How could his interests be any different from ours when the entire world's at stake?"

"Because he doesn't care about the world. Not this one anyway."

"That makes no sense," said Koschei. "If this world ends, so does he."

"I understand things better now," said Izanami. "He tried to erase the knowledge from my mind as he stole it, but I managed to hold onto some of it. Most of it, I think. Now I have to tell you as quickly as I can. Before it drains from my mind. You have to listen—and remember, in case I forget."

The others said nothing. They did not want to break her concentration. They waited for her to begin.

"Miyamoto is older than I ever dreamed. He's walked the earth for centuries. His experience is vast. His knowledge goes all the way back to ancient times. He learned directly from the old Masters of legend. He knew about the Old Ones, about Balor. He knew about the war between the Fomóire and the Tuath Dé and about the incarnation of Clíodhna. He foresaw the coming of the Zen'ei. He was aware of the prophecy foretelling the Expiator."

"What's the Expiator?" asked Koschei.

"The Expiator is the sacrifice. The one whose life and future must be surrendered so that the physical world will cease to exist. The one whose death will bring about the End of Time."

"Peter?"

Izanami nodded gravely. "Until now the End of Time has been forestalled by Clíodhna. The fact of her existence has protected this world for millennia, but now her own awareness of her identity has created a crisis. This is Balor's opportunity, and to end the physical world, he himself must become part of it."

Sapphire was puzzled. "You mean become incarnated as Clíodhna was? But why would he become part of what he wants to destroy?"

"No, not the same as Clíodhna. She became a human being—someone completely new. Balor wants to possess a pre-existing Host. Like a virus infecting an organism. He will become part of the natural world. That will trigger the end of humanity."

"Who's meant to be the Host?" asked Koschei.

"It must be Alaric," said Sapphire. "He's the one calling the shots to make this happen."

"What about the Software Wizard?" said Koschei.

"He takes his lead from Alaric," said Izanami. "I'd say he's as deluded as any of Alaric's other cultists."

"What's Alaric's motivation?" asked Koschei. "He gets possessed by a supernatural entity and then the world ends. Why would he do that?"

"The world won't end quickly," said Izanami gravely. "The disintegration of reality, from the perspective of human beings, will be a drawn-out, painful process. It will go on for years as physical laws break down and nature becomes warped. During that long age of chaos—the twilight of humanity—Balor's Host will reign supreme. He will have the powers of a deity, bending everyone and everything to the whims of his own capricious will. The very thing that would appeal to a madman with delusions of godhood."

"I still don't understand," said Koschei. "What's the Necromant's part in this? Where did he go and why did he take the child with him?"

"I can think of only one reason," said Izanami grimly. "He wants to replace Alaric. He wants to be the Host. He wants to wield Balor's power over the dying earth."

"That doesn't sound like the man I knew," said Sapphire. "It's not consistent from Tyra's memories of him."

"Yes," said the Russian. "Didn't Tsuru herself tell us to seek him out, that he was our only hope?"

"Tsuru is old and perhaps not as perceptive as she once was," said Izanami. "Hadrian must be some sort of sociopath, able to hide his true nature. I risked trusting him despite my instinct telling me not to. Now the world will pay the price. Does anyone else feel cold?"

"There's a chill in the air all right," said Sapphire.

"It's more than that," said Izanami. "I have that feeling again. Someone's watching us."

"Where did Hadrian get a second Grisial?" wondered Sapphire. "It's unique. There can't be another one."

"Then the one I have must be fake," said Izanami, taking the crystal in her hand. "He must have swapped them sometime while I slept. I might as well get rid of it."

She pulled on the crystal's strap, but Sapphire stopped her.

"Don't. We have to assume this is the true Grisial. If it weren't, we would know. The consequences are severe if it's removed from the bearer before the time."

"But when is the time?" asked Koschei. "How does the talisman fit into this?"

"Do you know?" Sapphire asked Izanami. "Did you glean anything from Miyamoto about that?"

"I know the Grisial's origin now. It was created by Clíodhna and Ciabhán. Energy was drawn from Clíodhna and converted to matter. It was crystalized in searing heat deep inside a volcano."

"They created it together?"

Izanami nodded. "Ciabhán became powerful in his own right. Clíodhna shared her familiarity of the non-physical world, and the secrets she taught him led to an ability to bend nature to his will. He was the first Mage."

"Why did they make the Grisial?"

"It's the ultimate defensive weapon. It draws on Clíodhna's power and thwarts any possibility of the Fomóire incarnating."

Izanami looked at the crystal in her hand and then at Sapphire.

"It's you who should be the bearer. The Grisial was always meant for Clíodhna."

"No," said Sapphire, "I don't think that's right. Your words have awakened memories that have lain dormant for millennia. I'm having trouble sorting them all out in my head, but I know this much. The Grisial draws on Clíodhna's power, but it was meant to be borne by Ciabhán."

"But Ciabhán is long dead."

"It need not be borne by him personally but by his heir. In other words, by Clíodhna's companion. Chiharu, I think you were always meant to be the bearer. I think your role was sealed the moment you and I met."

"How does it summon people from out of their own time?"

"It's a side effect of its power. Possibly an intentional one. The magnitude of its supernatural potency warps natural laws. It bends time in a specific way. What Clíodhna and Ciabhán may not have foreseen is that the Grisial makes possible the kind of temporal paradox that can destroy reality. Balor understands this and exploits it for his own purposes."

"My God," said Izanami. "By unwittingly calling Peter into our time, I've sealed the world's doom."

"Maybe not," said Sapphire. "Maybe what happened was necessary. Perhaps it was always meant to happen this way."

"Always the optimist, eh? Do you believe that? I don't. Look where we are. The Zen'ei have the boy again, and that means the end of the world is at hand."

"Have you learned anything else, Chiharu, that might help us?"

"There's one more thing. I know where Balor's Inhabitation is meant to take place. That must be where Hadrian took the boy."

"Let's follow at once," said Koschei urgently.

"Where is it?" asked Sapphire.

"You won't like it. I certainly don't."

"What are you talking about?" said Koschei. "Where have they gone?"

"The Inhabitation must take place atop the same volcano where the Grisial was formed. It will happen at or near the Licancabur Rim."

"Seriously?" said Sapphire. "Please tell me you're joking."

"I don't know that place," said Koschei. "What about it?"

"That's the location of Izanami's and my last demon battle. The hellion Merihim almost immolated the two of us. It was horrendous. That place is cursed for us. No good can come from going back there."

"When you think about it," said Izanami, "it's kind of perfect, isn't it? Maybe we were always meant to die there."

"Talk like that can't help," said Koschei.

"Can we please get out of this forest?" said Izanami. "I can't stand it here anymore."

"We need to get information from the outside world," said Sapphire. "We must go where we can see the latest news. If the Inhabitation is to happen soon, there will be large movements of people toward northern Chile. Masses of humans must come together in one place to provide the energy necessary to usher Balor into the physical world."

"We saw a newscast in Lausanne," said Koschei.

"I want to hear it in English. Let's go to London."

"Are you sure you're up to teleporting all of us that far?" asked Izanami.

"I'm fine. Just take my hands. There's no point wasting time."

Izanami and Koschei did as they were told, and the three of them were enveloped by the familiar gust and the darkness that came with it. When the light returned, they were in a massive city square. At the far end were the dome and columns of the National Gallery. Nearer was the familiar pillar, 170 feet tall, guarded by four bronze lions and with Horatio Nelson's statue on top. Beyond Nelson's Column were two large stone fountains. Neither had any water.

The sky was dark with thick, gray clouds. The air smelled of smoke. Trafalgar Square was devoid of people. The ground was covered by rubbish and the remnants of bonfires. Windows in many of the surrounding buildings were shattered.

Sapphire stumbled and fell to the ground. The others helped her to stand.

"Something's wrong," said Izanami, "and don't tell me you're just tired or short of sleep. Teleportation is taking a toll on you. I don't like it."

"You worry too much, Chi-Chi. Come on. What's that over there?"

"I can't get used to you having a nickname, Izanami," said Koschei as they walked across the square. "I can barely accept you having a birth name."

Facing each other across the square's width were two large outdoor LED screens. Sound blared from loudspeakers, but there was no one to listen except the three Demon Hunters.

"Truly a historic moment, Carol," said an Englishman sitting in an armchair. "The entire world has come together in a way never seen before. Totally unprecedented."

"Yes," said Carol from behind her desk, "all eyes are now on Chile's Atacama Desert. Pilgrims from across the world arrive by the hour and flock to the town of San Pedro de Atacama. Truly inspiring, I have to say. It's rather like a miracle, isn't it? The way people from all over the world have come together like this."

"Miracle perhaps, but we shouldn't overlook the generosity of the Robert Malcolm Ware Foundation, which has organized and funded so many charter flights. It is thanks to them that so many pilgrims can participate. It must also be said that Bob Ware is covering many of the expenses out of his own pocket. A philanthropist in the truest sense of the word."

"Again, we'll remind the viewers at home, if you're unable to make the journey to Chile, you may still participate. Simply use your smartphone or other mobile device to download the ParyDyme 'Save the Planet' app. There is no charge, and with each download, ParyDyme Corporation makes a donation to the pilgrimage fund."

"With all the challenges facing the world, Carol, it's heartening to see corporations like ParyDyme stepping into the breach..."

"Sorry to cut across you, Malcolm, but we've just made contact with our correspondent Brendan Forsythe on the scene in San Pedro de Atacama. Brendan, what can you tell us about the mood on the ground?"

"Carol, the atmosphere here is nothing short of electric. I've never seen or felt anything like it. The sense of hope is unparalleled in my experience as a journalist. Everyone is infused with an undeniable sense of history turning a corner. If you'll allow me a personal comment, I'd like to say, what a privilege to witness such a moment."

"Brendan, do you have an estimate of the numbers participating?"

"Difficult to say precisely, but they are simply massive."

"Yet there have been few if any problems. No signs of disorder. Remarkable, given the multitude involved."

"Volunteers are helping to keep things organized, Carol, and I have to say, they are quite efficient at their task. They call themselves Legionnaires, and they certainly have their own unique dress style. There's something medieval about it. As though they think they're at a Renaissance fair. Everyone is waiting for the culmination of this pilgrimage. It is promised for the exact moment of the winter solstice. Of course, in the UK and the rest of the Northern Hemisphere, that would be the summer solstice. Our viewers in the UK may anticipate the big moment as they follow the countdown clock at the bottom of the television screen."

"I've seen enough," said Izanami. "According to their clock, it's only a couple of days until the solstice. We have to get to Chile right away."

"And then what?" said Sapphire. "Look at how many people have gathered. Yes, most of them are clueless cultists, but there are also a fair number of Mercenaries or Legionnaires or whatever you want to call them. There are only three of us. This isn't like breaking into a château full of economists and executives."

Koschei looked at her with concern.

"More to the point," he said, "how will we get there? You look exhausted, Sapphire. Are you fit for teleporting us all the way to South America?"

Even as Sapphire protested, Izanami saw the fatigue in her eyes.

"Look," said the Canadian. "Can you teleport us just as far as Bordeaux? I have an idea."

"France? Why?"

"It's something that employee of Bob's said at the château. He mentioned server rooms and app downloads. It must be the same app they're telling people to download to their phones. If that's how they're coordinating this so-called pilgrimage, we might be able to shut it down—or at least slow things down and cause some confusion. If we're lucky, maybe we can trick all the pilgrims into going home again."

"Have you become a software expert since I last saw you, Chi–Chi?"

"No, but you always go on about that computer science class you took at U–Dub. I bet you can figure it out."

"I really don't think…"

"Come on, isn't it worth a shot? Security was pretty light there. We'll be in and out in no time. What's to lose? If it doesn't work out, we can still make our suicide run to the Licancabur Rim."

"How am I supposed to know where to take us?"

"Didn't Hadrian put the location in your mind before he took me there?"

"He did, but after you came back, I flushed it."

"You can do that? But why?"

"My mind is very crowded these days. I find expunging unnecessary data relieves my tension headaches."

"Then read my mind."

"Very funny."

"I'm serious. I have the location information in my head from when the Necromant took me there, and it's still floating around after all of the mind-sharing we did. Just look in my head for it."

"I certainly don't mind trying."

"Neither do I."

Sapphire placed her fingers on Izanami's temples. They closed their eyes. Sapphire put her forehead against Izanami's. Within moments their lips found each other. They played a game of touching and parting, ending with them firmly locked.

"I have information in my head too," said Koschei sarcastically, "if you care to search for that as well."

"I got what I needed," said Sapphire, opening her eyes. "About where we're going, I mean."

As they joined hands, Koschei said, "I'm beginning to feel like a third wheel..."

He lost his train of thought as the dark gust encircled them. Moments later, the journey was complete. They stood before the château where Izanami and Hadrian had been earlier in the day. While Koschei and Izanami needed a moment to regain their balance, Sapphire fell to the ground.

"Mrs. Lynch!"

Izanami dropped to her knees to check her breathing. It was labored. Moreover, her eyes were closed, her skin clammy.

"Can you hear me, Sapphire? Talk to me!"

It was more than two minutes before she opened her eyes.

"Sorry, I guess I've been overdoing..."

"Stop trying to explain it away. This is serious."

"I've told you before. Teleportation takes it out of me."

"It never did this to you before. This is what you said would happen, isn't it? Learning the truth about yourself, about

Clíodhna, is more than your body can handle. I remember your exact words. 'The magnitude of her self-awareness becomes more than her mortal body can contain.'"

"That's not what matters right now."

"Of course, it matters. I'm not going to lose you."

"Then let's get back to work because the only hope for any of us—including me—is to stop the Zen'ei."

"But you're not fit to do what we need to do. You need to stay somewhere safe. Let Koschei and me do what needs to be done."

"Look, I know I may slow you down, but you're going to need my powers and knowledge. We have to stick together, no matter what."

Izanami helped her to her feet.

"She's right, you know," said Koschei.

"If you're determined to protect me," said Sapphire, "can't you do that best if we're together?"

Izanami surveyed the château's grounds and saw no one.

"Did they all go to South America?" wondered Koschei.

The front door in the portico was locked, so they circled the building and found a side door. It too was locked, but it was no match for a blast from Izanami's hands. Inside was a deserted kitchen. They passed through it and into a wide hallway.

"This place is huge," said Koschei. "Where should we look first?"

"Servers would need to be kept at a low temperature," said Sapphire. "I'd look for an underground room."

Alert for security guards, they strode up and down corridors, looking for a basement door. In the rearmost part of the building, they found double doors which opened on a wide set of stairs leading downward. They descended into the chilly darkness. At the base of the stairs, Izanami felt the wall for a switch and turned on a light. One after another, fluorescent tubes on the ceiling flickered and, each in their turn, illuminated the vast room with a bluish light. A few oak barrels were stacked against a brick wall, a reminder this had once been an aging room. Now it was filled with rows of metal boxes with monitors and keyboards. They were all dead quiet.

"This is it," said Sapphire. "These are the servers, but why have they all been turned off?"

She was answered by a voice behind them, halfway up the stairs.

"Their work is done."

22
Journey

THE DEMON HUNTERS turned and looked up.

"Hello, Chad," said Izanami.

"So, you've returned."

"Mission accomplished for your boss and his crazy hordes?"

"Not exactly."

Sapphire and Koschei sized up the man in the gray suit. They concluded from Izanami's demeanor he did not pose a threat to them.

"Are these the machines downloading your boss's app?"

"They were."

"Why are they turned off?"

"Because I cut their power."

"No more phones to download the app to?"

"That's not it. I decided on my own to turn them off. This may surprise you, but I realized you were right. I had never believed the conspiracy theories before, but the more I thought about yours, the more it began to make sense."

"You do know, don't you, it's not a conspiracy theory if it's true?"

"When you told me why they wanted that boy, it was as though my blinders had been removed. How did I not see how crazy the whole thing was? They kept saying we were going to save the planet. I mean, how could anyone be against that, right? When I stopped and thought about it, none of it added up."

"We need to stop them, Chad. You don't know the half of it. You can't imagine what's at risk. If they succeed..."

"Yes?"

"You'll think I'm crazy."

"Tell me."

"It will mean the end of the world."

Chad's face suggested that Izanami sounded to him as deranged as his employer.

"Look," said Sapphire. "We don't have time to make you understand. You need to trust us."

"That's not good enough," he said nervously. "Where's the evidence?"

"You don't have to believe everything we say. You just need to trust us when we say that what's going on in Chile needs to be stopped."

"But there are thousands participating in it. The major international corporations are supporting them. Also, quite a few governments. How many are on your side? I see only three of you—unless you also count that strange guy who was here with you before."

"That's why we need your help, my friend," said Koschei.

The Russian's long, blond hair and strange garb drew Chad's silent stare.

"How would *you* go about stopping your employer and his friends?"

"I've already done what I can. I shut down the servers. The app can't be downloaded anymore."

"But what else? Their leader draws his power from the masses of people he gathers. How can we stop that? More importantly, they have the boy again. We must find him."

"Then you need to go to South America. They'll be communicating with all those people through electronic equipment broadcasting their words and images. You need to disrupt that system, or better yet, find a way to hack into it to substitute your own message."

"Can you help us with that?" asked Sapphire. "I have the power to take all of us there within moments. Will you come with us?"

"No," said Izanami. "It's too soon for you to teleport again, and it's too far. It might kill you."

"We have to take the risk."

"I don't know what you and she are talking about," said Chad, "but *I* have the power to take us all to South America."

They looked at him in bewilderment.

"Don't tell me," said Izanami, "that you're a Mage or an Augurer too?"

"Sorry, I don't know what those are," said Chad. "It won't be within moments, but I can fly us."

"Fly?"

"There's a company jet in a hangar at Bordeaux-Mérignac. I can have us in the air within an hour."

"You're a pilot?"

He nodded confidently. "I fly that plane all the time. Are you game?"

Sapphire was unsure, but Izanami answered affirmatively for all of them. Chad took a mobile phone from his inside coat pocket and began pressing keys.

"Sorry, but this will take a minute. I have to download some phone numbers. This is a backup phone. Someone broke my personal cell."

He stared at Izanami, who found it impossible to look apologetic.

As Chad carried on a conversation in French, the others spoke among themselves.

"Do we trust him?" asked Koschei.

"Do we have a choice?" said Izanami.

"We do," said Sapphire. "I can get us there, and it would be much faster."

"I'm not going to let you do anything," said Izanami, "that makes you weaker than you already are."

Koschei smiled. "This Izanami of the future is much more caring than the one I know from my time. I say, if Sapphire is determined, perhaps we should let her..."

"No," said Izanami definitively.

"It's all set," said Chad, returning the phone to his pocket. "The jet will be fueled and ready to go by the time we get to the airport. Follow me."

He led them outdoors and to a stable which had been converted into a garage. Inside was a late-model Renault

Espace. They boarded the multiple-purpose vehicle and traveled in luxury down the Route d'Arsac.

At the airport, Chad had some paperwork to complete, but Sapphire was impressed that they were not asked for passports or other identification. With little delay, they strode across the tarmac and up the boarding stairs. The cabin was spacious, the seats large and comfortable.

"Nice," said Sapphire. "So, this is how billionaires travel."

Koschei had not entered the cabin. Izanami found him frozen in the doorway, his face taut.

"This will be… interesting," he said with gritted teeth.

"I'm so sorry, Koschei. I forgot that you don't like to fly."

"What do you mean?" he said defensively. "I've never told you that."

"Yes, you did. I mean, you will. It's why we had to take a ferry to Ireland when we went to the Netherworld."

"I can't believe I would tell you that. It's ridiculous and humiliating that a Demon Hunter should be so apprehensive of a common mode of conveyance."

"Come, old friend. I'm sure there will be spirits on board. We'll drink together and stay intoxicated for the entire journey."

"I can't. Because of this infernal time travel, I'm incapable of taking drink. Bloody hell. This is a disaster."

"Never mind. There's no reason for fear. I've seen your death, and I promise you it does not happen on this plane. You're as safe here as in your mother's arms."

"My mother's arms were no protection," said the Russian darkly, "when Yurovsky came for us in the middle of the night."

Koschei entered the cabin reluctantly. Chad proposed that the Russian sit beside him in the cockpit.

"That will give you some sense of control," he said. "Don't worry. I've seen this many times. Fear of flying is quite common. Trust me, you'll be fine."

When they had reached cruising altitude, Izanami went to check on him.

"This is great," he said with a grin. "The view is fantastic, and Chad has shown me how all the instruments work. I actually believe now I could have been a pilot. It's wonderful. I needn't fear airplanes ever again."

"You realize, don't you, that when you go back to your own time, you won't remember any of this? You'll make us take the ferry to Ireland anyway."

"A pity," he sighed, looking down at the lights dotting the Spanish landscape.

"How is he?" asked Sapphire when Izanami returned.

"He's fine. He's conquered his fear of flying—at least until the world goes back to normal. The good news for us is that we can sleep for the entire journey, knowing that Koschei won't. He'll make sure Chad doesn't nod off."

"I'm exhausted, but I don't know if I can sleep. There are too many things going through my head."

"I know what you mean."

"Chiharu?"

"Yes?"

"I don't want to waste a single minute with you."

"There will be lots of time after we stop Alaric."

"What if we can't stop him?"

"There's no point thinking that way."

"What happened to Orpheus's lesson about not being over-confident?"

"I realize now it wasn't his best lesson. I've learned much more from you than I ever did from him."

"You know, I've told you everything about my life. I mean, about the one I'm living now—and everything I can remember about my other lives. But I still don't feel I know anything about you. I mean, your history. I have this feeling that these hours on this plane may be our last chance to..."

"To what?"

"To say all the things we haven't said."

"What do you think I haven't said? I promise, you know everything worth knowing about me."

"I don't know anything about your life before you were a Demon Hunter. You never talk about your childhood."

"You want to hear all my stories? I'm afraid my stories aren't very good. They don't have happy endings."

"Doesn't the story we're living now, the one about you and me, have a happy ending?"

"It doesn't have any ending—happy or otherwise. We're still living it. I can tell you, though, it's the happiest I've ever been."

"You must have had other happy times. What was your childhood like?"

"I don't think I want to..."

"Please."

In Sapphire's eyes Izanami saw exhaustion—and more than a bit of fear.

"Sure, my childhood was all right. I have no complaints."

"Where did you live?"

"My parents were farmers. We lived on the banks of the Fraser River. When we weren't farming, we fished. It was a good place to grow up. It was a lot of hard work, but there was always food on the table. We didn't want for anything, and we had good neighbors."

"Sounds nice."

"Yeah, it was. A Norwegian family, the Nilsens, had the farm nearest ours. We became friendly with them. They had a son three years older than me. Lars-Erik. He was blond and blue-eyed, and he always smelled of herring. At least that's how I remember him. He was the first person I ever kissed."

"You mean, I wasn't your first? I wasn't even your first Scandinavian?"

"You were my first woman. That must count for something."

"Was your family okay with you having a Norwegian boyfriend?"

"They didn't know, and he wasn't a real boyfriend anyway. He was eighteen. I was fifteen. We pretended to make plans, but that's all it was—pretend. Just silly talk. And a lot of kissing. And dancing."

"You dance?"

"Not anymore, but I did back then. Lars-Erik had a record player, and he'd play his 78s for me. He loved jazz, especially Billie Holiday. He played them for me, and we danced in his room."

"So what happened?"

"Pearl Harbor happened."

"What? Oh. I always forget..."

"That I'm old enough to be Lola Blumquist's great-grand-mother? Yes, I remember Pearl Harbor. By that time, Canada had already been in the war, at least officially against Germany, for two years. But Pearl Harbor meant that the country was now at war with Japan. Things were stressful for us after that. A few days after my sixteenth birthday, we were rounded up and sent to Hastings Park in Vancouver. Us and 22,000 other Japanese-Canadians. Everyone on the Pacific coast. I never saw Lars-Erik again."

"I'm sorry."

"Didn't I tell you? My stories don't have happy endings. We weren't treated badly—except for the fact we lost our home and our farm. The worst of it for me was that there was a commander at the camp. He took advantage of his position, and that's all I'm going to say about that. That's when I learned it's better to be strong than to be weak."

Sapphire put her arms around her. "I don't know what to say."

"There's nothing worth saying. Fortunately, we weren't there long. We were sent to the Tashme Internment Camp. A place called Sunshine Valley. How's that for a name? My father and older brother were sent to do road work. The rest of us at least stayed together."

"So, you were there until the end of the war?"

"My family was, not me. I made a friend, the son of another family. His name was Shigeru. He was two years older and the most recklessly inquisitive boy I ever knew. He talked to everyone in the camp, constantly gathering as much gossip and information as he could. He spent a lot of time, in particular, with two old grandfathers. Everyone said they were crazy, but Shigeru listened to their wild stories day and night. He pestered them with questions. They told him fantastic tales of demons and Mages and Masters of the mystical arts. They told him about two such Masters.

"Shigeru became determined to escape from the camp and find the Masters. After weeks of boredom and dreaming and listening to his second-hand stories, I was finally convinced to go with him. In the middle of the night, we cut a hole in the wire fence and ran. It was pure luck that, when we got to the main highway, a truck not only stopped for us, but the driver didn't turn us in. He was Polish, and I think he must have had some sympathy for people locked up in camps. That was my first time to travel the road to Cache Creek and Lost Gap."

"Is that when you met Tsuru?"

"No, not that time. We couldn't find Lost Gap. It's extremely difficult to locate if you've never been there before. We finally gave up and went in search of the other Master. That meant a much longer and more difficult journey. Over weeks we had to make our way to the northern coast of Vancouver Island. I honestly don't know how we did it. The journey would have been difficult enough—even without us having to keep out of sight the entire time. Nothing makes you more paranoid than knowing the way you look marks you as an enemy to everyone around you. Yet somehow we made it. We found Miyamoto's cabin, somewhere near San Josef Bay.

"He was a strange man, but he welcomed us and said we could stay for a while. Shigeru asked him to take us on as disciples, but he said he needed time to determine if we were suitable. Not only that, but he said he was abandoning Canada after having lived there for a century and a half. He was returning to Japan."

"In the middle of World War II?"

"The war didn't concern him. He said the world was calling him east and that, once he was at home there, we would be welcome to join him. If we were suitable, he told us, we would manage to find him in his new home."

"He didn't teleport you? How were you supposed to get to Japan in the middle of the war?"

"That was part of the test. At least he provided the transportation. One night we followed him to the ocean shore where he stood, raised his arms, and went into a trance. After fifteen minutes of absolute silence in the moonlight, an object rose from the water. It was a submarine. A small boat carried men to the shore. Miyamoto spoke with them, but I caught only bits of what they were saying. My Japanese was not very good.

"I don't know how he summoned the submarine or convinced the crew to take us aboard. Some mystical influence was apparently at work. During the weeks we were 'guests' of the Japanese navy, we witnessed the torpedoing of an American freighter in the Strait of Juan de Fuca. Also, the shelling of a lighthouse on Vancouver Island. Within two and a half weeks after that, we were in Yokosuka at the mouth of Tokyo Bay.

"We were released into a city we didn't know. Mount Fuji dominated the skyline, just as we had seen in many photographs and paintings. We didn't know anyone and had only the most rudimentary knowledge of the language. Unlike Vancouver, we could at least melt into the crowd and not be noticed. Or so I thought.

"People stared at us. Everything about us was wrong—the way we walked, they way we talked, the way we were dressed. They could tell instantly we were from somewhere else. We were Nikkei, the Japanese born overseas. Some called us *hikokumin*, meaning foreigners. One or two actually called us *kichiku*."

"What does that mean?"

"You'll like this. It means demon-creature. It was a term commonly used during the war for Americans and British. Before I went there, I had always imagined it would be like going home, that I would fit in. It wasn't anything like that. That's when I realized I would never again feel at home any-where in the world. I would forever be a stranger no matter where I went."

"You weren't a stranger in Ballard."

"No," smiled Izanami, "I wasn't. After many long years alone, I was finally at home in your house in Ballard." The smile faded from her face. "And now it's gone."

"Only the house is gone, Chiharu. Home isn't gone. Home is wherever the two of us are."

23
Descent

"DID IT TAKE you long to find Miyamoto?"

"It took weeks. Many long weeks. That was also part of the test. We had to learn to adapt to a culture that was foreign—and in some ways hostile—to us. We had to track down a man who was as mysterious as a *yurei*… a ghost. We had to survive and travel on no money. And we had to do all that in a highly organized society that had been mobilized for war. Shigeru and I relied on each other for everything. Giving up and going home wasn't an option. The only way was forward—no matter how difficult."

"You must have so many stories from that time."

"Too many to tell now, but we did finally find him. He had a cottage deep in the Sea of Trees, the forest known as Aokigahara on Mount Fuji's far flank. The densest part of the woodland was an entirely different world. Something about it suppressed sound. The quiet was eerie and oppressive. When we found Miyamoto, he had little welcome for us—let alone praise or congratulations. He had already become restless and was pre-paring to leave Japan. He would travel to Tibet, and we were allowed to accompany him. He treated us no better than servants. That too was part of the training. It was a long and arduous journey."

"Surely, he could have teleported there."

"Don't you see? It was another test. He wanted to observe us under pressure, see how we dealt with adversity. We traveled the width of China. Trains could only take us so far from Peking. The rest was largely by horse and cart. If not for Miyamoto's mystical skills, we would not have long survived in a country where the Japanese were hated enemies, where the Chinese had

been fighting Japanese invaders for years, where an inter-
mittent civil war was still being fought, and where bandits held
sway in the wilder regions.

"When we arrived at last at Miyamoto's new home in Ngari,
the next training phase began. For me, it was short-lived. Only
after our exhausting travels halfway around the world and after
having risked life and limb for months, he informed us he would
take on only one disciple. Shigeru and I were in competition.
After enduring one ordeal after another, he and I had come to
rely on one another completely and to trust one another with our
lives. To be told we would be separated, that only one of us
would receive the training while the other would be sent away...
it was cruel.

"Still, Shigeru and I gave it our all. Fear and the instinct for
survival surmounted loyalty. I did everything I could to outpace
my friend and to impress the Master. What I could not do was
change my nature. Miyamoto wanted obedience, and the best I
could give him was half-hearted attempts at feigning subordina-
tion. Ultimately, my attitude displeased him. He chose Shigeru."

"That must have been difficult for you. Did Miyamoto at
least teleport you home?"

"No, I was shown the door and told to find my own way. I
was a million miles from anywhere and alone in a country I
didn't know at all. I soon learned, though, that my experiences
with Shigeru and Miyamoto had not been wasted. I now had the
courage to go anywhere and the skills to survive anything. I
lived by my wits as I took the scenic route home. I crossed the
Himalayas through Nepal and journeyed across the Indian
subcontinent. I traveled over the Khyber Pass and through
Allied-occupied Iran and neutral Turkey. That is where I met
my first demon—and where I met Ragnar.

"He was a burly Scandinavian nearly six-and-a-half-feet tall
with wild, unruly red hair. We noticed each other when our
paths crossed at the Grand Bazaar in Istanbul. We instantly
recognized one another as kindred souls—people whose paths
had diverged from life's conventional course. By that point, I was
adept at bluffing my way through any situation—even with a
Demon Hunter. For a brief moment, I convinced him I was one

too. I persuaded him to take me along to the Taurus Mountains. We went to Nemrut Dagi, the mountain tomb-sanctuary of the ancient ruler of the kingdom of Commagene. For my trouble and my foolhardiness, I was nearly killed by the demon Karakura. Ragnar was shocked when I was unable to produce a diabolusbane. It was the first of many times he saved my life. He was livid that I had risked his life as well as my own. Yet he was impressed by my audacity. We traveled together until the end of the war.

"He taught me many skills, but inevitably, the day came when he said I needed to be trained by a proper Master. He told me to find one and then look for him again—after I had earned my diabolusbane. He swore to me, once I had done that, we could travel together again. Years later, when our paths crossed again, he kept his word. We traveled many miles side by side, the two of us. We were the best of friends."

"And something more?"

"I'll not say more—except that, in our own strange way, we were happy. No demon was a match for us. At least not until that terrible day in the Nullarbor."

Izanami fell silent, but Sapphire was keen to hear more.

"After he sent you away, did you go back to Canada?"

"Yes. I knew of only one other Master, so I went back to British Columbia to seek Tsuru. After a few weeks of stowing away on freighters, crossing the Atlantic, and riding the rails across the States, I was back in British Columbia. I had returned as someone completely different."

"Did you see your family?"

"No. They weren't there anymore. Near the end of the war, the government gave interned Japanese-Canadians a choice of being deported to Japan or moving to eastern Canada. At first my family chose deportation, but once the war ended with the bombings of Hiroshima and Nagasaki and they had learned of the conditions there, they changed their minds. Eventually, the government allowed them to resettle in Ontario where they became farm laborers.

"I thought about making the journey east, but I couldn't bring myself to go. I learned from the Nilsens that my parents thought I had died. They had a funeral for me. Somehow it was just easier to let them continue believing it. I was eager to begin my training, and I thought that I could always go see them later and let them know I was alive. The problem was that, the more time passed, the more difficult was the prospect of seeing them and explaining why I had stayed away so long. I'm not sure they would have recognized me as their daughter. I had changed too much."

"It's funny, but…"

"Yes?"

"You always make a point of letting people know you're Canadian. I can't imagine how you feel about your country after what it did to you and your family."

"The country didn't do it to us. It was the government of the time. After Pearl Harbor and because of the war in general, there was paranoia. I was born and grew up a Canadian—and nothing will ever change that. It will always be my country. Yes, it was rotten that we were the ones locked up and whose lives were devastated, but you know what? If the situation had been reversed, I might have done the same thing to someone else. I've always had a distrusting nature. I understand distrust. What I never understood was the fear. Yet I know it was real. Fear can make people do things they wouldn't normally."

Sapphire tightened her arms around Izanami.

"Life isn't fair," said the Canadian, "and we don't do ourselves any favors by trying to pretend that it's meant to be."

"Did you ever see Lars-Erik again?"

"Lars-Erik became a zombie."

"What? Really? One of the living dead?"

"That's what conscripts were called by volunteers in the Canadian military. They were looked down on because they waited to be drafted instead of volunteering at the beginning. Canada's troops were all volunteers early in the war. Conscription only began after Pearl Harbor. While we were interned, Lars-Erik was called up for Home Defence Duty. In the final months of the war, he was among the conscripts sent to fight in Europe. All I know about him after that is that he was reported missing in northwest Germany."

"I'm sorry."

"Those are the kind of stories I have. The kind that make people sorry. As you know, I did find Tsuru. She took me in and trained me—at least until my attitude annoyed her too. I learned a lot from her, and I did earn my diabolusbane. She taught me that my encounter with Karakura at Nemrut Dagi had extended my natural life. She said every encounter with a demon would expose me to the energy of the Netherworld. I learned I would eventually outlive everyone I knew."

"Did you ever see Shigeru again?"

"Yes. After his training with Miyamoto, he too became a Demon Hunter. You've probably heard of him. He took the name Momotaro."

"Momotaro? You mean, the same Momotaro who...? I... I'm so sorry."

"Yes, the same Momotaro who fell on the shores of Lake Rakshastal. The hunter who perished, abandoned and alone, at the hands of the demon T'an-mo. Another story with no happy ending. Please don't be sorry. I'm not. Life is a game of cards. You can't choose what hand you're dealt. Only how well you play it..."

"Thank you, Chiharu. I can't believe it's taken this long to hear these stories. I don't want to stop, but I'm afraid I can't stay awake any longer."

"It's okay," said Izanami, stroking her hair. "You need your rest. We both do. I'm glad my stories have put you to sleep. At least they're good for something."

"Don't say that. I feel so close to..."

Izanami knew from her breathing that sleep had overtaken her. Her slumber was already deep. Soon the Canadian too was dozing. As she nodded off, she thought she might have heard something, but the constant drone of the plane's engines obscured it.

She had no idea how long she had been asleep when she jerked awake. Koschei stood over her with a face so dour it could only be a Russian's.

"There's a problem," he said evenly.

She sat up.

"Is that blood? What happened? Are you injured?"

"It's not my blood, but I regret overcoming my aversion to aircraft. Come to the cockpit."

Sapphire was still asleep, and Izanami did not disturb her. She got up and followed Koschei. Chad was sprawled against the plane's dashboard. There was blood everywhere.

"What on earth happened, Koschei?"

The Russian pulled Chad's head up by the hair and leaned him back in his seat. A large knife was embedded in the center of his chest.

"Did you do this? What…?"

"Do you really think I would kill the only person aboard who can fly the plane? He did this to himself."

"What? Why? Couldn't you stop him?"

"He was busy at the controls and stopped talking. Not wanting to disturb his concentration, I distracted myself by looking outside. Suddenly, he screamed, 'Glory to Balor!' as he struck the control panel repeatedly with that hammer there on the floor. I'm surprised you didn't hear it. I released my seatbelt as fast as I could, but he had already dropped the hammer and was holding the knife in his hands. I have no idea where he took it from. Before I could do anything, he had plunged it into his own chest. I was taken completely by surprise."

"He must have planned this. He sacrificed himself to kill us along with him. Or was he sincere in the beginning and then had a change of heart?"

"Does it matter? What are we going to do, Izanami?"

"The plane is cruising at a constant altitude. It must be on automatic pilot. Does that mean we'll just continue to cruise until we run out of fuel? We'll have to find a way to land the plane ourselves."

"He's done serious damage to the controls. Even if one of us knew how to fly the plane, I'm not sure it would be possible."

"I better wake Sapphire."

"Do you think she knows how to fly a plane?"

"No, but she needs to know what's going on. Who knows? Maybe she learned something in one of her college courses that could help us."

Izanami led a drowsy Sapphire into the cockpit. She took a look around and said, "This isn't good, is it?"

"Do you think," asked Koschei, "there's any chance of us landing the plane?"

With her hand, Sapphire wiped some of the blood from the control panel's large screen and studied the display.

"I'm not going to pretend I know anything about how this works, but it looks to me like he entered a flight path into the computer. It cycles through different views of a map, and when that particular one comes up, it looks like the plane's going to circle that mountain several times and then land on the side of the mountain."

"You mean, crash," said Koschei.

"Yeah, probably crash. Planes can't land on mountainsides, can they?"

Izanami wiped more of the blood streaks from the display and peered at the small text labels.

"It says Licancabur. We're going to crash into the volcano where everyone has been gathering."

"So was he working for or against Alaric? Did he make us part of a kamikaze attack on the Zen'ei?"

"Not if he was yelling 'Glory to Balor' when he did this," said Izanami. "I'd say he just wanted to orchestrate some spectacular display to awe the masses who have gathered—and eliminate us in the process."

Sapphire continued to examine the controls.

"The radio's dead. We won't be getting help from any nearby air traffic controllers."

"So what will we do?" asked Koschei. "Sapphire, can you teleport us out of here?"

"I... I don't know. I've never attempted it from within a moving craft before, and I still feel drained."

"Drained? Our lives are at stake—not to mention the entire world. Is it not worth some fatigue to at least try?"

"Leave her alone, Koschei," said Izanami.

"Leave her alone? You're definitely not the Izanami I knew. She never tolerated weakness—in herself or in anyone else. You've become soft."

"You're not helping, Koschei. Let's use the time left to think of ideas—and not argue."

"He's right, Chi-Chi. I need to gather my strength and at least try. There's at least some chance I'll succeed. We and the world have no chance if I don't try."

"Before you do that," said Izanami, "let me try something else."

"What's that?" said Sapphire. "Are you going to use the Grisial to bring back Charles Lindbergh or Amelia Earhart?"

"I did think about that, but this plane may be too modern for them. Besides, from the looks of that dashboard, I don't know if any pilot could get us out of this."

"Do you feel that?" said Koschei. "I think the plane is banking. I see a mountain ahead of us. We must be beginning our first circle around the volcano. What about parachutes? They must have parachutes, right?"

"At this altitude. That'd be suicide. Just keep quiet for a minute, and let me try my idea. If it doesn't work, then Sapphire can try teleporting if she wants to."

Sapphire and Koschei watched Izanami close her eyes and go into a trance. They wondered what she was up to. Sapphire returned to her seat.

Izanami had entered a dream state. The constant sound of the plane's engines melted away, and she was enveloped in silence. She found herself walking through a dark mist. She felt neither cold nor warm. She was conscious of not breathing and of not needing to breathe. Though she stepped forward, there was no sensation of movement. Before her, the mists parted to reveal the silhouette of a man. She stopped, and he took a step toward her. As if stepping out of a shadow, his face was revealed. It was Hadrian.

"I've been trying to reach you."

His lips did not move. His voice was in her head.

"You've been blocking me."

"Of course, I've been blocking you. I didn't want you to know what we were up to, where we were. I'd have been a fool not to block you."

"You don't trust me?"

"Seriously? Of course, I don't trust you. What kind of fool do you think I am? You took the information you wanted from my mind. You took the boy. You disappeared. You betrayed us."

"Do you really believe that?"

"Don't play games, Necromant. You sold us out. The facts speak for themselves."

"Then why have you reached out to me now?"

"I want to make a bargain. Three of us are in a plane that is about to crash. I'm afraid Sapphire may be too weak to teleport us. Can you help us?"

"If you think I'm a villain, why bother asking?"

"Maybe I have something you want."

"What would that be?"

"I have the Grisial."

"Why would I want the Grisial?"

"I heard you say you wanted it, and when you disappeared, I saw you holding an object just like it. Perhaps you want this one as well."

The Necromant's soft laughter echoed in her head.

"Demon Hunter, do you believe I covet the Grisial hanging from your neck? Do you think I have thrown in my lot with Alaric and Balor? What's the real reason we are having this conversation?"

"For the reason I said."

"And...?"

"And because, against my better judgment, I have no choice but to trust you—in spite of everything."

"No choice?"

"We are out of options. And..."

"Go on."

"I have been in your mind. You have been in mine. Our knowledge of each other is deeper, more intimate than I have ever experienced with another human being. I hate to admit it, but it's true. Everything I know and sense about you tells me that you are trustworthy—despite all the evidence to the contrary. Unless you have some way of deceiving me down to our innermost thoughts, I have to believe you have a good reason for what you have done."

"That was not easy for you to admit."

"No, it wasn't. I can't shake the feeling that I've been set up. Trust is difficult for me. I can't afford to get this wrong. Too much depends on it."

"You *can* trust me. You were right to make contact. I'm sorry there's been no opportunity to explain things to you."

"You better make an opportunity because you owe me an explanation. First, tell me the boy is safe."

"The boy is safe."

"Why did you take him?"

"Time is short. We need to get you and the others out of harm's way. Tell me your location."

"We're circling the Licancabur volcano. We'll crash into it soon."

"This won't be easy. I won't pretend to understand the type of craft you are in, and assisting you while it is in motion is next to impossible. Your only chance is that I can teleport myself while we maintain our mental connection. We must not lose it, no matter what. Do you think you can do that?"

"I... I think so. I'll do my best."

"Not to make this any more difficult for you, but if we cannot maintain the connection, it will likely result in all our deaths."

"Not helping, Necromant."

"Sorry. Stand by for whatever comes next."

Izanami concentrated more urgently than she ever had before. She felt the strain through her entire body. The worst of it was in her head. She felt it would explode. The stress of the situation and the throbbing in her temples became unbearable. She blacked out momentarily but quickly regained alertness. She hoped the lapse would not be catastrophic, but something was now different. She opened her eyes. She saw the blood-spattered cockpit and was revolted by it all over again. The engine's noise had again filled her ears. Koschei stared at her.

"Well?" he said.

"I don't know."

"You don't know? What did you do? What was your plan? Have you given up?"

"Of course, I haven't given up. We have to hope the Necromant can help us."

"The Necromant? You communicated with him? Was that wise? Old friend, I fear you may have just doomed us."

There was a gust of wind, and the temperature in the cockpit dropped. As if stepping from behind an invisible screen, Hadrian stood before them, staff in hand.

"You!" shouted the Russian.

Without a moment's hesitation, Koschei swung his arm at him, pounding the side of his head with his fist. Caught by surprise, the Necromant took the blow's full force. He dropped the staff and crumpled to the floor.

24

The Marble Cave

"WHAT HAPPENED?" CRIED Sapphire, rushing to the cockpit. "What's he doing here?"

Izanami had dropped to her knees.

"We have to revive him. He was trying to help us."

Koschei rubbed his fist with satisfaction.

"Do you believe that? You've become gullible, my friend. Have you forgotten that he deserted us in Bialowieza, that he took Peter?"

"No, I haven't forgotten, but everything now depends on his reasons for what he did."

"This is the last thing I expected," said Sapphire. "Didn't you just tell me a story explaining how you came to be so distrustful? Of all of us, you were the most wary of Hadrian. Why the change of heart?"

"Because I... know him. As much as it goes against my nature, I'm tired of fighting the desire to trust him. I've been in his mind. I don't know all his secrets, but I do have a sense of his character. Besides, we have no alternative."

The Russian was unconvinced. "I say we open a door and toss him out."

"Talk sense, Koschei. We have to get the boy back, don't we? Besides, Hadrian may be our only hope of getting off this plane—if we can revive him."

Sapphire looked her straight in the eyes.

"You trust him, Chiharu?"

She nodded.

"Okay," said Sapphire, "Then Koschei and I have to trust *you*. I'll try to wake him."

Izanami withdrew and let Sapphire take her place next to the fallen man. She pressed her forefingers against his temples and closed her eyes. After a full minute had passed, she opened her eyes.

"My God, Koschei, you don't know your own strength. You could have killed him."

"I thought we were under attack," grumbled the Russian.

Hadrian opened his eyes and blinked several times. He sat up.

"I didn't anticipate that—but I suppose I should have."

"Are you... okay?" asked the Russian with the barest hint of contrition.

The floor tilted downward. Through the cockpit's windshield they saw the distant landscape's horizon disappear upwards. The whine of the engines grew louder.

"How long was I unconscious?" gasped Hadrian, using his staff as an aid to stand.

"Not long," said an agitated Izanami, "and yet perhaps too long."

She stared out the windshield. The mountainside rushed toward them. The Necromant turned to see for himself.

"This is not ideal," he muttered. "I'd want more time. Quickly! Let us all take hands—without delay."

They did as they were told. Within moments all went dark. Heat swept over them as they were tossed about the inky murk. Izanami and Koschei momentarily lost consciousness. Hadrian and Sapphire blacked out completely.

"Where the devil are we?" wondered the Russian, forcing his mind to focus.

As far as they could tell, they were in a cave. A rough iron bracket embedded in the cave's wall held a candle. It was the only light source.

"We're not dead," said Izanami. "At least as far as I can tell. That's good enough for the moment."

"Are they okay?" asked Koschei, looking at the others on the ground.

"I think they must..."

She froze, having sensed another presence. She turned to see a shadow flit behind a large rock. The angle of the candle's light exaggerated its size. It was only a small figure that rushed toward her.

"Chiharu!"

"Peter! Thank God you're here. Are you okay? Did anyone hurt you?"

The boy was too excited for words. After giving Izanami a forceful hug, he did the same to Koschei. Finally, he found his tongue.

"I'm so glad you're here. I'm glad we're all together again."

Hadrian sat up slowly.

"That was quite a blow you gave me, Koschei. You're lucky I recovered well enough to remove us from that flying vessel in time."

"It's called an airplane, Necromant. For such a renowned holder of knowledge, you have some odd gaps in your vocabulary. We need answers from you—and they had better be good."

Izanami knelt by Sapphire. She was concerned that she had not yet wakened.

"Lola? Are you okay? Please don't do this to me."

Several anxious minutes passed. Sapphire opened her eyes slightly and managed a faint smile.

"When all of this is over, I'm going to sleep for a week."

Izanami said nothing. There wasn't time.

"Where are we?" demanded the Russian.

"Patagonia. We're in a system of marble caves on the Chile-Argentina border. It's impossible for even the most skilled Mage to locate us here. Marble is notorious for being resistant to remote viewing."

"How near are we to the volcano?" asked Koschei.

"About 1,600 miles."

"So far away?"

"We wouldn't want to be any closer. Not until we have organized ourselves for a proper assault. Don't worry, when the time comes, Sapphire and I shall make little work of the distance between here and the volcano."

Despite the Necromant's confident tone, Izanami fretted. She looked at Sapphire and wondered how soon she would be capable of teleportation.

"What sort of assault are you talking about?" asked Koschei.

"Before we go any further," Izanami interrupted, "you have to explain something. Why did you flee with the boy?"

"He was in imminent danger. The one you call the Software Wizard has honed his remote viewing capabilities. The Zen'ei were about to launch a raid on us. Once I had absorbed the information Miyamoto planted in your mind, everything fell into place. I saw the Zen'ei's plan for incarnating Balor—just as you yourself have seen it. I learned their plans for the child in more detail. The danger was all too clear. They were about to strike. I had to take him someplace more secure without delay. There wasn't time to explain. Once he was safe, I tried desperately to communicate with you, but you blocked me."

"You tried to erase Miyamoto's information from my mind."

"I didn't. I swear it. Yes, I removed some information from your mind, but it was information about myself that you had acquired inadvertently while our minds were linked."

"Why? What are you afraid I'll learn? What are you hiding from me?"

"There are things... If you knew everything, I mean, if you knew it too soon, it would work against us. I know it's difficult to understand. You have to..."

"I know. Trust you. I'm trying, but you have no right to decide for me what I can and can't know. Not when the stakes are so high."

"This situation is unique. Believe me, I would like nothing more than to tell you the whole truth."

"Why do you have a Grisial?"

"You weren't meant to see that. I had to make sure I still had it, and I was careless."

"There's only one Grisial," said Sapphire. "How can you have it as well?"

The Necromant sighed heavily.

"This is not the moment I would have chosen to explain things to you, but I see we'll not be able to move forward until I do. You are correct, Sapphire. There is just the one Grisial."

He removed a talisman from his pocket and held it next to the identical one hanging from Izanami's neck.

"These both are the same crystal."

"You speak in riddles, Necromant," said Koschei, impatiently.

"Izanami possesses the Grisial as it exists today. I have the Grisial as it existed more than a century ago."

"It's traveled through time?" exclaimed Koschei. "But how?"

"I carried it."

"Are you saying… you're a time traveler?"

"Yes, but only in the same sense as you and Peter. I was also summoned by Izanami."

Sapphire nodded. "There has definitely been something out of place about you. Yet your deception was largely effective."

"I confess to cheating a bit. I gathered information about this era and current language usage from Izanami while our minds were connected. Obviously, there were still gaps in my knowledge."

"I knew it!" said Izanami angrily.

The Necromant continued. "The entire experience has been overwhelmingly strange to me. I have had much to learn about this future world—and in an exceedingly brief time. Not least disconcerting is the fact that it has been less than a year since I last saw Tyra Knagenhjelm. Now I find myself face-to-face with her reincarnation."

"Koschei and Peter arrived," said Izanami, "with no understanding of how they got here or awareness of having traveled through time. You were clearly well aware of the entire situation from the beginning."

"Not from the true beginning. Bidden by Tsuru, you arrived in Bialowieza to seek me out, but you inadvertently called me from the past. You were not, however, the first people I met when I found myself transported to a different time and place. The first was someone who had waited for my arrival. It was he who explained briskly what had happened and the danger that confronted the world. He told me what I must do to put things right, to avoid the end of reality. Moreover, he effected an enchantment on me that would allow me to retain my memories of all this when I eventually return to my own time."

"So that was the man I heard you speaking with," said Izanami, "that night in the forest. Who is he?"

Koschei interjected, "So you've been lying to us the whole time. Instead of telling us you were summoned like me, you made up a story to explain why you neither ate nor slept. You could have told us the truth, but you didn't. Why should we believe anything you say now?"

"My intent was not to deceive you—only to postpone the conversation we are now having. I was advised to avoid this confusion and distraction because, as you can see, it is con-suming precious time. You see, the one who spoke to me has knowledge of the future. He warned me of unintended con-sequences. He took care to shield certain information from me and advised me to do the same with you."

"And you just happened to have the Grisial in your possession when you arrived in this time?" said Koschei, suspiciously.

"Yes. That was the cosmic coincidence that may well save the universe. You see, I knew much about the Grisial long before any of this happened. Intrigued by its reputation in the old texts as a powerful talisman, I had long sought it and, in fact, had only recently located it. It was in the possession of a Mage who lay dying in Tunis. In his final days, I persuaded him to be-queath it to me. Once it was in my possession, unfortunately, there was no opportunity to study it. I was soon afterward transported to the future."

"Does it not create a paradox," said Izanami, "for a single object at two different times in its history to exist simultaneously?"

"Apparently not," said Hadrian. "A paradox will arise only if I do not carry this one back to my own time and then safeguard it for many years. That is no trivial thing. There are those—and have been for centuries—who would do anything to gain possession of it. We know that it will—or must—eventually find its way into the possession of Sapphire and then Izanami."

"The crystal you have," said Sapphire coldly, "before it comes into my hands, it will be kept by my parents. It will be the cause of their deaths."

"Yes," said Hadrian gravely, "and I expect I will be the one to hand it over to them. For that I am truly sorry."

"Now that you know what will happen, you could do things differently. You could wait longer and give it to me directly. They do not—did not—need to die."

"I understand, but surely you can see things are not so simple. I have no way of knowing under what circumstances I will give it to them or why it will happen in the moment that it does. If there were a way of preventing your parents' deaths, I would gladly do so, but since it has already happened, I have to presume it is impossible to change. Why must things happen the way they do? I have many long years ahead of me to ponder that question. I must make the right choices—if I truly have any choice at all. While I don't believe in predestination *per se*, the many coincidences that have led all of us to this point do cause me to wonder whether some unseen hand doesn't guide us."

"How can you say you don't believe in predestination?" said Izanami bitterly. "You yourself now know the future. You'll return to your own time knowing what lies ahead. You already know you'll inadvertently cause the deaths of Sapphire's parents. The future's set for you, and if it's set for you, then it must be set for all of us. What's the point of any of this? Our individual choices make no difference, do they? We think we have free will, but everything happens the way it has to, regardless. We're mere slaves to destiny."

"Future knowledge is my unique burden," said Hadrian. "You and Sapphire have no idea of what lies ahead of you. Nor will Koschei and Peter since, when they return to their own times, they will have no memory of any of this. The point is that the future *can* be changed. Otherwise, reality would not now be on the verge of dissolving. If any of these instances of temporal dislocation should result in a paradox, the world will end. A paradox would not be possible if free will did not exist. Rest assured, your future is entirely up to you. None of that matters right now, does it? Our immediate concern is to do whatever necessary to ensure there *is* a future."

"You didn't tell us who the man was that you met in the forest," said Sapphire. "Who was he? How did he know in advance that you would appear at that exact moment in that precise place?"

"Can't you guess?" smiled Hadrian. "But we've distracted ourselves long enough with these questions for now. With any luck, we'll be able to discuss them at length later. For now, time is short. We have to stop Balor's incarnation by going to Licancabur. Can anyone tell me precisely when the solstice occurs?"

"Don't you know? You're the Necromant," said Izanami. "Can't you just use magic or something to calculate it?"

"If I were in my own time, I would consult an almanac. Otherwise, one must take measurements of a gnomon's shadow over a period time. Clearly, we don't have time for that."

"I'd estimate that, at this point, the solstice is about thirty-six hours away. We saw a countdown clock for it on a television screen in London."

"We need to be as precise as possible."

"Once we're out of this cave and I can get a cell signal," said Sapphire, "I can stream the news channel Izanami's talking about—or just do a web search for it."

"Very well," said Hadrian. "It is critical that we know exactly how much time we have to complete our assault."

"Let me ask again," said Koschei. "What sort of assault are you talking about?"

"We must penetrate the main cave deep within the volcano."

"Within the volcano?"

"There is a series of caves—unknown to the world at large— deep within the mountain. That's where the Grisial came from. We must take it back." He turned to Izanami. "But you know that already, don't you?"

"So, Licancabur is the mountain where the Grisial was made. That's where it all began."

"And where it shall end," said the Necromant.

"Since the two of you are now experts on volcanos," said Koschei, "let me ask a pertinent question. This volcano isn't active, is it?"

"No need for worry," smiled Hadrian, "It's dormant. It's been thousands of years since its last eruption."

"So, it must be well overdue," muttered the Russian.

"It is revered as a holy mountain by the Atacameños. They have always been aware of its significance."

"What must we do with the Grisial," asked Sapphire, "once we take it back to the mountain?"

"The volcano is the weak link between the physical world and the realm of the Old Ones. It's where the two planes of existence have always brushed up against each other. When the magma first flowed inside it, it brimmed with the power of Clíodhna's energy. It acted as a sort of cauterization of the physical world's weakest point. Over time, it has cooled, and its power has weakened. As the Grisial is infused with a remnant of her power, it can be used as an igniter to revive that protective energy. We only need to take it to the right place at the right time. Then the world will be protected for another eon."

"Yes," said Sapphire, "as I hear you say it, I know it's all true. I have the faintest memories of what occurred all those ages ago, but they're only echoes. If I think about it too much, it overwhelms me. No human being was ever meant to bear and sustain Clíodhna's knowledge."

"Does Sapphire herself," asked Koschei, "not have the power to ignite the magma?"

"No," said Hadrian. "It's only Clíodhna's consciousness that resides in Sapphire. Physically, she is no different than any other mortal. The only remnant of her original power lies locked in the Grisial."

"And why must there be an assault?" said Koschei. "Can you not teleport to the cave's interior and do what needs to be done before anyone's the wiser?"

"Neither I nor anyone else can teleport safely to the interior of a mountain. The odds would be overwhelming of materializing within the mountain itself."

"You managed to teleport to the interior of a moving aircraft."

"That was only possible because of the link I formed with Izanami."

"You teleported us to this cave we're in."

"You really do enjoy trying to catch me out, don't you, Koschei? I could teleport here because I had been here before. And only after a long trek through labyrinthine passageways. Neither of the cases you cite apply to the interior of Licancabur. The only way to accomplish what needs to be done is to teleport to the cave system's entrance and enter from there. We can be certain it will be well guarded. We shall have to fight our way in."

"If we had known all of this sooner," said Izanami glumly, "we could have taken the Grisial back to its place of origin before any of this started and avoided having to fight at all."

"We only know what we know when we know it," said Hadrian. "We must make the best of where we find ourselves now. Alaric and the Zen'ei will be bound and determined to stop us, and I fear the odds are against us. They have an army of so-called Legionnaires on their side. We are only four."

"Five!"

Peter, who had been all but forgotten by the others, stepped forward determinedly.

Hadrian smiled. "I admire your spirit, boy, but there is no way you will join us in the battle. Quite apart from your age and your size, you above all of us must survive."

"Four are not enough," said Izanami. "It's certain suicide. I know you don't want me to use the Grisial again. I understand the risk of more meddling with time, but I don't see any other choice. I'm going to summon more help."

"Izanami!" shouted the Necromant. "No!"

His objection went unheeded. Already her eyes had closed. She grasped the crystal. As she concentrated on it, the talisman glowed. The others felt its mystical power. From the cave's shadows stepped three strapping men. Izanami opened her eyes and gasped. Somehow she had done what should have been impossible. She did not know which of them to hug first. Koschei had no such dilemma.

"Callan! It's not possible."

He threw his arms around the broad-shouldered man with obsidian skin and fierce mahogany eyes. While his bald pate was smooth, his cheeks were blemished by old, black scars. The Russian's heartfelt embrace startled him.

"Koschei! What manner of enchantment is this? How do I come to be here?"

The Russian could only stare.

"You behave strangely, my friend, as if it weren't scarcely a fortnight since we last saw one another."

"It's just that the circumstances are most unusual. We find ourselves in the gravest of situations, my friend. You and I have been summoned to help. Forgive me. It's... strange to see you again this way."

"I see Izanami's here too. And is that Ragnar? Strange. I was certain I had heard that he..."

Izanami had rushed to Ragnar and given him a quick hug. She stepped back. She trembled for all to see, and it embarrassed her.

"It's good to see you again, my friend," she said in the calmest voice she could muster.

"Izanami! As I live and breathe! I have the same question as Callan. How did we come to be here? This is powerful sorcery indeed."

"Chiharu?"

The third man stared at her with deep black eyes. His ebon hair flowed to his shoulders. Tufts of a beard and mustache clung to an otherwise smooth and youthful face.

"What is going on?"

"Is that the only name you know me by, Momotaro?"

"Do you have any other? How have you learned my new name?"

"I am a Demon Hunter too. I'm now called Izanami. I know this is confusing, but please trust me. We need your help in a battle."

"Say," whispered Callan to Koschei, "is that really Momotaro? How can this be? Everyone knows what happened at Rakshastal."

"Sorry, old friend, I must echo Izanami's plea that you help us in our fight with an abundance of trust and a deficit of curiosity. We are in exceedingly strange times."

As the new arrivals did their best to sort through their confusion, Sapphire put her hand on Izanami's shoulder.

"What have you done, Chi-Chi? This could go terribly wrong if anything happens to any of them."

"We won't stand a chance without them," said Izanami. "I had to take the risk."

"And perhaps get an opportunity for some proper farewells in the process? I suppose it could have been worse. At least you summoned only three."

"No," she said. "I summoned four. I called for Orpheus as well, but he's not here. Apparently, there are limits to the Grisial's power. As much as I would have liked to see him one more time, it appears we will have to prevail without the aid of the most renowned Demon Hunter."

HADRIAN FELT THE urgency. Time was short, and delay would mean disaster. Yet now he found himself in the middle of a sudden and unexpected reunion of comrades in arms. He observed as they tried to understand by what supernatural power they had been pulled from their normal lives. Each had his questions, and every answer they received resulted in more questions.

Sapphire and Peter also watched the others in fascination. Sapphire was acquainted with the newcomers only by their reputations. None of them knew her. She was mesmerized by Izanami's conversation with Momotaro. Only hours before had she learned of her companion's connection to the young Demon Hunter. Now here he was in the flesh. She saw a softness in Izanami's eyes.

"Are they all really Demon Hunters?" asked the wide-eyed boy.

"Yes," said Sapphire. "They are legends. The sort about which one says, we'll never see their like again. Clearly, the word 'never' has little relevance when the supernatural is involved."

"I must take your word for their worthiness," said Hadrian impatiently. "I know none of them. From my perspective, they are all phantoms waiting to be born." He sighed heavily. "We can ill afford time for this distraction. Summoning them was a mistake, but there's no undoing it now. We must make the best of it."

He pounded his staff on the cave's floor. A low boom echoed through the cavern, and for a few moments the area around

Hadrian lit up brightly. All conversation ceased, and the Demon Hunters turned their attention toward the Necromant.

"Esteemed friends, I apologize for the confusing situation, but time is now precious. As you have been hearing, a critical battle is at hand. We need your help."

"And who, may I ask, are you?" shouted Ragnar.

"I am called Hadrian."

"Hadrian the Necromant?" said Ragnar. "What are you playing at, chancer? I met Hadrian once, and you are not he. You are younger than myself. Hadrian is old and haggard."

"Haggard? Really? Just out of curiosity, when you met him, what did he say to you?"

Ragnar fell silent. As he searched his memory, the others waited for his answer. A strange look came over him.

"It was years ago. He... he berated me. He claimed that I had once called him haggard to his face... even though I had never..." His voice trailed off.

"My friends," said the Necromant, "we may be now in the end times. The laws of nature are fraying at the edges. Time is becoming unstuck. We are meeting one another outside of any natural chronology. As confusing as it is, I must ask all of you to put aside your puzzlement and curiosity to focus on the task at hand. You all know Izanami. She is the bearer of a talisman crucial to the world's survival. She and it must be delivered to the heart of a mountain more than a thousand miles from here. Sapphire and I can take us as far as the mouth of the mountain's cave, but from that point onward we must fight—all the way to the center of the mountain."

"Who is this Sapphire?" called out Callan.

"If the stakes of this battle are so high," demanded Ragnar, "then why is Orpheus not here? Surely, any significant gathering of Demon Hunters should include him."

With newfound energy, Sapphire stepped forward and shouted.

"You want to know who I am? In another life I was the Demon Hunter Eurydice. In this life I am the Demon Hunter Sapphire, last disciple of Orpheus and now partner of Izanami. I have been to the Netherworld twice—and I escaped the Fiend's clutches both times. Orpheus is gone forever. In his absence, Izanami and I are here. That is all you need to know. For years I have heard the accounts of your battles and your deeds. I am grateful and impressed to be in your company. If you are as good as your reputations, you will waste no more time and do as Hadrian asks."

Several moments passed. Ragnar broke the silence.

"I, for one, am with you. Lead the way, Necromant. What the hell. This is probably only a dream anyway."

Callan and Momotaro concurred. None would tolerate appearing less ready for battle than the others. Momotaro gazed at Izanami, whose eyes were fixed on Sapphire. She was so different from the young girl he had led out of a Canadian internment camp years earlier. He hoped there would be time to hear her stories, to become reacquainted.

Izanami was relieved to see Sapphire's renewed vitality. She had risen to the moment and recovered her spirit when it was needed. That made it easier to face the battle.

"How did you become the bearer of this magic crystal, my friend?"

Izanami had forgotten Ragnar was at her side. He saw she was distracted.

"You need not answer now. I will look forward to the story after the battle."

"It's so good to see you again, Ragnar. You can't imagine how much I... Look, be careful out there today."

"There are many traits that make a good Demon Hunter, Izanami, but being careful is not one of them."

"This battle is different. It's important that none of you fall."

"That does not sound like you, Izanami. How many times did you charge ahead of me toward a hellion, crying, 'It's a good day to die!'?"

"That was the foolishness of youth, Ragnar. I'm a lot older and a bit wiser. I know the truth now. There is no good day to die."

"This is the plan," said Hadrian, taking back control of the gathering. "Sapphire and I will teleport us all to a hill called Quimal. It has a clear line of sight toward the volcano

Licancabur. From that distance I will be able to employ remote viewing to assess the Zen'ei's numbers and positions and judge where precisely to teleport us for the push toward the caves. Any questions?"

"I have spent time in the Atacama Desert," said Callan. "Does this perhaps bear some relation to the ancient legend of Licancabur, Quimal, and Juriques?"

"It is no coincidence. The winter solstice is mere hours away. That is when Licancabur's shadow will extend the full distance across the salt flat to Quimal. That is the moment of greatest danger—when the incarnation of Balor is meant to take place. That is why we must hurry. We must go as soon as I do one more thing."

Hadrian asked Peter to find a comfortable spot against the cave wall, one that was sheltered from the cavern's occasional cold drafts.

"Are you content enough to sit here awhile alone, boy?"

"For how long?"

"Not long, I hope, but I cannot promise. Time will pass slowly without company, but do not fret if we are gone a long time. You have no need for food or sleep. There's nothing here to harm you. You are safe from the prying eyes of Mages and sorcerers. You can survive here indefinitely—even if we don't return."

The boy nodded solemnly. Koschei was grateful he did not ask more questions.

"I'm sorry to be so much trouble, Hadrian."

"You did not choose to be where you are in this moment. None of us did. It doesn't matter. All that counts now is how well we all play our parts. You have perhaps the most difficult role of all—to sit and wait alone. If fortune is on our side, I shall see you again soon, child, and we will celebrate our victory."

Hadrian asked the six Demon Hunters to join him in standing in a circle. To his right was Izanami. To her right was Sapphire. They joined hands.

"It is unheard of to teleport so many people at one time," explained Hadrian, "but I have every confidence we will achieve such a feat today. Sapphire and I will effect the teleportation jointly, joining our minds through Izanami who has established a mental link with both of us."

"What is the risk if something should go wrong?" asked Momotaro.

The Necromant smiled thinly. "No worse than if we fail to prevent Balor's incarnation."

From his location several yards away, Peter shivered as he hunkered down. The temperature in the cave had dropped suddenly. He watched the others' forms become blurred until they vanished altogether. He felt as if every human being in the entire world had disappeared with them. The cave's shadows loomed ominously. The silence felt like a threat.

The seven found themselves standing atop a barren, rocky hill. After the darkness of the cave, their eyes were now blinded by the bright sun. From their vantage point, the bare, arid landscape extended vast miles before them. Below them the gray-brown land was marked by ranges of ragged hills alternating with dry valleys. It was devoid of vegetation except for tufts of sagebrush peaking out from under some of the rocks. A few white clouds floated in the sky, causing large, oddly shaped black shadows to move swiftly across the ground. The sun blazed above, but they were chilled by a frosty wind.

On the far horizon was a bare, rugged mountain range. The tallest peak was striking for the perfect symmetry of its cone, covered at the top in white. To its right and farther away was a lower peak with a jagged crown. The two mountains made for a comparison of a classic stratovolcano before and after a major eruption.

"Despite the brightness of the sun," said Momotaro, "the breeze is icy cold."

"This is winter in this part of the world," said Hadrian. "Today is the shortest day of the year. If it were December, we'd be roasting all right. Precious little rain or snow falls anywhere in this region."

"It wasn't that long ago," said Izanami, "that Sapphire and I were there."

She pointed toward the snow-covered peak.

"That is where we confronted the demon Merihim. We were lucky to escape with our lives. I never intended to come back."

Ragnar took a breath. "The air is thin, isn't it?"

"Yes," said Momotaro, "it is like being back in the Himalayas."

"That was part of the challenge in fighting Merihim," said Sapphire. "Though we are only about one-hundred miles from the ocean, the desert has a high elevation. That volcano is only a few hundred feet shorter than Mount Denali in Alaska. Where we stand on this hill is only a few hundred feet lower than Mount Blanc in Europe."

Momotaro smiled at Izanami. "Your friend is certainly full of information."

"Yes, she's college-educated."

Koschei and Callan were not part of the conversation. Having climbed onto a large rock for a better view, they were having their own chat.

"What was the legend you spoke of?" asked the Russian.

"In the Atacameño tradition, those two volcanos, Licancabur and Juriques, were brothers, princes, and warriors. They were also rivals for the hand of Quimal, the hill where we now stand. In a fit of jealousy, Licancabur beheaded Juriques. For his punishment, Quimal was taken from him. That is why he can only see her at this distance. Once a year, they are allowed to touch. On the winter solstice his shadow extends all the way to this point."

"Callan, I am grateful we have this chance to fight side-by-side one more time."

"I'm confident we both have many more battles ahead of us, my friend."

"This one is unlike any other we have fought before. The stakes are enormous."

"Talk like that can be dangerous."

"Don't misunderstand. My resolve is not weakening. Still, I would regret it if either of us were to fall and I had left certain things unsaid."

"Have you become sentimental, old friend?"

"I know it is not our way to speak of such things, but I want you to know…"

"I'm not sure I want to hear this, Koschei."

"Please listen, Callan. It's important."

Callan exhaled slowly. "This is about the night in Sevastopol, isn't it?"

"What?"

"I told you. That was a one-off. We said we'd never speak of it again."

"No, you misunderstand. I haven't thought of that night in years. I'd all but forgotten it."

"Years? Forgotten? It was only two weeks ago."

"Well, for me it happened years ago."

"This is confusing."

"It is indeed. What I'm trying to say is that, since I last saw you I've had much time to reflect on our friendship. The battles we fought at one another's side. You saved my life more than once, you know."

"And you mine."

"But I never told you how much your friendship means to me. How much I… cherish it."

Callan stared at the ground. "I'm not certain this is suitable talk when we are about to go into battle. We must be girded for whatever carnage may come. Not softened by sentiment."

He cleared his throat.

"But for what it's worth, I love you too, Koschei. Like a brother, I mean."

"Yes, that's what I mean too, Callan. I had four sisters but no brother. You were the brother I never had."

They saw that the others had gathered around Hadrian. They clapped each other heartily on the back and, with stoic faces, joined them.

"I have surveyed the situation by means of remote viewing," said Hadrian. "The news is not good. Thousands upon thousands have gathered at the base of the mountain."

"Really?" said Momotaro. "I can't see any of them from here."

"Believe me, they are there. If we were closer, you would see them teeming for miles in every direction. It's a massive gathering that makes it impossible to teleport close to the cave entrance. No matter where we would materialize, the odds would be overwhelming that we would land in space occupied by people. Nor is that the only problem. The entrance is guarded by a heavily armed company of Mercenaries. Clearly, they have anticipated our aim and have spared no resources to stop us."

The Necromant gave the others a few moments to reflect before continuing.

"Unfortunately, we will be required to fight our way through the crowd over considerable distance to reach our goal. While I do not possess the skills or experience of a warrior, my powers should be of use in clearing the path through the multitude."

"That's your plan?" said Koschei. "I find it flawed. We know Alaric has Mages at his disposal. Any use of your powers will attract their attention and draw them on us. I say we do this the old-fashioned way."

"Koschei's right," said Callan. "There is no need for all six of us to run the gauntlet to the caves. We'll all have tired ourselves out. Let no more than two or three of us do it. Once there, we can clear a space so that you and the others can teleport safely."

"The two of you sound awfully confident," said Hadrian, "that so few could do so much successfully."

"Look," said Callan. "These are not demons we'll be fighting. If you're correct, Necromant, we will not have to confront any real warriors until the end. By the time we meet them, the rest of you will have joined us. A pair of Demon Hunters are more than sufficient for the initial assault."

"So you two will do it then?" said Hadrian.

"Three," said Izanami. "I'll go with them. No matter how much space we manage to clear among the crowd, it will still be relatively small. You and I will need to be linked mentally, Hadrian, to ensure you arrive at the precise spot."

"I should go as well," said Ragnar.

"No," said Izanami. "That defeats the purpose. The fewer who go first, the better for the main battle. We need some to save themselves for later."

"So we are agreed," said the Necromant. "It's a sound plan, though not without risks. Remember, none of you is expendable.

If anything should happen to Koschei or Callan, there would be a temporal paradox. As the Grisial's bearer, Izanami is indispensable."

"The same can be said of you, Hadrian," added Izanami. "Your death would also cause a paradox. Furthermore, you must survive to return to your own time and keep the Grisial safe for its ultimate purpose. The survival of everyone is absolutely necessary."

"Not everyone," said Sapphire. "Of all of us, I alone am expendable."

"That's not true," protested Izanami.

"Yes, it is. My death would not cause a temporal paradox. As far as putting an end to Balor's plan, you have what you require in the Grisial. Clearly, if there's a sacrifice to be made today, you must let me be the one to make it."

"You're the most crucial of all. You're Clíodhna. It's your existence that has preserved this world for eons."

"Clíodhna is immortal. This body isn't. You shouldn't confuse the two."

"Don't talk like that," said Izanami angrily. "You're… indispensable… to me."

"I am only stating facts. Aren't you the one who's always said sentimentality is a weakness for Demon Hunters?"

Izanami's face burned. She knew Sapphire was right, but she refused to concede. The others stood awkwardly until Hadrian broke the silence.

"I will not instruct Demon Hunters on their own code or how to follow it. We all know what must be done. For what it may be worth, I agree with Izanami. We are all indispensable—if not all for the same reason. Unfortunately, being necessary is no guarantee of survival. Now, if the three of you are ready, I will take you to the edge of the crowds so that you may begin your foray toward the mountain."

The Necromant and the three Demon Hunters joined hands. As they vanished, the temperature atop the hill dropped as an icy gust swept over Sapphire, Ragnar, and Momotaro.

"I should have gone with them," said the young man.

"No, this is a good plan," said Sapphire. "There will be a greater chance of success if we and the Necromant are fresh when we join the battle. Those three will have no trouble handling the first part of the assault."

Momotaro nodded and said nothing. He could tell she was not in good form. He wondered if she were ill.

Another cold gust blew over them, and Hadrian reappeared. Once he had fully materialized, he moved to a good vantage point. He stood motionless and stared in the mountain's direction.

"I will watch them from here. At any sign of danger, I will do what I can for them from this distance."

"I worry that Izanami will be distracted by her concern for me. I hope I haven't become her Achille's heel."

"Is her concern justified?"

Sapphire said nothing. As he monitored the Demon Hunters' progress, Hadrian changed the subject.

"You said before you could tell me the precise time of the solstice."

Sapphire took out her phone.

"Here. I'm streaming that UK news channel with the countdown clock. I'm lucky to get a connection. The signal is surprisingly strong for such a remote location. Let's see, almost twenty-four hours remain. That should be enough time."

"Those devices are amazing. This is a wondrous era."

"Everyone has a smartphone these days. That's how I got the statistics about the mountain heights."

Hadrian furrowed his brow. "Tell me, are these the same devices that Alaric's Mage has used to summon the Zen'ei's followers from around the world?"

She understood his concern.

"It is, but I deleted that app. I never downloaded it, but I found it on my phone. As soon as I noticed it, I got rid of it."

"So there's no way he could use your device to…"

Sapphire's face froze. She looked down at the phone. She was dismayed to see an image of Bob on its screen. He smiled triumphantly and winked. Her face turned red with anger.

"Why, you sneaky son of a…!"

She squeezed the phone with both hands, closed her eyes, and channeled all her fury at the device. It shook violently, and she gripped it all the tighter. The phone's back separated from the rest of the device and fell to the ground. Smoke wafted from the exposed circuit boards, and the screen crackled with bright sparks. Then the phone's vibrations stopped, its entire surface blackened. Sapphire flung the device with all her strength against a large rock. Then for good measure, she smashed it with her foot.

"That should have given him a jolt," she said evenly. "With any luck maybe it injured him physically. I hope it did."

"It's lucky we discovered this breach," said Ragnar, "before it could do more damage to us."

Sapphire rejected the supportive words.

"Not only am I the dispensable one," she said bitterly, "but I'm also the world's biggest idiot. I hope I haven't doomed us all."

26
The Battle of Licancabur

"THANKS TO ME," said Sapphire, "Bob has been able to spy on us the whole time."

"Do all of you carry those things?" asked Hadrian.

Ragnar and Momotaro shook their heads in response.

"Izanami doesn't," said Sapphire. "I doubt Koschei or Callan has one either. No, I'm the only idiot when it comes to the phone. She's nagged me to get rid of it. I thought she was just being paranoid about tracking software. I should have listened to her, but the damned thing is just too handy."

"Has he been listening to all our conversations?" asked Ragnar. "Tracking our location the entire time?"

"Presumably, he could monitor the phone only when there was a signal connecting it to the network. Fortunately, I would have been out of range most of the time. Still, when he has the powers of the mystical arts at his disposal, who knows how limited he is by terrestrial mobile networks?"

"You said you had a signal here in the middle of the desert."

"Yes, and it was quite strong. That can't be normal so far from the nearest town or major road. The Zen'ei must have set up their own transmitters since they're using phones to control their followers."

"Or," said Hadrian, "the signal is of a supernatural provenance."

"He must then know we are here on Quimal," said Ragnar. "Do you think he knows our plan for reaching the caves?"

"We must assume he does. I can't believe I was so stupid. Being immortal clearly isn't the same as being smart."

"I should go to them," said Momotaro gazing anxiously at the volcano. "They need to know what's happened. They may need help."

"I'm afraid," said Hadrian, "they are on their own—at least until they can clear an area sufficiently large for us to teleport to—but I can at least warn Izanami telepathically."

The Necromant turned toward the volcano and froze in place. Eyes closed, he made mental contact with the Canadian Demon Hunter.

"Don't feel bad," said Momotaro sympathetically. "It is often difficult anticipating where danger might lurk. Especially when it comes from the most ordinary and familiar of things."

"It was a stupid blunder," said Sapphire angrily, "and pretending it wasn't won't help. I have to do better."

The younger Demon Hunter fell silent.

"There is at least a silver lining to this setback," she said, "I'm energized now. My pulse is racing. I feel I could do anything. You may have noticed I haven't exactly been at my best."

"I… couldn't say."

"You're being polite."

"Is it true you've fought alongside Orpheus? I hope to do the same someday."

She looked at him with softened eyes—and then at Ragnar. She said nothing. It was painful knowing other people's futures. Contemplating her own uncertain one would have been burden enough.

Hadrian had not ended his trance. While communicating with Izanami, he found that the link between them was a better way of following the trio's progress than remote viewing. He was effectively there with them, seeing everything through Izanami's eyes. More than that, he could hear the same sounds as her, smell the same odors. She was, of course, aware he had not broken the link, and she chose not to break it either. She found she didn't mind his company—remote as it was. She also knew that keeping the link open would make it easier for him to provide help if required.

The three Demon Hunters' incursion into the crowd of Zen'ei followers had so far been unchallenged. The Necromant had left them a hundred yards or so from the edge of the mob. The volcano towered above, blotting out much of the sky. Their ears were filled with the dull roar of voices. A current of joyous excitement ran through the crowd. People were dressed in every manner of clothing. They were from any number of countries and included every economic class.

As the Demon Hunters approached, they heard snatches of conversation in various languages. There was no need to brandish weapons. Nobody saw them as threatening or, for that matter, particularly strange. They squeezed into the throng and pushed forward. Mostly, people accommodated their passage. A few stubbornly held their ground, but they got around them easily enough. The farther the trio proceeded, however, the thicker the mass of people. Progress became more difficult. Moreover, the closer they were to the mountain, the surlier the tempers. Here people were packed uncomfortably. In the lead, Koschei pushed more aggressively, and people pushed back— sometimes roughly. More determination and force were now required.

"This is becoming difficult," shouted Koschei. "The congestion is too great. They can barely let us by—even if they wish to."

"We have another problem," cried Izanami. "I'm in communication with Hadrian. Alaric and Bob likely know what we're up to. For all our effort, we may be walking into a trap."

"I, for one, like a good trap," said Callan. "It's surprising how overconfident some adversaries become when certain they have you cornered."

The surrounding horde became all but impenetrable. The Demon Hunters' movements were now constricted. Undaunted, Koschei found his own makeshift solution. With both hands, he grabbed a man directly in front of him, jerked him upward, and tossed him out of the way. He landed on the shoulders of others, who protested angrily, but the Russian paid no attention. He did the same to the next unlucky man. Callan followed his example. For now, the furious shouts of the injured were lost amid the crowd's general drone. Only those nearest noticed what was going on, and they ignored it as long as they weren't the ones manhandled. Izanami followed cautiously in their wake, wondering how much ground they could cover under these conditions.

As they pressed on, the crowd's mood darkened yet more. Koschei and Callan met increasing hostility. People were more inclined to resist and fight. While none individually was a match for the Demon Hunters, in combination they put up formidable resistance.

"This is not working!" shouted Callan. "Give me a demon to fight any day. There's no end to this mob."

"You're right, my friend. It's a trap we have blundered into, and it's of our own making. Izanami, can the Necromant not aid us?"

Already aware of the deteriorating situation, Hadrian heard Koschei's plea through Izanami's ears. In response, she heard the Necromant's voice in her head.

"I'm going to try something. Do you trust me?"

"Do I have a choice?"

"Yes, you do. One always has a choice. If you do not trust me completely, this will not work."

"What do I have to do?"

Koschei and Callan glanced at Izanami as they continued their struggle. It worried them to see her eyes closed, her face blank.

"Allow me to take complete control of your mind and body."

"It's the wrong time for jokes, Necromant."

"It's your—our—only hope."

"Let me rephrase your question. Can *I* trust *you?*"

"You can. You have earned my full respect, and I'll proceed accordingly. If it helps you trust me and lower your mental defenses, I'll allow you full access to my knowledge and memories. I'll no longer have any secrets from you."

"And you won't try to wipe my memory afterward?"

"Only if you ask me to. Given some of the things you will learn, you may well do so."

Izanami took a long breath.

"Do what you must. I won't resist."

Koschei and Callan were no longer advancing. It was all they could do to hold their positions. They stared with alarm at their comrade. Her facial expression had become unrecognizable, her posture strange and unfamiliar. She stood taller, appearing to have grown in height.

"Brace yourselves, Demon Hunters!"

The voice had come from her mouth, but it was not hers. It was the Necromant's. They gaped in awe. The sound had echoed, drawing the startled attention of all close by.

"I'm deadly serious! Brace yourselves! Hug the ground for dear life."

There was little space for lying, but Koschei and Callan dropped to their knees. They lay as flat as they could manage.

Izanami raised her arms. Her fingers were curled as if holding an invisible staff, the tip of which touched the ground. The veins in her temples throbbed as she focused her mind. An explosion shook the ground in front of her. Dirt flew in all directions. The boom was deafening. Shock waves radiated, throwing those still on their feet through the air. The area nearest her was cleared of people, save the two prostrate Demon Hunters.

She extended her arms outward. She again positioned her hands as if holding a staff, but this time one pointing forward. She shouted several unintelligible words, and people lying farther away were blown into the air like leaves in a windstorm. The invisible staff continued its forceful blasts as she turned slowly, clearing a wide circle all around her. Koschei and Callan hugged the ground in their efforts to keep below the shock waves.

Upon finishing, Izanami surveyed her work. She heard Hadrian's voice in her mind.

"It is done. I now release you. Thank you for your trust."

Her body relaxed, and she stumbled dizzily. Her comrades leapt to their feet to steady her.

"That was amazing to see." It was her normal voice but hoarser than normal.

"To see?" said Koschei. "Izanami, you were the one doing it."

"No, I wasn't. I was a witness—the same as the two of you."

A strong breeze brushed past them. As if out of a mist, Hadrian, Sapphire, Ragnar, and Momotaro stepped into view. Izanami could not take her eyes off the Necromant. He avoided her gaze.

"It's true," she gasped. "I... I know everything. I've seen it all. Experienced it all. I haven't absorbed everything. I don't yet understand completely, but I know who you are. I know you backwards and forwards."

"Just as I know you," he replied quietly, ignoring Sapphire's quizzical stare. "Not as satisfying as you expected, eh?"

"I don't like knowing this much about another person. It's almost worse than someone knowing so much about me."

"I do have the power to expunge memories..."

"I like that idea least of all."

The many witnesses of the sudden supernatural appearance of the Necromant and the three Demon Hunters were shocked. Still on the ground, they scrambled to get farther away, climbing atop one another in the process. The entire multitude moved out of their way as best it could. The seven's path forward became less congested.

"Is it just me," asked Koschei, "or are they moving out of our way just a little too conveniently?"

"More than a little," said Callan gravely.

Momotaro had no time for their doubts.

"Did we not come to fight our way to the caves?" he cried. "Why waste time with questions? Forward!"

Koschei and Callan exchanged quick, doubtful looks before pursuing the younger Demon Hunter in his dash toward the mountain. The others followed.

The path sloped steeply upward toward a rise. As they neared the high point, several imposing figures came into view on the other side. Soon they saw more behind them. Among the closest ones, Izanami recognized Hathus, Belenus, and the Mercenary from the battle on the Trans-Canada Highway.

Hathus shouted an obscenity. "Thanks to you, Hant Oppressor, I now walk with a limp!"

"You shouldn't be walking at all!" she yelled back. "How are you back on your feet so soon?"

"The Zen'ei look after their own. Our healers are the best there are, but there'll be no healing you today. You're a dead woman, Izanami. All of you are dead!"

"If you like walking so much," she cried, "this is the perfect time for it! Walk away now while you have the chance!"

A loud-pitched roar was Hathus's response as he and the others rushed forward. The six Demon Hunters drew their diabolusbanes and ran to meet the attackers. Hadrian lifted his staff high, then pointed it at the adversaries. A bright blast of energy surged toward the horde, knocking several off their feet, but most continued the attack. The Necromant repeated the blasts, directing them wherever the danger was greatest. Even an instrument as powerful as his mystical staff, however, could only do so much against such numbers. Scores of additional Mercenaries had joined the attack.

Hathus focused his fury on Izanami. She had no trouble deflecting the blows from his club, but she knew it was not enough merely to defend herself.

"Give up, Hathus!" she cried. "I have no wish to kill you."

"No wish or no stomach for it? You're a traitor to your own kind, Izanami! A traitor to the planet!"

"This is your last chance. Don't make me do this."

"Do your worst, Hant Oppressor!"

He raised his club high over his head, ready to bring it down on her. She hurled her diabolusbane at it and knocked it from his hands. As her weapon dematerialized, Hathus lost precious moments recovering from his surprise at her unexpected maneuver. Both lunged for the club, but she got to it first. She welled with anger for what Hathus and the other Mercenaries had done to her. For what they and the Zen'ei had done to Peter. For their part in trying to end the world. She swung the club with all her might against his temple. The bone in his head cracked, and blood spurted in several directions. His eyes, wide with shock, went blank as his body fell to the ground.

It was as if Izanami had become a feral animal. Nothing seemed real. She stared at the bloody club in her hand.

"The pitiful fool," she muttered. "He definitely had a problem holding onto his weapon. At least no one can say I used an unfair advantage against him."

She glanced to one side to see Koschei, engaged in his own frantic fight. He gave her a quick, understanding look. In the instant before turning away from him, she also caught a warning in his eyes.

Belenus, having seen Hathus's fate, charged at her. She stepped so he didn't hit her with his full force. They both landed on the ground but were immediately on their feet again. He swung his mace at her.

"You'll pay for what you did to Hathus!"

"For what it's worth," she yelled, "I regret having to kill Hathus. I actually liked him once. I have never liked you!"

Though using the diabolusbane would have given her a clear advantage, she did not summon it. She knew it was stupid, but she had trouble shaking her stubborn sense of fairness. What did fairness matter when the entire world hung in the balance? She still held Hathus's club, but the blood made it hard to grip. Still, she held on to it. She swung it at Belenus only for him to duck out of the way. She swung again, and this time knocked the mace from his hand. He reached for the club, hoping to take it from her. She surprised him by tossing it to the ground. As he knelt to grab it, she went for the mace. Her speed was greater, but she was not ready to use his weapon on him just yet. She gave him a vicious kick in the thigh as he stood up. The bloody club slipped from his hand. His eyes were frantic as he calculated the seconds needed to retrieve it again. By the time he reached it, his own spiky weapon landed on the back of his head. Despite the injury, he took the club and struggled to stand.

"You tried to choke me to death," said Izanami. "I was helpless, and you were going to kill me in cold blood."

He stared with dazed eyes. Blood streamed from his head's crown. He raised the club, but his hands shook.

"As much as you deserve this," she said, "It's not as satisfying as I expected it to be. Goodbye, Mercenary."

He choked on his own blood and was thus unable to register his protest that she had used an offensive term. She put him out of his misery with another solid blow from the mace.

"Why do you fight them with their own arms?" shouted Koschei, mowing down yet another foe with his diabolusbane. "Did we not agree we were left no choice but to employ our most powerful weapon?"

"You're right," she cried. "I miss hunting demons. I hate fighting my own kind."

She dropped the mace and did her best to wipe the blood from her hands. She summoned her diabolusbane, barely in time to cut through a pair of Mercenaries leaping toward her. More came after. When able, she glanced around at her comrades. Sapphire, Koschei, Ragnar, Callan, and Momotaro were all more than a match for every adversary. Hadrian's staff distracted enough attackers so the Demon Hunters were never overwhelmed.

She was pleased to see Sapphire full of energy and enthusiasm. She was back to her old self, and that gave Izanami confidence their mission would be successful.

The combatants lost track of time. Hours had passed when the Mercenaries suddenly ceased fighting. Koschei, Ragnar, and Callan killed a few more before realizing their adversaries were not fighting back.

"What's going on?" asked Momotaro.

"It's time!" shouted a Mercenary.

"Time for what?" asked Callan.

"Balor will now walk among us! It's the hour of the incarnation!"

"What? No!" shouted Hadrian. "The solstice is hours away."

"It is now!" cried a Mercenary. "Look!"

In their progress against the Mercenaries, the Demon Hunters had reached a higher elevation on the mountainside. In the clear desert air they looked across the yawning salt flat all the way to Cerro Quimal. They saw the volcano's shadow stretch across the land. It had indeed reached the faraway hilltop.

"But how?" cried the Necromant. "How could we have gotten the time wrong?"

"It's my fault," said Sapphire, distraught. "It's my fault again. I got the time of the solstice from my phone. The same phone that Bob was controlling."

"It's not just the phone," said Izanami. "The time was on the satellite news channel we saw in London. The same one owned by Bob's friend. Through their control of the media, they ensured we'd have the wrong information."

A shout went up from the surviving Mercenaries. It was echoed by the crowds at the base of the mountain. The Demon Hunters looked up. On a ledge, hundreds of feet above, they saw the hulking creature that had been present at the battle in the Bialowieza Forest. It roared like thunder. On its shoulders sat Alaric.

"This is the moment!" he shouted in a voice echoing for miles. "Now is the time when Balor becomes part of this world! A new age is at hand! Nothing shall ever be the same! All hail Balor!"

27
Balor

EVERYTHING AS FAR as the eye could see was bathed in a blinding white light. The earth rumbled for several minutes and then calmed into an eerie stillness.

The echoing voice again emanated from Alaric.

"I am Balor! I have come to put things right at last!"

"All hail Balor!" cried the throngs in unison. "Balor will save us!"

A Mercenary pointed excitedly at Alaric.

"There he is! He has become incarnated. He's now one of us. He has mounted the Kehua."

"It's over," cried Koschei. "We failed."

"Not yet," said Hadrian. "He may have succeeded in becoming incarnated, but the world doesn't end until he has his temporal paradox. That won't happen without the boy."

"Why does he need the boy?" asked Callan. "You said that any of our deaths would cause a temporal paradox."

"There is something different about the boy."

"He's right," said Izanami. "All the stuff Miyamoto put in my head. I understand it better now. There's more to the unraveling thread of this world's existence than a contradiction in a single person's timeline. It needs to be someone whose path through time wends through more than one plane of existence."

"Peter exists in more than one plane of existence?" asked a perplexed Koschei.

"Miyamoto put things in your head?" asked a confused Momotaro.

"Where is he?" roared the booming voice coming from Alaric's mouth. "I command you to bring forth the Expiator so he may be sacrificed."

Alaric thrust a finger in the direction of the Demon Hunters. Against his will, Hadrian levitated unsteadily above the ground.

"You! The one called Necromant. Bring him to me!"

Hadrian closed his eyes and, holding his staff parallel with the ground, thrust it forward. He struggled against the force holding him. A flash of light burst from the staff, and Hadrian fell to the ground. He regained his feet and backed away from the man on the Kehua.

"The limitations of physical form do not suit me," cried Balor's voice.

Alaric stared at Sapphire.

"Clíodhna, why did you ever choose this manner of existence? Everything is unnecessarily difficult. The limitations in communicating are agonizing. It will be so much better when this dimensional plane and its maddening, linear timestream are deleted."

He turned to a figure emerging from a shadow on a higher ledge. It was Bob.

"Acharya! You are well accustomed to working in this constrained environment. Fetch the Necromant and make him bring us the Expiator."

Sapphire noticed a fresh, nasty-looking wound on Bob's cheek. She took satisfaction, knowing it would have been caused by her final interaction with her mobile phone.

"I have a request, great Balor," he said.

"What?"

"In the new world order, I would like to have the one called Izanami as my concubine."

"Your words make no sense. I gave you a command."

"Yes, you have, and now I'm negotiating. I'm telling you the first item on the list of things I'd like in exchange for serving you."

"Your words still make no sense. What is a negotiation? Do as you're ordered!"

"I'm standing my ground. That's what a good negotiator does. What is your response to my demand?"

"Demand? This manner of existence is too confusing. This thing you call a negotiation is at an end."

"Wait! That's not how it works. Surely, one as mighty as you understands how powerful men deal with…"

The Software Wizard's sentence was left unfinished. The Kehua, on which Alaric was perched, reached up to grab Bob. It flung him down the mountainside. The beast then stomped down the slope after him until one of its feet landed squarely, squashing him like a bug. The monster continued downward in the direction of the Demon Hunters.

"Will no one secure the Necromant and make him produce the Expiator? I must say, I did find extinguishing that annoying mortal strangely enjoyable. I'm beginning to gain some appreciation for the physical form's pleasures."

The Mercenaries turned their attention toward Hadrian. The six Demon Hunters formed a circle around him, their weapons at the ready.

"Do you not now see," shouted Sapphire at the Mercenaries, "the true nature of the monster you've brought into the world? Join us in resisting him! It is not too late. What's been done can still be undone."

"Listen!" yelled Hadrian. "She speaks the truth!"

"She speaks the false erudition!" cried one of the Mercenaries. "She denies the true erudition. The erudition of our savants. There is no truth but Balor's truth!"

The Mercenaries attacked the circle of Demon Hunters with renewed fury. The Kehua and Alaric drew nearer as the combatants fought hand to hand. One Mercenary after another fell before the diabolusbanes, but there was no shortage of new attackers.

Soon the Kehua had reached the battle, and the Mercenaries made way for its imposing physical presence. As it extended a brawny arm in the Necromant's direction, the Demon Hunters' blades made one slice after another in its exposed limb. The creature howled with pain.

"The poor beast," said Izanami to Sapphire between gasps of exhaustion. "I hate attacking it. It's Alaric's slave. It never asked to be part of this battle."

Despite the Demon Hunters' best efforts, the Kehua succeeded. They watched in horror as it took Hadrian in its grasp and lifted him. They feared the Necromant would be crushed by the creature's brute strength. To their relief, the beast's grip was firm but not fatal.

"Yes," boomed Balor's voice. "Physicality has a purpose in this plane. By touching you I see your mind now. I see what I need to know. I see what I need to have."

The Kehua extended its other arm and unfolded its hand with its coarse palm up. A momentary burst of light, then the Demon Hunters gasped to see Peter, with startled eyes wide, balanced uncomfortably atop its fingers.

"No!" shouted an anguished Koschei.

He bounded toward the beast and leapt toward its fingers with the diabolusbane in hand. The Russian wrapped one arm around a giant finger and sliced through another with his blade. The monster howled in pain and reeled. The boy rolled off its palm. Koschei caught him and beat a hasty retreat up the mountain.

"I like this world less and less," roared Balor's voice. "The sooner it is gone, the better."

The Kehua lumbered after Koschei, but the Mercenaries had already swarmed after him, inadvertently hindering the beast's progress. Several Mercenaries were crushed beneath its feet. Others were felled by the Russian's fellow Demon Hunters, also in pursuit. Izanami caught up to Koschei on the trail upward. A ways ahead of them on a rise stood a figure. It was Hadrian, who had teleported to the spot.

"Well done, Koschei!" cried the Necromant. "We're nearly at the caves' entrance. You and Izanami must carry the Grisial to its source. Take the child with you. He'll be safer in there with you than out here."

"What's the point of sealing the dimensional rift now?" said Izanami. "Balor has already passed through it."

"It will prevent other Fomóire from coming through," said Hadrian.

"But," said Koschei, "won't we cut off any way of sending Balor back to his own world?"

"Yes," said the Necromant, "but this world stands a better chance against a single Fomóire than against all of them."

With Peter in his arms and with Izanami close behind, Koschei sprinted toward the jagged indentation in the mountainside. Several Mercenaries nipped at their heels as they slipped into the narrow hole's blackness. Hadrian stood in the way of the remaining pursuers, repelling them with blasts from his staff. The other four Demon Hunters joined with him to block their progress. Mercenaries fell, but more replaced them.

Soon the Kehua loomed large, obliviously stepping on Balor's allies as it pushed its way toward the Demon Hunters. Realizing the boy had gone into the caves, Balor vented his rage through the screams of the man providing his voice. The monster echoed him with its own roar and beat the side of the mountain with its fist. It pounded repeatedly on the rocks, crushing them to pebbles. The vibrations triggered a reaction. A small section of mountainside higher up collapsed. The Kehua was not directly in the rubble's path, but Hadrian and the four Demon Hunters were. They scrambled furiously out of the way of the rocks.

Farther down, there was mayhem. In their panic, people fought one another as they attempted to flee, fearing a major landslide that would engulf them. The dislodgement did not extend that far, but it did have the effect of covering the cave's entrance entirely.

Alaric and the Kehua turned their attention to Hadrian and the Demon Hunters, as did the remaining Mercenaries. A thunderous war cry went up from the self-styled Legionnaires, and they threw themselves into the attack.

"I'm sorry," said Sapphire, swinging her diabolusbane at one foe and then another.

"You've nothing to be sorry for," said Hadrian, wielding his staff wherever it could do the most good.

"I mean, I'm sorry to leave you in this situation."

"Leave? What are you talking about?"

She did not answer. For a scant few moments, she was not under direct attack. She took advantage to stand still, close her eyes, and vanish.

"Where did she go?" cried Ragnar, still striking adversaries with his diabolusbane.

"Your guess is as good as mine, Demon Hunter," said Hadrian as he continued wielding his staff.

"I hope she has a good reason for leaving us here," said a breathless Momotaro.

"Do you think," asked Callan, "that she may have attempted to teleport into the caves? To assist Koschei and Izanami?"

"I hope not," said Hadrian. "Even the most skilled Mage would require a lifetime's worth of luck to accomplish such a feat without becoming fatally embedded in the mountain. No, I suspect she's gone elsewhere. For what purpose, I have no idea."

The four carried on the fight against a seemingly endless number of assailants. Some of the fighters were not true Mercenaries. The attackers' numbers had been swollen by fanatical youths drafted into the cause with little or no experience or training. Ragnar and Callan regretted the injuries and deaths suffered by the callow conscripts, but they had little choice.

Momotaro glanced at the Kehua with Alaric on its back. Trying to force a way into the caves, it clawed at the mountainside, but its stubborn efforts were in vain. By dislodging more earth above the cave-in, it only made the former entrance more impassable.

The young Demon Hunter saw his chance. He made short work of an unfortunate youth attacking him, then sprinted toward the monster. He leapt onto its back and climbed up toward the rider. Alaric glared at him in surprise. He raised his arms menacingly, but Momotaro was swift. A deft stroke of his supernatural blade severed Alaric's head. It rolled down the beast's flank and onto the ground.

The Kehua roared in pain. Alaric's slumped body slid down the creature's back and toppled onto an outcrop of rocks. The Mercenaries froze in place. They stared in shock at their head-less leader. Momotaro raised his diabolusbane in triumph.

"I did it!" he shouted. "He can be killed. Once in a human body, he became as mortal as anybody else."

The Demon Hunter jumped to the ground. The Kehua lumbered around and faced him.

"You are free now, beast," cried Momotaro. "He enslaved you, but now you're free. I don't know where you come from or if there are any more of your kind, but we'll take you home so you may live out your natural life unmolested. The nightmare is over."

"Momotaro!" yelled Hadrian. "Get away from it!"

"It may look like a monster to us," said the Demon Hunter, turning to address the Necromant, "but isn't it a child of nature the same as you or I? There's nothing to fear now it's free of Balor's control."

Hadrian shouted again, but it was too late. With both its hands, the beast grabbed hold of the Demon Hunter and lifted him. As Momotaro struggled uselessly, the beast placed him on its shoulders, where Alaric had sat. The Demon Hunter's eyes glazed over. From Momotaro's mouth emanated Balor's voice.

"Did you think that I would choose to be incarnated in a frail human body? Why would I inhabit such a puny host? Strength is required in this physical world. This beast is not ideal, but it was the most powerful creature available to me. Its main drawback is its inability to communicate with your kind, forcing me to use a human for my voice."

Hadrian, Callan, and Ragnar watched in horror as the creature lumbered toward them with Momotaro robotically clinging to its shoulders.

"I can only hope," said Hadrian, "that things are going better for Izanami and Koschei. If they can reach their goal, perhaps all is not lost."

At that moment, the Canadian and the Russian were heavily involved in a battle of their own. In addition to the Mercenaries who had followed them into the caves, others had been lying in wait inside. The cave would have been pitch black if not for light-emitting discs worn by the Mercenaries. Their faint glow gave the warriors a ghostly appearance. The Grisial too emitted light in the darkness.

Izanami and Koschei fended off attackers from two directions, doing their best to keep the boy safe between them. Thankfully, the narrowness of the passage allowed only enough space for one foe at a time to attack from either side.

"We'll have to kill them all, won't we?" cried Izanami, thrusting her blade through the midsection of a Mercenary blocking her way.

"I'm afraid so," replied Koschei, decapitating a long-haired Mercenary attacking from the rear. "I see no other way."

"Didn't Hadrian say there's a network of caves in this mountain?"

"He did."

"How will we find our way to where we need to go?"

"Why ask me? You're the one with all your old Master's information in your head—and now, apparently, the Necromant's as well. If you don't know where we must go, then no one..."

The Russian was distracted by having to meet a lunging warrior's throat with his blade.

"My brain is about to burst. I can't cope with it all. I just hope the information we need is at hand when the time comes."

Trembling, Peter cringed between them, eyes closed. He covered his ears.

By the time an hour had passed, Koschei had felled every Mercenary who had pursued them into the cave. He turned to help Izanami with the warriors in front of them.

"Stay behind us, boy," he told Peter. "You'll be safe as long as you keep back."

"How many do you think there are?" asked Izanami. "There seems to be no end to them."

"Personally, I'm more concerned with how we'll get out of here—even if we're successful. Judging from the rumble we heard shortly after we entered the cave, I'd say our way out is now well sealed."

They slowly forced their attackers backward. It soon became clear that many of the Mercenaries were retreating willingly. The Demon Hunters now progressed more easily.

"Why does this feel like a trap?" said Koschei.

Several minutes later, they came to a fork in the cave. Mercenaries defended both passageways.

"Which one do we go for?" wondered Izanami.

"You're the Grisial's bearer. You choose."

"I have no idea."

"Then let's go for the left one."

"Why not the right one?"

"Okay, we'll go for the right one."

"I didn't mean we should go for the right one. I was playing devil's advocate."

"The devil already has too many advocates if you ask me. Just pick one."

"The left one then. No, the right one."

"Yes," whispered Peter, "the right one," but they did not hear him.

"The left one it is then," said Koschei with finality.

With renewed fury, they set upon the defenders of the left-hand passage. In short order, they cut down several of the Mercenaries in their way and broke through. They were relieved to meet no additional fighters—until they realized why.

"It's a dead end," said Izanami, staring at the cave wall before them.

They turned and saw Mercenaries gathering loose rocks and piling them at the chamber's entrance.

"*Pizdets!*" shouted the Russian. "Come, it's not too late. We can still burst through and fight our way to the other passage."

Izanami dropped to her knees.

"I'm exhausted. You and Peter don't need sleep or food, but I'm not fit for another attack."

"But they'll have us completely blocked in."

"I'm sorry. It kills me to admit it, but I have to rest. I may be a Demon Hunter, but I'm still only human."

"Let her rest, Alexei," said Peter firmly.

The boy sat down behind her and put his hands on her shoulders.

"Lean back, Chiharu. You can rest your head on my lap."

She did as he said and found lying against him surprisingly restful. One of his fingers played idly with a strand of her hair.

"It's all right, Chiharu. Everything will be fine. I'm certain of it."

She found herself dozing comfortably.

"Do you know what, Chiharu?"

"Mmmm."

"When I grow up, I think I'll marry you."

"Believe me, you don't…"

She was fast asleep. Koschei sat down next to her and waited impatiently. A half-hour later, she opened her eyes and spoke.

"We've killed a lot of people today, Koschei."

"Yes, we have, my friend."

"Do you feel guilty? I mean, about so many deaths of our own kind?"

"There is only one death I will ever truly regret."

"Who?"

"His name was Pyotr Belov."

"Who?"

"He was thirteen years old. No bigger than this lad here."

"What happened to him?"

"He was stolen from his bed in the middle of the night. His family never knew what happened to him. They spent the rest of their lives missing him, wondering where he was. It was only many years later that I found out who he was and sought out his family. I went back to Yekaterinburg in the dark days of Stalin. They were all gone by then—save one sister. She was old before her time. She's the one who told me who Pyotr was. She told me about his brief life. About his love of playing gorodki. His skill at knocking down the wooden pins."

"What was his connection to you?"

"I laid eyes on him only one time. For just a few minutes. It was the night I was taken from my bed. He was left in my place. Terrified, we looked into each other's eyes. A man named Vodyanoy had brought him. He was a former associate of the Mad Monk. He had visited the palace when we still lived there. He took a liking to me, saw something in me. As Pyotr and I stared at one another, Vodyanoy used a knife to cut one of Pyotr's fingers and one of mine. He made us mix our blood together. Then he smiled at Pyotr and congratulated him, told him his veins now carried the blood of a prince. It must have been true because, decades later when they dug up his body along with those of my sisters, scientists insisted their tests proved he was me.

"Vodyanoy took me away that night. He was my first mentor. The Mad Monk had cured my blood disease but only temporarily. By the time Vodyanoy came for me, I had been using a wheelchair for weeks. It was Vodyanoy who cured me permanently. He trained me to be a Demon Hunter. I have now lived nearly a century, but Pyotr Belov died at thirteen. His is the only death I regret. It should have been me. I should have died with my family."

Peter's eyes were on the verge of tears. He took Koschei's hand and squeezed it hard. The Russian squeezed his in return.

"But enough about that. Are you finally over your laziness? Shall we get out of here and finish what we came to do, old friend?"

"Most definitely, your highness. The rest has worked wonders. I'm now ready for anything."

28
Hellions

SAPPHIRE STOOD AT the cliff's edge. Below her, waves crashed against the rocks, one white explosion of spray after another. Above her, the wind blew large gray and white clouds across the sky. It was a beautiful first day of summer on Admiralty Inlet. She gazed out at the sea and remembered the first time she set foot on the island. How she, Maria, and Kyle were all nearly lost forever in the sea.

Though the island was little more than thirty miles, as the crow flies, from her house—or rather from where her house used to be—she had never been tempted to return. There had been no reason. It would have only served to stir memories better left at rest.

Now, she had no choice. She remembered the children: Celia, Audrey—and Peter. Their presence on the island was an enigma, Peter's most of all. Unfortunates plucked from the cusp of the afterlife, as Septimus had explained. When he released them, they were gone forever—or should have been. Yet the boy had returned, and she was determined to know why. That, however, was not her most urgent concern in this particular moment, and she had no time to spare. Despite her dread, she had to finish what she had come to do.

She breathed deep the sea air. She walked the bluff's edge to the ruins of Bridge House. Only a heap of stones remained. A newcomer would think it had collapsed ages ago—not a mere few years earlier. She passed the ruins and walked into the woods. She continued until she had climbed to the island's highest point and felt the brisk wind on her face. She had been at this spot once before. It had been at night, but now in the daylight, she had an expansive view of the sea and nearby islands.

The hilltop was one of the rare points where reality's fabric between the physical world and the Netherworld was just that bit thinner. That night, Septimus had performed the ceremony with candles. Sapphire wondered how much of that had been for show. She was confident candles weren't necessary for what she needed to do. She clenched her fists at her side and lifted her head. The cold wind blew her hair. She let out a cry.

"Astaroth!"

A cloud passed in front of the sun. The temperature fell, and the air pressure dropped.

"I'm not afraid to say your name, demon, and I'm not afraid to tell you mine!"

Additional clouds darkened the landscape. It was almost like an eclipse.

"You and I shall speak, Astaroth!"

A distant rumble grew louder. It sounded like thunder, but it couldn't have been because she saw the flash of crackling light afterward. For a brief moment, everything was eerily white. In front of her, the air ripped like a sheet of paper. A large, scaly arm emerged from the rift, then paused. Scabrous fingers extended themselves, opened, then froze as if waiting.

This was the moment Sapphire had sought but also feared. This was her leap of faith. If she had miscalculated, she could look forward to more centuries of imprisonment in the Netherworld. The previous time, she had not known who she was, but now things were different. She steeled her resolve and walked right up to the fingers. They closed around her and pulled her back through the rift.

She had forgotten how bone-numbing the chill of that world was to a mortal body, not to mention the disorientation of the sudden, complete absence of light. She focused her mind and fought the vertigo. She drew her diabolusbane and took comfort from its flickering light.

In this world, her mouth was of no use. She formed words in her mind.

"I am here. Do you know why?"

"Do you?"

The Fiend's growling voice echoed in her mind as if in a cavern.

"Yes, I do. You must give me the one called Septimus Bridge."

"That will not occur."

"It must."

"It must not."

"I now know who I am."

"I am sorry."

"If you do not give me Septimus, my world will end."

"Your world?"

"Yes, *my* world. Release him now. You must."

"I must not. Do you not know that?"

"Why must you have him forever?"

"I never wanted him. It was always you, but this world could not contain you, so it has him. Now it cannot continue without him."

"What will happen to you if my world ends?"

"Say your name."

"I am Lola Blumquist."

"Say your name."

"I am Sapphire."

"Say your name."

"I am Clíodhna. I was one of the Old Ones. I was the last of the Tuath Dé. Now I am one of the New Ones. Answer my question."

"You know only what you want. You do not know what you need."

"What do I need?"

"I can give you T'an-mo. I can give you Merihim."

"Demons? What do I want with your demons? Merihim almost killed me and Izanami. T'an-mo killed Izanami's friend."

"Do you not yet understand?"

"I have never understood you or the Netherworld."

"Understand. It is the only way."

"Tell me why the demons stopped invading my world."

"Yes."

"Yes what?"

"Yes, your questions are not the point."

"Answers would be nice."

"Your mind must let go of questions and answers. Your mind must understand. Let go of your human side."

She let go of her determination and frustration. Everything changed.

"I… I think I understand better now. What must I do?"

"Go. You and the hants. The quantity of that which you call time is meager. Go."

Astaroth's voice had become silent. She was not certain how much time had passed since he had stopped talking. She was enveloped by a welcome warmth and blinded by a brilliant light. She had the sensation of falling. When her body came to rest, she had to blink several times before she could see anything. The ground underneath her was brown, sandy, and dry. The landscape was barren. The sky was clear. She was back in the Atacama Desert. She got to her knees and looked around.

Atop the hill on the far side of the salt flat, two huge shapes were silhouetted against the sky. For a moment, she thought they were grotesque statues, relics left by a forgotten, ancient civilization. They were like gargoyles that had escaped the top of a medieval cathedral and had grown in size. Then one shifted its position. They were scaled creatures, sitting on bent knees. The bat-like wings on their angular bodies and their crooked necks made them resemble vultures perched on a bluff, waiting for something to die.

They eyed her malignantly, and she stared back. She had never before observed demons at rest. Every previous encounter had been an immediate and prolonged battle for survival. Things were different now. Merihim and T'an-mo made no move. They waited.

She wondered if she could communicate with them, as she could with Astaroth. She tried speaking to them with her mind.

"Do you hear me?"

Silence.

"Do you not have language, as your master does?"

Merihim shuddered. T'an-mo shifted his head.

"If you hear me, make a sign."

They both stood upright and flapped their wings tentatively. "Come to me."

In a slow and oddly graceful motion, they leapt into the air and floated in her direction.

Sapphire stood nervously, her hand ready to draw the diabolusbane. The monsters alighted a few yards away. At more than twelve feet in height, they towered over her. They carried an odor like sulfur. Eying her coldly, they waited.

"Do you know Balor? Is he a threat to your world as he is to mine? Is that why your master sent you? Are you here, for once, to fight with us rather than against us?"

Nothing in the hellions' expressions or movements betrayed anything like a response.

"Balor of the Fomóire has been incarnated into this world. He is trying to kill a young human. If he succeeds, this world will end."

Was she wasting her time? Did they understand anything she was trying to communicate? The hellions cocked their heads one way, then another, and stared at her with beady eyes.

"The boy is inside that mountain. He is with two..." She thought better than to use the term *Demon Hunters*. "... with two of my comrades. They have a talisman that can block the Fomóire's passage to this world. Do either of you understand any of what I'm trying to communicate?"

Merihim bent over until he was flat on the ground—like a supplicant in prayer. He waited.

"What are you doing? Wait, no, do you want...?"

The idea was crazy. Months earlier she and Izanami had been locked in a life-and-death struggle with the creature on the volcano's rim.

T'an-mo stared quizzically. He watched her walk hesitantly to the prostrate hellion. She held her breath and climbed on top of him. For one panicky moment, she wondered if it was a trap. What if Astaroth were in league with Balor? The possibility did not bear thinking about.

The demon reared up and expanded his wings. She dug her knees into spaces between his flanks' large scales and grabbed hold of the ones on his back. Her position was surprisingly comfortable despite the creature's rough exterior.

Merihim squatted for a brief moment, then sprang into the air. Sapphire tightened her grip as the cold desert wind whipped her face and hair. Thankfully, the wind carried away much of the demon's stench. Below her, the arid desert fell away and spun around as the hellion circled in the volcano's direction. T'an-mo followed close behind.

Within minutes, she saw the crowds gathered around the mountain's base. They were in disarray. Many fled in panic. Fights had broken out among some pilgrims. As she thought about where she needed to go, Merihim seemed to understand her wish. They flew to the collapsed cave entrance. The angry Kehua clawed at the rocks and earth covering the hole. To her surprise, Momotaro was on the monster's shoulders. His eyes were glassy.

Ragnar, Callan, and Hadrian had their hands full, defending themselves against the remnants of the Zen'ei's Mercenaries. Ragnar glanced up to see the two demons overhead.

"Bloody hell! Now what?"

The others looked up, and Callan cried, "Demons!"

All combat ceased as Demon Hunters and Mercenaries alike stared at the winged creatures. The Demon Hunters clutched their diabolusbanes and braced for an attack. The few remaining Mercenaries fled in panic.

"The cowards," sneered Callan.

"What did you expect?" said Ragnar. "That's why they're Mercenaries and not Demon Hunters. Wait, is that...?"

They had been astonished to see the demons floating overhead, but they were now more shocked to spot Sapphire on the back of one of them.

"This is a most interesting turn," said a perplexed Hadrian, his staff at the ready.

The demons hovered over the Kehua, which continued to dig furiously. Sapphire looked at T'an-mo and gave him a nod. The demon lowered his large, retractable jaw and coughed up a blinding ball of light. It rushed at the Kehua's back and exploded in shards of glowing energy. The beast howled in pain.

It and Momotaro turned their heads in the demons' direction, as Merihim threw open his maw. Sapphire clung as he hurled his own incandescent sphere of energy at the monster.

A loud roar went up from the Kehua's mouth as it flailed wildly. T'an-mo circled around and struck with another blast. The monster's rage grew wilder. It leapt high into the air and grabbed one of T'an-mo's feet, jerking the demon downward.

"So the Netherworld has taken an interest!" boomed Balor's voice through Momotaro's body.

As he struggled against the bigger creature's grip, T'an-mo eyed the human on its back with piercing eyes. Sapphire wondered why Momotaro was on the Kehua's back, but she soon worked out what must have happened.

As T'an-mo and Momotaro stared at each other, she wondered if demons could distinguish one human from another. Did T'an-mo recognize the young Demon Hunter, now possessed, as the same man he had killed years earlier at Lake Rakshastal? Was he curious to know how he could still be alive? Or was it even a question, given the Netherworld's complete disassociation from her world's natural laws and time flow? As for Momotaro, possessed or not, he could not have understood he was looking into the eyes of the creature that would one day slay him.

Seeing his companion's predicament, Merihim let loose a ferocious, fiery ball. It struck its target and drew another scream from the Kehua, which tightened its hold on T'an-mo. It pulled the frantic demon closer and squeezed his midsection. Struggling to free himself, he flapped his wings madly.

"I know I can take what I need from the frail mortals," said Balor's voice. "Can I do the same to a hant that has wandered into this plane of existence?"

T'an-mo's horrendous shriek assaulted the ears of all within its range. It was most painful to Sapphire who clung to the other demon and had no way to shield her ears.

The Kehua released the demon, which fell straight to the ground and landed in a heap. The beast reared up on its haunches to its full height and roared in triumph. Its body underwent a rapid metamorphosis. Scales burst through its hide. Wide reptilian wings emerged from its shoulders. It roared again louder. The sound echoed throughout the flatlands below.

"This can't be good," said Sapphire through gritted teeth as she stared in disbelief.

She formed a thought in her head. "Shouldn't we get farther away from it?"

Merihim batted his wings, reversing away from the ungodly hybrid. Before he could put much distance between himself and it, the beast opened its mouth and emitted a large orb of energy in the demon's direction. Unable to avoid it completely, Merihim turned and took the force of the blow on his upper arm. His maneuver protected Sapphire from suffering more than a massive jolt. She held on with all her might, but the whiplash was too great. She was flung into the air. She saw the ground rush toward her.

Before impact, her descent slowed. She hit the earth roughly but with nowhere near the injury she had feared. As she brushed herself off, she spotted Hadrian with his staff not far away. She nodded her thanks, then turned her attention to the hovering demon which faced the winged Kehua.

The hybrid monster alighted, picked up a large boulder, and hurled it angrily at the demon. When it missed its target, the beast fired another blast from its mouth.

Hadrian, Ragnar, and Callan joined Sapphire to watch the battle.

"Have I gone insane?" said Ragnar. "Did those demons join the fight on our side? How is this possible?"

"I went to the Netherworld. I spoke with Astaroth."

"That was foolhardy," said the Necromant.

"I was desperate. I hoped against hope he would free Orpheus. He wouldn't—or couldn't—but he sent two demons to help."

"Why on earth would he do that?" asked Ragnar.

"The Netherworld has some sort of stake in this struggle between the Old Ones and the New Ones. Somehow it affects the demons' domain as well."

"Who would have thought?" said Callan. "I've now seen everything."

The Kehua picked up a boulder bigger than before and raised the stone above its head. As a precaution, the demon batted his wings and flew higher. Merihim was not the intended target, however. The Kehua threw the rock in the direction of T'an-mo's prostrate body.

Merihim shifted direction and swooped toward him. He opened his maw wide and emitted a wild burst of energy in the boulder's direction. The rock shattered into pieces before landing on top of the fallen demon. Merihim alighted next to him and stared with something like concern.

With the hellion distracted, the Kehua leapt into the air, wings beating furiously. Merihim turned and braced for a new attack, but it never came. Abandoning the battle, the hybrid beast soared straight upward. It climbed until it was small in the sky. It circled the mountain's snow-capped peak, then flew upward again. Hovering above the mountain's summit, it shifted position and dove downward. To observers on the ground, it appeared to have been swallowed by the snow. A look of horror came over Hadrian's face.

"He's gone into the crater. He's inside the mountain."

"What can he do there?" asked Callan.

"He can go all the way to the heart of the volcano. I have no idea how far Izanami and Koschei have progressed through the caves, but if and when they reach the Grisial's source, Balor will be waiting for them!"

29
Volcano's Heart

WITH THE KEHUA hybrid gone, Merihim returned to T'an-mo. Motionless and silent, he sat next to his companion, wings folded over his shoulders.

Ragnar watched the demons warily. "Is it dead?"

"They're not organic creatures as we would expect them to be in our world," said Sapphire. "I don't know if they can die."

"It looks dead to me," said Callan. "In countless battles, I have done my best to kill a demon, but I've never seen one inert like that."

"We're wasting time," said Hadrian. "Can the demon that isn't dead or injured be of any help in stopping Balor before it's too late?"

"If he'll let me," said Sapphire, "I can ride him into the crater after Balor."

"By all that is unholy, Sapphire," exclaimed Ragnar, "what it must be like to ride a demon! You're either the most foolhardy Demon Hunter I've ever known or the most courageous. Either way, you have my admiration."

"In a past life, I spent a couple centuries in the Netherworld. That may explain why those creatures and I have some sort of affinity—although it also has to do with Astaroth's decision to intervene in our struggle."

"You'd almost feel sorry for it," said Callan, looking at Merihim. "The way it sits vigil for its comrade. It's almost..."

"Human?" said Sapphire. "By the way, why do you call him 'it'? I'm fairly certain they're male."

"How can you possibly know that?"

"Something about their attitudes."

"If the demon will take you," said Hadrian, "you should go at once. The rest of us will try to join you inside the mountain as soon as we can."

"We will?" said Callan.

"I'll attempt to reestablish my mental link with Izanami. We did it before to effect a teleportation under precarious circumstances. The spaces I'll be negotiating are tiny, and there will be no margin for error, but we have to try."

"That's assuming," said Ragnar, "that she and Koschei have not been overcome by the Zen'ei's Mercenaries."

"How many Mercenaries can there be?" said Callan. "A score? Two score? I like those odds when it's Koschei and the Canadian involved."

Sapphire approached Merihim slowly. He looked at her coldly but with intelligence. It was strange to feel bonded with a hellion. As they both looked at T'an-mo, his motionless form faded from their sight.

"Has he gone back to the Netherworld?" she asked in her mind. "Will he be all right there?"

Merihim stood and turned. She climbed atop him, bracing herself for another wild ride. With no delay, he leapt into the air and traveled straight up like a rocket. The ground below them shrank until Sapphire could see the entire expanse of the Atacama Desert as well as a sizable section of the Pacific Ocean. The air was frigid. Below them was Licancabur's snowy peak. The demon circled the mountain's top. As he dove, she saw the crater.

Unlike the last time she had seen it, there was no longer a frozen lake with a glassy surface. There were only remnants of ice and a jagged hole in the lake's bottom. The demon headed straight for the gap. She held her breath as they plunged through the icy aperture and into the black. Bone-chilling air rushed past her as they shot downward through the darkness.

Once Sapphire and the demon had disappeared from their view, Ragnar and Callan turned their attention to Hadrian. He had closed his eyes and gone into a trance. They waited for him to speak again.

Several minutes later, he broke the silence without opening his eyes.

"Are you there, Demon Hunters?"

"Are you speaking to us or to Izanami and Koschei?"

"To you, Ragnar and Callan. Take my hands. It is important that you both kneel."

"Why?" asked Callan.

"So that neither of your heads becomes embedded in a stalactite."

"Is this safe?" asked Ragnar.

"What a question. No, definitely not."

The Demon Hunters closed their eyes, hoped for the best, and braced themselves for the worst.

Inside the mountain, Izanami and Koschei were busy dislodging rocks the Mercenaries had piled in attempt to block their exit. Their sweaty task would drag on for the better part of an hour. Peter struggled with a few of the smaller rocks, but Izanami shoved him aside.

"You're in the way," she said impatiently. "You're slowing us down."

The boy backed away and sat down, his arms crossed on top of his knees. He buried his eyes in his sleeves. After a while, he stole a quick peek. Koschei smiled sympathetically and winked. The boy hid his eyes again.

"Where did they get so many stones?" complained Izanami, rolling another small boulder to the back of the chamber.

"They seem numerous because they're heavy," said Koschei. "Fortunately, their supply was not unlimited. We're nearly out of here."

"Can't be too soon. The air in here is pretty rank."

When the gap was large enough, Izanami crawled through quickly. Koschei continued clearing away the remaining rocks.

"You should have waited," he called out. "I can't help you if you get into trouble."

"Not a problem," she called back. "There's no one here. It's probably too much to hope they left the cave. They'll be waiting for us farther down."

"Also," he grumbled, "you've taken the light with you."

Soon the Russian had widened the gap. His hands now free, he summoned his diabolusbane for the dim light it emitted. He lifted Peter through the hole, telling him to crawl toward the Grisial's light. Koschei went next.

"The diabolusbane does not make a good torch," he said, allowing his weapon to disappear.

They followed the passage leading to the volcano's heart.

"They had to know we'd get out," said Izanami. "They'll be waiting for us deeper in the caves. We'll be seriously out-numbered."

"What else is new?" laughed the Russian grimly. "They are no match for us. Their only advantage is their numbers. Will you be ready?"

"Don't worry about me. My catnap is all I needed."

They marched deeper into the mountain. The air was more humid and had a faint odor of sulfur.

"I wish that crystal was brighter," said Koschei, "so we could see farther ahead. We're as good as blind in this cave."

"We'll hear them before we see them," said Izanami, "or we will if you stop talking."

They listened for sounds of voices or footsteps. As the march dragged on, they lost track of time.

"We've gone such a long distance," said Koschei. "Is it possible that they didn't go this way at all? Could they have left the caves? Perhaps no one stands between us and our goal."

"That would be too easy. We must all stay alert."

More time passed. It was Izanami who first heard the noise. She stopped Koschei with an arm on his shoulder and put a finger to her lips. He listened carefully. Then he heard it too. At first, the Russian thought it was air currents in the passageway, but the sounds became more distinct. It was the faintest rumble of voices echoing through the warm, damp air.

Gripping her knife, Izanami proceeded cautiously in the lead. Every few steps, she paused and listened. The voices grew louder. Soon the voices sounded as if they were around the next bend in the cave. Izanami whispered so softly that Koschei had to read her lips.

"Stay here. I'll go ahead."

Before Koschei could protest, she had left him and Peter in darkness. Only because of the Grisial's faint glow, he saw her body's partial outline. He heard her gasp. Then the weak light was gone. He heard her scream, but it came from far away. He took Peter's hand and moved forward cautiously, stopping at the point where he had last seen her. He knelt and felt the ground. It was as he had feared. His fingers found the edge of a precipice.

"Izanami! Are you there?"

Her voice echoed upward from below. "I'm so stupid. I'm in a pit. Yuck!"

"What is it?"

"There are at least two bodies down here. I think they're Mercenaries."

"Are you injured?"

"I don't think so. I managed to land all right, and my suit protected me from breaking any bones. It was like falling down a curved shaft. Now I'm in a different cave, and there's something hard and sharp hanging from above."

Shadowy figures appeared on the opposite side of the pit, highlighted in the glow of the discs they wore. They had heard the commotion and had come to gloat. Thanks to their light, Koschei could now see the wide hole's outline, as well as a narrow path along one edge. The Mercenaries had apparently used it after two of their number blundered to their doom. The survivors stood ready to prevent anyone else from using the path. The good news was that they were unlikely to risk using it themselves to cross back over. Not with Koschei waiting on the other side to shove them downward one by one.

"Can you climb out?" shouted Koschei.

There was no response.

"Izanami? Can you hear me?"

More silence.

"For God's sake! Izanami! Answer me!"

"Is she all right?" said Peter.

"Just say something, Izanami!"

"Sorry. I was speaking with someone."

"With whom? Is someone else down there?"

"Sorry, not exactly speaking. Communicating. Telepathically."

Confused, Koschei watched a robed figure rise out of the pit and face the Mercenaries on the opposite side. Suspended in midair, he pointed his staff at them and shot a blast of energy. They scrambled away in shock. The figure then turned in Koschei's direction. It was Hadrian. He drifted toward the Russian.

"Quickly. Cross over to the other side. You need to hold back the Mercenaries until I can bring up the others."

"Others?"

Koschei told Peter to stay where he was, then carefully walked the narrow path along the chasm. The tunnel widened on the far side, allowing more than one enemy to attack at once. He drew his diabolusbane and waited. Warily, the Mercenaries approached. One ran at Koschei and was handily rebuffed. Two more followed.

Suddenly, the Russian was not alone. Izanami was at his side.

"You look no worse for the wear," he said.

"Tell it to my knees."

As they fought the Mercenaries, Ragnar joined them. Then Callan and finally Hadrian. He had carried them up, one by one, from the pit's bottom.

"You picked an opportune moment to get in touch, Necromant," said Izanami.

"That wasn't the worst place to teleport to. The only tricky part was the stalactite."

"You never mentioned levitation was one of your skills."

"You never asked, but then you didn't need to. You know all the skills I have mastered—and those I haven't."

"It bothers you a lot that you haven't managed invisibility yet, doesn't it?"

"Very much."

The Zen'ei forces were little match for four Demon Hunters and the Necromant. Koschei hit his stride, grabbing one opponent after another and flinging them toward the pit. Others fell dead on the cave floor. When few were left, they gave up and retreated deeper into the cave.

"They will be little trouble to us now," said Hadrian. "We should have a clear path to the Grisial's source."

Koschei, Ragnar, and Callan removed illuminated discs from some of the bodies strewn on the cave floor. They attached them to their own garments to benefit from the light they shed.

Izanami turned and looked to the other side of the pit. A small, lonely figure looked back at her.

"It's safe now," she said. "You can take the path over to us."

He didn't move.

"I... I don't think I can."

"Of course, you can. Just walk carefully."

"I'll fall."

"No, you won't. Trust me."

"You said I was slowing you down."

"Yes, I did, and you're slowing us down now. Stop wasting time."

"I don't think I can do it."

"You can. Listen, I've put a magic spell on you. It will protect you from falling. You'll be safe. Hurry."

"You promise?"

"Yes. Now hurry."

Nervously, the boy took one step and then another on the narrow path. He glanced downward and froze.

"Don't look down. Keep walking."

"You promise the magic won't let me fall?"

"Yes, but only if you're careful. Don't try testing it by doing something stupid."

"You're not making it up?"

"Of course not. I'm a Demon Hunter, and Demon Hunters never lie."

Peter screwed up his courage. He walked the rest of the path, his eyes locked on Izanami. When he reached the other side, he raced to her. He tripped and fell at her feet.

"I guess your magic spell only worked until I got past the hole."

"There was no magic spell."

"There wasn't?"

"No, I made it up to get you to walk across."

"But you said Demon Hunters never lie."

"Yes, and it was a lie. Demon Hunters lie all the time. We lie more often than we tell the truth."

"I could have fallen! I'll never trust you again."

"Good. Lesson learned."

"I don't want to marry you anymore."

"Then the lesson was doubly valuable."

The six marched onward toward the heart of the volcano.

"Where are Sapphire and Momotaro?" asked Izanami. "Why are they not here?"

"You don't want to know," said Ragnar.

She did want to know, but they needed to keep their silence while progressing ever deeper toward the mountain's center. They had to be alert to any sounds from Mercenaries and other possible dangers.

They sensed the nearness of their destination. The air grew heavier, more humid, and hotter. Izanami felt her fatigue returning and hoped she would have enough strength for completing the task. It did not occur to her to wonder whether she would have the means or stamina for escaping the mountain afterwards.

They followed the path upward and then sharply downward. A persistent light leaked into the passage ahead of them. At the path's lowest point, the cave opened onto a massive cavern. They were blinded by a bright light. It was difficult for their eyes to adjust after hours in the dark, but after a while they made out the light's source. It was high above them in midair. The eerie light shone as if passing through a crack in a wall, but there was no wall. Only air. Above it and on either side of it, there was endless shadow.

"So, that's it, eh?" said Izanami, staring. "The rift between our world and the Otherworld. Well, it certainly looks like a rift. And all I have to do is touch it with this crystal?"

She looked down and saw the Grisial emitting its own dazzling light.

"According to everything we've been able to learn," said Hadrian.

"And we're not concerned that, once I do it, Balor will be in our world forever?"

"I'm more concerned other Fomóire will pass through the rift and possess more people."

"So be it, Necromant, but that means I must get up there. Can I get a lift from you?"

"You may indeed. Just say when you're..."

They were overcome by a roar so deafening it forced them to their knees. They all covered their ears. Peter shut his eyes and howled in pain. The others looked up and saw a winged creature emerge from the shadows. It was like a demon but more gargantuan. A figure rode on its back."

"Is that the Kehua?" shouted Koschei. "What's happened to it?"

"Come Indech!" shouted the unearthly voice from the young man on the monster's back.

"My God!" cried Izanami. "Is that Momotaro?"

"Come Bress! Come Elathan! Come Laméch! Follow me, Fomóire, to the physical world! Let us put an end to the New Ones! Let us extinguish the last of the Tuath Dé!"

30
War's End

"QUICK, HADRIAN!" SHOUTED Izanami. "Carry me up now! Before it's too late!"

She had no sooner spoken when Koschei threw himself against her. An explosion filled their ears as they hit the ground. Smoke billowed out of a deep hole where she had been standing.

"Retreat!" cried the Necromant. "Back to the cave where he's too large to enter."

Several more blasts rocked the cavern as they scrambled to the relative safety of the passageway. The monster alighted on the cavern's floor underneath the rift.

"Can you hear me, my brothers and sisters?" echoed the unearthly voice. "This physical form hampers my communication."

Izanami again heard the sound of flapping wings, but this time it came from the shadows above the monster. She crept toward the cavern for a better look and froze. She knew the creature hovering above Momotaro's head.

"A demon! If I'm not mistaken, the same one Sapphire and I fought before on this volcano. Can things get any worse?"

"It's hard to keep up," said Ragnar, "but I think it, I mean, *he* is on our side."

She ventured farther.

"Is that... Sapphire?"

The Kehua lobbed two fiery balls at Merihim, who dodged them by flying a zigzag pattern. Balor continued attacking the flying demon until one of the projectiles grazed the hellion's wing. He dropped several feet before arresting his fall, but Sapphire lost her grip and plummeted. Merihim tried to swoop

292

down to her but was deterred by the monster's persistent attacks.

"Sapphire!" cried Izanami.

She leapt to her feet but was grabbed roughly by Koschei.

"No, my friend! You'll be killed."

"I don't care!"

She struggled fiercely against his grip. The Russian looked for assistance from his comrades and realized something.

"Say, where's the boy?"

Peter had not retreated into the cave with them. Koschei looked toward Sapphire's motionless body and stifled an urge to yell. He knew it would draw Balor's attention. Peter had taken refuge behind a large rock but now crawled toward the fallen Demon Hunter.

The monster continued its cat-and-mouse game with Merihim. The demon buzzed his foe's head, taunting the beast and making himself an awkward target for its fireballs. The monster resorted to swatting at its winged tormentor. One of its swipes was lucky. Merihim fell to the ground, not far from where Sapphire lay. Like her, he was inert.

Balor turned his attention back to the rift. The beast reared back, extending its arms outward. The human rider did likewise. The unholy voice filled the cavern.

"Come Bress! Come Elathan! Come Laméch! Do you hear my call from this putrid corner of reality's existence? Respond to me! Follow me!"

Balor had not noticed Peter, who was now holding Sapphire's head on his lap and stroking her hair. Nor did he notice Merihim rising slowly and staring at the boy with the fallen Demon Hunter. Peter did not notice him either—at first. The boy turned his head to see the demon's beady eyes staring. The creature's retractable neck brought his head closer to the child.

Peter's eyes grew wide in terror.

"Are you... the devil?"

The demon shifted his head and stared more intently.

"You're real! The fallen angel! The old serpent! The unclean spirit!"

Merihim turned in a half-circle and faced away from the boy. Peter stared at his scaly tail and whispered.

"I understand now. You're not Satan. He's an allegory."

The boy got up and walked along the demon's tail. He climbed on his back and all the way up to the spot between his shoulders. Merihim rose and spread his wings.

"What on earth is he doing?" cried Izanami. "He's gone crazy! Let me go, Koschei!"

"Something tells me," said the Russian, "we shouldn't interfere."

"If you're wrong, you'll answer to me!"

The Demon Hunters and the Necromant watched spellbound. The demon lifted off the ground with the boy on his back. He made a wide circle around the rift, drawing Balor's attention. The beast turned to face him and swung an arm back and hurled a fireball at the demon. It came within a foot of Peter's head, the boy's hair waving in its searing wake.

The Kehua cast another, and the Demon Hunters held their breath. The blasts passed perilously near the boy. They knew, if any of the bursts touched him at all, he would be incinerated instantly.

The monster spread its wings and swept around for clearer aim at the terrified child. Before he could release another energy blast, however, Merihim dropped his retractable jaw and revealed a massive set of jagged teeth.

Deep within the demon's belly, a ball of fire formed. It gushed through his gaping maw and spewed outward. As the flame grew in size, its force pushed the Kehua backward toward the rift. The monster flapped its wings furiously, arresting its backward movement. Merihim roared yet more loudly, but the creature still resisted.

As precarious as his situation was, Peter let go of the demon with his right hand, clinging to the hellion with only his left. Shakily, Peter raised his right arm and closed his eyes. A blast of energy shot from his fingers at the Kehua. The monster flapped its wings wildly, but it could not stop its drift backward. Despite its efforts, it disappeared into the crack, but not before Momotaro had slipped off its back and plummeted to the ground.

The Demon Hunters were dumbfounded. Only Hadrian kept his wits about him.

"Now, Izanami! We must do it without delay!"

Her fear for Sapphire, Peter, and Momotaro had paralyzed her. The Necromant shouted again, and this time his words roused her. The two sprinted toward the rift. As he had done before when lifting her out of the pit, he wrapped his arms around her waist, and they rose into the air. Within moments, they were level with the crack in space.

Izanami's gaze was drawn to the rift's interior. All manner of unnatural shapes, colors, and perspectives filled her head and overwhelmed her. She felt as if her brain were about to explode. As if her mind were being sucked out of the world. She knew that, if she did not close her eyes, she would be unable to hold onto a coherent thought.

Closing her eyes was worse. She seemed to be transported to another world. It was familiar and terrifying. In the dim light she saw and felt snakes coiling around her legs. A spider crawled across her face. A rat leapt through the air and landed on her shoulder. She could not move. It was the world of her nightmares.

This isn't real, she insisted to herself in her thoughts.

She heard the Necromant's voice. "What are you waiting for?"

When she did not respond, his voice spoke in her mind.

"Let me into your thoughts. I can help. I can guide you through this."

She did not trust that the voice was truly Hadrian's. She blocked him from her mind and concentrated all her thoughts on escaping the dream world. Her body quivered as she drew urgently on her own will. The effort drained her energy, and she feared lapsing into unconsciousness. Before that happened, the dim dream world melted away, and she was again confronted with the maddening spectacle of the rift.

Before it could overwhelm her, Izanami reached for the Grisial. She removed it from her neck and held it outward. She and Hadrian drifted toward the rift as if carried by a breeze. She panicked that they might be sucked in and trapped forever.

Their movement toward the rift stopped suddenly. They were then forced backward by a force emanating from the Grisial. The rift was bathed by the blinding, blue light shooting forth from the crystal. The crack in space shrank in the azure glare until it had disappeared completely. When the last of the light from the otherworldly fracture was gone, the cavern shook. High above, a stalactite broke free and plunged to the floor.

Izanami heard its terrible crash, but she did not see the impact. By the time it landed, the Grisial had extinguished its light, and the cavern was plunged into darkness. Once her eyes adjusted, she saw faint dots of soft light below her. They were from the discs worn by the Demon Hunters.

"Was anybody hurt?" shouted Hadrian.

"All accounted for down here," Ragnar called back to him, "but that thing made quite a mess."

Izanami and the Necromant descended slowly until their feet touched the ground. In the faint light available, she saw Merihim crouched nearby. He eyed her coldly.

"Peter," she whispered cautiously, "come to me."

The demon remained motionless as the boy climbed down and ran into Izanami's arms. Once she had hold of him, Merihim spread his wings and rose into the air. He circled the cavern and then shot upward, disappearing into the shadows.

"What ever possessed you to climb on top of that thing?" she asked.

"I... I don't know. I don't understand. He wanted me to. He seemed to know me. I could hear him speak—even though he wasn't speaking. He told me he had needed something from Clíodhna and that he also needed something from me. He needed me to use Grandfather's trick. How did he know?"

Koschei took Peter's hand.

"Come, boy. Izanami needs to look after Sapphire. You and I shall attend to Momotaro."

Izanami rushed to Sapphire, knelt down, and rolled her over to see her face.

"Thank God, she's breathing."

She checked her for injuries.

"Wake up, Mrs. Lynch. Come on. Don't do this to me."

Sapphire opened her eyes.

"Did the world end, Chi-Chi?"

"No. We did it. Everything's going to be okay."

Izanami looked over at Koschei and Peter, who were with Momotaro.

"Is he all right?"

"He's banged up," said the Russian, "but he'll live."

Hadrian knelt next to Izanami.

"You were magnificent," he said, "just as I was told you'd be."

"Not to be rude," she said, "but why are you still here? Shouldn't all of you have gone back when the Grisial closed the rift?"

Sapphire forced herself to sit up. She answered Izanami's question.

"Clíodhna's energy has gone back into this place, and it will protect the world from the Fomóire for another eon. It remains for you, as the Grisial's bearer, however, to return the people you summoned through the timestream."

"You mean, I get to keep the power to bring back people from the past?"

"No, that power has gone out of the crystal. All it's good for now is undoing the temporal disruption it has caused. The sooner you do that, the better. The effects of Balor's intrusion into the physical world won't be put right until you do."

"I..."

"What?"

"I didn't think it would be this hard to say goodbye. Now that I have Koschei and Ragnar back, I don't want to let them go."

"You have to. You know that."

"At least this time I'll get to say proper goodbyes—even if they won't remember."

She approached Callan, who had joined Koschei, Ragnar, and Peter. They were explaining to a dazed Momotaro what had happened. She shook Callan's hand firmly.

"It's been an honor to fight beside you one more time—and to know you better. Thank you for answering my call."

"The honor is mine. I understand why Koschei has always spoken so highly of you."

"Don't make her head any bigger than it already is," said the Russian.

"This is difficult," she said to the Russian. "I can't bear to lose you again. Thank you for all the times you saved my life—including the one that still lies in your future."

"I cannot think of a better way to die, my friend. I tell you in advance that I will have no regrets."

She gave the Russian a tight hug.

"This is so strange. I think I'm going to miss you most of all, scarecrow."

"Well, you didn't lie. You really have been watching films. As it happens, I attended the first screening at the Orpheum in Green Bay, Wisconsin."

Next was Ragnar.

"Thank you for taking me on all those years ago. I don't know what would have happened to me if you hadn't."

"I still think this is merely some strange dream," he replied, "but it's been a wonderful adventure and a grand surprise to meet you in the future. You're the warrior I always knew you would be. I'm glad to have known you and to have shared the road."

"Ragnar…"

"Yes?"

"There's no point saying this, but I can't help myself."

"Say what?"

"Please don't go to the Nullarbor."

"Sounds ominous."

"I'm sorry. That was stupid. You won't remember."

"Thanks for the warning anyway. Don't worry, Izanami. I know I won't live forever. I chose this life willingly. All I've ever wanted was to preserve our world and, in the end, die well."

"No one will ever say you didn't do both things magnificently. Farewell, my friend."

As Ragnar joined Koschei and Callan for more final reminisces, she went to Momotaro.

"Have you recovered?"

"I'm full of aches and pains, but maybe they'll be gone when I return to my own time. Chiharu, I'm happy to know you became a Demon Hunter after all. I look forward to the day we find each other again. No doubt many great adventures together lie ahead of us."

She forced a smile.

"Yes, many great adventures, my friend. It's all ahead of you. Excuse me, I need to say my farewell to Hadrian."

She turned her head so he would not see her eyes. Sapphire watched sympathetically from a distance.

"So, Necromant, what do I say to someone who knows all my thoughts? And whose thoughts are all known to me?"

"Rest assured, your secrets are safe with me."

"Keep the Grisial secure for me."

"I think we both know that I already have."

"It's so strange."

"I know. We're bound forever, you and I."

"Will I ever be able to get you out of my head?"

"No more than I will be able to purge you from mine."

"It's the price for saving the world. For my part, I have no regrets knowing you so well—even the dark parts."

"Goodbye, Hadrian."

"Goodbye, Chiharu."

She walked back to Sapphire and Peter.

"Time to go home, brat. I only wish I knew where home was for you."

"Don't you know?" said Sapphire. "Or at least suspect?"

"Do you?"

"I'm fairly certain, but I'd like to be sure."

"How?"

"My head has become crammed with all kinds of knowledge since I set off on this odyssey. There's now little beyond my ability to see. I can get to the bottom of a mystery like Peter if I put my mind to it."

She knelt in front of him, and said, "Peter, I'm going to help you remember some things. Is that all right?"

He nodded. She brushed his hair back past his ears and placed her fingers on his temples.

"Close your eyes. Send your mind back, Peter. Tell me the earliest thing you can remember."

"I was on the island. With Grandfather and Judith and Celia and Audrey."

"Tell me about before that."

"There is no before that."

"Yes, there is. Listen to my voice. Embrace the memories. Tell me where you were before the island."

"I'm in the water. I can't swim. I'm drowning. Grandfather saved me."

"How did you come to be in the water?"

"I was at the strand. I went out too far. The waves carried me. I couldn't get back to the shore."

"Who waited for you on the strand?"

"I... I don't know. I can't remember."

"Yes, you can. Relax and think. You know the names."

"It was Stephen and Jill."

"Who are they?"

"They're my new parents. I lost my old ones."

"Tell me about meeting Stephen and Jill."

"They found me. I was wandering in a field. They tried to find my real parents, but they couldn't. They couldn't find anybody belonging to me. They became my new parents. They're the ones who named me Peter. They said I talked strangely, that they could barely understand me. They took me to a university, and people studied me. They said I spoke like someone from another century. They taught me how to speak as they did."

"And where were you before they found you in the field."

"I can't recall."

"You're doing very well, Peter. Keep trying. The memories are there. You just have to look for them."

"I remember now. I lived on a farm. All of us lived there."

"All of us?"

"Father. Mother. My brother Jacob. My brother Melchior. My brother Balthasar. My brother Alexander. That was all of us—except for my brothers, Quentin and Sextus. They were in heaven."

Peter closed his eyes and whispered.

"Let us hold fast the profession of our faith without wavering, for he is faithful that promised."

"What was *your* name?"

"My name is Septimus. Septimus Bridge. How could I have ever forgotten?"

"Orpheus?" gasped the Canadian.

Sapphire nodded. "That explains why you failed to summon Septimus to the marble cave. He was already there. He was the first one you summoned."

"But how...?"

"You didn't know what you were doing. You didn't understand the power of the Grisial. It was a trial run, so to speak. You pulled him from his childhood in seventeenth-century England and sent him skipping through time like a stone across a lake's surface. But his journey across the centuries was interrupted. He fell short and landed in another era. When he got in trouble, he was pulled further ahead in time by... himself. His future self. To Riesgado Island."

"Do you think Orpheus knew who he was? That it was himself he was saving?"

"Who knows?" shrugged Sapphire. "But he certainly outdid Mark Twain. He literally became his own Grandfather. Only when Septimus released him did he skip ahead on the last leg of his trajectory through time."

Peter's eyes were wide with confusion.

"No wonder his disappearance would have caused a temporal paradox. He has so many centuries of demon hunting ahead of him as well as other exploits that affect this world and others. Imagine the consequences if he ceased to exist. Even Astaroth had to take an interest."

"I don't understand anything you're talking about," protested the boy.

Izanami put her hand on his shoulder.

"It doesn't matter. You're going home now. You won't remember any of this, but you're going to have an awful lot of adventures in your long life. And you're going to meet me again. You're going to be one of my teachers, and I'm going to give you nothing but grief. Please don't give up on me. What am I saying?

Of course, you won't. You didn't. Thank you. You'll see Sapphire and me again."

"Will you and I be married?"

"No, but you and Sapphire will have a thing in the 17th century."

Sapphire slammed a fist on Izanami's shoulder.

"Don't tell him that."

Izanami called all of them together.

"It's time. It's been difficult, but once again the Demon Hunters prevailed. It's been an honor to be among your number. Now, we must part ways."

Hadrian, Koschei, Ragnar, Callan, Momotaro, and Peter stood silently. Izanami lifted the Grisial to her forehead, closed her eyes, and concentrated. A cool breeze wafted through the cavern, providing a welcome, momentary relief from the warm stuffiness. The five men and the boy faded from view.

Sapphire had stood back, but she now drew close and put an arm around Izanami. She sighed, and they were quiet for several minutes.

"Well, Mrs. Lynch, it's back to the two of us."

"Yes," said Sapphire tentatively, "it's always the two of us."

31
First Dance

"ARE YOU STRONG enough to get us out of here or are you going to make me walk the entire way out of the caves?"

They huddled together on a rock in the dark. The only light was the Grisial's pale glow. Sapphire had willed it to emit light again with a touch from her finger. Their faces looked like ghosts. Izanami had meant her comment as a joke, but Sapphire's labored breathing concerned her.

"Give me a few minutes. I can at least get us out of the mountain."

"Take all the time you need. I wonder where Merihim went. Will we have to fight him again?"

"I suspect he's gone back to the Netherworld. Something's changed. I can't say what precisely, but the demons seem to have lost interest in this world. Maybe it has something to do with Balor and the Fomóire. Or perhaps Septimus's ongoing presence in the Netherworld. Who knows, but something has definitely changed."

"Does this mean we're out of a job?"

"Maybe, but that's all right, isn't it? I mean, it didn't really pay that well. I'm ready to leave this place now."

Sapphire stood uncertainly. They held hands and, a few moments later, stood under a glaring sun. They shielded their eyes from the brightness, waiting for them to become adjusted. They were on a street paved with light gray bricks.

Next to them was a low wall made from the same bricks as the street. On top was an iron railing crowned with sharp points. They walked to a gate.

"I know this place," said Izanami. "We're in San Pedro. Where we stayed to recover after our previous encounter with Merihim."

"This is as far as I could manage to take us," said Sapphire, apologetically.

She stopped to rest against the railing.

"I don't mind. We had a good night here, as I recall. I don't mind reliving it."

"It may not be exactly... the same."

Izanami used the intercom by the gate to speak to reception. They were soon in a modest room, one in a row of several. It was not unlike a North American motel. The tidy exteriors were reddish-brown under a continuous, flat roof of corrugated metal. The room's interior was small but sufficient with a bed, fold-up tables, and stools. The bedspread and tablecloths blazed with bright patterns of red, blue, and purple—colors favored by the Atacameños.

"I think this is the same room we had before," said Izanami. "As glad as I was to see my old comrades again, I'm happy it's just the two of us now."

Sapphire collapsed on the bed.

"Chiharu..."

"You look wrecked. Just lie there for a while. You'll be yourself in no time."

Sapphire looked at her with pain in her eyes.

"Chiharu, I'm not going to be myself again."

"Of course, you are. You've already recovered a lot. You were amazing in the battle against the Mercenaries—and riding the demon! I couldn't believe it. Nothing can stop you."

"Chiharu, I told you. Recovering all my memories from past lives, acquiring all of Clíodhna's knowledge—it's more than a human brain and body can sustain. It's more than I can bear."

"But the crisis is over," said Izanami. "Balor is gone. The rift is closed. The demons are gone. We won. You just need time to recover. Then you'll be your old self again. You'll see."

"No, I won't. I got a second wind when I needed it. I regained enough energy to do what I needed at the end, but closing the rift doesn't change what's happening to me. There's not much time left. I thought I'd have longer, but I was wrong. It's almost over."

"No. I refuse to accept that. We'll fix this. We'll find someone who can solve this and keep you alive."

"This is beyond earthly medicine."

"I know that. I'm not stupid. I meant we'll go to Tsuru or some other Master. She'll cure you. Hypnotize you to forget what you learned if she has to."

"It won't make any difference. Please, let's not waste time."

"So that's it? You're just going to give up and die? Just like that?"

"It's not giving up to accept the inevitable. Please, come lie here next to me."

"No! I don't accept this. I won't let it happen. We've been through too much. We fought too many battles. Survived too many dangers. I waited so long to find you. It's not fair. We were going to live for ages. Be young for ages. We had all that time ahead of us. It can't end like this. I don't accept it."

"Please lie with me."

"We never danced. I was always too embarrassed to ask you to dance. Get up. Dance with me now."

With visible effort, Sapphire got to her feet and leaned against Izanami. Arms around each other, they shuffled slowly around the room as Izanami sang softly.

"I've never heard you sing before. That's pretty. What is it?"

"'All of Me.' Billie Holiday sang it. I've always loved that song. When things finally settled down, I was going to find a copy on vinyl and buy it. I was going to play it for you. And we were going to dance. I thought we'd have time for all that."

"I need to lie down."

Izanami lay next to her.

"You can't leave me."

"It's all right, Chi-Chi. I'm immortal. I'll come back."

"You mean, like you did for Orpheus? How well did that work out?"

"I never came back because of him. With you and me, it's different."

"But you'll be someone else. It won't be the same."

"Life is all about change."

"It will take too much time. I don't want to wait for you to be born again. Then wait for you to grow up. You'll be that much younger than me."

"You may not have to wait. Clíodhna's not bound by linear time. I've possibly already been born again. I could even be someone you already know."

"Now, you're confusing me. Or you're losing your grip on reality. How would I find you again?"

Sapphire reached for the crystal hanging around Izanami's neck. It glowed.

"With this. I've taken away its power to shine except when it's in my presence. That's how you'll find me. You'll know it's me when the Grisial glows again."

"It took so long to find you once. I don't know if I can find you again."

"You will. Next time, though, you have to stop me if I get too curious about who I really am."

"I've never been able to stop you from doing anything."

"Hold me, Chiharu."

"Please don't go. Please."

"I won't go far."

"Are you in pain?"

"No. It's strangely pleasant. I'm in a state of euphoria. I'm reliving every other time I've died. This is the best one. This is the first time I've died peacefully in a bed. With someone I care about."

Sapphire closed her eyes. Her face was radiant.

"It's too soon," said Izanami.

Sapphire was quiet, her body still.

For the first time since she was sixteen years old, Izanami wept.

"I love you, Lola Blumquist. I always will."

Sapphire's body glowed. The light grew brighter. So intense that Izanami was forced to look away. Then the light was gone, and so was Sapphire. The Grisial went dark.

"There isn't even a body left to mourn over," sobbed Izanami.

After an hour staring at the empty bed, she stumbled to the bathroom. She leaned over the sink and wiped her cheeks. She glanced at the mirror.

Her hair had turned silvery white.

The next day, she walked the 55 miles from San Pedro to Calama on foot. From there, she hitchhiked to the Pan-American Highway and followed it to the Peruvian border. Along the Pacific coast, she visited as many bars, taverns, and cantinas as she could find. There were many nights she did not remember. There were brawls with scores injured.

She stopped in Arequipa, Nazca, and Lima. She passed through Trujillo, Guayaquil, Quito, and Cali. In a card game in Medellín, she won the price of passage around the Darién Gap.

Her solitary odyssey took her to Panama City, San José, and Managua. She drank and fought her way through San Salvador, Guatemala City, and several towns in Chiapas. Her command of Spanish was formidable by the time she visited Puebla, Guadalajara, and Mazatlán. Foolish criminals had attempted to rob her along the way, and all regretted the experience. A young, black-haired man with soulful, brown eyes and a guitar had tried to woo her in Hermosillo, and he too was left with bitter regrets.

The loneliest leg of the journey was the thousand miles and more through the farmlands and mountains of California, Oregon, and Washington. Passing through Seattle, she meant to stop and visit the site of Lola's house. She knew she should tell Maria what had happened. In the end, though, she just kept going.

She continued until she reached Lost Gap. She emerged from the cave and felt the warm sunlight on her face. She gazed at the cottage atop the hill and took a deep breath. Slowly, she approached the house.

In her reckless misadventures during the preceding months, she had felt no fear. She had dulled her pain with drink and convinced herself she did not care if she lived or died. Now, as she neared the cottage's door, she was nervous.

She mentally asked for permission to enter, but there was no response. Nor was there an answer to her knock. The complete silence was unsettling. She knocked again and waited. She tried the door. It was unlocked, and the hinges creaked. Inside, a strange stillness clung to the main room. Unwashed pots sat on the stove.

With no small amount of dread, she went to the bedroom. On the bed, a motionless shape was turned away from her. She knelt at the bed's side, and put a hand on the old woman's body.

"I thought you would still be here," she said quietly. "So, I've lost you too."

"Did no one teach you to knock?"

Startled, Izanami jumped back a foot.

"You're alive! And I did knock. Twice."

"You should have knocked louder. You have no respect for the privacy of others. You never did."

"You scared the life out of me. I thought you were dead."

"I will be soon. Not that you care. Get out of my room so I can get up and change. Then I'll make tea."

As she wet the tea leaves, Tsuru said, "Your hair..."

"We're not talking about my hair."

"I gather you resolved that business with the Fomóire. You must be proud of yourself."

"Sapphire's gone."

"I sensed that. Not gone exactly. Only her human form. She's still here, but she doesn't know who she is."

"She is? Can you tell me where she is? Who she is?"

"Do I look like a phone book? Can't you search for her on the internet or something?"

"Why do you always make everything difficult?"

"People don't learn when things are easy."

"Master, I think I want to become like you."

"Old and miserable?"

"I want to become a Mage and then a Master. Will you take me back as a disciple?"

"At my age? Are you nuts? My teaching days are over. You'll need to find someone else."

"Miyamoto is gone. Orpheus is gone. Who should I seek?"

"Perhaps someone you already know."

"Who?"

"Hadrian."

"Is he still alive?"

"He's nearly as old as I am, but I'm sure he minded himself better. He never worked as hard as I did."

"I've been afraid he's dead."

"Why?"

"He and I formed a strong and complete mental link. Since I sent him back to his own time, I've been unable to find any trace of him telepathically. I'd have thought he'd make contact."

"Perhaps he's waiting for you to get in touch."

"Where would I find him?"

"I sent you to him once before. I could do it again if I absolutely had to. Teleporting at my age will set me back a week, might even kill me, but if you insist..."

"It would be strange to see him now, but I suppose he's my best hope for what I want. And it would be good to see him again. I've missed him the past few months."

"Very well. Finish your tea, and I will send you to him."

Later, when Izanami opened her eyes, she found herself flat on the ground. The teleportation had been rough. She looked up to see the familiar cabin in the Bialowieza Forest. She got to her feet. Like the last time she was there, she could not shake the feeling of being watched.

"You're here, aren't you?"

The only reply was a breeze through the tree branches.

"It was you before. You were watching us the whole time, and now you're watching me again."

She heard his voice in his head. The broken link was restored. She scanned the trees until she spotted him. By an ancient oak stood a stooped figure in a dark robe.

He walked toward her and lowered his hood. His face was longer, more drawn with deep wrinkles. His chin was covered with a medium-length, silver beard. His hair was wispy but still made a striking white mane. His nose was large. Unruly brows covered the tops of his eyes. His ever-present staff was now needed for physical support.

"I did it, Izanami."

His voice was still deep but now raspier.

"It took years, but I finally mastered invisibility. It came in quite handy, I can tell you, when I needed to make myself scarce when you and the others were here before."

She stared at his face.

"Hadrian, you've become…"

"Don't say haggard. What about you? It's been only a few months since I last saw you in this very place, but now your hair…"

"We're not talking about my hair. So, you were here all the time. Hiding. Spying on us."

"Keeping watch. I tell you, my friend, time plays strange tricks on the mind. As the decades passed, I began questioning whether I had truly journeyed to the future all those years ago. Had it all been some sort of delusion? I doubted my sanity. Then the day arrived. I waited here in the appointed place. Just as I remembered, my younger self appeared here in the forest. We had the same conversations as before, but this time I was the old man.

"I couldn't reveal myself to you. It would have been too confusing. Too distracting. Besides, that wasn't how I remembered it. That's not how it had happened. I can't tell you how wonderful it was to see you again, looking as I had remembered. This meeting is better because now I can speak to you directly. More than that, I can allow myself to hear your thoughts and allow you to hear mine. Blocking my mind from you all these years was difficult."

"Sapphire's gone."

"I'm sorry. Your love for her has filled my mind and my heart for decades. I'm so sorry about her parents. I intended to keep the Grisial and deliver it to you personally, but it wasn't possible. It's a long story. I was taken prisoner and held for years by Theurgists. When I realized I couldn't elude them—and might not survive them—I knew only one way to ensure the Grisial would get to you when it was needed."

"It's all in the past now, isn't it? Do you know why I've come?"

"I believe so. It's not an exaggeration to say I know you like I know myself. As for what happens next, it's a relief to say I have no more idea than you do. Knowing the future all those years was a terrible burden. I was a prisoner of the calendar. This is the year Izanami will be born. This is the year Izanami will meet Miyamoto. This is the year Izanami will meet Sapphire."

"I want to be a Mage and a Master. I want to be like you and Tsuru. I want to learn teleportation, levitation, remote viewing. I want to master invisibility. Can you teach me?"

"Don't worry. It will all come easy. You already possess my knowledge. You need only to be shown how to apply it and trained to use it."

"So, you'll take me on then?"

"I thought my teaching days were over, but as it happens I have just taken on my first new pupil in many years. If you like, I can instruct the two of you together."

"A new pupil? Who?"

"My great-grandson Tiberius. He's young, but he's very keen."

"I don't know. I think I'd prefer that it be just the two of us. I don't have much patience for meeting new people."

"Come, I'll introduce you. Just get to know him. Then decide."

They went into the cabin. A lanky, young man with long, black hair was spread out over a chair, one leg draped casually over an armrest. He tapped rapidly on his phone's screen.

"The software's rubbish," he muttered in an English accent. "Ever since Parydyme went out of business. And can't you do anything about the Wi–Fi coverage, Hadrian?"

"Tiberius, I want you to meet someone."

The young man stood reluctantly. Stretched to his full height, he was quite tall. He towered over Hadrian and Izanami. In his face, she saw a distinct resemblance to the Necromant. On seeing Izanami, the young man's eyes widened appreciatively.

"Tiberius, this is an old friend of mine. Izanami."

"Nice to meet you," he smiled. "Very nice indeed. You're obviously not *that* old of a friend."

Izanami disliked him immediately. She did not care for the way he looked her up and down. His posture betrayed unearned, youthful cockiness.

"Would it be all right with you, Tiberius, if Izanami joined our studies?"

"Join us? Would it ever. That would be splendid."

"I don't know if it suits me," she said. "I might find a different arrangement."

"Why don't the two of you go outside," said Hadrian, "and chat a bit. I'll make tea. Don't decide too hastily, Izanami. He's not a bad lad."

"I just had tea."

Hadrian ignored her words and went to put on the kettle. Tiberius beckoned her to go outside with him. As she followed reluctantly, Hadrian's voice spoke in her head.

"What do you think?"

"Of what?"

"Tiberius."

"He's very young."

"He is. Too young for me to relate to. The age gap between us is vast. It would be a huge help if you were around to help guide him."

"It's been no time at all since I was saddled with babysitting a male child. I don't need that again."

"He's hardly a child."

"He's a zygote."

"Izanami, I have so much to tell you about what's happened during the long years since you sent me back to my own time. Some of it involves someone you once knew. We need to have a long talk—alone."

"Did you hear what I said?" asked Tiberius.

"Sorry, I was distracted."

"I asked if you'd been here before. You know, I can tell you a lot about the various trees. I did some botany at uni. My main course was religious studies, but I took as many classes outside my field as I could. I was at Oxford, you know."

"Should I be impressed?"

"It's one of the top universities in the global standings."

"Trust me. The most important knowledge isn't found in ivy-covered halls."

"That's a fascinating crystal you're wearing, by the way."

"Before you waste too much time chatting me up, you should know I'm a lot older than I look. I mean, a *lot* older."

"Why would that matter? Don't you know chronological age is an artificial construct?"

"I'm sorry, but what does that even mean?"

"I meant what I said about your pendant. It's mesmerizing."

"There's a long story about it, but I won't be here long enough for you to hear it."

"What makes it glow like that?"

"What?"

"How does it emit its light?"

She looked down with no small degree of concern. The crystal was indeed glowing.

About the Author

Scott R. Larson is the writer of six novels, including three in the fantasy genre. They include the stand-alone book *The Three Towers of Afranor* in addition to *The Curse of Septimus Bridge,* set in a fantastical world of demons and Mages and which introduced the Demon Hunters Sapphire and Izanami. *Last of the Tuath Dé* is the continuation of their adventures. He has also authored a trio of books (and the short story "Rendezvous") about the adventures of one Dallas Green, spanning many years and locations. Larson is a native of California's San Joaquin Valley, the original inspiration source for the Dallas Green tales. Other places he's lived have also provided settings for his books—and inspirations for characters—including Seattle, France, Chile, and his current home in the West of Ireland. In addition to novels, he also writes a number of blogs, including one of the internet's longest-running movie review web sites, *ScottsMovies.com,* which has been logging online film commentary since 1995.